Sammy Rambles
and the
Land of the Pharaohs

J T SCOTT

Praise for the Sammy Rambles series:

*"The JK Rowling of the South West" - Brad Burton,
The UK's #1 Motivational Business Speaker*

*"A tale of finding yourself and achieving great things, the Sammy
Rambles series of books keep readers of any age hooked through the
myriad of adventures. JT Scott is the modern-day fantasy author
whose stories are being brought to life by youngsters in the sports hall
and playgrounds around the world." - Caroline Bramwell, Author of
'Loo Rolls to Lycra' and Inspirational Speaker*

*"Two hours to do the school run tonight. Sammy Rambles to the
rescue, I turned on my Sammy Rambles and the Floating Circus
audio book and kept everyone happy." - Francis, Plymouth.*

*"I loved it, only problem was I couldn't put it down. It's the first time
in ages I have spent the entire day ignoring work and reading it from
cover to cover." - L. Watts*

*"Great to hear about these fantastic books!" - Councillor Terri Beer
(Cabinet Member for Children and Young People).*

*"It's a fantastic read, Lily is totally engrossed in the story, as am I!
It's a huge hit here! We're looking forward to reading the rest of the
Sammy Rambles books." – Jayne W.*

"I've read all of the books and I'm starting to read them again. I think they're really good. They have a good story to them and they have a meaning behind them as well about the bullying and it can encourage other people to stand up for themselves." – Natasha, Dragonball Player

"A great read. Jenny has a very vivid imagination. Her descriptive writing style makes it easy to create your own picture in your mind. Looking forward to reading the rest of the series." – Peter Clarke

"If you've read the Floating Circus you'll know how captivating the story is! It draws you in on every page. A book for all ages. Great on every level." – G. Singh

"Sammy Rambles and the Floating Circus is a beautifully written and well-crafted story. It's pacy and a 'page turner' with unexpected twists and turns. Gentle writing and great fun!" – Amazon reader.

"I bought this book on a Friday. By Sunday I'd finished reading it. OK, so I'm not a child any more (a grandfather now, actually) but as a fan of Tolkein & Lewis, this appealed to me and I was not disappointed." – Amazon reader.

"I bought as a present for my grandson who loves dragons. It's been a fun bedtime story for us both." – Amazon reader.

Sammy Rambles and the Land of the Pharaohs

First published in 2016
This edition published in 2019

ISBN-13: 978-1530137923
ISBN-10: 1530137926

J T SCOTT

J T Scott lives in Cornwall with Ari and Sam surrounded by open countryside, sandy beaches, lots of historical castles, pens, paper and a very vivid imagination.

Also available in the Sammy Rambles series:

Sammy Rambles and the Floating Circus
Sammy Rambles and the Land of the Pharaohs
Sammy Rambles and the Angel of 'El Horidore
Sammy Rambles and the Fires of Karmandor
Sammy Rambles and the Knights of the Stone Cross

Find out more about Sammy, Dixie and Darius and their adventures on the Sammy Rambles website.

www.sammyrambles.com

Sammy Rambles and the Land of the Pharaohs

Chapter List:

Sammy Rambles and the Land of the Pharaohs

For Ari & Sam

CHAPTER 1

THE GREEN SPARK

It was ten past three on a sunny August afternoon and two boys and a girl were sitting in a red and white spotted mushroom shaped treehouse situated halfway up an old oak tree.

'Dr Lithoman was really called Eliza Elungwen,' said a dark skinned, dark haired boy as he poured lemonade out of a plastic orange jug into a glass, 'who would have thought it?'

'That's all you've said Darius since your parents dropped you off ten minutes ago,' said the small, green eyed, green haired girl, grinning at him. She held out three glasses for him to fill with a hand unsteady from laughing.

'I know,' said the dark haired boy. 'But it's just so weird. She's a teacher and my parents said I must respect the teachers, but why should we when all she was doing was threatening to kill all our dragons and close the school?'

'Dragamas,' said the second boy. He had dirty blond hair and pale blue eyes that were sparkling. 'I can't wait to be back there, uh, not that it hasn't been nice staying here,' he added quickly as the green haired girl looked indignantly at him. 'Dixie, you know I've loved staying here while my parents are in Switzerland, but I'm ready to go back. We get to play Dragonball and Firesticks properly this year, with our dragons.'

'Like you haven't played it enough, Sammy, you and that dragon of yours,' said Darius, shaking his head. 'Anyone would think you're playing professionally, flying round the pitch on Kyrillan all the time.'

The boy with dirty blond hair looked out of the tree house window. He could see six long shapes lying side by side on the grass below. Each of the shapes was a live dragon, hatched from an egg that each student received on their first day at Dragamas School for Dragon Charming, the only school in Britain that encouraged dragon breeding and allowed its pupils to learn unusual skills.

The shimmering blue-green dragon at the far end was Sammy's dragon, Kyrillan, whose name he had discovered meant "strong and wise".

'He's awake,' said Sammy as the shimmering blue-green dragon shook its tail. 'I can't believe how much Kyrillan has grown.'

'All dragons grow,' said Dixie matter of factly. 'At six feet, they're only half grown.'

'Swot,' said Sammy, grinning at her.

'Me?' asked Dixie indignantly. 'What about you Mr Medal of Bravery?'

'Cross,' corrected Sammy, touching the metal Celtic-like cross he wore on a black cord around his neck. It had been his reward at the end of term last year for helping raise the ransom and saving the school from closing. 'Hopefully Eliza Elungwen, has told Sir Ragnarok who else is in the Shape as well as her.'

'Yeah,' said Darius. 'Then we can all go back to school in peace.'

'After last year I need a bit of peace,' said Sammy.

'You nearly came home in pieces!' giggled Dixie and they all laughed.

'There are only two more days of holiday,' said Sammy, checking their homemade calendar on the curved treehouse wall. 'That's enough time for three games of Dragonball, maybe some Firesticks, packing our cases, then we go back to school.'

'If I hear another word about Dragonball, I'll ask Sir Ragnarok to make you give your Excelsior Dragonball set back,' said Darius.

Sir Ragnarok was the headmaster at Dragamas, an ancient man with grey hair, bright blue eyes and a quick thinking mind that was fair in judgment. At the end of the summer term, he had granted Sammy's wish and given him a silver briefcase containing brand new equipment to play the popular sport called Dragonball, which people with dragons play all over the country.

'I thought you said you didn't like school anyway,' said Dixie. 'You said you were glad to get home each afternoon.'

Sammy looked at her, his eyes wide open. 'You really don't understand, do you? Dragamas is completely different. It's a boarding school and there aren't any people like the Shape out to get me.'

'I'd rather have those Rat Catchers you said about after me than the Shape,' said Darius, a worried look in his eyes. 'At least at your old school you weren't going to die.'

Sammy shrugged. 'I'll find out who else is in the Shape this year,' he said firmly. 'If any of them try anything,' he added, picking up his staff, a long wooden stick with a

11

glossy black onyx gemstone at the top. He waved it high above his head in a long sweeping movement.

As he waved the staff, a handful of green sparks flew from the onyx and fizzed and crackled in the air.

Sammy leapt back in surprise. He had no idea his staff could do that.

Darius burst out laughing. 'That's a new one. The Shape will be terrified of that!'

Dixie looked thoughtful. 'I've seen green sparks before. My brothers use them sometimes. How about trying just one big green spark Sammy? Open the window first though.'

'Ok,' said Sammy. He moved the chairs, unhitched the latch and pushed the window wide open. 'Stand back.'

'On three,' said Darius, holding up his hand with his fingers outstretched. 'One…two…three.'

On "three", Sammy held his staff tightly and threw his arm forward.

There was a loud BANG and a huge green flame spurted from the onyx followed by a jet stream of tiny green candle sized flames that followed the green fireball out of the window, across the sleeping dragons and into the field behind Dixie's house.

'Wow!' shouted Darius. 'That was amazing.'

Sammy leaned out of the window and drew a deep breath. He turned to face Dixie and Darius, grinning broadly at them. 'I think it's landed in the field.'

'Let's go and find it,' said Dixie. She opened the tree house door, swung herself on to the rope ladder and climbed down out of sight.

Darius went next, climbing hand over hand until he reached the bottom.

As Sammy took his turn, he was glad he'd asked his parents to buy the sturdy new ladder, replacing the old ladder with its broken rungs, as a thank you present to Mrs Deane for having him to stay. She had refused to take any money but, knowing they would go up into the tree house whether the ladder was safe or not, she had accepted the ladder, preferring to know that they were safe.

It was very safe. It didn't budge when Sammy swung himself on to the strong wooden rungs, holding on to the knotted rope to guide him down on to the muddy circle below.

Even though Dixie and her triplet older brothers, Serberon, Mikhael and Jason hadn't used the mushroom shaped tree house built by their father shortly before he disappeared four years ago, the grass refused to grow. Mrs Deane joked that it hadn't grown because it knew the tree house would be used again and it couldn't be bothered to try.

'It's over there!' shouted Darius, standing with Dixie in a gap in the high, overgrown, brambly hedge separating the row of houses from the training grounds of the Woodland Ranchers, the local Firesticks team some of the pupils at Dragamas supported. A keen Firesticks supporter herself, Dixie even had a poster of Nitron Dark, the captain of the Nitromen Firesticks team, on her bedroom wall.

'Look Sammy!' shouted Dixie. 'It's exploded! There's bits of green flames everywhere.

'Where?' demanded Sammy. He ran to the hedged bank at the end of Dixie's garden and leapt up beside Dixie and Darius. 'Oh no,' he said, looking at the hundred or so dancing flames, each no bigger than a candle flame, spread out across the neatly mown Dragonball and Firesticks pitch.

CHAPTER 2

ANGEL WHISTLES

Sammy leaped down the other side of the bank, landing on a rugged stone in the middle of a shallow stream that separated the pitch and the hedgerow. In Dragonball games, the stream was used to supply water to put out fires created by over enthusiastic dragons.

He held out his hand to Dixie and she jumped down on to the stone beside him. They jumped across the rest of the stream on to the pitch.

'Watch this!' shouted Darius, taking a flying leap from the hedge, trying to cross the stream in one go. Arms flailing, Darius landed mid-stream, splashing water everywhere.

'Oi!' shouted Dixie, rubbing the water off her jeans with her jumper sleeve pulled down over her hand.

'Sorry,' said Darius, bursting into a fit of giggles. 'Hey, isn't that Gavin and Toby?'

Sammy followed Darius's pointed finger. High up in the stands surrounding the pitch were two dark haired boys playing catch with an oversized black football, bouncing the ball between the rows of seats.

'Looks like it,' said Dixie, shielding her eyes against the sun. 'Hey Gavin! Toby! Is that you?'

The two boys playing catch stopped and looked in their direction. Remembering his previous visit to the Woodland Ranchers where the Shape had appeared and chased them, Sammy crossed the stream, ready to run up the bank if the boys turned out to be the Shape.

The boys waved and ran down from the stand, across the pitch to Dixie and Darius. Sammy jumped back, feeling a little foolish.

'Hi Sammy,' said one of the boys with jet black hair.

'Hi Toby,' said Sammy, double checking which of the brothers he had spoken to. Gavin and Toby Reed were identical twins who were in his Dragamas house and the same year at school.

'Have you had a good holiday?' asked the other twin.

'Really good thanks Gavin,' said Darius. 'My parents took me all round Europe looking at ruins, then dropped me off at Dixie's for the last few days.'

Gavin yawned. 'Sounds really good,' he said sarcastically. 'How about you Sammy? Been anywhere?'

Pretending he didn't care that Gavin wasn't interested, Darius went over to the flames on the pitch, stamping out any that were still alight.

'It's been ok,' said Sammy, grinning as Dixie elbowed him in the ribs. 'Yeah, really good. I've been staying at Dixie's for most of the holiday. My parents came back for a few days and we went to London to get some new clothes and books.'

'Awesome,' said Gavin. 'We went to London as well. We saw a show in the theatre up there.'

'The Legend of Karmandor,' added Toby. 'It was a bit boring really, nothing like what Dr Shivers says about it.'

'Isn't Karmandor the dragon that belonged to King Serberon of the Dark Ages?' asked Sammy, thinking back to their Dragon Studies lessons, taught by gaunt, grey haired and ghost-like Dr Shivers who brought history to life with his entertaining practical lessons helping Dragamas students learn the skills needed to take care of their own dragons.

'That's right,' said Dixie. 'My brother is named after King Serberon.'

Toby nodded, bouncing the black leather ball on the ground. 'Are you here to play Dragonball?'

'Can do,' said Dixie. 'Have you brought your dragons?'

'No,' said Toby. 'Ours have to help out more on the farm since, you know…'

Sammy nodded. Gavin and Toby's mother's dragon had been killed by the Shape who had stolen the draconite stone buried in her dragon's brain. Without draconite, a dragon cannot perform spells, cannot fly, cannot breathe fire, cannot breathe at all. Without its stone, a dragon would die.

'Dad did give us this Angel whistle,' said Toby, holding up an orange, half-moon shaped plastic disc. 'It's been programmed to call both our dragons to come to wherever we are.'

'That's brilliant!' said Sammy looking at the orange whistle. 'Where did he get it?'

'I don't know,' said Toby. 'It was a birthday present last week.'

'Happy birthday,' said Sammy. 'Sorry, I didn't know.'

'Yeah, we're both twelve now,' said Gavin.

'Happy birthday,' said Darius, coming back now that all the green flames were out. 'Hey, that's really cool,' he said looking at the device. 'Is that an Angel whistle?'

'Yes and it was really expensive,' said Gavin, grinning.

'Use it!' said Dixie. 'Our dragons are just over the hedge. There should be time for a game before it gets dark.'

'Ok,' said Toby and he blew hard into the orange half-moon whistle. The sound came out as a low hissing, making hardly any noise at all.

Darius let out an explosive giggle. 'That won't go far! My parents use Angel whistles when they train dragons in the wild. Theirs are much louder.'

'Ooer,' said Gavin, taking his turn to blow the orange whistle.

'I bet it does work,' said Dixie. 'Just because we can't hear anything doesn't mean it doesn't work.'

Toby nodded. 'It's a special whistle.'

'Really expensive,' repeated Gavin.

'Yeah all right,' said Toby, ruffling his brother's hair. 'They get the picture.'

'How long do we…' Sammy broke off in mid-sentence as a whooshing noise sounded overhead.

'Look!' yelled Gavin, pointing at the sky.

Sammy shielded his eyes from the sun. He could see two large shapes flying towards them. As the shapes got nearer, he could make out the bodies of two dragons, their wings beating in perfect synchronisation. A grey-green dragon circled twice and landed in the middle of the pitch.

'Puttee!' shouted Toby, running over to his six foot long dragon that had landed perfectly on its feet and throwing his arms around the dragon's neck.

'Syren!' yelled Gavin, frowning as his dusty pink dragon landed on one foot and collapsed in a muddled heap on the grass.

'You need some practice!' said Darius, pretending to duck as Gavin shook his fist at him.

'Let's get our dragons,' said Dixie. She leapt on to the stone in the middle of the stream and then across to the gap in the hedgerow where she called for their three dragons. 'Kiridor, Kyrillan, Nelson!'

From the other side of the hedge, Sammy heard the crackling of scales as the dragons lifted themselves on to their hind legs and crawled up the bank, slithering past Dixie and through the hedge. Kyrillan and Nelson splashed through the shallow stream and stood by their masters.

Shimmery blue-green Kyrillan nuzzled against Sammy's shoulder and navy blue Nelson marched around Darius before lying at his feet.

Dixie's dragon, Kiridor, was also shimmery blue-green in colour like Kyrillan. He waited patiently on the bank, allowing her to climb on to his back before carrying her safely across the stream.

'Come on!' shouted Dixie, pulling her green hair into a ponytail. 'Let's fly two laps to warm up, then throw your ball in Toby. I'll play in goal this end,' she said, pointing towards the far end of the pitch where there was a small chink in the otherwise solid hedgerow.

Sammy looked uneasily at the gap. It was where he had crawled through with Gavin and Toby at Easter and the Shape had stood in front of it, blocking them inside the Woodland Ranchers training ground.

'Me and you against Gavin and Toby,' shouted Darius from ten feet in the air. He had mounted his dragon and was flying around them in circles.

'You're on,' yelled Gavin. 'Come on Toby! We'll show 'em!'

Toby threw up his hands. 'Fine! We'll play on a team next time Sammy.'

Sammy nodded. He would have preferred to be on a team with Toby since after Dixie, who breathed the sport like air, Toby was the next best player.

He swung his right leg over Kyrillan's scaly back, rested his hands on the dragon's shoulder blades and kicked off.

Kyrillan responded and plodded forward, breaking into a run and then from beneath Sammy's knees two enormous wings sprouted and uncurled into beautiful blue-green shimmering flying wings that took Sammy's feet off the ground and propelled him into the air. The rush of air blew back his hair and made his eyes water but it was worth it because they were flying higher and higher. Sammy looked down and Dixie's house was tiny. He was high above the treetops, circling around the Dragonball pitch.

When they played at school, each dragon would have a metal harness and leather saddle, but Sammy much preferred riding his dragon bareback, using his knees and thoughts alone to guide Kyrillan who, to Sammy's delight, seemed to have an innate idea of how the game should be played.

'Let's go!' shouted Toby, throwing the ball to Gavin.

Fumbling the first pass, Gavin dropped the ball from only three feet up. As quick as lightning, Sammy steered Kyrillan to collect the ball. He scooped it up and threw it in an overarm pass to Darius who was close to the goal. Darius punched the ball over Dixie's head and into the netting.

'Goal!' shouted Darius.

'Cheat!' yelled Gavin, his face contorted with rage. 'She let it in!'

'I did not!' shrieked Dixie. 'You're a bad loser Gavin.'

'Am not!' yelled Gavin. 'Fine! We'll start from five goals down. Then we'll see who can play.'

'Can we play as well?' came a shout from across the pitch.

Sammy looked down. Dixie's three green haired brothers, Serberon, Jason and Mikhael, were beneath him, each wearing their black and gold Nitromen Firesticks shirts and sat astride their dragons.

'Sure Serberon,' said Sammy without hesitating.

'Ok,' said the tallest of the green haired boys. 'Mikhael, you and Jason go in goal, then me, Dixie and Sammy against Darius and you two,' he added pointing at Gavin and Toby.

'Not fair,' said Gavin. 'I'll go in goal and you, Sammy and Toby can be on my team.'

'Ok,' said Serberon, the tallest green haired boy. 'Us against Dixie, Darius, Mikhael and Jason. Everyone happy?'

'Yes,' said Gavin, sweeping his dragon into a steep curve towards the far goal.

Jason flew to the opposite goal, his ponytail streaming behind him, and started pacing from post to post to protect the netting.

Toby stood in the middle of the pitch beside the golden dragon and threw the leather ball high into the air. With the training ground officially closed, the central dragon and Shute tunnels under each goal were switched off and they had to simulate the action.

'Go!' yelled Toby, leaping on to his dragon, taking off and banking into a climb to collect the ball.

Mikhael beat him to it and punched the ball in Dixie's direction. The pass caught her off guard and knocked her off her dragon on to the floor. Since she hadn't taken off, no damage was done. Serberon flew across to her and offered her his hand.

'Oi! Serberon!' yelled Gavin. 'She's not on our team.'

Serberon stuck his hand up at Gavin and helped his younger sister to her feet.

'Thanks Serberon,' said Dixie, picking up the ball. She threw the ball to Darius and climbed back on to Kiridor's back.

Some three hours later, Sammy made the score eighty to seventy one in their teams favour. With so many goals handed back, either when Gavin objected, or as penalties for unfair tackles, Sammy was glad someone had found out how to turn on the large scoreboards used in official matches and he could see for himself that the score was indeed eighty versus seventy one.

'We won!' shouted Sammy as they grouped in the centre of the pitch as the light began to fade.

'What time is it?' asked Toby. 'Must be quite late, it's getting dark.'

Sammy pressed the clip on the Casino watch he'd been given by his uncle to illuminate the numbers. 'It's eight twenty two.'

'No way,' said Toby, clutching Sammy's wrist to check the time himself. 'Mum will go up the wall. She made us promise to be home at seven to help Dad with the sheep.'

'Oops,' Darius giggled.

'She'll murder us,' said Gavin, his face draining to a pale ivory.

Having been on the wrong side of Mrs Reed, Sammy wasn't keen to repeat the experience.

'Telephone her from our house,' said Serberon, scratching his head. 'Tell her you're here and either she can pick you up or I expect our mum will drop you home.'

'You don't understand,' said Toby. 'Mum thinks it's Sammy's fault her dragon is dead. She's always saying she wishes it was Kyrillan that the Shape had caught and killed.'

'I see,' said Serberon stiffly. 'Then perhaps you'd better fly home yourselves.'

'No,' said Dixie. 'Sammy wasn't to blame. Gavin and Toby know that.'

The twins nodded. 'We know what really happened,' said Toby.

'Ok,' said Serberon. 'Come over the bank into our house. You can call her from the telephone in the kitchen.'

CHAPTER 3

SHAPES IN THE NIGHT

Half an hour later, Mrs Reed drove into the driveway at Three Chimneys in her sleek and shiny Land Rover.

She refused the cup of tea from Dixie's mother and glared at her sons, not daring to ask in front of the five stony faced, green haired members of Dixie's family exactly what Gavin and Toby thought they were doing there.

She wouldn't look at Sammy or Darius and stayed just long enough to turn the car in the driveway, calling to Gavin and Toby to tie up their dragons rather than getting out and doing it herself.

'What a rude woman,' said Mrs Deane when the Land Rover had disappeared from sight.

'The smell has gone,' said Jason.

'The air is clear,' added Serberon with a grin. 'Come on, let's sort out some tea.'

Sammy had found it strange at first to be helping with so many household chores he didn't have to do at home. With their father gone, Dixie and her brothers helped out at home in many ways, from fetching groceries and chopping firewood to preparing meals, cleaning and various DIY jobs as and when they came up.

He went with Darius to fetch the cutlery and plates. Dixie disappeared into the walk-in fridge and Serberon turned the oven on and started peeling potatoes.

Jason and Mikhael followed Mrs Deane into the lounge muttering something about "too many cooks" and "better taste good" as they closed the door and switched on the television.

Fifteen minutes later, all eight were sitting in the lounge watching a real-life chat show hosted by the bizarrely named Dr Livitupadup who brought the show to life with his exaggerated impersonations of his celebrity guests.

They sat on the two flower patterned settees, Sammy, Dixie, Serberon and Jason on one sofa, Darius, Mikhael, Jason and Mrs Deane on the other. Each person sat with a cushion on their lap, supporting a plate piled high with sausages and homemade chips cut into zigzags by Serberon.

To Sammy, they looked like "S" shapes. If Serberon's name hadn't started with an "S", he would have thought they'd been designed especially for him. Or for Sylvia, he thought, remembering Mrs Deane's first name. Sammy, Serberon or Sylvia, he thought to himself with a grin wondering if his mum would make him chips like that at home one day.

'What?' asked Dixie, snapping him out of his thoughts.

'Huh?'

'Look,' said Dixie, her mouth full of ketchup and chips. 'He just said he'd throw his dragon out on the streets because it's too old to breathe fire.'

Sammy stared with interest. Thinking about his parents, who he wasn't a hundred percent sure if they knew about dragons or not, had reminded him that they hadn't said anything about dragons before letting him go to Dragamas and not a single word about dragons, staffs or magic during the entire short length of time he'd spent with them over the holiday.

Even though his parents hadn't said a word about dragons, they were interested in his choice of books and were happy when Sammy spent twenty minutes looking at what they described as a charity shop, but which Sammy knew was actually Excelsior Sports Supplies, the leading stockist of all Dragonball and Firesticks clothing and equipment.

At that moment, whether his parents could see dragons or not, one thing Sammy was certain of was that he'd never seen a TV show as funny as Dr Livitupadup's and with the amount of TV he'd used to watch, that was saying something.

'Shocking,' said Mrs Deane. 'Why, even with my dragon up in the attic to keep the house warm, I could never imagine getting rid of her. A replacement if she died yes, but I'd rather go without hot water than lose her.'

Sammy hadn't given any thought to the heating and electricity supply in the Deane's house. He frowned, thinking it through. To him, the basics of the house just worked.

Mrs Deane leaned over towards Sammy. 'My dragon sleeps in the attic next to the hot water tank. She blows fire in her sleep which boils the water for the hot taps.'

'Is it safe?' whispered Sammy as the others roared with laughter at another impression from Dr Livitupadup.

Mrs Deane laughed. 'Why of course it is honey. The roof is fully insulated and of course we're insured. Kyrillan may do the same in your house one day.'

Sammy stared at her. 'My house?'

'Of course that's a long way off for you,' said Mrs Deane, throwing back her head and laughing out loud. 'At your age, I couldn't see past my sixteenth birthday, but I expect even that seems old to you.'

Sammy nodded. 'I'll be twelve at the end of November.'

Mrs Deane clapped her hands. 'A Sagittarius, same as me.'

'Not more star signs,' said Sammy, rolling his eyes. 'It's bad enough at home. My mum swears by them. Once she wouldn't drive her car because the horoscope said there would be unforeseen problems with transport.'

Mrs Deane looked keenly at him. 'And, were there?' she asked, pushing her reading glasses up into her short green wavy hair.

Sammy scratched his head. 'She wanted to catch the bus instead but the first bus driver didn't have any change for a ten pound note. If I remember, we waited an hour for the next bus in the rain.'

'You poor dear,' said Mrs Deane. 'I like reading my horoscopes. I always read them first thing in the morning with my cup of tea.'

'Shh,' hissed Dixie. 'Dr Livitupadup is going to pour a bucket of water over that old man!'

Sammy was glued to the television screen until Mrs Deane shooed them all up to bed.

When Darius arrived, Dixie had moved into Mrs Deane's room to make space for Sammy and Darius, who, despite Serberon's objections, the five boys simply wouldn't have fit into the room he shared with Mikhael and Jason.

Dixie had tried to make her room more masculine for Sammy and Darius, but there was no getting away from the pastel pink walls and bedroom furniture. Several soft toys bulged from under the bed. She had left out her posters of

Nitron Dark and the Nitromen Firesticks team along with Firesticks and Dragonball memorabilia; badges, sticker books, a black and gold striped scarf and black baseball cap with the initials "ND" embossed in gold.

Both boys had chosen to sleep on the floor, tucked up in sleeping bags and resting their heads on Dixie's pastel pink bean bag.

Exhausted from the flying, Darius had gone to sleep almost as soon as his head touched the makeshift pillow. He slept soundly beside Sammy, snoring every few seconds, stopping when Sammy pushed him with his foot.

Despite trying every trick he knew, Sammy found it impossible to fall asleep. The sleeping bag was hot against his skin and it held him in a fixed position. He couldn't stick his legs out of the end to cool down like he could in a proper bed with a duvet.

After spending ages wriggling to get comfy, he sat up and reached for the glass of cola he had brought upstairs. Above his head, Nitron Dark was staring at him from the poster on the wall.

Sammy reached up to open the arched window overlooking the garden. He leant across the wide windowsill that, judging by the cushion, the copy of Nitron Dark's autobiography and chocolate wrappers, Dixie used the windowsill as her reading seat. He pulled the curtain aside and stopped in his tracks, screaming and dropping his glass to the floor.

Outside the window, four pairs of blood red eyes inside dark hooded capes stared straight at him. Unable to move, Sammy stood rooted to the spot, his fingers white with terror, gripping the windowsill for dear life.

Darius jumped to his feet and rubbed sleep from his eyes as the door burst open and Mrs Deane and Dixie ran into the room.

'What's…' started Mrs Deane, her eyes widening, her mouth dropping open. She pulled her knitted shawl around her shoulders. 'Oh my,' she whispered. 'The Shape are here.'

Breaking his trance, Sammy reached down into the hold-all bag he was using to store his holiday clothes and pulled out his staff, the hand-picked branch of a Horse Chestnut tree he had found in the woods within the school grounds at Dragamas.

At Dragamas the staff was used in a number of ways, from casting magic to stirring potions. Now though, Sammy planned to use it to drive the four figures suspended from the second floor window, away from the house and away from him.

Mrs Deane was already holding her own staff. She marched forward and pushed open the window, knocking it into the hooded figures.

Sammy jumped as the red eyes wobbled and disappeared.

Mrs Deane turned back into the bedroom, her cheeks crimson with rage.

'Serberon!' she yelled. 'Mikhael, Jason. In here! NOW!'

Sammy edged forward to the window. He saw the red eyes dangling underneath the window ledge. A long wooden pole was propped against the wall, the dark cape swaying in the breeze.

'They've gone Mrs Deane,' said Sammy. 'Look.'

Mrs Deane clenched her fists. 'Oh they'll be going all right. The nerve of those boys, especially to you Sammy, you'd think they'd be more sensitive.'

'Sensitive?' asked Sammy. 'What's it got to do with them?'

'Wake up Sammy,' said Darius. He grinned and let go of the sleeping bag he'd been clutching. 'It's a joke.'

'A joke?' spluttered Sammy. 'How can it be a joke?'

Mrs Deane put her arm around him. 'I'm so sorry Sammy,' she said quietly. 'You three go back to bed. I'll deal with my sons.'

Twenty minutes later, Mrs Deane returned with four large mugs of hot chocolate. She sat at the end of Dixie's bed until all three children fell asleep. As Sammy's eyes closed, he saw her lift Dixie up and carry her daughter out of the room, closing the door softly behind them.

CHAPTER 4

BACK TO DRAGAMAS

The following morning, Serberon, Mikhael and Jason came down to breakfast with extremely solemn faces. Each brother offered an apology to Sammy and they showed him the twelve metre garden poles and bed sheets they had rubbed in soot to disguise them and pretend to be the Shape.

Serberon held out a cardboard box with eight glass balls inside. He poked them with his forefinger and they gave off an eerie red glow that bounced off the kitchen walls.

'They're joke rubies from the Floating Circus,' explained Serberon. 'We got them last year.'

Sammy picked up one of the marble sized balls. He held it up to the light, remembering how much it had frightened him.

Serberon shifted his weight. 'I'm sorry Sammy, really, we all are.'

'Yeah sorry.' Mikhael and Jason spoke together and nodded.

Sammy swallowed hard, surprised he had a lump in his throat.

'It's ok, really,' he said, putting the ruby coloured marble back in the box.

'Good,' said Mrs Deane. 'Now that's sorted, why don't you enjoy the morning.'

Sammy didn't need telling twice. He crammed the rest of his toast into his pocket for Kyrillan and ran out to the garden with Dixie and Darius.

'Be back by three,' Mrs Deane called out of the kitchen window. 'You need to pack for tomorrow.'

In reply, Dixie waved at her mother and they mounted their dragons to play a last game of Dragonball with her brothers before the end of the holiday.

As they swooped from end to end of the Dragonball pitch, Sammy knew his flying had improved dramatically over the seven weeks since the end of the summer term. He had been impatient waiting for Kyrillan to learn to fly and even more impatient whilst painstakingly learning the techniques to mount and dismount.

Mrs Deane had insisted he and Dixie were shown the correct way to fly so that, in her opinion, they were less likely to come into any mischief or break any bones.

As Sammy glided to the far end of the pitch, he thought that apart from his first fall (from two feet up when Kyrillan had thrown him off backwards) flying dragons was something that almost came naturally to him.

He was still pondering this thought back in the house at ten past three when he was piling freshly ironed shirts, trousers, socks and a pair of smart leather shoes his parents had bought him in London into his grey school suitcase with the initials S.R.R. stitched in green thread in the top right hand corner.

He had taken Serberon's advice and packed his books at the bottom, followed by his towels to keep his school clothes and evening and weekend clothes free from the dust his books had accumulated over the holiday. Sammy rested his night things and wash bag on the top of the suitcase, ready to throw inside in the morning.

Mrs Deane cooked a huge farewell meal for her three sons, Sammy, Dixie and Darius. After gorging on pizzas, pasties, crisps and chocolate ice cream, Sammy walked up to bed with hundreds of butterflies swarming in his stomach, caused partly from overeating at dinner and partly with excitement at the thought of going back to Dragamas.

If Sammy had fallen asleep with butterflies in his stomach, it was nothing compared with the surge of excitement he felt when he opened his eyes.

Darius was already up, his sleeping bag tightly rolled and standing vertically next to his suitcase with the initials D.M. inscribed on the side.

Sammy made a special point of looking out of the window where the "Shape" had been.

'Nothing there,' he said out loud.

'Nothing where?' asked a voice behind him.

Sammy spun round. 'Oh, hi Dixie, uh, nowhere.'

'It was open,' Dixie looked embarrassed. 'I just wanted to get a few things from under the bed.'

Sensing she wanted to do it alone Sammy nodded. 'Ok, I'll go to the bathroom.'

'Thanks. I'll only be a minute. Mum's done a bit of breakfast and a packed lunch. We go back a day after the first years and Serberon says there's never any nice food left.'

Sammy turned away from the window, leaving his thoughts of the Shape behind him. 'Seems ages ago, doesn't it,' he said, picking up his clothes and wash bag.

'Yeah,' said Dixie, kneeling down and peering under the bed.

'I'll see you in a minute,' said Sammy, sure she wasn't listening.

'Mm.'

Sammy stole a glance back into the bedroom. Dixie had pulled out a teddy bear wearing a Nitromen t-shirt from under the bed. He grinned and went into the bathroom to get ready.

He swapped his pyjamas for his black school trousers and long sleeved white shirt and fumbled his tie into shape. He slicked spikes into his blond hair and after a quick glance in the mirror, he ran back to Dixie's room and threw the crumpled pyjamas and wash bag into his case, then ran downstairs to the kitchen.

Contrary to Dixie promising a "bit of breakfast", Mrs Deane had prepared a huge assortment of freshly baked bread rolls, a large dollop of butter in the shape of a dragon, marmalade and six different types of jam.

She had even provided oversized purple serviettes to keep the food away from their neatly pressed school uniforms. Sammy, Dixie and Darius were going into their second year at Dragamas, whilst Serberon, Mikhael and Jason were starting their penultimate fourth year.

'Don't you all look good,' said Mrs Deane, beaming at them and dabbing her eye with a serviette. 'Here Sammy, let me fix your tie.'

Sammy looked down, his tie seemed to be ok, but he let Mrs Deane untie his effort and pull it straight. He loved the breakfast banter at the Deane house.

When the last crumb of breakfast had been eaten and the breakfast plates had been washed and put away, Mrs Deane ushered the six of them out of the house.

Outside and despite knowing that he was with his best friends and was going back to his favourite school, Sammy found the butterflies in his stomach were back. His hands shook a little as he helped Dixie's brothers heave their suitcases into the back of Mrs Deane's rickety blue Land Rover. Behind them, the six dragons stamped and hurrumphed as if they too were keen to get moving.

Mrs Deane revved the engine and a cloud of blue-grey smoke shot out of the rusty exhaust.

'Come on, come on,' said Mrs Deane, tapping the steering wheel and laughing as she reversed around the old oak tree in the middle of the gravel driveway.

With a whooshing and whirring of wings, the dragons took off and circled the car. Mrs Deane checked her mirrors and swung the Land Rover out of the drive and on to the village road, singing the Dragamas school song.

'At Dragamas we are brave and strong,' she sang, turning into the village high street.

'At Dragamas,' chorused everyone in the back.

Sammy leaned out of the open back of the Land Rover as they passed the shops and caught a glimpse of his uncle (on his mother's side) Peter Pickering's jewellery store.

Almost unconsciously he checked his Casino watch as they went past. It was the watch his uncle had given him as a birthday present, a watch Sammy had found had hidden powers and was the same watch worn by Commander Altair, the Armoury teacher at Dragamas.

In almost no time at all, they followed the road out of the village, into the long, high hedged lane, until finally they stopped opposite a pair of wooden gates hanging from two stone pillars. On the left hand pillar, a wooden sign read "Dragamas School for Dragon Charming" in black gothic swirl writing.

Sammy remembered his parents first words when they had arrived this time last year. Neither his mother nor his father had been able to see the sign or the castle beyond. Until one of the teachers had arrived, his parents had been sure Sammy was seeing things that simply weren't there.

During his first year, Sammy had learnt that Dragamas was protected by a shimmering bubble shaped dome that only allowed people with links to dragons to see in.

To the rest of the world, when they looked at the school, they saw neither the bubble, nor the castle. Instead they would see a desolate farm building that no matter how long they looked, or how badly they wanted to get there, they would be unable to set foot inside the large grounds surrounding the school.

This was the work of Dragamas headmaster, Sir Lok Ragnarok, a Dragon Commander of the highest rank before he had retired and taken the post of headmaster of his former school.

Mrs Deane pulled into the small layby opposite the gates and checked her watch.

'We have fifteen minutes in our slot to unload your cases and say goodbye,' she said, pushing open the car door. 'This is the worst bit for me,' she explained, 'dropping off all my children, then back to an empty house.'

'It won't be for long Mum,' said Serberon. 'Then you'll wish we'd all go back and leave you to your peace and quiet!'

'I know,' sniffed Mrs Deane, pulling out a purple serviette.

Sammy shifted his weight uncomfortably. He wanted his own mother to be there, giving him the big hug Mrs Deane was giving to Dixie, Serberon, Jason and Mikhael in turn.

Then he had the wind knocked out of him as Mrs Deane gave him and Darius a goodbye hug as well.

'Nice to meet you Darius honey,' said Mrs Deane. 'See you again Sammy. Boys, take care of your sister, yes goodbye Dixie as well. Work hard all of you, but don't forget to have a good time too!'

Before Sammy had a chance to thank her for having him to stay, Mrs Deane slammed her door shut and drove off at break-neck speed. He watched as the cloud of orange muddy dust subsided.

Between arriving and goodbyes, Serberon, Jason and Mikhael had unloaded their six suitcases which were stacked up in the layby.

Sammy sat on his suitcase. 'So what happens now?'

'We go in,' said Serberon, grinning at him. 'There should be more people though. Last year, we went in the Shute.'

'The what?' asked Darius. 'Do they shoot you?'

Mikhael laughed. 'It's a different kind of Shute. Inside the gates there's an underground passage from here to the castle doors.'

'Yeah,' said Serberon. 'There's a conveyor belt, you just put your luggage on and walk beside it.'

'Cool,' said Darius, picking up one end of his case. 'Give me a hand with this will you?'

'I'll help,' said Dixie, drowned out by a sudden snort from the usually silent Jason. 'I could carry it by myself if I wanted,' she retorted.

Jason snorted again, followed by a giggle from Mikhael.

'Like to see that,' said Serberon.

'Won't be necessary,' came a gruff voice from behind the gates.

Sammy recognised the voice and the person behind it as the gates split open and Captain Duke Stronghammer, leader of the dwarves who mined gemstones under the castle, appeared.

Captain Stronghammer was wearing his usual blue denim dungarees, grubby white shirt with the sleeves rolled up to the elbow and red and white spotted neckerchief. His calf length black boots matched his hair to perfection. Like the dwarves Sammy had read about in picture books, the dwarves he had met in real life came complete with shaggy beards and only came up to his waist in height.

'Hi Captain Stronghammer,' said Sammy.

'Hi Sammy,' replied the dwarf as he surveyed the group. 'See you're still hanging around with the trolls.'

Sammy looked at Dixie and her three brothers with their genetic green hair. "Trolls" Captain Stronghammer had called them. Enemies of the dwarves for their height and plundering interest in stealing gemstones. It had been Serberon who had explained this to him and he remembered how Dixie had been embarrassed of her hair which made her stand out from the crowd when he had first met her.

'Nothing wrong with green hair,' said Serberon, patting his own spiky green haired head. 'Doesn't like our ancestors, does he?'

Although Serberon grinned, Sammy knew it hid the pain of taunts from the villagers.

'Do you blame me?' growled Captain Stronghammer. 'Murderers, plunderers, thieves, should be shot the lot of you.'

Darius coughed. 'Talking of shot, can we use the Shute? These bags are heavy.'

Captain Stronghammer laughed. 'Just a joke boys.'

Sammy noticed the dwarf looked a little nervous and cast a glance behind him. Dixie was standing rigid, her arms folded and a look of thunder in her eyes. Her face was flushed pink under her green hair and Sammy had never seen her so angry.

'You know nothing about our family,' she shrieked, high pitched and close to tears. 'You know nothing about me, or my brothers, or my parents.'

Before it happened Sammy knew, instinctively, that it was too close to the bone for Dixie whose father had left home when she was seven. Even four years later, the wound was deep and she had been affected by it. Tears streamed down her face as she ran over to the dwarf and pulled at her hair.

'Doesn't make us any different,' she shrieked, shrugging off Serberon as he stepped between his sister and Captain Stronghammer, taking her wrists before she could do any damage to the dwarf.

Mikhael and Jason pushed past Captain Stronghammer, each carrying their cases. Sammy and Darius followed with their own grey suitcases. Sammy gave Captain Stronghammer a long stare, trying to read his mind.

This was another skill taught at Dragamas and one he hoped to become good at. He found it hard to focus as the dwarf's mind flittered in a mix of thoughts, looking up at the brother and sister in front of him.

Eventually Serberon let go of Dixie and she slumped to the floor, still crying.

Captain Stronghammer bent down and whispered into Dixie's ear. She sat up straight, her cheeks returning to their normal colour and she straightened her green ponytail with a smile back on her face.

Sammy helped Serberon carry the remaining cases into the school grounds. Captain Stronghammer closed the wooden gates behind them and peered out between the rails.

'That was close,' muttered Captain Stronghammer as two men on horses rode towards the gate.

Sammy turned to look as the horses clip-clopped past them.

'Old Samagard Farm,' said one of the riders. 'Should be Old Samagard Ruins.'

The other rider laughed. 'It's been in ruins for as long as I can remember. Should tear it all down really, but it's a listed building, can't be touched.'

Sammy turned to the riders, his mouth wide open. 'Can't you see the forest, the road, the castle?' he asked in amazement.

The riders, just a few feet away, ignored him as though he hadn't spoken, pulled on their reins and clip-clopped down the lane.

'Can't hear you,' wheezed Captain Stronghammer. 'Old Samagard Farm. I always wondered what the sign said if you couldn't see, you know,' he tipped his head towards the castle, 'the school.'

Captain Stronghammer led them a short way up the tree lined road that led to the castle. To their left the trees formed the start of the forest that surrounded the school. Under the shelter of the trees, ferns, bushes and heathers grew alongside snowdrops and bluebells that, Captain Stronghammer informed them, grew all year round.

They stopped between two large rhododendron bushes and Sammy peered over Serberon's shoulder. About five paces in front of them, there was a small stone entrance with irregular sized bricks forming an open passageway that led down into the ground.

'The Shute,' said Captain Stronghammer, pointing towards the darkness. 'Go down the steps, then follow the passage to your right and it'll take you all the way up to the castle.'

No sooner than Captain Stronghammer had helped Dixie down the steps, he raised a hand to his ear in a salute and marched back towards the gate.

Sammy watched as the dwarf pulled open the school gates and let in a large white minibus, driven by a man Sammy recognised as Professor John Burlay, his Astronomics teacher and head of the North school house.

At Dragamas, students were divided in to four houses, North, South, East and West, representing the four points of the compass. Each house was symbolic of an element as well as a direction.

Sammy was in the North house, which represented the element Earth, which Sammy had been led to believe would play a part in his future, hopefully as a Dragon Knight.

'Hi Sammy!' Professor Burlay shouted out of the minibus window. 'Plenty of time to stare into space in my lessons, but I think you're needed here to help with your luggage!' He laughed along with the group of older children in the back of the minibus.

Sammy snapped himself out of the daydream and waved as Professor Burlay drove off with what looked like a group of fifth years who were arriving at Dragamas for the start of their final year.

Captain Stronghammer pulled open the gates and waved in a family of four students. The two boys and two girls had small blue stripes on their collars, on the boys' ties and on the girls' shirt pockets. They gave Sammy a frosty stare, muttering "West is best" as they helped each other into the entrance of the Shute.

Sammy followed them a few paces behind, down the uneven stone steps and into a passage lit by pools of candlelight, jumping in the darkness as the flames moved in a cool wind that whistled through the tunnel.

'Thought you'd got lost,' said Darius, making Sammy jump. 'We've been waiting ages for you.'

'Sorry.' Sammy took a close look at the passage. The ceiling was only a few feet above his head and it looked as though it had been hacked out by hand.

It was slightly claustrophobic with a damp, old, musty smell hanging in the air. Next to the narrow pathway at his feet, a belt-like black line snaked alongside a shallow stream.

'Put your case on that,' said Serberon. 'It's a conveyor belt. Our cases are already on it. We'll catch them up at the castle.'

Sammy followed Serberon's instructions and his case jolted along the black belt, pulled towards the castle by the hidden mechanism.

'Keep out of the water as well,' said Serberon. 'It's really cold this time of the year.'

Sammy nodded. He'd just noticed tiny glittering shards under the water. They were jewels and gemstones, worth pence individually, but collectively they would be worth a fortune.

It was with stones like these that Dragamas headmaster, Sir Lok Ragnarok, had used to pay the Shape's ransom. He had been forced to pay an enormous sum to prevent their enemy, the Shape, from carrying out their threat to kill their dragons and close the school.

Sammy felt around his neck, his hand closing on the warm metal cross he had received at the end of term for his bravery against the Shape. He had finally admitted to himself the unpalatable truth that the Shape were searching for him, believing him to be the key to their plan.

To make matters worse, Sammy had identified one of the members of the Shape as his Gemology teacher, Dr Margarite Lithoman, also known as Eliza Elungwen. He had been awarded the cross for bravery and had then helped Sir Ragnarok raise the final amount of money to keep the school open.

Sammy kept an eye on his suitcase as they walked in silence along the dark passageway.

Serberon, Mikhael and Jason walked ahead, behind the boys and girls from the West house, leaving Sammy, Dixie and Darius to make sure their cases arrived safely at the end of the passageway.

They needn't have worried as the jerky movement pulled the conveyor belt in a perfectly straight line and before Sammy knew it, they were climbing up another set of roughly hewn steps that led into a circle of light.

As they climbed up, Sammy looked back into the passage and saw two dwarves in the shadows pulling on some kind of machinery that he guessed kept the conveyor belt moving.

Beyond the dwarves, the passage carried on and Sammy guessed it linked up with the passage under the castle that led to the small house in the school grounds belonging to Mrs Grock, Dragamas school secretary and nurse.

Sammy climbed the steps, dragging his case behind him. The light was daylight and they emerged in the gravel courtyard that ran around the castle walls. Up close, the grey stone castle with its nine turrets looked as impressive as ever.

Professor Burlay has already parked the white minibus outside of the castle's main entrance, between the South and West towers.

There were two towers at each compass point, one for girls dormitories and one for boys dormitories with a shared common room for studying and socialising underneath.

Each tower contained five floors, one floor per school year with the first years sleeping in the coned turret roof, the second years on the floor below, the third years on the floor below the second years, then the fourth years on the floor below the third years and finally the fifth year dormitories were at ground level. Sir Ragnarok had his own tower in the centre of the castle.

This year, Sammy remembered, because their dragons were getting bigger, they would have to sleep underground in the Dragon Chambers underneath the North tower.

As if reading his mind, Dixie leaned over to him. 'Lucky first years, hatching their dragons and they get to keep them in their rooms,' she whispered.

Sammy nodded. 'I was just thinking that.'

'I'm glad we've done the hatching bit,' whispered Darius. 'It wasn't quite as good as I imagined.'

Sammy laughed. 'Nelson's ok though, isn't he?'

Darius nodded. 'Thanks to Dr Lithoman.'

More students joined them in the castle courtyard, emerging in twos and threes from the underground passageway. Captain Stronghammer was a tiny blur on the horizon against the shimmering pearlescent bubble surrounding the school.

'Welcome to Dragamas,' came a croaky voice from the castle entrance.

Sammy recognised the voice. It belonged to Sir Lok Ragnarok, headmaster of Dragamas.

'...slight cold...have to come closer...' Sammy caught as he, Dixie and Darius mingled among the first years, who seemed to be very small.

Small and nervous, thought Sammy, bet we were never like that. He smiled at a girl clutching a green envelope. She shrank away from him, staring over his shoulder.

Sammy turned around. Dixie was behind him. He grinned to himself and turned back to explain, but the girl had gone.

'First years please follow your heads of house,' said Sir Ragnarok. 'North students with Professor Burlay, East students with Professor Sanchez, South students with Commander Altair and West students...West students, follow me.'

Sammy stared at Dixie. It didn't look as though Sir Ragnarok had found a replacement for Dr Lithoman.

They watched as Professor Burlay, dressed as in a grey cotton suit, led the ten nervous North first years through the castle entrance and out of sight. The North students were followed by the East students, led by Professor Sanchez.

Professor Sanchez waved to her son Simon, who was in Sammy's year. Simon went very red and turned away.

Commander Altair followed Professor Sanchez, leading his South students into the castle. He was still as tall and handsome as ever, dressed casually in dark blue jeans with his belt studded with three silver stars and a grey jumper with the sleeves rolled up, his fair hair slicked away from his keen blue eyes that scanned his students, daring them to step out of line.

Sammy wondered about his belt with the three silver stars. Were they awards he had been given to become a Dragon Commander?

Sir Ragnarok followed, taking the ten West students inside. He beckoned for the older students to follow, accompanied by staff chaperons.

Sammy was pleased to see gaunt, ghost-like Dr Shivers, their teacher for Dragon Studies, was escorting the remainder of the North house to their tower. Dr Shivers led them through the castle to the North common room, identified by a tarnished plaque with the single word "North" written in scrawled Gothic writing.

Inside the circular common room, Sammy was even more pleased to see that it remained exactly the same as he remembered with the bookshelves, tables, chairs, sofas and a large grandfather clock on the left as they walked in. At either end of the common room, two staircases spiralled up to the tower dormitories where boys and girls slept separately.

Dr Shivers split the boys from the girls and led the way up the boys' spiral staircase, dropping off five boys at each floor.

When just Sammy and Darius were left, Dr Shivers took them up to the next level.

'Here you are boys,' said Dr Shivers with a pale smile as they reached another solid wooden door.

As Sammy had expected, there was a silver plaque in the middle of the door that read "Second Years" in the same Gothic scrawl as the "North" plaque on the door leading to the common room.

Above the door was the familiar old fashioned gold bell that would be used to tell them when to get up in the morning.

'This reminds me of my time here,' said Dr Shivers, holding the door open for them.

'You stayed here?' asked Darius, peering into the round room.

'I certainly did,' said Dr Shivers, with a hint of a smile curling at the corners of his lips. 'Me and John Burlay, we had some good times here.'

Sammy ducked under Dr Shivers's arm and walked into the room. It was laid out exactly the same as their old room above them with five windows, five beds and five chests of drawers. The only difference was that the second year dormitory ceiling was flat and didn't extend into the cone roof.

There was a large reddish brown stain on the far side of the ceiling, running down the wall. Sammy stared hard at Dr Shivers, but he offered no clue to the cause of the stain.

'Hey Sammy, you're next to me again.' Darius pushed past Dr Shivers and leaped on to the bed nearest the door. He waved to the next bed along and Sammy crossed the room and lay his suitcase on the green duveted bed.

The five beds were evenly spaced, with the feet end pointing towards the centre of the room. Deep green curtains were pinned to the wall, ready to swing out around the bed and chest of drawers to give the occupant privacy.

Sammy knelt at the foot of his bed to check the nameplate. It was definitely his bed, carried down from the floor above with the plaque:

North House
Samuel R. Rambles
5 years

He checked Darius's plaque, it still read forty-five years which Darius had explained that he hoped to become a teacher at Dragamas when he was older.

Next to Sammy's bed the name plaque read Toby Reed and the bed closest to the stain was laid out for Toby's twin brother, Gavin Reed. On Gavin's other side, next to the door and opposite Sammy, there was a bed made up without a name plaque.

'Just the four of us,' said Sammy.

'Yeah,' said Darius in a hollow whisper. 'We share with a ghost!' He giggled, sending a shiver down Sammy's spine.

'A ghost,' whispered Sammy. 'I don't know if I can do that. Maybe Amos could come back.'

Darius laughed louder. 'It was a joke Sammy!'

'What was?' demanded a familiar voice from the doorway.

Sammy spun round. 'Gavin! Toby!' he exclaimed, clapping his hand on the back of Gavin, one of the dark haired Reed twins.

'Nice room,' said Toby, coming through the door with a suitcase in each hand. 'Where are we sleeping?'

'You're here,' said Darius, still grinning, 'and you're there Gavin.'

Gavin frowned as he saw his name on the bed next to the brown stain. 'I'm not sleeping there,' he said, pulling at the fifth, unnamed bed. 'Whoever's going there can have the worst place.'

After a few minutes of huffing and puffing, Gavin switched the beds and threw his suitcase on the bed furthest away from the stain.

'Much better,' said Gavin, taking his black Dragamas rucksack off his shoulder and laying it next to his suitcase on the bed.

Gavin threw open his case and started unpacking, chucking his clothes haphazardly into the wooden chest of drawers beside his bed.

'You should have switched the name plaques,' said Toby. 'That would have been less work.'

Gavin grinned and threw his pillow across the room, aiming for his brother. The shot was wide and hit Darius on the shoulder.

Darius grabbed his own pillow and before long, Sammy joined in with Toby, thumping each other with their pillows. At a heavy clash with Gavin, Darius's pillow exploded and sent feathers and stuffing high into the air.

They were so busy yelling and thumping the pillows that they didn't notice a shadow slide up the staircase, followed by a boy no more than five feet tall, carrying a black rucksack and dressed in a pair of grey jeans and the navy school jumper with the North compass point logo over his heart.

The first any of them saw of him was when he coughed loudly at the door.

CHAPTER 5

THE NEW BOY

Sammy stopped first. He put down his ruffled pillow and waved for the others to stop.

'Hi,' said the short boy at the door. 'I'm Jock Hubar. I've transferred to Dragamas from St. Elderberries.'

'Hi Jock Hubar from St. Elderberries,' said Toby, doing his best to keep a straight face.

It was no use. At one hysterical giggle from Darius, Toby and Gavin collapsed on the floor in a fit of laughter.

'St. Elderberries,' howled Toby, thumping his pillow. 'Elderberries!'

The boy at the door said nothing and walked past the twins, setting his rucksack down on the empty bed with no name.

'Come on, let's not have another Amos,' said Sammy, remembering how they'd alienated their fifth housemate, Amos Leech, who had been so unhappy in his first year that he'd asked to change houses.

'But Sammy,' said Toby, still giggling hysterically, 'you don't understand. St. Elderberries is a school for girls!'

The new boy looked at Sammy and nodded. 'Officially for girls. My mother was headmistress there. She got me this place at Dragamas. Sir Ragnarok owed her a favour.'

'Must've been a big favour,' said Gavin, scooping his short hair into pretend bunches. 'Why did they let you out, Jock Hubar from St. Elderberries?'

'None of your business,' snapped Jock. 'It's between Sir Ragnarok and my mother. I should have been in West but there was only room in North. I wish I wasn't here.'

'I'm sure that could be arranged,' said Sammy without thinking. 'Uh, if you're not happy here that is.'

His words were drowned out as Gavin yelled "Yes" and leaped across the room, bouncing from bed to bed, and thumped Sammy on the back.

'Good one Sammy! Let's get Sir Ragnarok to send him...'

Sammy turned around to see where Gavin would suggest sending the boy. His jaw dropped. Gavin was standing rigidly still, his mouth half open in mid-sentence. Toby and Darius were equally frozen, each holding their tattered pillows. A faint red mist surrounded them.

'What have you done?' demanded Sammy. 'Undo it!'

'That's why I'm being transferred,' said Jock, grinning wickedly. 'I did it to my science teacher. 'Course it wears off after about five minutes. Gave me long enough to nip round to his desk and get the exam answers I was missing. What?' finished Jock. 'You never done anything like that?'

Sammy felt his cheeks burn. 'I, uh,' he flustered, 'not like that anyway. How's it done?'

Jock held out his hand, revealing a blood red stone. 'It's the gemstone we get given in the second year,' he explained. 'It's a ruby.'

'How did you...'

'My Mum,' Jock answered without bothering to let Sammy finish. 'She's the new Gemology teacher. The three of us come as a package, me, my Mum and my Dad. You probably know him, Fignus Hubar.'

Sammy felt his jaw drop again as he recognized the name. 'Duke Stronghammer is your father?'

'Captain Stronghammer to you I expect,' said Jock. 'Mum calls him Figgy. He's supposed to be the best miner in the school.'

'You're having me on,' said Sammy. 'There's no way your dad's a dwarf.'

'He is so,' said Jock. 'I bet that girl from downstairs with the green hair is related to trolls somewhere along the line. They take all sorts at Dragamas!'

Sammy nodded, knowing full well that Dixie was indeed from a troll-related family.

'Dixie Deane,' he said out loud. 'She's in our house.'

'Figures,' said Jock. 'Green hair and everything.'

Sammy nodded again. 'When will…'

'…it wear off?' finished Jock. He checked his watch. 'About twenty seconds. I only did it a little bit. Let's go before they wake up. Most people get really mad at me!'

'No, I'll stay,' said Sammy.

'Bor-ing!' yelled Jock, vaulting over Sammy's bed. He ruffled Gavin's hair, leaped out of the room and clattered down the spiral staircase.

As promised, Gavin, Toby and Darius came back to life. The faint red mist evaporated.

Toby was grey faced, as though the colour had been drained from his skin. 'What was that?' he whispered.

'He'll wish he'd never done that,' shouted Darius. 'The ruby is a stone of peace.'

'Wait until I get my hands on him,' said Gavin, straightening his ruffled hair.

'Where did he get the stone?' demanded Darius. 'They're for advanced magic only.'

'We all get one,' said Sammy. 'His mum's the new Gemology teacher and Captain Duke Stronghammer is his dad.'

'Duke who?' asked Gavin. 'Is this a joke?'

'How come you weren't affected?' demanded Darius, clenching his fists together.

'Didn't he get you as well, Sammy?' asked Toby.

Sammy held up his hand. 'I can explain,' he said slowly, 'I think.'

'So he didn't get you as well?' asked Toby, sitting on his bed, his hand pressed against his eyes.

'Like being in a mine,' said Gavin. 'All dark, can't see anything, can't hear anything.'

'It's illegal,' said Darius. 'That's what my parents taught me: Only use the stones for deeds of kind, unless on the receiving end you don't mind.'

'So he'll get that done to him?' asked Sammy.

'By the rule of three times three,' chanted Gavin with Toby joining in, 'he'll receive what's done to me.'

Sammy felt a cold shiver run down his spine. He wanted to get out of the room, suddenly afraid of his friends.

'Where are you going?' asked Gavin, wobbling slightly, the effects of the ruby not quite worn off yet. 'It's just a song from a T.V. programme. Nothing will come of it.'

Sammy paused in the doorway, staring at a shimmering surface of pale blue liquid which had spread from floor to ceiling.

'Then explain that,' he said, pointing at the oily blue wall in front of him where the door should have been. He poked his finger at the shimmering substance and his hand fell back as if it was as solid as the wooden door. He stared around at his friends. 'I think we're locked in.'

Sammy pressed both hands against the oily liquid. It rippled slightly but wouldn't let his hands or arms go through.

'It's no good,' muttered Sammy. 'We're stuck here.'

Toby walked up to the doorway and scowled. 'Magic,' he grumbled. 'We're here until we're let out.'

'Magic?' exclaimed Sammy, wishing he wasn't so constantly surprised at the seemingly endless powers of the dragon folk.

'Yeah,' added Gavin. 'Mum uses this on our bedroom door to keep us inside.'

'She lets us out when our room is tidy,' said Toby. He grinned. 'Once we were in there for twenty-four hours.'

Sammy stared. 'How did she know when it was clean? he asked in amazement.

'Like that,' said Toby, pointing at the doorway. 'You can see figures behind the shimmery stuff, like looking through a mirror from the other side.'

'Oh,' said Sammy. He peered into the blueness. 'Woah, what's that?' he asked as shapes appeared behind the pool of shimmering silver-blue oil.

'Probably Jock using his stone,' said Darius. 'If he's any good, he'll be able to cast spells from a distance.'

As they leaned closer, there was a soft rumble and the pool of oil slid from the top of the doorway to the floor and evaporated into thin air, revealing a hunched over Sir Ragnarok, his arm around Jock Hubar's shoulders.

'Hello boys,' croaked Sir Ragnarok, his silver white beard barely moving as he spoke. 'I hear young Jock hasn't received the friendly welcome I promised him.'

'Tell-tale,' hissed Gavin.

Sir Ragnarok took a gold disc out of his robe pocket. He stared briefly at the disc, then at Gavin, Toby and Darius.

'I see,' said Sir Ragnarok, holding up the disc.

Sammy recognised the Directometer, the device used to give directions and replay events recorded by the school monitors in Sir Ragnarok's office.

'I see,' repeated Sir Ragnarok. 'Events have been tit for tat, an eye for an eye, a white cat for a black monkey.'

Sammy looked at Sir Ragnarok, wondering what was going to happen next. Sir Ragnarok scratched his head.

'Gavin and Toby,' said Sir Ragnarok slowly. 'You would be wise to make friends before enemies. Darius, you too have much to learn, especially about the stones.'

Sir Ragnarok held out his hand. Four red stones glowed brightly in his outstretched palm.

'One each,' said Sir Ragnarok. 'Please use them for good, not evil.'

He threw stones to Gavin, Toby and Darius. Then he turned to Sammy and came so close, Sammy could feel the tip of the headmaster's beard tickling his chin.

'Ah yes,' whispered Sir Ragnarok. 'Samuel R. Rambles, Dragon Knight in training. Tell me Sammy, how was it that you alone were able to shield yourself from the spell? Indeed, many things about you suggest powers beyond your years. Choose your friends wisely Sammy. A man is known by the company he keeps.'

As Sir Ragnarok backed away, he pressed a ruby the size of a golf ball into Sammy's palm. 'For good, Sammy, not evil.'

Sammy nodded as Sir Ragnarok left the tower room. He felt heavy, like he was in a trance. Events had happened so quickly. He had a new roommate and now a new gemstone to add to the end of his staff.

'Hey Sammy?'

Sammy looked up.

Darius was looking strangely at him. 'What did Sir Ragnarok say?'

'Uh nothing,' said Sammy. 'He just looked at me like I'm weird or something. Just because I didn't turn to stone.'

'Weirdo,' said Gavin, grinning at him.

'I don't know why I didn't turn to stone,' repeated Sammy.

'Weird.' Gavin shrugged and turned to Jock, who was sitting at the end of the nameless bed. While Sir Ragnarok had been speaking with Sammy, Jock had packed away his belongings in the bedside chest of drawers.

'Hey Jock,' said Gavin. 'I'll have my space back now.'

Jock looked up and surveyed the stain trickling down from the ceiling.

'Ok, it's all yours.'

'I'll make you,' said Gavin, squaring up his fists. 'No tell-tale's going to sleep between me and my brother.'

'Hey Gavin,' said Sammy, stepping forward. 'He said yes.'

Gavin stared sheepishly and lowered his fists. 'Thanks.'

Sammy and Darius helped Jock move his bed back towards to door. Gavin and Toby dragged Gavin's bed across the stone floor, back to its original position.

'Phew! That was hard work,' said Sammy when they had finished. 'What's next?'

'Lunch I hope,' said Darius, grinning. 'That was definitely hard work.'

'Sounds good,' said Jock. 'You'll be able to meet my mum.'

'Great,' said Gavin sarcastically. 'Like we'd want to do that.'

Jock glared at Gavin. 'Just watch it,' he muttered, holding out his red stone.

'Another few weeks and I'll be able to do that,' said Gavin. He kicked his bed back against the wall and stormed out of the tower room with Toby hurrying in his wake.

Sammy, Jock and Darius followed at a slower pace and met up with the second year North girls in the Main Hall, the huge auditorium where they congregated for meals and assemblies.

The four house tables were pointing, as always, vertically down the room with their ends facing a horizontal table up on the stage which was used by the teachers. Even in the bustling hall, the North girls were easily recognisable by Dixie's vividly green hair.

Sammy was pleased to see there were still pieces of pumpkin flesh brushed in the corners and a stray piece of tinsel was wound around the arm of Sir Ragnarok's throne like chair. School hadn't changed much over the holiday.

'Over here, Sammy,' Dixie shouted as they approached the North table.

'She's saved you a seat,' said a second girl, angel-like, with silvery blonde hair tied into neat plaits.

'Thanks Milly,' said Sammy, sitting on the wooden chair next to Dixie.

'Sammy's got a girlfriend!' Gavin giggled at him and sat next to Milly.

Sammy noticed the dreamy expression on Milly's face and thought it looked very much like Gavin had a girlfriend too.

Jock sat the other side of Dixie, staring at the sparkling clean, empty plates which were white with a green edging to symbolise the North house.

'They might have given us something to eat,' grumbled Jock, reaching out to pick up his knife and fork.

Sammy grinned, knowing the second Jock picked up his cutlery, there would be a noise like thunder and the plate would fill with a delicious pile of hot food, the welcome feast for students on their first day back at Dragamas.

At the front of the hall Sir Ragnarok smiled, there was always one student who didn't heed the notice pinned to the entrance door that read "One star deducted per impatient student".

Everyone looked up as Jock's plate made an explosive sound and filled with hot food.

Jock went crimson. 'You could have told me that would happen,' he snapped, putting down his knife and fork and scowling as a black star floated from the teachers table on to the noticeboard.

Sir Ragnarok coughed and stood up. The school fell silent and stood up, their chairs creaking across the stone floor.

'Good afternoon Dragamas,' Sir Ragnarok coughed again. 'I wish all of our new first years a very warm welcome to Dragamas School for Dragon Charming,' he coughed a third time.

'We are one of a small number of schools remaining in Britain to instill the discipline and scholarship of the ancient art of dragon charming,' he paused, smiling as the first years gasped, 'and welcome back to everyone else!'

Sir Ragnarok clapped loudly. 'Welcome back everyone!'

The teachers, watching from the side of the room joined in the clapping as did the students from Sammy's table. Further down, Sammy saw that the girl from earlier had been given a place in the North house. She didn't seem to know what was going on, but had joined in the clapping as well.

Dixie elbowed him. 'Do you reckon we were that nervous on our first day?' she whispered.

Sammy shook his head. 'They've been here a day already, remember, the rest of the school returned while we were on our tour of the school on our first day.'

Dixie nodded. 'I don't think I was that nervous, especially after my brothers told me what to expect.'

Sammy looked back up the table. Dixie's three brothers were sitting at the fourth year table looking very grown up, even though they were only two years older.

'I suppose,' Sammy agreed as they sat down. 'I didn't want it to be like my old school in Ratisbury.'

Dixie nodded again. 'It sounds a lot different than Dragamas.'

'It was horrible,' whispered Sammy. 'Come on, let's eat!'

They picked up their forks at the same time as the rest of their table. A thunderous roar echoed down the Hall followed by a succession of loud "pop", "pop", "pop", as food materialised on their plates.

'Cool!' shrieked Milly. 'I've got fish!'

'Traitor,' said Dixie, looking at her own sausages and chips.

'Is it "choose your own"?' asked Sammy.

'Looks like it,' said Darius, staring wide eyed as a giant chocolate cake appeared on his plate. 'Anyone want to share?'

'You pig Darius, you'll never eat all that,' said Dixie, shaking her head.

'Bet I do,' Darius retorted. 'I could eat twice that!'

There was another loud "pop" and a second cake, dripping with chocolate icing and sprinkled with hundreds and thousands and mini marshmallows, squeezed itself up through the first cake.

'I was only joking,' wailed Darius as he stared at the mountain of cake.

'Bet you can't eat it all now,' giggled Dixie, helping herself to some of the marshmallows on top of the cake.

If Sammy had started to wish he'd thought of chocolate cake when he'd picked up his knife and fork, he was glad that he hadn't when his favourite dish, a full English breakfast with all the trimmings, except tomatoes and mushrooms appeared on his plate along with a glass of his favourite drink "Lerryade" that he, Dixie and Darius had discovered by mixing limeade and cherryade last year.

Everyone tucked into the food, laughing, joking and exchanging stories of what they'd done over the holidays. Sammy looked up and down the tables and smiled. It was perfect.

CHAPTER 6

DRAGON MINDERS

After lunch, the first years were led away by the housemasters, Professor Burlay leading the North students, Professor Sanchez leading the East students and Commander Altair leading the South students. In Dr Lithoman's absence, Sir Ragnarok escorted the West students.

Dr Shivers stepped up to the second year tables as gaunt and ghost-like as ever, his grey suit only a shade darker than the greyness of his sallow skin.

'We are starting with a warm up lesson,' he said, making the idea itself sound cold. 'In this Dragon Studies lesson I want to see how much you remember from your first year. We'll start outside, with your dragons please,' he said, leading them outside and into the rain.

Sammy turned around, meaning to tell Dixie about their new ruby stones but she had gone. He nudged Milly who held out her hands, mouthing "I don't know where she is" to him.

Sammy clutched his new timetable without really looking at it and ran after Gavin and Toby. When he asked, they hadn't seen Dixie either.

'She'll be late,' he said to Gavin.

Gavin shrugged. 'So what, as long as we're there on time. We can't afford to lose any more stars.'

Sammy knew this was directed at Jock and shook his head. 'We lost stars on our first day too,' he said, but Gavin wasn't listening.

Dr Shivers it seemed had been listening. 'You'll see in a moment Sammy,' he said with a grey tight lipped smile. 'Dixie will be there before us.'

Sammy stared at Dr Shivers. 'Wh..how?'

'Wait and see,' Dr Shivers laughed. 'We have a new Dragon Minder,' and he would say no more until they were outside and looking at forty brightly coloured dragons which were lined up in four neat rows on the grass lawns at the front of the castle.

The dragons were all shapes and sizes, different breeds, some with long necks and pointed faces and others with sharp spikes protruding from their backs that were in fact quite fleshy to the touch.

All of the dragons were one year old, between four and eight feet in length and covered from head to toe in shining scales.

At the front of the class, Dixie was sitting astride her blue-green dragon. Kiridor was some six feet long and, Sammy noticed, Dixie was wearing thick black leather trousers.

She waved as she saw Sammy and pulled the reins around her dragon's neck.

Kiridor, lolled over towards Sammy, who was standing at the back with Gavin and Toby.

'Hi Sammy.'

Sammy looked up. Dixie was level with his shoulders.

'You're the Dragon Minder?'

'Yeah.' Dixie grinned, her eyes shining. 'Captain Stronghammer asked me to be one this morning.'

'Lucky,' grumbled Gavin. 'Wish he'd made me a Dragon Minder. They get loads of time off lessons for feeding the dragons.'

'Really?' asked Sammy. 'That sounds good.'

'You could be a Dragon Minder,' said Dixie, steadying herself on Kiridor's back. 'There are two Dragon Minders for each house and Captain Stronghammer said I could choose the second North Dragon Minder. He'll recommend people from the other houses to Dr Shivers. He said you've got to be really committed and he doesn't want just anyone doing it.'

'I suppose he can't really have just anyone do it,' said Sammy thoughtfully, 'not with the Shape still around.'

'Funny that Sir Ragnarok didn't mention the Shape in his speech this year,' said Dixie.

'That's because the school's not closing,' Gavin grinned. 'There's no need to worry because the Shape are long gone after Sammy finished them off.'

'It wasn't quite like that,' Sammy tried to explain.

'Yeah, whatever,' interrupted Gavin. 'So, Dixie, who are you going to choose?'

Dixie didn't get a chance to speak as Dr Shivers came over.

'Hush please, we're about to start the lesson.' Dr Shivers whisked himself up to the front of the class. 'Ready when you are Captain Stronghammer.'

Captain Duke Stronghammer stood up from behind a pure gold scaled dragon with a blue underbelly.

'Morning all,' he said in his earthy dwarf voice. 'Ah, Jock there y'are. Would you go first?'

In front of the entire class, Jock marched up to the gold dragon. He put his left hand firmly on the dragon's back, bent his left knee and pushed up, swinging his right leg over the dragon as if mounting a small horse.

The dragon wobbled but stood firm. Jock pretended to take off a hat and bowed to the class audience.

Captain Stronghammer coughed, his cheeks pink with pride. 'There's a gud'un Jock. Shows 'em how it's done.'

'Quite,' said Dr Shivers with an icy smile. 'That will be all Captain Stronghammer. Please return at the end of the lesson to take the dragons back to their secret location.'

Sammy grinned at Dixie, knowing full well that the dragons lived under the North tower.

As Captain Stronghammer marched back to the castle, his head held high on his short body, Dr Shivers turned to the class.

'Do you think you can do that?'

They nodded, Gavin shouting from the back of the class "Yes Sir!"

Dr Shivers smiled again, thin laughter lines appearing in wrinkles beneath his grey eyes.

'Very well. Mount your dragons!'

Having practiced nearly all summer, Sammy was able to mount Kyrillan with the skill of a professional Dragonball player. He rested his foot on one of the spikes on Kyrillan's tail and hauled himself up on to the scaly back of his blue-green dragon. He rubbed a spot of dust off Kyrillan's neck and looked around to see how everyone else was doing.

Most of the class had managed to successfully mount their dragons and were taking their first tentative steps. Gavin and Toby were trying to get Milly to climb up on to her pastel pink dragon. She had her arms firmly folded. Even her dragon, Bubbles, was refusing to take part by lying on the ground, her head tucked between her front legs.

Gavin leaped down from his own dragon. 'Look Milly,' he shouted, loudly enough for the whole class to hear, 'it's like this,' he said cockily, 'watch me.'

Gavin rested his hand on the back of his own pale pink and grey dragon and pushed upwards to mount his dragon, Syren.

But as he leapt up, his dragon arched her back and Gavin flew face-first over Syren and landed heavily on the other side.

Everyone burst out laughing and clapped. Sammy noticed Jock laughed especially loudly.

Gavin went red and picked himself up as quickly as he had fallen down. Dr Shivers was next to him and helped pull Gavin to his feet.

'You need to see Mrs Grock,' said Dr Shivers. 'She'll clean you up and look after your cuts.'

'I'm fine,' snapped Gavin.

'I'm your teacher,' Dr Shivers replied coolly, sucking in his cheeks, making him look thinner and gaunter than before.

'I'm not going,' said Gavin, his cheeks flushed. 'I'm fine.'

Dr Shivers picked up his staff from where it was leaning against the castle wall. 'I'll give you a choice,' he said briskly, 'either go to Mrs Grock's and get cleaned up, or go to Sir Ragnarok's office and lose twenty three stars.'

'Twenty three?' spluttered Gavin. 'What kind of a stupid number is that?'

'It is the entire number of stars North has scored since term began,' said Dr Shivers stonily. 'I doubt you would be so confident when the fifth years find out they've lost all the stars awarded to them in their Alchemistry pre-term exam. Professor Sanchez has been unusually generous.

Gavin went very pale. 'Ok, I'll see Mrs Grock,' he whispered.

'Good.' Dr Shivers smiled. 'Take Milly with you, perhaps she will be of more use at Mrs Grock's than she is in her Dragon Studies lesson.'

Milly nodded enthusiastically. 'Oh yes,' she said giggling, 'Mummy says I'll make a good nurse one day.'

Dr Shivers rolled his eyes. 'Go, before I change my mind.'

Without a second thought, Milly scooped up her bag and grabbed Gavin's hand, almost skipping with excitement at leaving the Dragon Studies lesson early.

'Right,' said Dr Shivers. 'Now that's sorted, has everyone managed to mount their dragons? Good, that's really good everyone. Let's begin the lesson.'

Dr Shivers put his staff back against the castle wall and guided the class of students riding their dragons in figures of eight around the gravel courtyard.

'This is so tame,' Dixie muttered to Sammy as they crossed in the middle.

'Yeah,' agreed Sammy, 'but even Nitron Dark must have done this once.'

Dixie nodded. 'It's actually the standard warm up in Dragonball.'

'No talking please, Sammy,' said Dr Shivers from the bottom loop of the "eight".

Dixie grinned and mouthed "sorry" as she passed Sammy and started the upper loop.

After seven figures of eight, Dr Shivers called them back into a semi-circle.

'That was perfect,' he said, smiling at them. 'A little tame perhaps for those of you who have already flown,' he

looked directly at Sammy and Dixie, 'but necessary none
the less. I have marked you all out of ten so that I will
know who to spend more time with. Please dismount and
we will return to the classroom.'

Dixie raised her hand.

'Oh yes,' Dr Shivers scratched his head. 'There is one
last task, the small matter of allocating the Dragon Minder
pins.'

Jock's hand flew up past Sammy. 'Sir, please may I be a
Minder? My father is…'

'I know who your father is,' snapped Dr Shivers.
'However, I would prefer to give the chance to students
with less experience.'

'That's discrimination,' said Jock, scowling.

'Spell it and it's yours,' Dr Shivers smirked.

'Hey!' exclaimed Dixie. 'Captain Stronghammer
promised me I could choose the second North Minder.'

Jock screwed up his face. 'It'll be me,' he muttered.
'D..i..sc, um, r..i..m, ey, discrimey, i…'

Dr Shivers smiled.

'…n..a..t..i,' Jock carried on.

'I..T!' shouted Gavin, returning from Mrs Grock's with
a variety of mummy-like bandages sticking out from under
his clothes.

'I..T,' repeated Dr Shivers with a chuckle, 'indeed.'

Jock stamped his feet. 'You said spell it.'

'That's right,' agreed Dr Shivers. 'Now, Dixie, who
would you like to be your number two?'

Dixie grinned. 'That's easy.'

'Dixie's got a boyfriend!' chanted Gavin. 'Dixie's got
a…'

'Enough!' shouted Dr Shivers. 'Out of my lesson Gavin
Reed! You may come back when you apologise!'

Gavin shook his head in surprise, his mouth open for a comeback that never came.

'And take those twenty three stars with you,' growled Dr Shivers, clapping his hands twice.

His staff materialised in his hands. 'Twenty three stars from North,' commanded Dr Shivers, 'now,' he added, shaking his staff.

One by one twenty three black stars squeezed themselves out of Dr Shivers's wooden staff and flew at a snail's pace in through an open castle window.

'Well that's got North off to a good start,' Dr Shivers grumbled. 'Dixie, have you decided?'

'Yes,' said Dixie, firmly fixing her eyes on a spot in the distance. 'I choose Milly.'

If Dr Shivers looked surprised, it was nothing compared with the way Sammy felt his jaw drop.

Dr Shivers recovered first. 'Very well, Sa…er, Milly, would you like to come to the front?'

Milly dragged her high-heeled feet, staring warily at the dragons. There was a look in her eyes that said "do I have to".

Dr Shivers nodded. 'Yes Milly. Now, who else?' He rested his hand on the side of his face. 'We'll have Simon Sanchez and Amos Leech from East, Tristan Markham and Rachel Burns from South and Samantha Trowt and Peter Grayling from West. Come here please so that I can give you your Dragon Minder pins which will allow you to access the Dragon Chambers.'

The other six students left the semi-circle of the class and walked over to Dr Shivers. Sammy saw him hand out small silver dragon shaped pin-badges to each of the chosen students. Once each person received their pin, they clipped it to their shirt or jumper and went around to the ten dragons from each of their houses.

'Follow Dixie to the Dragon Chambers please Minders. Everyone else, please follow me back to the Dragon Studies classroom.'

Sammy made a point of marching with the front of the class up to the East wing.

As they reached room fifty five, the Dragon Studies classroom, Sammy was so busy keeping his brave face that he didn't notice the first years filing out of the classroom.

He bumped straight into the fair haired girl from the courtyard, almost knocking her over.

Her books fell to the floor and Sammy bent down to help her. She stood up as he stood up and their heads banged together.

'Sorry,' said the fair haired girl with a giggle.

'No problem,' said Sammy, laughing as well. 'Hope you're ok.'

She nodded. 'I'm fine.'

'Good,' said Sammy, offering a hand to help her up. 'See you around,' he added, but she had gone, scurrying after her friends, invisible in the wave of first years.

'Weird,' muttered Sammy, wondering why his cheeks felt warm.

Inside the classroom, Dr Shivers was talking to a thin woman at the front of the class. She nodded and packed up her books. As she left, she smiled at Sammy.

Dr Shivers closed the classroom door behind her. Sammy wondered why he bothered since the windows didn't have any glass and the room was already chilly.

'So,' said Dr Shivers, 'how did it feel to ride your dragons?'

A boy from the West house raised his hand.

'Yes James,' said Dr Shivers, beckoning the scrawny boy to the front of the class to speak.

'It was great!' beamed James. 'Just like I thought it would be.'

Sitting next to Sammy, Darius scowled and folded his arms.

'Yes Darius?' said Dr Shivers. 'Do you have something to share?'

Darius shook his head. 'No Sir, it's just that I was expecting to fly.'

'Quite,' said Dr Shivers. 'You'll understand I have a responsibility to your parents to ensure your safety.'

Darius nodded begrudgingly. 'At least we get to fly in our Sports lessons and play Dragonball.'

Dr Shivers smiled. 'I'm sure Mr Cross will start you on the ground with the basics as well. Now, would you all turn to page two thousand and seventy three in your textbooks. I want to introduce you to the fine art of descaling your dragons.'

Sammy exchanged a dark look with Darius. He wasn't looking forward to descaling any more than he imagined Kyrillan would be.

He shut this thought out of his mind, still feeling a pang of what he could only describe as "left-out-ness" that Dixie hadn't chosen him to be a North Dragon Minder.

They only had time to read the first paragraph on descaling before the end of the lesson and the bell above the door clanged loudly.

'Answer the questions on page twenty one hundred please,' said Dr Shivers. 'Pass the message on to the Dragon Minders please.'

The class filed noisily out of the classroom talking eagerly about descaling and possible answers to the questions.

As Sammy and Darius followed Gavin and Toby out of the classroom, Dr Shivers called Sammy to wait behind.

Used to this, Darius nodded with his usual, 'I'll wait for you.'

'Thanks,' Sammy muttered under his breath.

'Thank you Sammy,' said Dr Shivers.

Sammy wasn't sure if he was being corrected on his speech, or commended for staying behind.

'Now Sammy,' Dr Shivers went on, 'you mustn't blame Dixie for the incident earlier.'

'But...'

'No buts,' said Dr Shivers firmly. 'She is, in my opinion, one of your better classmates. She wanted to choose you,' Dr Shivers smiled, 'but she lost her nerve when Gavin teased her. She's had a lot of criticism about her family and heritage that she handles better than anyone else her age.'

Sammy nodded.

'She cannot however, handle criticism involving you.'

'Commander Altair said that in the forest.'

'Ah yes, that was your first encounter with the Shape,' Dr Shivers smiled again. 'I remember,' he coughed, 'hearing about that. Very brave, it has to be said.'

Sammy looked at his feet. 'So she likes me, so what?'

'Patience Sammy, Milly will tire of being a Dragon Minder. I will arrange it. There may be an election, a ballot to find a suitable candidate, which you will win. Or, perhaps something else, I'll have to see.'

'You can predict the future?' asked Sammy in surprise.

Dr Shivers laughed. 'No, for that you should speak with Professor Burlay. I can create the future.' Dr Shivers laughed again, his cheeks sucked in firmly. 'To predict the future, talk to Professor Burlay. To create it, come to me.'

Dr Shivers waved Sammy out of the classroom. 'Give her two weeks.'

Sammy stared in horror. 'Two weeks,' he repeated. 'You can't do that, please don't. Dixie chose Milly and I'm ok with that, honestly,' he added, sure Dr Shivers knew he was lying.

Dr Shivers pressed a long grey forefinger to his lips and pushed Sammy gently by the shoulders out of the door. 'Go and join your friends. In two weeks time, you will have full access to the Dragon Chambers.'

CHAPTER 7

DRAGONBALL

Sammy left the Dragon Studies classroom with a worried look etched across his face. He met Darius at the end of the corridor and told him what Dr Shivers had promised.

'Do you reckon it'll happen?' Darius asked, staring Sammy uncomfortably in the eyes.

'I hope not,' whispered Sammy. 'He can't do that, he's a teacher.'

'So was Dr Lithoman and look at her.'

Sammy nodded. 'They're both doctors too.'

'My parents are Healers. That's a type of doctor,' said Darius. 'They aren't part of the Shape.'

'It's just a similarity.'

'Yeah,' retorted Darius. 'A co-incidence.'

'Has everyone else gone to Dragonball?' asked Sammy, hastily changing the subject.

Darius nodded. 'I kept tying and untying my shoelaces every time a teacher walked past. They all thought I was up to no good.'

Sammy laughed. 'Come on, hopefully Mr Cross'll let us fly.'

'Be nice to be back in the air,' said Darius. 'I know it's only been a few hours, but...'

'I know what you mean,' said Sammy, checking his timetable. 'Hurry up! We're going to be late!'

They ran all the way through the castle, down the stone stairs into the lower corridors. Spotting caretaker Tom Sweep, they slowed to a walking pace and sped up as soon as he disappeared out of sight.

It was cold and blustery when they reached the Gymnasium. The trees beside the Dragonball pitch were swaying wildly in the wind.

The rest of the second years were already changed into their white short sleeved shirts and navy shorts with the house colours and compass emblems stitched down the side.

Their sports teacher, Lance Anderson Cross, former captain of the Southampton Seals Dragonball team, was dressed as usual in his navy tracksuit with the zip done up to the collar and his pink plastic whistle hanging out of the front. He waved for Sammy and Darius to get changed with one hand, whilst directing a vigorous warm up with the other.

By the time Sammy and Darius came down from the changing rooms, Mr Cross had finished the warm up and was passing out several of the black leather balls used to score in the Dragonball goals at each end of the pitch.

'Next lesson,' Mr Cross was saying enthusiastically, 'we'll have a go at airborne Dragonball. For some of you I expect it'll be your first time, so we'll start out nice and slow.'

Sammy nudged Darius and rolled his eyes.

'At least we get to fly next time,' muttered Darius.

'For now, pair up and practice catching,' said Mr Cross. 'We should have time at the end of the lesson to practice a real game, say North and West against South and East.'

'Great,' grumbled Darius. 'Look at them, they can't even pass to each other.'

Sammy looked across to where Darius was pointing. Two boys from the West house were gawkily rolling their football sized Dragonball along the ground. The pass went wide and Mr Cross kicked it back to them.

Sammy and Darius paired up, throwing the ball to each other and taking a step back each time to make it harder.

Eventually Mr Cross blew his pink whistle and called them together in a circle in the middle of the pitch.

'That was good. Take a five minute break, then get into your houses. Work together as a team and whoever plays the best wins this,' he held up a bag of sweets.

'Bet it won't be like this every lesson,' said Gavin as they clustered into teams.

'Who wants sweets anyway,' said James from the West house. 'They're bad for you.'

'Just because you won't win it,' sneered Gavin. 'Useless, the lot of you.'

'Says you,' said James. 'You think you're something special.'

'I am,' said Gavin in his most arrogant voice, flinging his arm around his twin brother. 'Me and Toby, we're extra special!'

Toby ducked out of Gavin's grip. 'Come on, let's sort out some tactics.'

'Tic tacs,' said Gavin.

They huddled round, forty students in two clumps of twenty, at each end of the Dragonball pitch.

As Gavin predicted, the West house weren't any good at Dragonball. They dropped passes thrown to them and gave the balls away to the other team.

Sammy even found himself elbowed out of the way as a tall boy from the West house ran past him and drop-kicked the ball into their own goal. He was glad when Mr Cross finally blew his whistle three times to end the game and called them back into the middle of the pitch.

Mr Cross held up the sweets. 'One winner,' he announced. 'One man of the match, well actually a woman, well not yet, a girl, from the North house.'

'North?' asked the tall West boy.

'Yes Peter,' said Mr Cross.

'But…'

Mr Cross smiled. 'The winner is a girl from the North house, Milly in fact, for her splendid efforts in goal.'

'Milly?' spluttered Gavin.

Everyone turned to look at Milly who had gone a bright crimson. Sammy stared open mouthed, had Mr Cross gone mad? Milly had let every single shot at their goal into the back of the net and blamed it on not messing up her new hairdo.

Milly stumbled forward, the class parting as she walked up to Mr Cross to take her prize.

Mr Cross looked keenly at her. 'This is not a reward for playing badly, it is a reward for playing at all.'

Several students laughed, silenced at a fierce stare from Mr Cross.

'As Professor Burlay often tells me in the staffroom, playing is more important than winning.'

'That's not what Nitron Dark says,' said Dixie, scowling.

'Yeah,' said Gavin. 'He always wins.'

Mr Cross looked at them. 'What do you think Sammy?' he asked suddenly, catching Sammy off guard.

Sammy paused. 'Well if you don't play, you can't win,' he added helpfully.

Mr Cross raised his right eyebrow. 'Hmm…hey stop it!' he shouted as a scuffle broke out between Peter and Jock.

In a flash, Mr Cross pulled his staff from under his tracksuit and with, 'Four stars from North and West,' he sent them back into the Gymnasium to change.

The first evening back at Dragamas was spent in a lengthy library tutorial hosted by petite grandmotherly school librarian, Mrs Skoob.

In the dark and dusty library, she wasted no time in telling the second years they had made a wasted journey visiting her and it wasn't worthwhile coming to the library since most of the books were too long, too heavy, irrelevant or out on loan.

Looking around, Sammy thought she must have been in the wrong room since the shelves at the Dragamas library were bulging from top to bottom with literally thousands of books of all shapes and sizes. There were more books here than at Mrs Grock's house, and she had loads.

'And so,' Mrs Skoob concluded, 'Music books are to your left, History books are to your right, and,' she added, a glint appearing under her half-moon glasses, 'if you need anything else, there is always the "self-help" section.'

She paused, twiddling with her glasses cord. 'But don't let me hear you ask where it is,' she finished with a chuckle and turned away to stack some papers.

'Why not?' demanded Gavin.

'Why my dear,' said Mrs Skoob, giving Gavin a disapproving look, 'it would completely defeat the purpose.'

CHAPTER 8

MINDERS AND MENTORS

The following morning, Sammy woke in a cold sweat, his hand gripped tightly around the paws of his soft toy lion. He had been dreaming that the Shape were behind a pool of pale blue liquid covering the tower room door. They hadn't been able to get in, but he hadn't been able to get out either.

'Kyrillan,' mumbled Sammy, still half asleep and feeling stupid as he remembered Kyrillan wasn't under his bed like last year, but underground in the murky Dragon Chambers underneath the North tower.

'Hey stupid,' said Gavin, whisking open the curtain and grinning at him. 'Dragons are downstairs.'

'Yeah, I know,' said Sammy, shoving the toy lion out of sight.

'What's up?' asked Toby, peering his round face over Gavin's shoulder. 'What's going on?'

'Sammy's having hallucinations,' said Gavin, still grinning.

Sammy rolled his eyes. 'I was asleep.'

'Oh Kyrillan,' moaned Gavin, 'where are you? The Shape have eaten you,' he roared with laughter, punching his pillow.

'Yeah ok,' said Sammy, feeling this was a little too close to the bone. 'What's our first lesson this morning?' His words were drowned out as Gavin and Toby started a pillow fight waking Jock and Darius.

Unnoticed, Sammy slipped down to the bathroom where he found a timetable stuck to the mirror with chewing gum. With half-hearted interest, he read the lessons whilst splashing his face with cold water.

'Higher Astronomics, Higher Alchemistry,' he muttered, 'doesn't sound too bad.'

'You're joking, right?'

Sammy spun round. Serberon, wearing just a towel round his middle, stepped out of the showers into the changing area where Sammy was standing with his toothbrush and toothpaste poised in mid air.

'I, er...' started Sammy.

'Third year wasn't too bad,' said Serberon, reaching for the timetable, drops of water splashing from his sodden green hair on to Sammy. 'But look at this,' he grumbled, 'Higher Astronomics, Higher Alchemistry, Higher Armoury, Higher Dragon Studies and I've been asked to captain the Firesticks team in the summer.'

'Really?'

'Yeah, it's a lot of work.' Serberon threw on his shirt and tie, ducking behind a row of lockers to put on his trousers. He took out a black cylinder and squirted drops on to his neck.

'Mary-Beth's favourite,' he grinned.

Sammy stared, goggle-eyed. 'Her what?'

'Aftershave you idiot.'

'But?'

'So what I haven't shaved,' said Serberon, 'don't need to yet, do I? Now Jason, that's another matter.'

As Sammy laughed, a group of three fifth year boys burst into the bathroom, talking and shouting. Spotting Sammy and Serberon they stopped in their tracks and the largest of the three stepped forward.

He was head and shoulders taller than Sammy, wearing a gold chain and there was a cigarette packet sized lump in his breast pocket. The boy leaned uncomfortably close and tipped his head as if he couldn't quite believe they dared to be in the bathroom at the same time as him. He blew a smoky breath at them and tucked an unlit cigarette behind his ear.

"Op it squirts!' he yelled, making Sammy almost jump out of his skin.

Sammy and Serberon took his advice and bolted, the bathroom door banging shut on a roar of laughter behind them.

'Bully,' spat Serberon as they stopped in the corridor. 'Anyway, I'll see you Sammy.' Serberon grinned and, leaving a musky scent behind him, he skipped down the stairs two at a time.

Sammy paused on the stairs, drying his hands on his green towel. He rubbed his thumb along the gold weave that spelt out his name. Hearing the voices of the boy with the gold chain and his gang on their way out of the bathroom, Sammy marched as quickly as he could back up to the second year tower room.

When he arrived on the fourth floor, Gavin and Toby had disintegrated another set of Dragamas pillows. Darius had a cut above his left eye and Jock was standing on Sammy's bed holding a pillow in each hand, glaring at Toby.

'Hi guys,' said Sammy.

Jock jumped down and threw a pillow to Sammy. 'You're on my side.'

Sammy caught what was left of the pillow and raised it above his head.

'Enough!' roared Dr Shivers, who had appeared as if by teleport in a shimmering mist behind Sammy. 'I do not expect boys in my house to behave like hooligans,' he added, surveying the damage and frowning.

Feathers covered the floor. Strips of torn cotton flapped from Toby's pillow. Darius rubbed the cut above his eye.

'Hooligans,' repeated Dr Shivers, opening the window beside Gavin's bed. He brushed a cloud of feathers into the courtyard below and shook his head. 'Think of the example you're setting.'

Sammy looked at his feet. If they were only given a detention, or lost a few stars, they would be doing well.

Dr Shivers seemed to read his mind. 'Your choice boys,' he said. 'Lose ten stars each, a week of detention, or collect me a big bag of dragon scales.'

'Scales,' said Toby and Darius at the same time Gavin and Jock said "Detention".

Gavin looked horrified he'd chosen the same as Jock and said "Scales" at the same time Toby changed his mind to join Gavin's first choice of "Detention".

Dr Shivers laughed. 'I came here to tell you about the Dragamas Mentor Programme, where each of you has a responsibility to introduce a first year to the school. It's usually reserved for third year students and really quite a privilege.'

Sammy stared at Gavin and Toby. Both looked absolutely horrified.

Dr Shivers held out five slips of paper. Each was roughly A4 in size with a black and white photograph of the first year along with a short description.

Sammy turned to Dr Shivers. 'Did we...' he started.

Dr Shivers pointed to Sammy, 'Your Mentor is Serberon Deane.' He pointed to Darius. 'Mikhael Deane.' He pointed to Gavin and Toby, 'Raymond Heathfield, John Sycamore.'

'Did Amos have...'

'Jason Deane,' finished Dr Shivers. 'I believe he did. Anyhow, one of you will need to take two. It's not fair to ask Jock since he's only just arrived.'

'But,' started Gavin.

'I'm sorry Gavin, I don't make the rules' Dr Shivers smiled. 'Would you like to volunteer?'

'No,' said Gavin quickly.

'Right,' said Dr Shivers. 'Two for Gavin, one for Toby, Darius and Sammy.'

'That's not fair!' shouted Gavin. 'I don't want one, let alone two!'

'Shh,' hissed Dr Shivers. 'They can hear you.'

Gavin stared, his eyes blazing. 'They'll wish they weren't here when I've finished,' he growled. 'They'll want to be back home before the week's out.'

Dr Shivers frowned. 'I'm sure you'll do a good job. The idea is that they don't know they're being mentored. I don't believe any of you realised last year.'

Sammy shook his head. 'Serberon told me at the end of last year. He said he was looking out for me all the time.'

'Good.' Dr Shivers smiled. 'I'll award him some stars for that.'

'Why don't we mentor them next year?' asked Sammy. 'Serberon's two years older than us. He was in the third year last year.'

Dr Shivers smiled again, his thin lips parting slightly. 'As I mentioned Sammy, I don't make the rules. In my opinion, third years are usually preoccupied with sport and girls to concern themselves with first years. However, I believe Sir Ragnarok has made the change because he feels that you second years must be more responsible, sooner, because of the Shape.'

'Oh,' said Sammy, half wishing he hadn't asked.

Dr Shivers handed out the five pieces of paper.

Gavin let out a huge snort as he read his papers. 'Herbert and Montegue Smythers!'

Sammy grinned and Darius gave one of his famous giggles.

'Herbie and Monty,' giggled Darius, 'Herbie and Monty!'

'Who have you got?' snapped Gavin.

'Kyle Hilton,' said Toby, without looking up from the photograph on his paper.

'Matthew Hill,' said Darius, 'aged ten years and two months. He likes skiing and water polo. Parents are in the Army. He knows nothing about dragons.'

'It says all that?' asked Sammy, studying his paper. 'I've got Nigel Ashford.'

'Yep, under "Hobbies",' said Darius.

'I see it,' said Sammy, skim reading about how Nigel Ashford liked football and horse riding. 'Says here his mother is in finance and his dad is a healer. He scores 52% on the Dragon Knowledge scale.'

'Good,' said Dr Shivers. 'You'll be able to get acquainted this week.'

'What was my score?' asked Sammy, sure the answer would be zero.

Dr Shivers raised his right eyebrow and squinted. 'From memory,' he muttered as if mentally scanning through hundreds of student records, 'you had an exact 50%.'

Sammy stared. 'I what?'

'That's right. 'You scored 100% on heritage. Your ancestors would have been fine dragon folk, but your parents I understand have kept you in the dark which gave you a zero percent. I would imagine Sir Ragnarok thought you deserved the benefit of the doubt.'

'The...' Sammy stared harder. 'I didn't know dragons existed this time last year.'

Darius exchanged a knowing glance with Jock.

Dr Shivers raised his hands. 'I daresay you have questions your parents will be able to answer.'

'Can't you answer them?'

'No,' said Dr Shivers, kindly but firmly. 'Some things in life you have to find out for yourself. I'm sorry. I shouldn't have told you this much.'

'That's not fair,' Sammy snapped angrily, stamping his foot. 'It's worse than you not telling me at all.'

Dr Shivers shrugged. 'It's not my place. Perhaps not even the right time.'

Leaving Sammy in a spin, Dr Shivers turned around and left. Two seconds later he appeared at the tower door. 'No more pillow fights please,' he said with a smile, 'and if you'd be so kind as to bring a full bag of scales to my next lesson, I'll forget all about detentions and losing house stars.' Dr Shivers winked at Sammy and held up two fingers. 'Two weeks,' he whispered, although Sammy was sure no one else had heard.

As the tower door closed, Gavin groaned loudly. 'Two posh brats and a sack of scales, can today get any worse?'

Outside, there was a flash of lightning and marble sized hailstones hurtled in through the open window.

Gavin surveyed his sodden chest of drawers and damp quilt. 'Great,' he muttered at the sky and pulled the window shut with a bang.

Sammy grinned to himself and threw on his black trousers and white shirt with the North house compass logo embossed on the shirt pocket. Two weeks was a long way away.

CHAPTER 9

THE DRAGAMAS CONSTELLATION

Professor Burlay was waiting for them as they filed into the Astronomics classroom on the third floor. Dressed smartly in a navy pinstripe suit, he was standing with his back to the door, staring through a small telescope out of the window.

Outside, the hailstones pounded the windows and the double doors leading to the balcony where students could stand outside and use larger telescopes to look at the sky. Today, Sammy noticed, the outdoor telescopes were stacked together and wrapped in green tarpaulin to protect them from the stormy weather.

As they shuffled to the desks arranged in two horseshoe rings facing the front, Professor Burlay turned around.

Sammy caught a fleeting worried look that vanished as Professor Burlay gave a beaming smile, ignoring Jock and Gavin jostling for the free desk next to Toby.

'Good morning second years,' he said, waving his free hand towards the desks. 'Sit down please. We have lots to learn this year.'

'Good morning!' shouted Gavin, elbowing Jock and sitting next to Toby in the back row.

'Indeed,' said Professor Burlay. 'Tell me, did we cover the Dragamas Constellation last year?'

With the exception of Sammy, Dixie, Darius from North and Amos Leech, now in East, the class shook their heads.

'Then that is what we must cover this morning,' said Professor Burlay, the worried look crossing his face again.

He turned back to face the window. 'It's too wet to use the equipment outside.'

'Good,' said Gavin from the back of the class. 'The rain came in our tower room and got my bed wet.'

'Are you sure it was the rain and not you that wet the bed?' asked Simon Sanchez, grinning as the East house roared with laughter.

'Yeah,' added Jock. 'We didn't see any rain, did we Darius?'

Darius shook his head. 'Dry as a desert,' he said giggling.

'Enough,' said Professor Burlay, smiling himself. 'I have sketched the formation on the blackboard.'

'It looks like the number five on a dice, Sir,' said Peter Grayling from the West house.

Professor Burlay nodded, looking a little taken aback that a student from the West house had spoken up in an Astronomics lesson.

'Put your hand up,' said Gavin. 'No shouting out in class!'

Professor Burlay raised an eyebrow. 'Thank you Gavin.'

Gavin nodded. 'It's ok, Sir, don't mention it.'

Sammy grinned to himself. Professor Burlay's lessons never seemed quite in control.

'Does anyone else know about the Dragamas constellation?' asked Professor Burlay, rubbing his clean shaven chin.

Amos cast a bitter stare at Gavin and put his hand up.

'Yes Amos,' said Professor Burlay.

Amos cleared his throat. 'The four coloured stars, yellow, red, blue and green, represent the four Dragamas houses and the white star in the middle represents the dragons that we protect.'

Sammy looked across at Amos and smiled at him. The rest of the class were in silence, taking notes about the new constellation.

'Very good Amos,' said Professor Burlay. 'Do you remember why the four outer stars sometimes circle around the inner star?'

Sammy, Dixie and Darius shot up their hands.

'Amos?' asked Professor Burlay.

'Yes Sir,' said Amos quietly. 'They circle the inner star when a dragon is being attacked.'

'Yes, the stars move in a circle to protect the dragon,' said Professor Burlay. 'To the trained eye, the coloured stars can be used as co-ordinates for where it is happening.'

'They didn't save my Mum's dragon,' shouted Gavin, shoving himself up from his chair and standing, staring at Professor Burlay. 'Her dragon is dead!'

'My Grandfather's dragon died,' said Simon Sanchez.

'Mine too,' added Samantha Trowt from West, 'and my Great Aunt Sarah's.'

Professor Burlay held up his hand. 'There is a difference between a dragon who dies from illness or old age compared with a dragon who has been murdered for his or her stone.'

'Draconite,' whispered Sammy, an image of Kyrillan flashing into his mind, an x-ray picture with the blue-green pearlescent stone shining through the skull bone. He shivered, remembering Mrs Reed's dragon dead and motionless in the field behind their house.

'They stole her stone!' shouted Gavin, his face flushed crimson.

'Murdered!' added Toby, standing next to his brother.

'I'm truly sorry to hear that,' said Professor Burlay. 'Please, sit down, so that I can continue the lesson.'

With an angry stare, Gavin sat down, followed closely by Toby.

'Good,' said Professor Burlay. 'Now, where were we?' He rummaged among the papers on his desk and handed out charts with a diagram and notes on the Dragamas Constellation to each student.

As they stuck the charts into their notebooks, Sammy was glad they wouldn't need to write anything. Judging by the weather, which had cleared up, and the way that Professor Burlay was whisking the covers from the telescopes, the rest of the lesson would be spent on the balcony overlooking the Dragonball pitch.

He was right. Professor Burlay called Gavin, Toby, Amos and Jock to help move the heavy telescopes. They always reminded Sammy of the binocular stands he used to see on the pier at Torston Sands, just outside of his home town of Ratisbury. They were tall and blue and when you put coins in them, you could look at the boats far out to sea until the money ran out. The school telescopes were on white stands and had much stronger lenses than the binoculars. Using the telescopic lenses, you could see up to the stars many miles high in the sky.

'As usual please,' said Professor Burlay, 'ten groups of four. Gavin, since you've helped move the telescopes, your group can go first.'

Sammy looked up and caught Gavin giving Jock and Amos a vicious look that said "of everyone in the class, you're the last people I'd choose". Sammy recognised the look of hate from his time at his local Ratisbury school where the bullies, the Rat-Catchers, chased him time after time, cornering him, untying his tie (which they knew he couldn't redo himself), tying his shoelaces together, pushing him, kicking his shins until they were black and blue, shredding his work and spitting in his packed lunch.

He shivered, erasing the memory with happy thoughts using the advice the Ratisbury school counselor had offered him. Thinking about his parents coming to meet him from school had usually worked. He'd heard the counselor had left Ratisbury shortly after he had transferred to Dragamas. The Rat-Catchers had been dragging locker keys down the side of her car for months, then they had taken it for a joyride and left it, burnt out, fifteen miles away.

Sammy smiled to himself, glad he didn't have to go to school there anymore. Glad he had friends like Dixie, Darius and Toby and even Gavin as well.

Just as he was counting his new friends on his fingers, Professor Burlay flustered back from the balcony into the classroom.

'All of you, come quickly, see the stars. The sky is just right.'

Sammy creaked his chair back and joined Dixie, Darius and Milly on the stone balcony next to the first telescope.

Professor Burlay pushed his hand against Sammy's back. 'I think you should see this,' he muttered.

Sammy peered into the dark glass of the telescope, adjusting his position as Professor Burlay swung the lens towards the Dragamas stars. Sammy drew a sharp breath. The four coloured stars were spinning around the white centre star, first clockwise, then anti-clockwise.

Sammy pulled his eye away from the bright constellation, knowing a dragon was in danger.

Professor Burlay nodded. 'Look again, Sammy.'

Ignoring Dixie and Darius, who were both nudging him and muttering "we want a go", Sammy stuck his head back towards the telescope.

He zoomed in on the Dragamas constellation, which, if anything, was spinning faster and faster. He searched a little to the left and saw a second group of stars, in a star shape, moving towards the constellation.

Forgetting he was looking through the lens, Sammy swatted at the new stars. 'No,' he muttered. 'Get away.'

He stepped back as Professor Burlay touched his shoulder. 'Sir, those second stars...'

Professor Burlay nodded gravely. 'We understand them to be the form of the Shape. When they took five stones from five dragons, they are believed to have been given a second life among the stars.'

Next to Sammy, Dixie, Darius and Milly gasped.

'But Professor,' started Milly, 'surely the stars can't be people?'

Professor Burlay shook his head. 'Worse,' he muttered, 'far, far worse. Each member of the Shape is said to have incorporated their powers into the star. Even if the human body, like Dr Lithoman, has been imprisoned, the Shape can harness her powers using her star.'

'So what?' scoffed Gavin, from the doorway. 'Stars can't hurt us.'

'Perhaps I haven't explained myself,' said Professor Burlay coldly. 'The stars are the power. To stop the power, someone must sacrifice their life and the life of their dragon. They would become a star without human form, yet remain pure and good. Then,' Professor Burlay paused, 'well, take this as you will, but it's said that they will join the Knights of the Stone Cross and battle to the immortal death.'

'Are there no volunteers?' whispered Darius. 'Not even in the whole world?'

'Well,' Professor Burlay looked uncomfortable, 'that is a good question Darius…perhaps you could research it, as a class project perhaps?'

'He doesn't know,' cackled Gavin, snorting loudly. 'Professor Burlay should go. Be replaced!'

'Shut it Gavin,' Toby elbowed his brother in the ribs.

'Perhaps he is right,' added Simon Sanchez, peering back from under his telescope. 'The Dragamas stars are fading. Perhaps someone is volunteering.'

'Perhaps,' Professor Burlay smiled. 'But it's unlikely. Outside of this school, there aren't many like Sir Ragnarok who campaign for the safety of dragons worldwide.'

'My Mother would volunteer,' said Simon, 'and my Grandmother.'

'That's interesting Simon,' Professor Burlay sighed. 'I'm sure if she had it in mind, she would speak with Sir Ragnarok. It's not a decision to be taken lightly and no one knows if it is true.'

'She doesn't like you,' snapped Simon. 'She thinks you are incompetent.'

Behind Simon, cackles of laughter grew louder as Professor Burlay's face became redder as he tried to regain control of the class.

'Perhaps,' Professor Burlay mopped his forehead with a grey silk handkerchief, 'perhaps we could go back inside.'

'You aren't going to take that, are you Sir?' yelled Gavin. 'Not from that Rat Muncher.'

'Catcher,' Sammy muttered under his breath, rolling his eyes. 'Rat Catcher.'

'Yeah Professor,' added Dixie, 'give him detention!'

'Cane him!' shouted Peter Grayling from West, covering his mouth with his hand as soon as he'd spoken.

'Cane them both,' added Darius, Jock nodding his approval.

Professor Burlay didn't get the chance to reply as the whole class, with the exception of himself, Sammy and Jock, suddenly froze, rock solid, still and silent.

'Everything all right in there?' came a soft, feminine voice carried from the classroom doorway.

Sammy peered in through the window. A small woman, "petite" his mum would have described her, with a bob of fair hair framed around a face heavy with makeup, overshadowed by the striking contrast between her jet black trousers, pale violet scarf and sparkling white fur coat, was standing at the entrance to the Astronomics room.

Professor Burlay ducked under Gavin's frozen arm and marched into the classroom. 'Can I help you?'

'It looks as though you need the help,' the woman chuckled, pulling the coat around her shoulders. 'It's chilly in here.'

Professor Burlay pushed Gavin's arm outside and slammed the balcony door.

Jock joined Sammy at the window and they watched as Professor Burlay made sweeping movements with his hands and mopped his forehead whilst the woman inspected the classroom and shook her head from time to time. Sammy caught a glint of red in her right hand as she approached the balcony doors and the class began to unfreeze.

Without knowing why, Sammy decided it was important that the woman in the fur coat didn't know her stone hadn't frozen him. He rested his hand on the nearest telescope and bent his head, copying Simon Sanchez's rigid pose. He coughed to signal to Jock, but he had turned away and was ruffling Gavin's hair, slicking it into girly bunches.

Professor Burlay opened the door and the woman barged in front, the ruby stone on full display.

Instantly there was a rush or warm air that sparkled through the still class. Sammy sneaked a look at Simon Sanchez, waiting for him to move.

A second later, Simon kicked his foot against the telescope stand. 'The counter-spell didn't work,' he grumbled. 'Think harder next time.'

Sammy pretended to stretch and caught looks of thunder from Dixie and Darius.

'Who does she think she is?' shouted Dixie. 'Using stones like that!'

'They're all like it,' shouted Gavin, spitting furiously into his hands and trying to straighten his hair. 'Dirty little dwarves, good for nothing little…'

There was a loud crack and Gavin fell to the floor holding the side of his head. 'You!' he screamed. 'You'll pay for that!'

Jock grinned and pushed past Sammy as he walked into the classroom. 'Hello Mum, you all right?'

'Mum?' Gavin spluttered, hoisting himself up. 'Makes sense, whole little family's like it, dirty little…'

'Twenty stars for foul language,' said Professor Burlay briskly. 'I apologise Mrs Hubar. Gavin are you like this in Dr Shivers's classes as well? You weren't like this last year.'

'Only twenty?' demanded Mrs Hubar, rubbing Jock's shoulders. 'After that abuse against my race and my family?'

'Thirty,' groaned Professor Burlay, assembling his staff.

'Fifty!' screeched Mrs Hubar, her own staff poised. 'Fifty from South.'

'South!' Gavin giggled. 'Take two hundred from South.'

'Two hundred from South,' repeated Mrs Hubar, shoveling black stars out of the classroom, 'and another fifty for insolence.'

'This cannot be right,' snapped Simon Sanchez. 'He is North, you stupid dwarf-breath.'

Gavin laughed louder, his hand still rubbing his head. 'More!' he giggled. 'Take more!'

As Mrs Hubar raised her staff, Professor Burlay took hold of the end to call a stop to the event. 'Enough!' he commanded in the most authoritative voice Sammy had ever heard.

But it wasn't Professor Burlay's voice. Sir Ragnarok was in the doorway, Directometer in one hand and a glass fishbowl, full of Mrs Hubar's black stars, in the other.

'Quite enough already,' said Sir Ragnarok. 'No damage has been done.' He tapped the glass with his forefinger and the stars fizzled and imploded, turning to a thin film of grey dust at the bottom of the bowl.

'Professor Burlay, would you care to entertain me with what in the dragon's name is going on in this circus?'

Sir Ragnarok waved his staff, unfreezing a girl from the East house who hadn't been in range when Mrs Hubar had unfrozen the class.

Professor Burlay looked down at his feet. 'It won't happen again Sir Ragnarok,' he muttered, looking every inch the guilty schoolboy about to be punished for being naughty in class.

Sir Ragnarok opened the door and walked out on to the balcony. 'Is everyone back?' he asked, as the students filtered into the classroom. He paused as Sammy stepped forward and checked the Directometer. 'Still unaffected Sammy?'

'Yes Sir,' Sammy whispered, conscious that people were listening. He caught Mrs Hubar's eye and although she gave no sign, he was sure she had heard.

'As I thought,' said Sir Ragnarok mysteriously.

Simon Sanchez raised his hand. 'Surely she isn't allowed to use the stones on children?'

'Pah!' Gavin snorted. 'Like it stopped him,' he said, poking Jock in the stomach.

Jock held out his ruby and Sir Ragnarok tapped him on the wrist.

'Enough Jock, there will be time enough to show your skills.'

Jock nodded and pocketed his stone.

Sammy felt a shiver run down his spine. He'd just thought how good it would feel to try to freeze the class using his mind alone. Hadn't he been told often enough that he was going to be a Dragon Knight and that staffs and stones were used to channel energy rather than create it? "It comes from within" is what Professor Patrick Preverence had told him last year. He caught Sir Ragnarok's eye.

Sir Ragnarok shook his head. 'I believe you can, but now is not the time.' He smiled and Sammy ducked under his arm and stepped into the classroom.

Professor Burlay was sitting hunched up at his desk reading a complex star chart and marking the paper with neat lines using a protractor and pencil.

Mrs Hubar was checking her appearance using the glass in the classroom door as a mirror. She pulled the ends of her violet scarf, adjusting the length until they hung evenly around her neck.

Sir Ragnarok coughed politely.

Mrs Hubar turned around. 'Oh Sir Ragnarok,' she gushed. 'How good of you to unfreeze the class. Are they ready for me?'

Sir Ragnarok nodded. 'Everyone, I would like to introduce your new Gemology teacher, Mrs Hubar. As some of you may already know, Mrs Hubar's husband is our head miner and dragon keeper Fignus Hubar, better known as Captain Duke Stronghammer. Mrs Hubar is a great friend of mine and although she has no formal title, she is more than qualified to teach Gemology.'

'Does she know the silly-bus?' demanded Simon Sanchez, smacking his hand against his fist.

'Her knowledge,' Sir Ragnarok paused, 'is worth more salt than anything our government can put together.'

'Our government,' said Sammy, suddenly wishing he hadn't spoken as forty two pairs of eyes seemed to scream at him that he didn't know what he was talking about.

'She has been given the syllabus,' said Sir Ragnarok. 'It is exactly the same as they teach in other schools and although she may be a little more flexible in her interpretation, I have received permission to let her teach at Dragamas.'

Simon clapped. 'Then this is ok,' he said smiling broadly.

Sammy exchanged a worried look with Dixie. 'What if we don't get taught enough for the exams,' he whispered.

'Trust Sir Ragnarok,' Dixie whispered back. 'He wouldn't be allowed to do it if it wasn't ok.'

'Please stop whispering children,' said Mrs Hubar in her soft silky voice. 'If you're ready, we shall move to the Gemology classroom.' She unfolded a timetable with the map on the back. 'Would someone please lead us to room 7.'

There was a snigger from the back of the class.

Mrs Hubar gave a disapproving stare. 'I'm sure it was your first day once too,' she said, turning to face the class. 'Ooh, a green-hair,' she added, suddenly catching sight of Dixie. She took a step forward and frowned as Dixie towered over her by several inches.

Dixie looked down at Mrs Hubar. 'I'll show you where room 7 is,' she said, smiling sweetly.

Sammy grinned, knowing Dixie would be seething inside. She hated attention drawn to her hair and her troll heritage.

'A troll,' said Mrs Hubar, examining Dixie as if under a microscope. She walked a full circle around Dixie, staring intently and holding out her hands, comparing them in size.

Dixie glared at Mrs Hubar. 'Shall we go?'

Oblivious to her tone, Mrs Hubar nodded and linked arms jovially with Dixie. 'Let's go,' she giggled. 'A troll in my class, who'd have thought!'

Behind them, Gavin and Darius fell about in a fit of laughter.

CHAPTER 10

DWARVES AND TROLLS

Downstairs, behind the long purple curtain, they went through the glittering door that led into the passageway down to the Gemology classroom and further down into the jewel mine under the school.

The sloping passageway was the same as it had been the year before, with the wheelbarrow tyre groove deeply ingrained into the floor.

As they walked downwards, Captain Stronghammer rumbled around the corner towards them. He was pushing a wheelbarrow half filled with shining diamond gemstones.

He stopped when he caught sight of Dixie and Mrs Hubar and grinned. Dixie grinned back as he made an elaborate show of kissing his wife on both cheeks, then heaving the wheelbarrow onwards and out of the classroom.

'Oh Figgy!' Mrs Hubar blushed. 'You shouldn't do that in front of my class!'

Sammy nudged Dixie's elbow. 'Figgy,' he giggled as quietly as he dared without drawing Mrs Hubar's attention.

'Dwarves,' whispered Dixie, raising herself up on tiptoe.

'Which way now?' asked Mrs Hubar, flustered by the sudden show of affection. 'Oh, there's only one way in,' she added as they walked the short corridor and out into the circular Gemology classroom underneath the West tower.

'I remember now,' Mrs Hubar smiled. 'Turn left through the classroom and down that passage to our rooms.' She paused, scratching at the sparkling glitter on the rocky walls with a fingernail painted in a pale violet matching her scarf.

A shower of tiny crystals fell into the palm of her right hand.

'Diamonds,' she breathed. 'I thought Fignus was joking.'

'Mi-iss, can we go in yet,' Gavin called out from the back in his best put-on whining voice.

'Yes, yes of course,' said Mrs Hubar, still sounding flustered. 'Sit where you like and we'll start by talking about the stones you have been given.'

Sammy sat in the same seat as last year when Dr Lithoman had taught Gemology. Dixie sat on his right between himself and Milly and Darius sat on his left, pulling the large Gemology textbook from his rucksack.

'Not necessary,' said Mrs Hubar, chuckling. 'You probably know more in that book than I do!'

'Then what is the point?' demanded Simon Sanchez from the far corner. 'We are here to learn.'

'We are here to learn,' mimicked Gavin. 'From the booooks!'

Simon glared at Gavin, his fingers wrapped tightly around his black and red tipped staff. 'Shall we take this outside?'

'Boys, please,' begged Mrs Hubar. 'Not in my first lesson.'

Simon nodded and sat down. In Sammy's opinion it probably wouldn't have been a bad thing to take Gavin down a peg or two, but he knew Simon wouldn't mess around in class for fear of his mother. Alchemistry teacher, Professor Sanchez wouldn't look kindly on her son causing trouble for a fellow teacher.

Sammy cast a glance over to Jock, who was sandwiched between Amos and Simon, each with their hands clasped and resting on the desk, looking as though butter wouldn't melt in their mouths.

The North table however looked close to being given a detention. The raised voices of Gavin and Mrs Hubar caused everyone in the classroom to stop and watch.

Gavin was pointing his staff inches from Mrs Hubar's nose, the red and black stones glinting at the tip, reflecting on her cheeks.

'You leave her alone!' roared Gavin. 'She's just like the rest of us.'

A chill ran through Sammy. Next to him, Dixie was shaking, tears streaming down her face. She was his best friend and he had no idea what Mrs Hubar had said to upset her. He stared at Dixie, shaking her shoulder.

She looked back at him, her bottle green eyelashes dripping with fresh tears.

'She should be locked up with Dr Lithoman,' choked Dixie. Clutching her rucksack, she ran out of the classroom.

Sammy stared at her empty chair, then at Darius.

'Come on,' said Darius firmly. 'Let's go after her.'

Sammy nodded numbly and ran after Darius, their chairs clattering to the floor behind them.

Captain Stronghammer was coming back in as they burst out of the passage door.

He pointed towards the North tower. 'She went that way,' he grumbled, stooping to pick up some fallen gemstones.

'Thanks!' Darius yelled over his shoulder, pulling Sammy along by his jumper sleeve. 'Come on!'

'She's gone,' puffed Sammy as they turned the corner at the bottom of the corridor. The door to the North tower common room was on their left and the passage to the East wing lay empty to their right. Dixie had vanished.

'Our tower?'

'Got to be,' said Darius, pushing open the heavy oak door.

The common room was empty apart from two older students who broke away from each other as Sammy and Darius burst in.

Sammy recognised the boy from earlier in the bathroom. If it was possible, he looked even less pleased to see Sammy than before.

"Op it squirt,' he commanded, stubbing out his cigarette on the back of his hand.

The girl sitting next to him whispered in his ear and he laughed out loud.

'She says you're the Dragon Knight.'

Sammy stared. 'Mary-Beth?'

The girl giggled and tossed her hair back. It was Mary-Beth.

'Everything's changed Sammy,' she said, smiling at him. 'There was nothing serious going on between me and Serberon anyway. Not that you'll tell him about this, right?'

'Right?' said the cigarette-smoking boy. 'Else I'll set my mates on you. They're at college and they'll knock you into little pieces.'

Sammy felt his cheeks flush. He wasn't going to get pushed around anymore.

'Fine,' he said, surprising himself. 'Mary-Beth, you'll wish you hadn't done this. Have you seen Dixie?'

'No,' Mary-Beth looked surprised herself. 'Should I?'

Sammy turned to Darius. 'She's not here.'

'Where did she go then?'

The cigarette-smoking boy stood up and came close to Sammy and Dixie.

'Me and Mary-Beth,' he nodded over to Mary-Beth who was checking her make-up using a compact mirror, 'we want you to leave.' He poked Sammy's shoulder blade with a grubby finger. 'Right now,' he added, shoving them outside and slamming the door.

'What is she doing?' asked Sammy, picking himself up off the floor. He dusted his trousers with his jumper sleeves rolled over his hands.

'No taste,' agreed Darius. 'So anyway, Dixie isn't here. Do you want to go back to Gemology?'

Sammy shook his head. 'She has to be here somewhere. Check the paintings, curtains, there might be a hidden passage.'

'To where?' asked Darius.

Sammy shrugged. 'I don't know,' he replied, tapping at the walls and looking at the paintings and tapestries that hung on them. 'Look, "Shaping the Future of Dragons",' he read aloud from one of the paintings. 'Knights of the Stone Cross, Castle of Karmandor. Hey Darius, look at this Karmandor painting. It's got a castle here that looks the same shape as Dragamas.'

'Duh,' said Darius. 'It is Dragamas. Look, here are our towers, the main entrance and the school gates.'

'Less trees,' said Sammy, 'and Mrs Grock's house is missing.'

'Must be quite old,' said Darius. 'Thought we were looking for Dixie anyway.'

'Yeah,' said Sammy, giving the painting one last look. 'Hey, wait! It looks like there should be some steps here leading downwards.'

Darius shook his head. 'It's old Sammy. You said so yourself. There aren't any secret passages here.'

Sammy grinned. If Darius only knew the secret passages he'd seen already. He knelt beside a radiator under a large window embossed with a stained glass golden dragon and started tapping the wall. 'I reckon it's here somewhere.'

'Try turning it,' said Darius, pointing at the radiator dial. 'No, the other way.'

'I'll thank you to leave the school heating to me,' came a gruff voice from behind them.

Sammy and Darius spun round. Dressed in his brown overcoat, baggy trousers and carrying a large broom, the Dragamas caretaker did not look pleased to see them.

'Tom Sweep! Run!' shouted Darius.

They ran away from the caretaker at top speed, down the long corridor and burst out of the North entrance. Darius stopped as they reached some tall bushes and leaned against the wall, breathing heavily.

'I bet it opens a secret door,' puffed Darius. 'A hidden passage.'

Sammy checked around the side of the bush. The caretaker was nowhere in sight. He scanned up the wall and scratched his head.

'In theory this would be where it would come out.' Sammy pointed up to the stained glass window, depicting a golden dragon breathing fire, above them. 'The radiator was under that window.'

Darius's eyes sparkled. 'Yeah, so that means…'

'…it's here somewhere!' finished Sammy, pressing at the bricks in the castle wall.

After five minutes of searching, they measured how far the steps would have reached from the castle wall.

'It's no good,' said Darius, sitting on the grass and plucking pieces out. 'Any steps here are long gone.'

'I guess,' said Sammy, a little downhearted. He had been sure they would have found at least one brick from one step, or rubble buried in the grass from where the steps had been. He stared up at the window, the stained glass dragon frowning down at him. 'Where did the steps go?' he said out loud.

'Perhaps the painting was wrong,' suggested Darius, picking himself up. 'Perhaps the steps never went outside.'

Sammy paused. 'What, so they might go inside instead?'

'Whatever,' said Darius, chewing the stalk of a long piece of grass.

'No, seriously,' said Sammy, getting excited. 'Where are we?'

'North Tower, duh!' said Darius, looking at Sammy as if he'd gone mad.

'And what's under the North Tower?'

Darius's eyes lit up. 'The Dragon Chambers! You don't reckon...'

Sammy nodded. 'It makes sense. Dixie's a Dragon Minder so she would have known about the passages so she could get to the dragons quickly, if there was any trouble.'

'Like the Shape,' added Darius, throwing away the chewed grass. 'But we don't know if there is a passage behind the radiator.'

'I bet there is,' said Sammy. 'Lift me up. I'll see if Tom Sweep's still about.'

Darius knelt down and arched his back.

Sammy pushed his right foot on to Darius's back and holding on to the wall for balance, he peered through the thick glass window.

'Gone,' he whispered, jumping down.

'Ug,' groaned Darius. 'You're heavy.'

Sammy grinned and picked up his rucksack. 'Back inside then?'

Darius nodded. 'Quick though, we've been ages.'

Back in the corridor, Sammy was glad Tom Sweep was nowhere in sight. Keeping an eye out for teachers and fifth years who considered it their duty to check that the younger students were in lessons, they crept back to the golden dragon stained glass window with the radiator underneath. Except the radiator was no longer there.

'It's gone,' said Darius, staring at the gaping hole.

Sammy crouched and felt the sides of the rectangular hole. He peered into the darkness. 'It's a passage,' he said excitedly. 'It goes downwards!'

They jumped back as they heard echoing footsteps from within the dark cavity.

'Back,' cried Darius, clutching his staff, pointing it into the hole, poised to strike anyone or anything that came out of the passage.

'I'm allowed to be down here,' came a muffled voice. 'Put that staff down or I'll blast you with my Nitro-staff!'

'Your what?' said Darius, peering into the darkness.

'My Nitro…uh…staff,' said the voice, a little uncertain this time.

'Dixie?' Sammy called into the hole. 'Is that you?'

'No,' said the voice, unmistakably Dixie's.

'It is,' said Sammy. 'Come on out. It's just me and Darius.'

'Ok,' came the reply, followed by the clamp-clamp of footsteps on stone stairs.

Dixie's green haired head emerged at ground level. She looked very serious.

'You can't tell anyone you know about this,' she whispered, using the thermostat as a handle to hoist herself back into the corridor.

'Why not?' demanded Darius. 'You know about it.'

'Yes,' said Dixie, her eyes narrowing into a worried frown, 'but you shouldn't. There's one for each of the towers,' she paused, looking unsure if she should tell them more.

'Go on,' Sammy encouraged her. 'Do they lead to the Dragon Chambers?' He pointed to the painting of Dragamas and showed her the steps leading down into the tower.

'Castle Karmandor,' said Dixie scanning the picture thoughtfully. 'It looks just like Dragamas.'

'Ug,' said Darius, putting his head in his hands.

Dixie looked at him strangely. 'Are you ok?'

'It is Dragamas,' explained Sammy. 'I said the same thing.'

'Less trees,' said Dixie.

Darius groaned louder.

Dixie frowned. 'Seriously, you can't tell anyone about the North Tunnels. They have to be kept secret. Only Dragon Minders can use them.' She removed her "Minder" pin and pressed it on the top of the temperature dial. The pin clicked into place and the radiator swung down, closing with an invisible seal.

'Wow!' Sammy took a deep breath, 'so your pin opens the door to the chamber.'

Dixie nodded. 'So does Milly's. They probably have different pins for the other entrances.'

'That makes sense,' agreed Sammy. 'We'll have to keep an eye out, passage spotting, watching for people disappearing!'

'The passage spotters,' Dixie grinned.

'That's a terrible name,' Sammy laughed. 'Hey, we could try the library and see if Mrs Skoob can recommend anything.'

'Just don't ask for the self-help section,' said Darius, putting on his new "Mrs Skoob" voice, 'why my dear…'

'Yeah we know,' said Dixie. 'It would…'

'…defeat the purpose,' finished Sammy grinning at his friends. 'So what were you doing down there anyway? Did you have to check on the dragons?'

Dixie coughed awkwardly. 'Well, you'll tell me I'm stupid.'

'You're stupid,' said Darius helpfully.

Dixie frowned at him. 'Yeah well Mrs Hubar said if the Shape were going to kill any dragons, they'd kill dragons belonging to trolls first.'

'Oh,' said Sammy, wishing he'd stuck up for Dixie in class.

'Yeah, so I had to check on Kiridor, you know, make sure he's ok. I checked Kyrillan too Sammy. He's ok as well.'

'Thanks,' said Sammy. 'How about Darius's dragon, Nelson?'

'Mm, I'm sure he's ok' said Dixie, her cheeks going pink. 'What's for lunch?'

Sammy and Darius had to jog to catch up with Dixie. The three of them arrived in the Main Hall a little out of breath.

'What's – for – lunch?' puffed Darius, throwing his rucksack under the North table.

'Sausages, chips, peas and gravy,' said Dixie. 'Yuk, who has gravy with chips?'

'We do I guess,' said Sammy, moving up as Gavin, Toby and Jock arrived clutching steaming plates.

'It's serve yourself today,' grumbled Gavin. 'No one seems to know why.'

'Out of magic,' suggested Sammy.

'Hardly,' said Jock, sitting next to Dixie. 'My Mum didn't mean that stuff you know. She's just not used to your kind.'

'My kind?' spat Dixie. 'She's just another short, fat, narrow minded, dwarf breath, little scavenging, dirty, fat, short, stupid…'

'Yeah?' Jock interrupted Dixie's stream of insults. 'Well I bet your Dad thinks you're his ugly frog princess with your stupid green hair, hook nose and spade hands and feet.'

'You know nothing about my family,' said Dixie icily. 'Sammy, would you pass the salt please.'

Clearly taken aback, Jock reached for the salt and passed it to Dixie. 'Here.'

Staring straight ahead, Dixie reached across Sammy's plate to get the second salt cellar. 'The other one's dirty,' she explained, shaking a dribble of salt on to the gravy sodden chips. 'Ug, it's empty,' she groaned.

'Here, have some of mine,' said Jock. 'Look, I'm sorry ok.' He tipped up his salt cellar and shook it. The lid jumped off and salt flew out of the shaker smothering Dixie's food like snow on fresh ground.

'Oops,' said Jock, drowned by a roar of laughter from Gavin.

'Sorry for that as well, huh?' said Dixie, trying hard not to laugh.

'Here, have mine,' said Jock, looking horrified at the mess. 'There's no gravy, but I expect it'll be ok.'

Dixie winked at Sammy. 'Well, I suppose it'll have to do,' she said accepting Jock's plate with a grin.

In bed that night Sammy was glad Dr Shivers's lesson had passed smoothly, reading in silence from their new "Ye Olde Arte of Descaling" textbook that although it had been first published nearly a century ago was still current once you got used to the funny spelling (like "ye" instead of "the").

He had to admit the pictures were as good as the text with hand drawn detailed sketches of dragons with arrows pointing to various parts of the dragon's body that could be pressed lightly to start a chain reaction to remove a large number of scales at once.

'Always use light fingers and descale on a surface that will be easy to clean,' Dr Shivers had said, then he'd winked at Sammy. 'Dragon Minders will go first before Christmas to show the rest of the class how it is done.'

Sammy had looked at Milly, who had been sitting next to Gavin looking over his shoulder so she could pretend to read his textbook, whilst propping her own textbook up so she could paint her nails without Dr Shivers seeing.

He thought Dr Shivers was probably right. Milly wasn't going to be much good at saving dragons when she hated even going near them. But he didn't like to think he would cheat her out of her place, or her pin, he thought enviously.

'Night all,' said Gavin, interrupting Sammy's thoughts.

'See you tomo-o-o-rrow,' yawned Sammy, pulling his toy lion close to him.

CHAPTER 11

THE SHAPE RETURN

Sammy woke early again on Friday morning to the late autumn sun streaming in through the tower windows. Milly's Dragon Minder pin was still bothering him even though it was ten days later than the day Dr Shivers had promised Sammy he could be a Dragon Minder.

He dressed quickly in a t-shirt and his leather padded trousers and made his way outside. By the time he was outside, spots of rain were falling.

Sports was the first lesson of the day and they practiced flying with their dragons. Sports master Mr Cross was watching and making notes on his clipboard, recording the abilities of the second years.

The first years were watching from under umbrellas, many of them as open-mouthed as Sammy had been when he'd seen his first Dragonball match.

The second years were playing against the third years who, in Sammy's opinion, didn't seem to fly any better, smoother or faster than himself.

Since their discovery of the radiator, Dixie had kept her distance from Sammy and Darius, afraid, she explained, that she would be dismissed as a Dragon Minder for discussing the secret passages.

This had suited Sammy and Darius and to Mrs Skoob's annoyance, they had spent many hours in the school library looking up the history of Dragamas and its relationship to Karmandor Castle, which was, as everyone at Dragamas was taught, the castle that had belonged to King Serberon of the Dark Ages and his loyal dragon Karmandor.

'Oi! Catch it Sammy!' yelled Gavin, aiming a wild pass.

Sammy swung his left arm past a slippery, spinning, leather-bound Dragonball. His fingers closed round the solid stitching and he pushed it to Darius who was flying upside down in a loop the loop.

Darius shunted the ball back to Sammy and completed his roll to a volley of applause from the ground.

Sammy squeezed his knees against Kyrillan's girth and sped off towards the goal. The wind howled around his ears disorientating him. A tall third year girl dressed rather unsuitably in a short games skirt showing long tanned legs was standing, arms outstretched, ready to block his shot on goal. She flashed a green gum guard smile at him and took a step forward.

Sammy froze. Behind her, staffs outstretched, were four hooded figures, their red eyes flashing at him. Sammy jerked, the ball poised, his shot ready to take.

'It's a joke,' he said to himself, feeling Kyrillan quivering beneath him, 'just Serberon and Mikhael.'

Ahead, the hooded shapes seemed to sway in the wind.

'Illusion,' muttered Sammy, 'using the power of the stars. They – are – not – there.' He swung his arm, lobbing the ball into an arc that he calculated would land in the far corner of the goal, his goal Sammy realised with a bolt of anger. How had he got mixed up, taking a shot at his own goal. No wonder everyone else was at the other end.

He stared transfixed as the ball curved. The wafting, cloaked figures were moving forward in slow motion. Sammy spun his head round. There was a large scuffle in the middle of the pitch that Mr Cross was sorting out. No one was looking at his end of the pitch.

His goal went unnoticed as the shapes enveloped the girl in goal. Her gum guard was coughed out of her mouth as one of the hooded figures wrapped its cloaked arms around her middle. There was a flash of red lightning and a roar of unearthly thunder that drowned out her scream. Sammy couldn't move a muscle. He was frozen solid.

Fully conscious, he could see directly ahead but couldn't move his eyes. Blood poured out of the girl's mouth, her eyes as wide open as Sammy's. There was another flash of red lightning and the hooded shapes vanished. The girl slumped to the floor. Everyone came running up the pitch. All went black as Sammy passed out.

'Ooch no lassy, don't disturb him yet,' came a rough Scottish voice that Sammy knew belonged to Mrs Grock, school secretary and nurse. He guessed he was in the hospital wing on the second floor of her house in the Dragamas grounds, not far from the Dragonball pitch.

'He's had a nasty shock,' added a male voice that sounded like Professor Burlay. 'This was written in the stars. I sent warnings. No one takes any notice of me.'

'Perhaps he is awake now?' came a third voice. 'I saw the boy's eyes twitch. He is awake.'

Sammy felt a hand gently shake his shoulder. He opened his eyes. Professor Burlay, Professor Sanchez and Mrs Grock were standing one side of his bed. His mother, father, Dixie and Darius were standing on the other side.

Sir Ragnarok was standing facing the window with his back to the room.

'Mum? Dad?' said Sammy, rubbing his eyes.

Julia Rambles looked at him with tears in her eyes. Her fist was tightly closed around a giant grey silk handkerchief that Sammy recognised belonged to Professor Burlay.

'I'm ok,' said Sammy, twisting round in the bed. 'Why are you here?'

Sir Ragnarok turned around, his hands clasped tightly together. 'There is something you should know Sammy. Something I would prefer to tell you alone.'

Sir Ragnarok waved his hands towards the door. Professor Burlay and Mrs Grock left first, followed by Professor Sanchez, Dixie and Darius. Sammy felt his mother stroke his hand, whispering "hang in there Sam" and kissing him on the cheek. His father squeezed his shoulder.

'Lucky we were passing,' Sammy heard his father tell his mother.

'Funny place this Samagard Farm. I still think he'd be better in a proper hospital,' came her reply.

Sammy sat up as Sir Ragnarok rested his hands on the metal rail at the end of the bed.

'Do they know?' Sammy whispered, staring at the door where his parents had just left.

Sir Ragnarok shook his head with a glimmer sadness. 'Your parents used to be the very best. I knew them from King's College. They were some of my first students when I taught there. From memory, it's where they started courting properly after their friendship began at Dragamas.'

Sammy stared at Sir Ragnarok. 'No one ever told me.'

'Not usually the sort of thing I suppose,' said Sir Ragnarok, pulling a dead fly from the matting of his beard.

'Still, you must have guessed you have dragon blood in your family?'

Sammy shook his head, he felt his eyes could go no wider. 'No,' he whispered. 'My first day here was the first time I've ever seen a real dragon.'

Sir Ragnarok laughed. 'I had hoped you would say that. It's what makes you different from boys like Gavin and Jock and even Darius.'

'How?' asked Sammy. Sir Ragnarok wasn't making any sense and his mind was still reeling from the Dragonball match and the reappearance of the Shape.

'You can learn from scratch,' explained Sir Ragnarok. 'Nothing to prove, no one to live up to. There's no pressure. You can grow up into your own person, make your own choices from the things you have learned, not the things you have been told.'

'So?' said Sammy, wishing his parents would come back. 'How come I'm here?'

Sir Ragnarok frowned, clearly annoyed at being interrupted mid flow of a speech he had obviously been preparing for some time. He clicked his tongue.

'You are here, Sammy, because I carried you frozen stiff from a direct hit of red lightning. A girl is dead. The Shape are back,' he softened his tone, 'but you are here at Dragamas because your parents, grandparents, great and great, great grandparents were at Dragamas. Your children and your children's children will study here too. Their names are already written in the stars.'

'But?' puffed Sammy, the wind taken out of him. 'I'm eleven, twelve in November. I don't even want any children!'

Sir Ragnarok laughed out loud and slapped the bed rail. 'You have so much to learn. I'm quite looking forward to it.'

'This is stupid,' snapped Sammy losing his patience. 'Why did I have to go to that other school if I have this dragon blood?' You saw my parents. They know nothing about dragons. They think this is Old Samagard Farm. They probably think I'm in some pokey ruins!'

Sir Ragnarok laughed louder, vibrating the rails. 'For your benefit I presume. Possibly even your safety.' Sir Ragnarok leaned forward and looked Sammy straight in the eye. 'You realise,' he frowned, 'that you cannot tell the Shape what you do not know.'

Sammy felt his mouth fall open. 'I what?'

Sir Ragnarok tapped the rail. 'Remember that and keep with your friends at all times. The Shape believe you are the key to their plans to kill all dragons.'

Sir Ragnarok turned on his heels and swept briskly out of the room before Sammy had the chance to breathe, let alone ask any of the million and one questions that were burning red hot in his mind.

He thumped his head back on the pillow, confident from previous encounters with Sir Ragnarok that he would be left alone until Mrs Grock returned to see if he was well enough to go back to the castle.

Sure enough, half an hour later, Mrs Grock returned with Dr Shivers, whose gaunt like face seemed to have grown some extra wrinkles.

'How long have I been here?' demanded Sammy.

Dr Shivers glanced at his watch. 'Three hours and forty two minutes. Short really for the lightning you were exposed to.'

'How come it's just me in here?'

'Ooch,' said Mrs Grock. 'There's no need to be like that. It was just you. You were the only one who got hit.'

'They know,' said Sammy, things suddenly snapping into place. 'They knew it had to be bigger than the ruby stone to work.'

'A trial run you think,' murmured Dr Shivers. 'No, Sir Ragnarok considers this a warning. A girl has died.'

'Ooch, this is terrible,' said Mrs Grock. 'I had hoped I would not live to see the Shape again.'

'Mrs Grock, is Sammy ready to go back?' asked Dr Shivers. 'I would like to escort him to the castle.'

'I should say,' beamed Mrs Grock. 'It'll take more than a bolt of red lightning to hurt this Dragon Knight.'

'We'll see,' said Dr Shivers. 'Sammy, are you decent?'

Sammy nodded and pulled back the covers, glad to see he was still in one piece and wearing his t-shirt and leather trousers. He bent down to put on his trainers, which had been removed.

'Ready,' said Sammy, picking up his watch and staff from the bedside chest of drawers. 'Is Kyrillan all right?'

Dr Shivers nodded. 'Unaffected you'll find. Dixie took him down to the chambers.'

It wasn't until they were outside and waving to Mrs Grock that Dr Shivers bent close to Sammy.

'Milly was the girl who died,' said Dr Shivers in a half whisper. 'She would have wanted you to have this,' he smiled, pressing a Dragon Minder pin into Sammy's suddenly sweating palm.

'Well?' said Dr Shivers, his voice sending a shiver of its own down Sammy's spine. 'A "thank you" may be in order. Everyone from the second year up wants one of these.'

'I...er...thanks,' said Sammy, a strange lump forming in his throat.

Dr Shivers relaxed. 'Good, good,' he said slowly, drawing out the vowels. 'Now do you know why the pins are important?'

Sammy shook his head. 'I know they let you get into the Dragon Chambers.'

Dr Shivers smashed a fist into his palm. 'Bingo!' he exclaimed. 'The dragons and the hidden walkways.'

'Secret passageways?'

'Yes!' said Dr Shivers, vigorously rummaging through his pockets. He pulled out a crumpled piece of paper. 'Here are the four entrances to the Dragon Chambers - North, South, East and West.'

'But...' started Sammy, wishing harder that his parents were there.

'No use,' smiled Dr Shivers tapping the side of his head. 'They're on their way home.' He pieced together his staff and drew a square in the air. He turned to Sammy. 'Watch this.'

Dr Shivers sent a blue-grey spark from the end of his staff into the empty space. The spark seemed to hit something solid, even though the air was empty. It crackled into a pool of liquid that rippled like a stone thrown in water, hundreds of circles moving to the edge of the square.

When the ripples stopped, Sammy blinked in disbelief. The square had turned into a television screen with his parents waving to Sir Ragnarok at the school gates.

'They're going,' he exclaimed.

'Indeed,' said Dr Shivers, looking keenly at Sammy. 'But you still have me, and your friends here at Dragamas.'

'They didn't say goodbye...' said Sammy, the strange lump forming in his throat again.

'They're staying with your uncle in the village I believe. They'll be back again at Christmas.'

'Oh,' said Sammy feeling foolish.

'And maybe for your birthday,' added Dr Shivers with a smile. 'Can't miss the big one-two.'

'Twelve,' echoed Sammy.

'If you like,' said Dr Shivers, folding the piece of paper. 'I said "one-two" at your age. It was the fashionable thing to say at the time.'

'So I'm now one-one,' Sammy grinned.

'One-one indeed,' said Dr Shivers. 'One all.' He pressed the folded square into Sammy's hand. 'You may find this puts you at the advantage,' he smiled. 'Shall we go back to the castle now?'

Sammy nodded dumbly, knowing without knowing that something was wrong. When they reached the castle he paused.

'Does Sir Ragnarok know I have the Dragon Minder pin and directions to the four entrances to the Dragon Chambers?' he asked, stopping suddenly.

Dr Shivers flinched. 'I couldn't say,' he replied, pushing open the heavy wooden door for Sammy. 'You'll be all right from here,' he added, closing the door firmly behind them.

Halfway down the corridor, Dr Shivers pulled aside a large painting to reveal a door labelled "Staff Only".

'Good night Sammy,' said Dr Shivers, disappearing into a dimly lit passage behind the door.

'Good night Sir,' said Sammy. He took the pin and the paper out of his pocket and stared hard at them. 'For good not evil,' he said to himself as he walked back to the North common room.

Inside, the common room looked as if it had been turned upside down. The chairs and beanbags were scattered like an obstacle course between the two doors at opposite ends leading to the girls and boys' tower rooms.

'What happened here?' Sammy spoke out loud, although he couldn't see anyone there. He bent down to pick up one of the chairs and found it splattered with red liquid reminding him of Sir Ragnarok's red berry potion. A handful of white stick cigarettes lay on the floor nearby.

'It's blood,' said Dixie, standing up from behind a chair and looking incredibly pale. 'There was a big fight tonight.'

'A fight?' exclaimed Sammy.

Dixie sniffed. 'It's not funny. Everything's gone wrong.' She turned her back on him and walked towards the girls' tower.

Sammy shook himself. 'Hey wait! Look what I've been given.'

Dixie paused and stared at the Dragon Minder pin in Sammy's hand. 'Where did you get that?'

'Dr Shivers gave it to me,' said Sammy. 'He said Milly would have wanted me to have it…but she's…dead.'

Dixie frowned. 'Milly still has hers. We went together tonight to check on the dragons. She used her pin to get through the radiator.'

'Milly's alive?' Sammy coughed the words out.

'Could be a fake,' said Dixie. 'Lots of them about.'

'Yeah?' said Sammy, getting defensive. 'Then why did he give me this?' he held out the folded square.

Dixie unfolded the paper. 'A map?'

Sammy nodded. 'The map shows all the entrances to the Dragon Chambers.'

Dixie folded the paper back up. 'I think you should give this to Sir Ragnarok.'

'No,' said Sammy so quickly he surprised himself. 'It's mine. Dr Shivers gave it to me.'

Dixie shrugged. 'It's up to you,' she muttered. 'Something's not right with it.'

'You're jealous,' said Sammy, his forehead burning. 'Just because you don't know where the other entrances are.'

'And neither should you,' snapped Dixie coldly. 'Two Dragon Minders per house, per year. Just make sure you haven't been given the map so the Shape can use you to kill the dragons.'

'Liar!' shouted Sammy. 'You want it for yourself!' He stormed off feeling really light-headed, unsure why he had shouted at Dixie.

'She's wrong,' he said as he marched up the tower stairs. 'The Shape can't use me. I'm going to be a Dragon Knight. She's wrong. She's got to be. They can't use me. They wouldn't.'

By the time he reached the second year bedroom, he was less sure he was right and more sure there was some truth in what Dixie had said. He barely noticed the blood spots on the stairs, nor that it was unusually quiet. He stomped into his bedroom, glad the others were asleep. He put the pin and the map into the toes of one of his socks in his chest of drawers and climbed into bed.

As his head touched the pillow, he realised he hadn't got changed for bed and that he hadn't even read the map properly to find out where the other entrances were. He wasn't even sure what Dixie had meant when she said that Milly was still alive.

CHAPTER 12

BEING A DRAGON MINDER

Sammy found himself alone again in the tower the following morning. He'd heard Gavin and Toby get up first, racing each other as usual to the bathroom on the floor below. Jock and Darius had left next, arguing about the powers of the ruby stone compared with the bolt of red lightning. He had been glad when they had left so he could take a second look at the Dragon Minder pin and the map with the secret passageways.

As he reached for his drawer, there was a knock and the tower door burst open.

'Hi Sammy!'

'Hi Dixie,' said Sammy, shoving the sock back into his drawer. 'What are you doing here?' He pulled his duvet back over his pajama legs in time as Dixie flung herself on to the end of his bed.

'Are you going to the funeral?'

'Uh...' said Sammy.

'Mary-Beth's, oh, I didn't tell you last night?'

'Look about last night, I'm really sorry I was angry,' said Sammy. 'I don't know what happened.'

'It's ok,' said Dixie. 'Anyway it was her. She was in goal.'

'Dead?' said Sammy, stunned. 'Mary-Beth?'

'She shouldn't have cheated on Serberon,' said Dixie grimly. 'I wished the Shape would hurt her and they did,' she folded her arms, 'and good riddance.'

'But she can't have,' said Sammy. 'She wasn't even playing.'

'Yeah she was,' said Dixie. 'Dr Shivers told her to. It was weird though. He called her Milly.'

'No!' said Sammy, his brain snapping into gear. 'He thought she was Milly.'

'What?' said Dixie tapping her head. 'You've lost it.'

'No I haven't. Dr Shivers. He promised me I could be a Dragon Minder. He said he'd get Milly's pin. So I could be a second year Dragon Minder.' Sammy pulled the sock drawer open. 'Look, it's here,' he pulled out the dragon shaped pin and showed it to Dixie.

'That doesn't make any sense,' said Dixie, pulling her ponytail straight. 'Milly would have given you her pin anyway. She wants to chuck it in.'

Sammy shrugged. 'Well I don't know what's going on. You said the Shape killed Mary-Beth. Dr Shivers put her in goal.'

'Hey wait, you can't accuse Dr Shivers.'

'I was right about Dr Lithoman.'

'That's different,' said Dixie, standing up. 'Completely different.'

'His name starts with an "S". He could be the "S" in Shape.'

'So does yours,' retorted Dixie.

'It can't be him. You're probably right,' said Sammy. 'Maybe I should give the pin and map to Sir Ragnarok.'

'You wanted to keep them last night,' said Dixie. 'It might not be such a bad thing if you were a Dragon Minder.'

'Yeah,' said Sammy, cheering up. 'We can look after the dragons together.'

'So, where are these passages then?' asked Dixie.

Sammy pulled the map out of the drawer. They had time to memorise the four entrances and the passageways between them before Darius and Jock came back into the tower room.

'What's she doing here?' demanded Jock.

'Just leaving,' Dixie grinned as Jock pulled his towel tight, even though he seemed to be wearing full pyjamas underneath.

'This is the boys' room,' said Jock, pointing to the door. 'Get out!'

Dixie stood up straight. She was already two or three inches taller than Jock and tapped her hand on his head as she walked out. 'See you Sammy.'

Sammy waved, feeling his cheeks redden.

'Hey Dixie,' came Gavin's voice from the stairwell. 'This is the boys' tower.' He entered the room and looked sharply at Sammy. 'What's she doing here?'

'Nothing,' said Sammy. 'Just came to tell me about the girl who died yesterday.'

'Mary-Beth,' said Toby, arriving at the tower door, his hair slicked back from his shower, his towel astride both shoulders. 'Are you going to the funeral?'

'No,' said Gavin firmly. 'Sir Ragnarok's assembly this morning will be more than enough for me.'

'What will happen to her dragon?' asked Sammy.

'Dr Shivers will take it back I expect,' said Toby. 'Do you remember? It was a gold dragon. He grew it for her.'

'I wish mine was gold,' said Gavin, 'but then Milly wouldn't like me as much!'

Sammy laughed. 'Is that why she hangs around you?'

'Apparently,' Gavin scowled. 'All she ever does is go on and on about pink dragons.'

Toby threw a pillow at Gavin. 'Gavin's got a girlfriend!'

There was a thud as Gavin flung his pillow back at his brother.

'Having fun are we boys?' came a voice from the door. Dr Shivers stood in a dark grey suit frowning at them. 'You'll go straight to Armoury this morning. There won't be a Dragon Studies lesson this morning.'

'Sir really?' Gavin punched the air. 'No Dragon Studies!'

'Because Mary-Beth was North,' said Sammy, looking out of his tower window.

Two black limousines had pulled up outside the school gates. He could see a group of students walking down to meet them. In the middle were three green heads. Dixie's brothers were going despite Mary-Beth cheating on Serberon. Sammy couldn't see the cigarette smoking fifth year.

'I shall be attending the funeral,' finished Dr Shivers. 'Are you listening, Sammy? Please go straight to Armoury.'

'Yes Sir,' said Sammy, wishing Dr Shivers would stop staring at him.

In Armoury, Commander Altair had prepared an action-packed lesson, perhaps hoping to take their minds away from the Shape and the tragedy from the afternoon before. He asked them to stand on chairs and block red sparks, a cut down version of the red lightning.

Sammy found the lesson exhausting. He'd been able to block every single spark heading his way and Commander Altair had awarded him twenty stars as the end of the lesson bell sounded.

'Lunch!' said Sammy, squashing the last red spark and tucking his staff into his rucksack pocket.

'Not yet,' said Commander Altair smiling at him. 'The rest of you may go. Sammy, a quick word if I may.'

'Sammy's in trouble,' Gavin chanted as he left the classroom, flanked, as always, by Toby and Milly. 'Sammy's in trouble!'

Commander Altair waited until the classroom had emptied, shooing Dixie and Darius out from behind the classroom door. When they were out of sight, Commander Altair looked closely at him as if he thought Sammy might faint. 'Are you ok Sammy?'

'I'm fine, thank you,' said Sammy.

'Sir Ragnarok asked me to give you a message.'

'What?' asked Sammy, wishing Commander Altair would hurry up. He had seen they were to have giant sausage rolls with stir-fried vegetables for lunch that he didn't want to miss.

Commander Altair frowned. 'Sir Ragnarok says you may keep the pin.' He stared Sammy straight in the eyes. 'I trust you know what this means.'

Focusing hard on the sausage rolls and stir-fried vegetables, Sammy nodded, picked up his bag and half walked, half ran out of the classroom.

From the single swear word that followed him, Sammy knew Commander Altair hadn't been able to read his mind. He stopped running at the bottom of the staircase and grinned. His practice had paid off.

'Yeah but did Commander Altair know that Dr Shivers gave you the pin, or did he just mean that you have to be responsible with it?' asked Dixie.

'Sammy, responsible? You're joking!' laughed Darius as they sat down to their sausage roll and stir-fried vegetable lunch. 'Chance would be a fine thing.'

'I think he knows,' said Sammy slowly. 'I blocked him. I think he was trying to read my mind.'

'Freaky,' said Gavin. 'So, this pin-thing, what do you do with it?'

Sammy bent down to rub his ankle where Dixie had just kicked him under the table. 'Don't know. Just a pin that says I can look after the dragons.'

'Cool,' said Toby.

'Yeah,' added Gavin. 'You get to go in all the secret passages!'

'Probably,' said Sammy, his mouth full of pastry. 'What's for pudding?'

'You know you can't talk about it,' Dixie whispered furiously as they left the dining hall. 'No-one talks about it. Not even to Darius,' she added picking up on Sammy's thoughts.'

'You're getting good at that,' he whispered back.

They spent the rest of the afternoon in a drizzly September shower, flying under Mr Cross's supervision in their Sports lesson. Orange flamed torches had been placed at one metre intervals around the Dragonball pitch and any balls that went out of play were rebounded back onto the pitch as if some invisible wall held them in. Sir Lok Ragnarok was taking no chances in the safety of the pupils at Dragamas.

Exhausted, Sammy was glad when Mr Cross called himself, Dixie and Milly along with the other Dragon Minders to help lead the dragons back to the chambers.

They walked around the edge of the castle to where Sammy and Darius had been when they were searching for Dixie.

"Open Sesame," said Simon Sanchez.

Amos giggled.

Standing on tiptoes, Simon waved his staff. 'Open and reveal the Dragon Chambers!'

Sammy wished Darius was there. He would have found Simon funny, even if they didn't get on too well.

'Yeah, enough Simon. Sammy's impressed.'

'Just open it Simon!'

'Come on Simon, our dragons are getting impatient.'

Busy watching Simon capering at the front, Sammy had almost forgotten that they had forty dragons with them. He reached out for Kyrillan's blue-green scaly back and was greeted by a puff of smoke that sailed over his head and landed around Simon's neck like a garland.

He laughed as Simon coughed, blowing the smoke away from him and on to Amos who started coughing as well.

''Oo was that?' coughed Simon.

Sammy turned to look behind him and shrugged.

Simon coughed again.

'Open Sesame!' He said, pushing one of the stones in the castle wall.

Sammy stared. He and Darius must have missed it earlier.

He felt a nudge in his left forearm.

'That's why you need the pin!' Dixie grinned at him. 'Sends some kind of signal to the dwarves below. No use tapping without the pin.'

'Oh.'

'Come on, it should be open by now!'

Sammy and the other Dragon Minders led the dragons down the ramp that had appeared from behind the bushes. He had seen the entrance before, except it had been on the way out when he and Darius had got in a different way.

Sammy was annoyed when Kyrillan, expecting him to wait at the entrance, trundled inwards, following Dixie and her dragon Kiridor.

He helped Samantha Trowt, a short dumpy girl with teeth braces, from the West house who was having trouble leading two large red and gold dragons down the ramp.

'Thanks,' she puffed at Sammy giving him a silver smile.

'It's ok', muttered Sammy, still cross with Kyrillan.

'You can take Kyrillan if you want, it's just he's not expecting you to be here,' Dixie tried to reassure him.

'Wish she'd stop doing that,' he muttered crosser still as Dixie turned around again to check that he was ok.

'Sure,' said Samantha with another brace-filled smile that flashed in the evening sun. 'Oooh,' giggled Samantha, touching the side of her head, 'no need to be like that Dixie Deane.'

Sammy grinned, he thought he'd heard in his head the stream of abuse Dixie had silently projected at Samantha. He needed to practice, he thought, and jumped as Dixie grinned at him, reading his mind again.

He soon found out why Samantha had been having trouble with the dragons. She was useless with them, thinking that a kick to the back of the leg would make it move. Instead, the dragon thrashed its tail and would have crushed Sammy if Simon hadn't reacted with a freeze effect from the ruby on his staff.

Simon vaulted over a green dragon to shove Sammy aside before bringing the dragon back to life and its tail thumping a foot into the ground where Sammy had been standing.

'Thanks,' said Sammy, catching the breath that had been scared out of his lungs.

'It is not a problem,' said Simon, ruffling a hand through his dark hair. 'Dragons do not obey the kick,' he said, scowling at Samantha Trowt.

Samantha tossed her head obstinately 'My mother teaches dragon flying. She kicks, thumps and spits at dragons all day long and it works for her.

'Then your mother is evil,' said Simon flatly, 'Sir Ragnarok should hear of this.'

'Sir Ragnarok already knows,' retorted Samantha.

'I doubt this is true,' said Simon.

Samantha went pale. 'Please don't tell Sir Ragnarok, I only saw her kick a dragon once.'

'That's not what you said, train-track mouth,' snapped Dixie.

'Troll,' spat Samantha.

'Oh yeah?' Dixie glared at Samantha and pushed up nose to make it wrinkle like a monster. 'I'll get you!'

'Oooh,' said Samantha, 'I'm so scared!'

'Stop it!' shouted Peter Grayling from the West house. He had come back up the ramp from delivering his dragons. 'You'll get the teachers down here! We'll all get stars deducted.'

'She isn't worth it anyway,' said Dixie, letting go of her nose. 'Come on Kiridor, let's get you to bed.

Obediently, Kiridor and Kyrillan, along with the thirty or so remaining dragons, followed Dixie like lambs following a shepherdess into the torch-lit cavern. Their footsteps echoed on the stone floor along with the clatter and scrape of scales and sharp toenails scratching and scrabbling as the dragons found their beds for the night.

Five minutes later, Dixie came back out of the Dragon Chamber with a singe of soot on her cheek and her green hair a little ruffled. She wiped her hands on her jeans and said, 'all done!'

'Very good,' said Simon Sanchez, beaming, 'you are a natural!'

'Yeah,' added Amos.

'Come on,' said Dixie, grinning as she fastened her pin to her jumper. Linking arms with Sammy and Milly, she skipped with them back to the castle door.

Sammy turned just in time to see Simon press one of the stone slabs in the castle wall and the entrance to the Dragon Chamber closed tightly as if it had never been there at all.

'Hotel de la Draco,' said Milly, 'that's what Mummy calls it. She was a Dragon Minder when she was here.'

Sammy felt a jolt in his stomach. What had happened to his family to make them forget about dragons, except, he remembered, his Uncle Peter Pickering, on his mother's side, who worked in the jewellery shop in the sleepy village beyond Dragamas.

He desperately wanted to say "I wish my mum called it that" but he didn't think it would do his reputation any good. "Not cool" he decided, "not the done thing" his mother would have said when talking across the fence about fashion with the next door neighbours.

Besides, Dixie got funny with him if he thought he was as dragonish as she was. Which, as he found out more and more about his parents, it looked as if he and Dixie might be equals. If only he could convince his parents and make them see dragons again.

Instead, he laughed. 'Hotel de la Draco, that's French, isn't it?'

'Ask Darius,' said Milly snootily as she pulled her hair into a ponytail, copying Dixie.

'Copycat,' said Dixie, noticing.

'Don't know what you're looking at,' giggled Milly.

'Honestly,' thought Sammy, didn't girls ever stop giggling. It was almost as bad as when Darius did one of his pig like snorts.

They entered the castle through the thick oak door and were met by Gavin running frantically towards them.

'It's official!' Gavin shouted from halfway up the corridor. 'We're going to the Land of the Pharaohs at Halloween!'

CHAPTER 13

OFF TO THE
LAND OF THE PHARAOHS

The next few weeks evaporated into a blur of Mrs Hubar's Gemology lessons, where she taught them about the five stones they would be given in their five years at Dragamas. She explained how they had received onyx in their first year and received a ruby in their second year which would be joined by amber, sapphire and emerald.

Simon Sanchez's mother, Professor Sanchez had allowed them to create their own healing potion in their Alchemistry lesson. They used the familiar recipe of turnips, eggs and amberoid, supplied by Mrs Grock. Professor Sanchez asked each pupil to prick their thumb with a pin and then repair the wound. She awarded fifty stars to Samantha Trowt who created a perfect potion on her first attempt.

Samantha had impressed Professor Sanchez when she wiped some of the healing potion on to her teeth and her metal braces fell out, revealing a glowing smile that any dentist would be proud of.

However, a few days later, Professor Sanchez deducted half of the stars when she found Samantha had kept a bottle of the potion and started selling it to the first years so they could have perfect teeth as well.

To Sammy, it seemed like Professor Sanchez was preparing them for some unimaginable terror at the Land of the Pharaohs. She kept checking his mixture three times and handed him a bottle of her own potion at the end. 'Just for emergencies,' she had whispered to him, making his skin crawl.

Sammy found that he couldn't sleep when they were finally sent to bed, talking nineteen to the dozen about pyramids. He had felt bad when he snapped at a first year who asked what the weather would be like.

'It'll be snowy, wear your wellies', he had snapped, angry that unlike Dixie and Darius, he didn't know anything about the Land of the Pharaohs because he had missed out on going on the visit last year.

Even Gavin and Toby, whose mother had refused to let her sons go, had allowed them to visit when she heard Sammy hadn't been given his parental permission slip. Without Sammy at the land, she thought Gavin and Toby would be safe.

'Bit of luck she doesn't know I'm going this time,' Sammy had said.

Making matters worse, the first year had stared at him, and to Sammy's annoyance, the boy had laughed and run away, shouting over his shoulder in front of all of the first years, 'you're joking! It's going to be at least thirty degrees!'

Sammy had snapped, 'we'll see,' and stomped up to bed. He had flung his curtains around him, changed into his pyjamas and was trying to sleep.

He could hear footsteps coming up the spiral staircase and thought it was probably Gavin and Toby. The twins chatted quietly as they got ready for bed.

Jock was already asleep, judging by the faint snoring from across the room. Darius had been given a detention by Dr Shivers for forgetting to feed Nelson for three days in a row.

As a punishment, Darius had been asked to collect forty sacks of grain from Mrs Grock's cellar and drag them to the food section in the cellars of the castle kitchens. According to Dr Shivers, each sack would weigh half as much as Darius himself. Not known for his athletics, Darius had looked horrified.

'You won't forget to feed Nelson again,' Dr Shivers had said, with a gleam in his eye.

It had gone long past 10pm when Darius arrived, accompanied by the stench of dusty grain that smelled to Sammy like decaying rabbit droppings.

'Yeugh,' said Darius, 'I can't believe Nelson eats that stuff. It stinks!'

Jock snored loudly.

'You stink,' came Gavin's voice from the other side of the room.

'You always stink,' retorted Darius throwing his dirty clothes into the middle of the room and swapping them for pyjamas.

'It's the Land of the Pharaohs tomorrow,' said Toby. 'Did you see we get to stay overnight?'

'What?' exclaimed Sammy. 'Who told you?'

'No one. It was on the noticeboard.'

'You don't read that do you Toby?' sneered Gavin.

'So?'

'Nothing.'

'What?'

'Nothing,' repeated Gavin. 'Just you never read anything except Dragon Strike comics.'

'Stuff you,' retorted Toby. 'Anyway, we leave at half past nine. We're the third group to go up.'

'Cool,' said Gavin, 'bit of luck you read that noticeboard.'

Toby threw his pillow at Gavin.

'Do we get wristbands to get free stuff?' asked Sammy, 'like at the Floating Circus.'

'I don't know,' said Toby, 'Maybe.'

'Cool,' said Gavin with a yawn, 'night all.'

'Night.'

Jock snored again.

After a therapeutic eight hours sleep, Sammy found he was wide awake at the first opening of his eyelids. Seeing that the others were still asleep he got dressed making as little noise as possible and went down to check on Kyrillan.

He pressed his Dragon Minder pin in the groove of the radiator, the first time he had done it alone, and feeling his way carefully into the dark passage he started climbing down the stone spiral staircase.

At the bottom, still in darkness, he found a door that he could push open. At the same time, there was a "clunk" above him and he guessed that the two were connected and the radiator door had closed.

'One door shuts and another one opens,' he whispered to himself, jumping as a bright white fluorescent light snapped on.

'Hey stupid!' came a shout that interrupted his thoughts. 'You're supposed to shut the radiator door first. It turns the light on.'

'Dixie?'

'Sammy?'

'Yeah, is that you, Dixie?'

'Yeah, I suppose no one told you about the light switch?'

There was a clatter on the stairs and Dixie appeared.

'Nope,' Sammy grinned.

'Right,' said Dixie, 'there's a few things you should know.'

By the time they had shown their pins to Duke Stronghammer and found Kyrillan and Kiridor asleep behind one of the pillars, Dixie had explained almost fifty rules and regulations required of the Dragon Minders.

'Finally,' she added, making Sammy's head spin with all the new instructions, 'Captain Stronghammer said to have fun!'

'Oh,' said Sammy. 'Most of the rules are just common sense anyway.'

'Aren't they all,' said Dixie stiffly. 'Just remember a door left open at the wrong time might let the Shape in.'

'I don't understand.'

'Stupid,' said Dixie. 'If the Shape get in, they'll kill...'

'No, I get that bit,' Sammy scowled, 'I don't understand why they would want to kill the dragons in the first place.'

'My mum reckons the Shape are immortal and they don't want anyone else being immortal either.'

Sammy bent down to pick up a blue-green scale from the floor.

'Darius says the Shape's brains have draconite in them.'

'Probably,' said Dixie,' immortality is supposed to be draconite and lions blood.'

'Oooh'

'What?'

'Maybe Dr Lithoman is the only immortal one?'

'Maybe she was the last,' came Simon Sanchez's voice from the shadows.

'Eavesdropper,' exclaimed Sammy.

'Snoopy,' said Dixie, 'big ears!'

'Draconite is what keeps the dragon alive,' said Simon. 'It is very rare for the dragon owner to want to kill a dragon for the draconite.'

'I couldn't do it,' said Sammy.

'Maybe you don't have to,' said Simon.

'Freak,' snapped Dixie grabbing Sammy's wrist. 'Come on, if Simon's leaving then the dragons are all ok.'

Sammy dropped some sausages he'd salvaged from last night's dinner into Kyrillan's clawed paw. Kyrillan puffed a halo of smoke that landed on Sammy's head like a crown.

As they walked back up the stone stairwell, Sammy paused and checked the mirror in the passage roof that Dixie had told him to use to check to see if anyone was in the corridor above them.

'All clear,' he said, pushing his pin against the trapdoor to open it.

'Wonder what he meant,' Dixie muttered, 'about you killing dragons.'

'He said I didn't have to kill dragons,' Sammy reminded her.

'Maybe you already have draconite in your head Sammy,' Dixie laughed.

'Maybe that's why the Shape are after me,' Sammy laughed as well. He didn't see Dixie's wide eyed stare, nor hear her say "you reckon" as they were met by the rest of the second years, escorted by Dr Shivers, all talking at the tops of their voices about visiting the Land of the Pharaohs.

Dr Shivers smiled at Sammy. 'Good,' he said, 'I am glad you are looking after your dragons. Are you using your Dragon Minder pin Sammy?'

A rock-like lump formed in Sammy's throat and his mouth went dry as he nodded, wondering if Dr Shivers had been responsible for Mary-Beth's death.

'Good,' repeated Dr Shivers, his voice making Sammy's skin crawl.

Sammy looked at his arms, goosebumps had appeared from his shoulders to his wrists.

'Creepy,' muttered Dixie. She walked beside Sammy as they joined Milly who, as usual, was sandwiched between Gavin and Toby with the other North girls giggling at them.

'Have you got everything?' asked Dr Shivers, handing Sammy his staff and his rucksack with clothes for the trip in it.

Sammy was surprised at himself for being unnerved that Dr Shivers had been through his things. Overnight, he kept his staff in his sock drawer, next to the map.

He focused again on sausage rolls and stir-fry as he took his staff, dismantling it in to three parts and tucking it into his jeans pocket. It was a handy trick Mrs Deane had taught him. Looking at the great willow bough Toby was tucking inside his jumper, Sammy was very grateful for her advice.

'Yes Dr Shivers,' chorused the ten North students, except Gavin who, trying to be clever, was holding his nose and gave a "Yesss Drr Shivvverrrsss" he had been practicing under the duvet.

'Do you have a cold Gavin?' enquired Dr Shivers. 'Perhaps you'd better not come with us.'

'I'm fine Sir,' said Gavin so fast his words ran together. 'My Mum signed the form and everything.'

'Our Mum,' corrected Toby.

'Enough boys,' said Dr Shivers, 'a pipsqueak from either of you and I shall deduct ten stars.'

'Ooer,' grinned Gavin, marching ahead towards the leafy glen where they would queue up for the lift that would take them up to visit the Land of the Pharaohs.

As they stood in a crocodile line, Sammy found that the palms of his hands were suddenly very sweaty and that his throat was dry.

They had been divided into the North, South, East and West houses at the mouth of the Dragon's Lair. Dixie was standing next to him, her green eyes fixed on the sky where a pearlescent tube extended from the hill into the sky above them.

'Looks like a dragon's mouth, doesn't it,' she whispered in Sammy's ear. 'Look, those rocks could be eyes, the cave is the mouth and these are the teeth.'

Darius joined in, 'yeah and the tube is the tail going up into the door at the top.'

'Are you trying to be funny?' snapped Dixie. 'I meant it. Look, those rocks look like Kiridor's eyelids when he's asleep, the purple and blue heather could be the scales.'

'Frozen,' Darius laughed, 'frozen rock solid like a fossil.'

'If you're just going to make fun of me, then go away.'

'Yes Mrs Troll!' Darius laughed and ducked away.

'What are you laughing at Sammy?' Dixie demanded, her hands on her hips.

'The tail in the sky,' said Sammy with an angelically straight face. 'Come on. I think it's our turn now.'

He went forward up the stone steps, pausing by the milk white row of stones outside the Dragon's Lair.

'The Dragon Knight goes first,' Professor Sanchez cooed admiringly.

'First to be last,' said Commander Altair who was standing with a group of third years. He checked his watch. 'They are late.'

'Ssh,' said Dr Shivers, 'Sammy will lead them there.'

'I hope I know where we're going,' Sammy muttered groping for the lift inside the cave. 'It is my first time going to the Land of the Pharaohs.' He stopped suddenly as his hand patted something warm.

'Ooh,' said Sammy, holding on to the cave wall and resisting a sharp nudge from Milly, who for someone not wanting to go to the Land of the Pharaohs, wanted to be out of the dark cave even more.

'Just ten at a time,' grumbled Captain Firebreath, pushing Sammy's hand away from his head. 'Any more and the lift will break.'

'Nonsense Firey,' Mrs Hubar's soothing voice came wafting into the cave, 'you've just had fifty in that lift. That I know for sure.'

'Nufin like spoiling the kiddies day,' growled Captain Firebreath. 'Anticipation, that's what they had in my day. Besides, you just wanted to make sure your son gets up there.'

'Anticipation you'd grow tall,' laughed Gavin, and the rest of the second years laughed with him, with the notable exception of Jock, who shouted for Dr Shivers to take Gavin back to the castle.

Gavin flung himself into the lift, sticking his fingers up through the glass window in the metal gate at Jock.

'Stuff you,' Sammy heard Jock mutter as he was left behind and the third and fourth years spilled into the cave.

The ride to the Floating Circus had taken seven minutes, Sammy remembered their first year tutor Professor Burlay saying he set his watch to circus time. Consequently, he was seven minutes late to everything, everywhere, all the time.

Guessing that the Land of the Pharaohs would be at the same place, Sammy clicked the stopwatch setting on his Casino watch.

Looking at the seconds ticking helped him to forget the lurching of soggy cornflakes in his stomach and the feeling that his brain was either going to explode or dribble out of his nose.

He saw the seconds flick to 06:58, 06:59, 07:00, 07:01, 07:02.

'We're not stopping!' Sammy exclaimed, clutching his stomach with a hand that suddenly seemed fuzzy around the edges before splitting into five hands as his head spun.

'Of course not silly,' said Dixie, matter of factly, 'the Land of the Pharaohs is much higher.'

She had sea-legs, or air-legs, thought Sammy, reminding himself not to laugh as a chunk of sick gurgled in his throat.

'It would cause a crash,' Dixie explained. 'Think of it like a motorway. The lands have to follow a set path. Can you imagine what would happen if two lands bumped together?'

Sammy, green in the face as well as in uniform, declined to answer.

'It's a pity she doesn't put that effort into her studies,' Mrs Hubar said silkily to Dr Shivers, who had his hands on his stomach and was also looking a little green in the face.

At eleven minutes and thirteen seconds there was a loud crunch and Captain Firebreath threw open the gates.

'Enjoy,' he muttered as his thirty passengers stumbled out.

Sammy, to his embarrassment, got out of the lift and spotting a grey gargoyle holding a card that said "get it all out", did just that.

He emerged moments later having removed all the soggy cornflakes from his stomach.

The gargoyle dribbled water out of its mouth like a toilet flushing and washing Sammy's sickness away.

Dixie laughed at him. 'Everyone did that last time.'

Unlike the glass reception at the Floating Circus, Sammy was intrigued to find himself in what appeared to be the centre of a towering pyramid. The four yellow-orange sandstone walls arched together into the darkness, the top completely out of sight.

The lift had transported them on to a large square platform within the pyramid. The platform seemed to be made up of four glass triangles that joined together to form a glass cover over the lift shaft.

They opened like an envelope to let the students out of the lift and then the triangles dropped back into the square, closing over so that whilst the lift was going back down, you could walk over the glass safely.

Sammy skirted around the glass edges, allowing himself a quick peek into the eleven minutes and thirteen seconds drop. He got down from the platform as quickly as possible, glad when his feet touched the sandy pyramid floor.

'Imagine falling down there,' said Dixie, grinning as she walked boldly across the middle and jumped up and down.

'I wouldn't do that if I were you,' said Dr Shivers, looking equally afraid as Sammy.

'It's ok Dr Shivers,' said Dixie, 'my brothers stand in the middle of the glass so when it breaks into the four triangles they just slide out of the way when the lift comes up.'

'I would prefer it if you came here,' said Dr Shivers firmly. 'It opens like a tipper truck,' he added, seeing Sammy's blank face.

'Oh right,' said Sammy, trying not to look into the deep hole.

'It's re-enforced glass,' said Dixie. 'Look!' She pointed to thin lines running through the glass, pale cream twists of metal that creaked as they swung upwards to let another group of students into the land.

Sammy recognised Dixie's green haired brothers in the middle of the lift. He watched open mouthed as the glass panels split open and the next group of students disembarked.

Jason and Mikhael were first out of the lift. They quickly disappeared, each holding hands with their blonde girlfriends.

Serberon came over to Sammy and Dixie, putting an arm around his sister's shoulders.

Dixie shrugged it off. 'She isn't coming back Serb.'

Serberon nodded. 'They keep telling me that.'

'He's seeing the school counsellor,' Dixie whispered in Sammy's ear.

'Shut it sis,' growled Serberon.

Sammy thought Serberon seemed to have lost a lot of weight recently. His cheekbones looked even more sunken than Dr Shivers's gaunt features. All of Serberon's green freckles had vanished from his nose, leaving him looking very pale and ghostly.

'Are you really ok?' Sammy asked finally.

'He's fine,' said Dixie, 'come on, me and Darius will show you around.'

Serberon gave a mock bow. 'As the lady says,' he said giving Dixie a hug. 'Come and find me later and I'll get you into the Great Pyramid,' he added, grinning at them.

'But it's only for fourth years and above,' said Dixie, 'after that accident the Great Pyramid is in ruins and no one our age is allowed to go in.'

'Staged accident,' said Serberon, 'rumor has it that Paulo wanted to join the Shape.'

'Paulo Preverence?' asked Darius.

'Yep.'

'The son of Professor Patrick Preverence?'

'Yep,' said Serberon again.

Sammy exchanged a look with Dixie and Darius.

'Just a little bit further,' said Serberon enthusiastically. 'They say that if Sir Ragnarok hadn't got there in time the whole pyramid would have fallen in and it would have crashed through the land and fallen slap bang on Dragamas!'

'Bit of luck really then,' giggled Darius. 'If it had, we wouldn't have had to go to school.'

'They would've sent you to Excaliburs or Pont y Cross instead,' said Serberon matter of factly.

'We might never have met,' said Sammy.

'Scary!' said Darius.

'So anyway,' said Dixie, changing the subject, 'how are you getting us into what's left of the pyramid?'

Serberon tapped his nose and infuriatingly told them to be outside the Great Pyramid an hour before teatime.

'It's awesome we get to stay here isn't it,' said Gavin, breezing past with Toby and Milly.

'Darius nodded. 'Yeah!'

'We're staying in Hotel de la Pyramid,' said Milly, her cheeks flushed with a mix of blusher and glitter. She paused, holding a hairband in her teeth, drawing her pale blonde hair into a bun. 'Mummy says...'

'Aargh!' said Darius, running off.

'See you later,' yelled Sammy and Dixie together as they stormed after Darius.

'Well!' they heard Milly say shrilly. 'That was rude!'

Sammy and Dixie found Darius crouched behind rolls upon rolls of ornately decorated rugs being sold by a dark skinned man with gold capped teeth, dressed from head to toe in a white robe with a white turban would tightly on top of his head.

'All rugs for sale,' he was calling, 'two thousand pounds for a small rug, five thousand pounds for a medium rug and fifteen thousand pounds for a large rug. Buy your rugs from Vigor's Rug Stall,' he chanted.

'He's got no chance,' said Darius, 'two grand for one of these manky things.'

Dixie laughed. 'It's those rugs over there,' she pointed across the stall, 'these ones are just camel bedding.'

'Camel bedding,' exclaimed Sammy. 'But there aren't any camels here!'

Darius giggled. 'Of course not!'

Sammy followed Darius's outstretched pointing hand and he could see another dark skinned man in a white robe leading six golden camels towards them. The camels were carrying heavy looking, brightly coloured rugs, stretched between the humps of two camels at a time.

'Allay, allay!' The man shouted at the camels.

Obediently, each pair of camels stopped, knelt on their front legs and allowed the two men to hoist the rugs down from where they were balanced between the humps.

'Hey-Hoop!' The two men shouted as they heaved the rugs over the camels' heads and on to the pile of rugs closest to Sammy, Dixie and Darius.

They stayed a minute longer, watching as the delivery man accepted a small brown parcel that they guessed contained payment for the rugs. The man waved, flashing a gold toothed smile at the rug seller who flashed an equally gold toothed smile back at him.

'That's amazing!' said Sammy. 'I've never seen anything like that before.

'Cool huh,' said Darius, 'yeah when we were here last...'

'First,' said Dixie.

'Second actually,' said Darius, 'I came with my parents when I was four.'

Dixie folded her arms. 'What happened?'

'I saw the same thing but me and my mum, we counted fifty big camels and twelve little ones. The little ones were carrying these,' Darius pointed at the camel bedding. 'I thought it was really cruel at the time.'

'No different than we use dragons,' Sammy felt his cheeks go pink as he said the words. It was the first time he had counted himself among the dragon folk, admitting he was part of their world.

'I guess,' said Darius, taking no notice, 'it just seems strange. They could have dragons here as well.'

Dixie shook her head. 'It's the wrong climate. Dr Shivers told Mrs Hubar the other day. He said it's too hot for dragons up here.'

'Hey! Look over here,' said Sammy, spotting a pool of water surrounding by palm trees. 'Palm Café ,' he read the sign out loud.

'It's rubbish in there,' said Dixie. 'Fake. They put on all this stuff to make it look Egyptian. The waiters are dressed as mummies and you drink out of a sarky glass.'

'They're not sarky glasses,' Darius laughed, 'it's...'

'Shut it Darius,' said Dixie, 'I'm not going in there and that's it!'

'Ok, ok,' said Sammy nervously. He hated it when Dixie and Darius squabbled.

'How about we go outside?' asked Darius.

'Good idea,' snapped Dixie, 'we'll get a sun tan.'

Looking again at how pale and fair Dixie's skin was under her green fringe, it didn't look like a week of sun would make her tan. Throughout the summer holiday, she had been in the sun as much as he had, but had tiny green freckles on her nose compared with his, admittedly fading, golden bronze sun tan.

'Hah!' snorted Darius. 'You'll get as much sun tan as me!'

Dixie shrugged and grabbed their hands. 'Come on, let's go to the Oasis!'

CHAPTER 14

EXPLORING AND NEW FRIENDS

Sammy followed Dixie and Darius out of the pyramid, shielding his eyes as they stepped into bright sunlight.

Outside, the sun was almost directly overhead, burning down on to the land.

'Funny,' muttered Sammy, 'it wasn't this warm at Dragamas.'

'The sun follows the land,' said Dixie marching ahead towards some palm trees. 'Hi Milly!' she shouted and ran forward, disappearing out of sight.

Sammy and Darius jogged after Dixie. As they reached the palm trees Sammy felt his mouth fall open.

In front of them was a giant aquamarine pool, surrounded by leafy palm trees and green shrubs. A wooden swing bridge was suspended from one side of the pool to the other side and there was a small wooden hut with a serving counter and a blackboard by the door advertising a variety of drinks and snacks.

Lots of students were swimming in the pool, others were playing games or sunbathing in deck chairs beside the water. At the far end, Milly, Gavin and Toby were dangling their feet in the pool and drinking brightly coloured cocktails from large triangular shaped glasses.

'Hiya!' said Gavin, holding up his glass. 'These are only 50p!'

'Yeah, you can choose from strawberry, raspberry, apple and lemon and lime flavour,' said Toby.

'And passionfruit,' added Milly, holding up her own glass which was filled with a sparkling pink liquid. 'They're really good.'

'Here you go,' said Darius, thrusting a fifty pence piece into Sammy's hand. 'I'll have a lemon and lime.'

Darius took off his shoes and socks and jumped into the shallow Oasis pool, splashing water and making Milly squeal.

'Mine's a bit of each, if they'll do it,' Dixie grinned with what looked to Sammy like a flutter of green eyelashes. She held out a pound coin. 'I'll get yours.'

'Thanks,' Sammy grumbled, feeling he'd been taken advantage of, but cheering up at the prospect of walking across the wooden swing bridge to get to the café counter.

A large, bald headed man with a bushy black mustache and a wide smile greeted him. He was wearing a loose white shirt with the sleeves rolled up to his elbows, revealing plaited leather bracelets adorned with small camel shaped charms.

'Hullo young Sir, what can I get you from the Oasis?' The man waved a chubby hand towards the blackboard with different flavours scrawled almost illegibly in yellow and red chalk. At the top of the blackboard it read "Antonio Havercastle - Oasis Café".

'Um, a lemon and lime, a strawberry and a bit of each.'

'For the young lady with green hair?' asked the man.

Sammy nodded.

'Ah yes, I remember her from last time. She told me you could have a bit of everything at the Floating Circus. Well! How am I, Antonio Havercastle, to compete with my brother, eh?' said the large man, looking closely at Sammy. 'So, I said to her, "You can have a bit of everything and I'll do it for free!"'

'Did she take it?' asked Sammy, his eyes open wide.

'Good gracious no,' said Antonio Havercastle, 'she seemed concerned it would go on the school bill. In my days at Dragamas, when Sir Bonahue was headmaster, we took what we could get!'

'You must know Sir Ragnarok,' said Sammy.

'That I do,' said Antonio Havercastle. 'I know him very well indeed. My brother Andradore, who owns the Floating Circus, and I were in the North house with old Lok Ragnarok, right from our very first day.'

'I'm in North,' said Sammy.

'I know,' said Antonio Havercastle, handing Sammy three large triangular glasses. 'It's in your eyes.' He held out his hand for the coins.

Sammy handed over the one pound and fifty pence coins. 'Thank you.'

'You're welcome,' Antonio Havercastle smiled and stroked his bushy black mustache. 'Very welcome.'

Sammy chose to walk around the Oasis than chance his footing on the wooden swing bridge.

The pool was large with lots of Dragamas students swimming and some diving from a platform into the cool blue water. He nodded at Mikhael and Jason who were with Miranda, Mary-Beth's best friend, and several other girls he didn't know.

Mikhael waved back. 'Have you seen Serberon?' he shouted.

Sammy shook his head, concentrating on the three drinks, one a sickly yellow-green, lemon and lime, his own strawberry flavoured drink and Dixie's "dollop of everything" that was turning a murky brown as the colours mixed together.

'Wow!' shouted Darius as Sammy reached the other side of the Oasis. 'Lemon and Lime!'

'Looks like someone's been sick in it,' said Dixie. 'Yuck!'

'Well,' retorted Darius, 'if it's sick in mine, I dread to think what's in yours!'

'What?' asked Dixie.

Sammy put his hands over his ears as Darius explained in great detail exactly what he thought had gone into Dixie's glass. After a moment, he took off his shoes and socks and rolled up the legs of his trousers, splashing his feet in the cool refreshing water, closing his eyes.

He was interrupted by a loud splash and opened his eyes to find Darius had fallen over backwards into the Oasis.

'Serves you right,' said Dixie, rubbing a patch of lemon and lime iced drink out of her hair.

'It was a joke!' shouted Darius, standing up, dripping wet. 'All I said was you're a green-haired troll and should have had my drink because it's green.'

'Yeah, well you can keep them both!' Dixie shouted back, raising her glass ready to throw the contents at Darius.

'That will be quite enough,' came Dr Shivers stern voice from behind them. 'Don't forget that you're representing Dragamas here. Ten stars from all of you!'

'Sir, that's not fair,' exclaimed Gavin. 'We didn't do anything.'

'Exactly,' said Dr Shivers. 'What would it have cost you to help your friends, to stop them from fighting?'

151

'Darius got beaten by a girl!' Gavin chanted. 'Darius got...'

'Thank you Gavin. Please escort Darius to your hotel where he can change into dry clothes.'

'It's Ok Dr Shivers, I'm fine,' protested Darius as Gavin gave him an angry look.

'I insist,' said Dr Shivers firmly. He gave Darius an icy stare, drawing in his thin cheekbones. 'Now go.'

Darius got out of the water shaking droplets over Dixie and Milly who both squealed that it was cold. Toby and Milly followed Gavin and Darius, heading out of Oasis Café and back to the hotel.

'Sheep,' sneered Dr Shivers. 'If he told them to kill their dragons, they probably would. Do you want any sun block?' Dr Shivers held out an orange see-through plastic packet with cream inside.

'No need,' said Dixie, showing Dr Shivers her pale white arms. 'I never get sunburn.'

'How strange,' replied Dr Shivers. 'Sammy?'

'Ok,' said Sammy, squirting the cream half-heartedly on to his arms and neck.

'Good. Next time, try and help your friends. I'm sure you would be sorry if you lost either one.' Dr Shivers pulled his cloak around his shoulders and vanished.

'What did he mean by that?' asked Sammy. 'What could I have done?'

Dixie shrugged. 'Nothing I guess. Darius is like the rest of them now. He thinks trolls are evil.'

'But you're not.'

Dixie yawned. 'No but I can be!' She pushed up her nose so it wrinkled. 'Grrrr!'

Sammy laughed and checked his watch. 'Come on, they won't be back for a while. Let's go and find Serberon and the Great Pyramid.'

CHAPTER 15

THE GREAT PYRAMID

The sun was now directly overhead. There were no shadows and no shade and it was blisteringly hot.

Sammy and Dixie walked past the rug delivery man they had seen earlier. He was herding another, larger, procession of camels with rugs tucked snugly between their humps. They counted twenty four camels plus the one that the man was riding.

The man held a thick black rope which was tied between the pairs of camels to keep them together. They walked in synchronization, taking one step at a time, so that the rugs stayed perfectly in place.

It was so hot that Sammy and Dixie rolled up the sleeves of their t-shirts to keep cool. Dixie had brought a bottle of water and she shared it with Sammy, both grateful for the refreshment in the heat.

They walked through the market stalls, twisting and turning through narrow streets filled with people and animals hustling and bustling about their daily business.

When they reached the end of the stalls the crowds of people thinned out and Sammy and Dixie walked unhindered into the expanse of desert filled with yellow sand dunes rising and falling as far as the eye could see.

They found the Great Pyramid in the centre of the land. It was easily the tallest and by far the biggest pyramid in sight.

As they approached, Sammy could see that two of the four pyramid sides had caved in, leaving a gaping hole among tons and tons of rubble and pebble sized rocks.

Sand spilled like yellow blood seeping from the wound in the side of the pyramid.

'They say the sand won't stop running out,' Dixie told him as they got nearer.

Up close, the Great Pyramid towered high above them, almost as if it was daring them to enter the forbidden place.

Professor Burlay and Mrs Grock were standing outside the pyramid entrance, checking for underage Dragamas students and turning away a group of interested first years.

'Fourth years only,' said Professor Burlay.

'Ooch, why not visit the Oasis,' said Mrs Grock in her Scottish accent. 'Come back lassies when you're a little older.'

Sammy grinned as Professor Burlay put his arm around Mrs Grock's shoulders.

Dixie nudged him. 'Serberon said to meet him round the back.

'Good,' whispered Sammy. 'Mrs Grock might think I'm going to be a Dragon Knight but I still don't think she'll let us in.'

Checking that they weren't seen by Professor Burlay or Mrs Grock, Sammy and Dixie crept around the side of the pyramid, ducking under fallen slabs of rock and making no sound as they navigated the rubble from the collapsed side.

Around the back of the Great Pyramid, the sun had moved from overhead and was casting a cool shadow as they crouched beside a fallen slab waiting for Serberon.

To pass the time, Sammy reached into the rucksack Dr Shivers had packed for him to see what his teacher had packed.

'Socks, jeans, jumper,' he said out loud. 'Jumper?'

'Two jumpers?' asked Dixie. 'We're only here for one night and it's so hot you probably won't need one anyway.'

'No, just one jumper,' said Sammy, 'but look,' he squeezed the socks.

'What?'

'No map,' Sammy whispered. 'I put it in these.'

'You sure?'

'Yes, these are my only clean socks. The rest are in the laundry.'

'Why would he take the map? He only just gave it to you.'

'I don't know,' said Sammy, feeling a lump forming in his throat. 'It's a good job we can remember what it looked like.'

'Yeah,' said Dixie quietly. 'I'll re-draw it when we get back. Have you still got the Dragon Minder pin?'

Sammy felt in the toes of his sock. 'Yeah.'

'That's good. We can check your room back at school. Perhaps Dr Shivers moved the map somewhere?'

'And he didn't take the pin?' asked Sammy. 'No way. He has taken the map away from me.'

'It's ok. I said I'd draw you another one.'

'It's not the same,' Sammy said, sniffing loudly.

'Think about it,' said Dixie. 'He gave it to you so I suppose he can take it back. He is a teacher after all.'

'Uh, sorry,' said Sammy, composing himself. 'That would be great if you redraw it. Now, shall we climb up and see if we can get inside the Great Pyramid?'

'Ok,' said Dixie enthusiastically. She jumped nimbly across on to a small tower of rocks. The rocks let out a low hiss and sand fell out of the cracks. 'Come on slowcoach!'

Sammy reached up to a rock jutting out above his head. Using his fingers, he hoisted himself up, loose stones falling as he scrabbled with his feet, trying to keep his balance.

'How did you get up there? Sammy shouted to Dixie, who was already several feet above him.

'Easy!' shouted Dixie. 'Take that stone, then that one, then use the two together there, then you're up.'

'Right,' muttered Sammy, finding it harder than it looked. Two minutes later he heaved himself on to the platform where Dixie was tapping her hand on an imaginary watch. He checked his own watch. The dial on the Casino watch read half past four.

'Pyramid time,' grinned Dixie. 'Moves at least three times as fast as our time. This is the South Entrance. There's a shaft that leads in to the centre of the Great Pyramid.'

'How do you know so much all of a sudden?'

Dixie moved aside revealing a plaque with white text on a black marble background.

'South Entrance,' Dixie read out loud.

Sammy grinned. 'Leads into the centre of the Great Pyramid. Let's go in!'

'No you don't!' A voice shouted at them from down at the foot of the pyramid.

Fearing Professor Burlay and Mrs Grock, Sammy and Dixie knelt behind a large boulder. They heard sand and loose pebbles fall as someone climbed up.

Poised and ready to jump into the Great Pyramid, Sammy held himself and Dixie steady as a tuft of green hair came into view.

'Serberon?'

'Yeah,' replied Serberon. 'Bit of luck I arrived when I did. They said it was just Sammy...'

'Just Sammy what?' snapped Dixie. 'I'm here too.'

Serberon hoisted himself up, crowding the narrow ledge.

'Uh, down there. They said it was just Sammy climbing up.'

'Liar,' snapped Dixie, 'I'm going in too.'

'Sorry sis,' Serberon frowned, 'Professor Burlay is asking for you. Sarah Hillcroft, your first year, she fell over. He wants you to take her back to the hotel to get some, um, bandages.'

'Bandages?' Dixie looked horrified. 'Can't Mrs Grock deal with it. I haven't got an overnight bag, let alone any bandages. What does he think I am a Healer or something?'

Sammy rummaged in his rucksack. 'Here, take this,' he said, giving Dixie his healing potion.

Serberon shrugged. 'It was Sammy I wanted to show anyway.'

'Fine,' snapped Dixie and picking up Sammy's rucksack, she made her way down the pyramid as sure footed as a mountain goat muttering, 'I'll show Sarah Hillcroft I'm not a Healer. Serves her right for asking for me. She'll wish...'

Dixie's voice faded away as she stomped off to find Professor Burlay. Able to read her mind at a short distance, Sammy laughed as he heard her cursing her first year, threatening to tie her up in more bandages than the Mummy at Palm Café .

'Are you ready?'

As Serberon turned to face him, Sammy saw a dark shadow passing behind his friend's eyes.

'Ready to see what the Great Pyramid has to offer you?'

Sammy nodded dumbly.

Serberon gave a small bow and held his arm towards the South Entrance.

Slowly, Sammy stepped inside, holding tightly to the warm stone. As his eyes grew used to the darkness, he found he could see a stone slope curving downwards into the pyramid.

He felt a cool breeze rush past his neck and then a huge push in his lower back that sent him flying face first down the slope, rolling head over heels down and down until he felt his head spin and he wished harder and harder that he would stop spinning.

His hands and bare arms dragged stones tearing his skin as he tumbled deep into the heart of the Great Pyramid.

After what felt like an eternity, Sammy stopped falling. He had reached a soft bed of fine sand. He rubbed the loose stones from his arms and cheek. Some of the stones seemed to be stuck to his face.

'Blood,' whispered Sammy, tasting the metallic stickiness. He stood up, banging his head on stone. 'Ouch!'

It was too dark to see what he had hit his head on, but he had the feeling that it was more solid than he was.

Looking up, there was a faint glimmer high above him. Not able to judge properly in the darkness, Sammy felt like he had fallen the height of a department store.

'Serb?' Sammy shouted, feeling a bit panicky. 'Serberon!'

There was nothing. No echo. No Serberon. Just darkness and silence.

'Serberon! Help! Dixie! Professor Burlay! Help!'

There was still nothing nearly five minutes later when Sammy had found his feet and run out of breath from shouting. He assembled his staff and whispered, 'fire.'

A small flame jetted out a short distance in front of him. The fire forced him to concentrate and he split the flames into five smaller fires that he sent in different directions, guiding each one with his thoughts and an occasional wave of his staff when a flame got stuck behind a rock.

Sammy was waving his staff at an obstinate flame that had got caught between two upright pillar slabs when all of a sudden there was a gust of wind and the lights went out.

The flames hissed and vanished.

'Fire!' shouted Sammy, suddenly scared. 'Fire! Fire! Fire!'

There was nothing. No matter what he tried, the faint candlelight would not return.

Even a jet of green sparks that he created disappeared the second they left his staff. He cowered as voices boomed within the pyramid.

'Have you had enough yet?'

'Let him be. This is fun watching him try.'

'Doesn't he know it won't work?'

'Quiet,' commanded the first voice. 'Now Sammy,' said the voice. 'You understand we control what happens.'

'Ok,' said Sammy, fearing the voices and hoping it was another of Serberon's jokes.

'Good. Now lay down your staff.'

Sammy laughed. 'Why? You just said you control everything. If I can't use my staff, why should I put it down?'

There was another gust of wind that whistled through the Great Pyramid. Sammy felt his staff whipped out of his hands. It landed with a soft thud on the sand.

'Now do you understand?' boomed the first voice. 'We control everything.'

'Yeah, yeah,' said Sammy, braver than he felt. 'Any minute you'll turn on the lights and it will be just Serberon, Jason and Mikhael. I've had enough jokes about the Shape. They seem real enough to me.'

'He knows we're real!' came a high pitched voice. 'Does he know we're immortal?'

'Silence Eliza,' boomed the first voice.

There was a shriek. 'No names! The boy must not know our names!'

There was laughter. 'You are not really here Eliza. You are a projection, a SideSplit, an image from your cell at the Snorgcadell.'

There was another shriek and a flash of blue light followed by another roar of laughter and a thud.

In the darkness, Sammy's head was almost bursting. He couldn't make up his mind. Was it the Shape? Were they really talking to his ex-Gemology teacher Dr Lithoman, otherwise known as Eliza Elungwen? He had wondered if she was the "E" in the Shape.

'Can, can I go now?' Sammy stuttered.

'No!' shouted the first voice. 'No, now you must see why you are here.'

There was a flash of green light and a spotlight fell from high in the Great Pyramid ceiling. Sammy blinked, getting used to the light.

The beam fell on a kneeling figure of a boy, arms tied behind his back, his legs shackled to a grill in the floor.

'Serberon?' Sammy yelled, trying to run forward. He couldn't. His feet were stuck.

'Yes!' shouted the first voice. 'He has betrayed you. He has brought you to us.'

There was a loud crack and the room flooded with light.

Sammy screamed.

Ahead of him, wearing the all too familiar black cloaks were four figures. Looking closer, shielding his eyes, he saw another shape, a jet black cloak draped over what looked like a boulder.

The boulder moved, rising into the dwarven height of Dr Margarite Lithoman, also known as Eliza Elungwen, with a halo around her head.

'Let Serberon go!' Sammy shouted. 'Let us both go!'

'No,' came back an icy, gravelly voice that hadn't spoken before, 'not until you listen to what the boy has to say.'

The figure raised a pale hand and held it, palm facing towards Serberon and aimed a green beam of light.

Serberon's head was thrown back and he yelled in obvious pain.

'Stop!' shrieked Sammy. 'You're hurting him.'

'Why yes,' came the gravelly voice. 'He has failed.'

The green light faded and Serberon collapsed on his side.

'Serberon. No!' Sammy found himself angrier than he had ever been before. 'You've killed him! He's Dixie's brother!'

'A troll!' shrieked Dr Lithoman, rising from the floor, floating towards Sammy, her body ghostly and see-through, wafting in the light. 'After all the dragons are dead the trolls must die too!'

'Tell him why he is here,' commanded the loud voice. 'Quickly.'

A beam of light shot from underneath Serberon, forcing him to stand. The ropes binding him disappeared and a door of light appeared in the South side of the Great Pyramid, lower than the entrance where Sammy had been thrown inside but higher than the ground they stood on.

To Sammy, the room seemed to go dark as the light in the doorway grew bigger and they could see the blue sky outside. Soft singing filled the air and a figure appeared in the doorway.

'Mary-Beth,' Serberon whispered. He turned to the Shape. 'Thank you.'

The ghostly figure lowered into the pyramid, swaying to the sound of the soft singing.

As she drew closer, her mouth opened. No words came out, but inside his head and knew somehow, that everyone inside the pyramid could hear Mary-Beth's soft voice scolding Serberon "Why have you done this? It is no longer my time. I cannot return".

'No!' shrieked Serberon, clutching at the figure as the pyramid descended into cruel darkness. 'Mary-Beth, come back! I need you!'

Serberon reached into the darkness where Mary-Beth's shadow had been. 'I...I love you,' he whispered, kneeling down, his head resting on the sand floor.

Mary-Beth, wherever she had been conjured from, had gone. The singing faded and was replaced by cruel laughter and clapping.

'You promised,' Serberon wept, making Sammy's blood chill. 'You said if I brought you Sammy you would let me see Mary-Beth again.'

'And did you?' came the gravelly voice. 'Did you see her?'

Serberon nodded, his green hair pale against his pale almost luminescent skin. 'You promised she could come back.'

'You failed. The boy will never join us.'

'He wants to forgive your pathetic traitorous self.'

'You want me to join the Shape?' Sammy whispered.

'Yes,' said the loud voice. 'To join us. Help us in our quest to recover all draconite from where it is scattered in dragons' brains. To restore the Stone Cross.'

'Why?'

'Did he say yes?' squealed Dr Lithoman. 'I told you it would work.'

'Silence fool. Surely boy you know of the Stone Cross, protected by those Dragon Knights you claim you want to be.'

Sammy shook his head. His hands were shivering, his body shaking. His mind was racing. He had to get out. He had to beat the Shape.

'You cannot escape.' The third figure tapped a cloaked hand to its hooded head. 'We can read your mind.'

'So, if he will not join us, we must surely kill him?' The gravelly voice asked the group.

'Indeed!' boomed the loud voice. 'This is your last chance boy. Will you or will you not join us?'

'I'll think about it!' yelled Sammy, finding depths of bravery he had never thought possible in his days against the Rat Catcher school bullies. 'Let Serberon go first!'

Sammy focused hard on sausage rolls, stir fry vegetables, pink ice cream, the toy lion, anything but his plan to escape from the pyramid.

'You are strong,' sneered the gravelly voice, 'and yet your mind is full of clutter. Try this!'

Sammy screamed as a beam of white light was directed at him. Out of the corner of his eye, he saw Serberon run towards the North entrance of the Great Pyramid. Leaping over fallen rocks, Serberon disappeared from sight.

The white light hurt his head so badly Sammy closed his eyes, seeing instead of blackness, a grassy valley from a viewpoint on a hilltop. A river ran through the valley with cottages dotted on each side.

The pain in his head grew as he was guided, almost like flying on Kyrillan, to give him an overhead view of the valley, the clear blue water reflecting in hidden sunlight. He jerked as he was swung round to face a monument with inscriptions laid up the base to a cross encircled in a stone wheel.

'This is the Stone Cross,' Sammy heard a faint whisper. 'Bring all the draconite here and lay it inside the Stone Cross and whoever lays the final stone, the stone from human origin will rule the elements. Whoever rules earth, air, fire and water will rule the world.'

Before the vision faded and the white light released him, Sammy saw that more than half of the statue was covered in blue-green stone he knew to be draconite.

'How many dragons have died?' he whispered.

'Thousands,' said the gravelly voice, 'and thousands more must die before we succeed. Join us. Help us restore the Stone Cross.'

Things swam before Sammy's eyes as he lurched back into the pyramid. It was still dark, maybe the Stone Cross wasn't so bad. It was pretty with the stones. The sort of thing Milly would like.

'Join us!' boomed the loud voice. 'Together we will succeed.'

Sammy felt his mouth open, ready to do as they wanted, to say "yes", to join them.

Then, like a stabbing pain, he felt his cross for bravery around his neck burning and his head cleared. The Shape were evil. They wanted him dead. They wanted to kill all dragons. They would kill Kyrillan. He could not let that happen.

'No!' he shouted. 'I'll never join you!'

Sammy clutched for his staff, sending jets of green sparks as he ran for the doorway that Serberon had disappeared through.

'Seize him!' commanded the loud booming voice.

Sammy heard a flurry of sandy footsteps, the cold breeze chasing him through dark unknown tunnels.

'Get the boy!'

'H...Help!' Sammy shouted, struggling for breath. 'Help me!'

'Sammy!' A voice shouted ahead of him. 'Sammy!'

Sammy ran on, feeling the cold breath of the Shape close behind that faded into warm air as he stumbled into a solid figure. He yelled, terrified that the Shape were both in front and behind him.

'It's ok Sammy. It's us.'

Sammy opened his eyes. Serberon, still looking white as a sheet was in front of him, with Professor Burlay, Commander Altair and Professor Sanchez each holding their staffs, poised ready to strike.

He looked back at the passage behind him. Rocks had fallen. Nothing could get in or out anymore.

'You're safe now,' said Professor Burlay, smiling and draping his suit jacket around Sammy's shaking shoulders. 'What on earth were you thinking going in there?'

'What indeed?' growled Professor Sanchez. 'Even Simon knows better than to go into the Great Pyramid. I say ten stars from North.'

'Sammy was tricked,' growled Commander Altair, 'betrayed, I hear. Perhaps the stars should be taken from Serberon instead.' Commander Altair gave Serberon an icy stare.

'No matter,' said Professor Sanchez. 'They are both in the North house.'

'But...the Shape were here,' said Sammy, pulling Professor Burlay's jacket closer around his shoulders.

Commander Altair herded Professor Sanchez, Professor Burlay and Serberon forward down the tunnel. 'Go on,' he said to them, 'Sammy and I will be right behind you.'

'But,' he whispered, so only Sammy could hear, 'would the Shape have been here if you hadn't disobeyed Sir Ragnarok's rules. Rules he put in place for your protection.'

Sammy felt sick. He knew Commander Altair was right. If he hadn't wanted to see inside the Great Pyramid so badly this would never have happened.

'It's all my fault,' he whispered.

'We all want what we can't have,' said Commander Altair matter of factly. 'Look at Professor Burlay and Mrs Grock.'

'Commander Altair, what is the Stone Cross?' Sammy asked quietly.

Commander Altair looked keenly at him. 'I wondered when you were going to ask me that.'

Sammy stared. 'I'm just curious.'

'Curiosity used wisely is a good thing,' Commander Altair said softly. 'Take Serberon. His curiosity to save Mary-Beth would have got you to join the Shape. That wasn't very wise.'

Sammy nodded, glad he could see daylight ahead of them.

'Bear that in mind,' continued Commander Altair, 'as you find out more about what you don't understand.'

'How...What?' started Sammy, angry to find himself alone. Commander Altair had left him in the entrance of the pyramid and was nowhere in sight. Sammy blinked, getting used to more darkness as he found he was in the early evening dusk with night time shadows creeping towards him.

CHAPTER 16

HOTEL DE LA PYRAMID

Sammy slowly made his way back to the market stalls and followed a group of fifth years, who were celebrating finding a shop that didn't care about serving alcohol to underage drinkers. They were merry, leaping and laughing on their way bay to the row of hotels where the Dragamas students were spending the night.

Sammy checked his staff and put it back into his pocket. It didn't seem to be broken. He was glad he had given his rucksack to Dixie. At least his Dragon Minder pin would be safe. He rubbed a smear off his Casino watch. It was nearly eleven o'clock.

'Pyramid time,' he muttered, hoping he wouldn't get into any more trouble for being out late alone. He stared down the row of hotels, all pyramid shaped. He looked at the signs. Excelsior Hotel, St. George's Castle, Raa Palace.

'Hotel de la Pyramid,' he said thankfully reading a sign on a small gold gate. He opened the gate and walked into an exotic garden full of palm trees and brightly coloured flowers. There was a pebble path leading up to a pillared entrance with a gold and white front door.

Sammy knocked on the door, bending down to brush the dirt and sand from his trousers, looking in dismay as he saw his arms were streaked with mud and blood. There was no answer so he knocked again a little harder.

Eventually footsteps pattered towards the door and it swung open to reveal the gold toothed grin of Vigor, the rug seller, and Antonio Havercastle from the drinks stall at the Oasis.

'Hullo Sammy!' The men chorused, thankfully not mentioning his un-hotel-like appearance.

'I'm sorry I'm not...' Sammy started to apologise for being dirty.

'It is to be expected,' beamed Antonio. 'Come in! They tell me you saved my brother's lion.'

'Yes, come in,' said the rug seller, flashing his mouth of gold. 'We have feasting! Come!'

Sammy let himself be led into a spotless dining room where the entire group of second year students were sitting at a large table waiting to eat from silver plates stacked high with food.

'Hey Sammy!' shrieked Dixie, running up and hugging the breath out of him. 'You're alive! I'm so sorry I left, Serberon said...'

'I know,' Sammy whispered.

'You're cut!'

'He's dirty!' squealed Milly. 'He needs to change. Mummy never lets me eat unless I'm clean.'

'No need,' said Antonio, still beaming. 'Come Sammy, bring your green haired girlfriend. Sit with us.'

Sammy grinned, leading a pink faced Dixie and grabbing Darius's hand as well, he led the three of them to the table at the top where Antonio and Vigor seemed to have kept the best food for themselves.

Sammy saw Antonio close a Directometer and knew that he had made everyone wait until he returned before letting anyone start eating.

Antonio waited for Sammy to sit between Dixie and Darius before waving his hand, signalling that the second years could start eating the feast.

'Where's Dr Shivers?' asked Sammy.

'He's gone to bed,' said Dixie, laughing. 'Look at all this food! This is instead of our Halloween feast at Dragamas this year!'

'Yeah, Antonio and Vigor told the all the teachers we would be fine,' said Darius.

'Oh,' said Sammy. 'I completely forgot about the feast, you know what with seeing the Shape and everything.'

Dixie nodded. 'You're ok now though. This feast is amazing. It's an Egyptian theme. Pyramid cakes, Mummy sandwiches, Pharaoh Brains and Sarcophagus soup.'

'Have you seriously waited for me to get back?' asked Sammy.

Dixie nodded again. 'Antonio let us have a glass of pumpkin water. He's had you on the Directometer ever since you left the Great Pyramid.'

'Yeah, those fifth years are going to get into big trouble drinking alcohol,' said Darius.

'Oh, right,' Sammy sighed, thinking back to the Great Pyramid. 'It was horrible seeing the Shape, again.'

'I don't see really what's so bad about them,' said Darius, picking up a Mummy shaped sandwich.

Sammy glared at Darius. 'They tried to kill me.'

'Only because you didn't join them. I would have.'

Sammy and Dixie stared at Darius.

'He doesn't understand,' Sammy whispered. 'Maybe one day he will.'

'I saw you in the pyramid,' Dixie whispered in Sammy's ear. 'Everything.' She tapped her forehead. 'I see things, not everything, just flashes of things inside your head. It's weird, I keep seeing these giant sausage rolls.'

Sammy laughed until he felt his sides were close to splitting. 'That's the funniest thing I've ever heard!'

The following morning Dr Shivers knocked on the hotel room door. Sammy was already awake, lying on luxurious cream silk sheets in a four-poster bed. He was in a hot sweat as he recalled every detail step-by-step of his nightmare encounter with the Shape. He decided Commander Altair was right. There were so many unanswered questions.

'Morning boys!' said Dr Shivers.

'Why is he so happy in the mornings?' Darius grumbled from the other side of the room.

Sammy heard the other four poster bed creak as Darius got up and let Dr Shivers in.

'Morning Darius! Morning Sammy! Did you sleep well?'

'Fine,' said Darius. 'I fell straight asleep.'

'Fully dressed I see,' said Dr Shivers, taking in the crumbs on their midnight feast plates and the half full glasses of pumpkin water.

Sammy could almost hear Dr Shivers making a mental note for his school report card.

'Are you dressed as well Sammy?'

Sammy wiped sweat from his forehead. He was still wearing the torn t-shirt and jeans from yesterday. The six feather pillows and ornate cream bedding were covered in dirt and sand. He moved his arm, hoping Dr Shivers would leave without noticing. He was out of luck.

'Perhaps you would take those sheets to Mr Havercastle downstairs. He will make sure they are clean for the next visitor.

'But...' Sammy started.

'Quiet,' snapped Dr Shivers. 'You will take your dirty bedding downstairs so it can be cleaned.' Dr Shivers swept out of the room, calling, 'breakfast is in ten minutes,' as he slammed the door behind him.

'I was only going to say there's a laundry bin there,' said Sammy.

Darius laughed. 'You look a right mess.'

'Thanks!' said Sammy, laughing and throwing a dirty pillow at Darius.

'Let's get some food!' shouted Darius, throwing a torch and book into his rucksack.

Sammy reached for his own rucksack, then remembered Dixie had taken it back with her. Lucky she had taken it, he thought. If he'd had it with him then his possessions, including his precious Dragon Minder pin that Dr Shivers had packed, would be lost forever inside the Great Pyramid.

Downstairs, he found that Darius had asked if he could sit at Antonio's table with Gavin and Toby. Unusually, Dixie was sitting with Milly. She looked pink and flustered and, he noticed, she was wearing his jumper. Sammy overheard a snatch of their conversation.

'For the last time Milly, Sammy is not my...'

Milly and the other North girls, Holly, Helana and Naomi giggled.

Dixie went scarlet. 'Hi Sammy.'

Sammy grinned to himself. 'Hi Dixie, can I sit here?'

If it was possible, Dixie went crimson and looked beseechingly at him. 'No, um, not today. Milly's telling us girly stuff. You uh, you probably wouldn't be interested.

Holly threw her auburn haired head back and she cackled, setting off Milly and Naomi. Helana had her head in her hands and was in tears of laughter.

Sammy felt his cheeks burn. Everyone was looking at them, including Dr Shivers who had a faint amused smile on his thin lips.

Sammy spotted an empty seat next to Simon Sanchez and Amos Leech.

'East only,' Amos grinned at him. 'You can't sit here.'
'Fine,' said Sammy, braver than he felt. Horrible memories of the Rat Catchers from his old school returned. He found an empty seat next to Tristan Markham of South, whose father was the vicar in the church in the village just outside of Dragamas.

'How's it going?' asked Tristan.

'Fine,' snapped Sammy, seizing a slice of hot toast that had just popped out of his plate. 'Ow, that's hot!'

Tristan laughed. 'That's coz it's freshly toasted, look.'

Sammy watched as another slice popped up. 'That's so cool!'

'We've got one at home,' said Tristan proudly. 'Ours does two at a time.'

Breakfast dragged on for Sammy. He felt he was on the receiving end of a few nasty stares from Dr Shivers and Professor Sanchez, who both seemed to be annoyed he had outsmarted Professor Burlay and Mrs Grock and got into the Great Pyramid. Milly was still teasing Dixie in her shrill "Mummy says" voice so that everyone could hear.

As they left the Hotel de la Pyramid, Antonio shook Sammy's hand.

'It is an honour to have met you,' he said quietly. 'Thank you so much for all you have done and all that you will do.'

It was even hotter than the day before and most of the Dragamas students seemed content lounging in the café s sipping cool drinks and trying different ice creams.

Dixie was keeping her distance from Sammy and he was grateful not to attract any more attention. She had thrust his rucksack back into his hands and disappeared straight after breakfast with Mikhael and Jason and he hadn't seen her since.

Darius kept Sammy busy. He organised a camel riding tour with Vigor, who was taking the day off from selling rugs.

For two pounds per person, Vigor had been more than happy to take a group of students around the perimeter of the land. He spent the day pointing out sights and telling them about the different pyramids. The day passed quickly with his interesting stories of how the pyramids were built and who had owned them.

Sammy was sorry when they arrived back at Hotel de la Pyramid. He had enjoyed being up high on his camel's back, bobbing up and down as the camel plodded, as surefooted as Kyrillan, on the sandy roads.

Just like at the Floating Circus, the edge of the Land of the Pharaohs was protected by a steep curve to keep residents inside. In the far corner, they had paused for lunch and let the camels drink from a fountain. Sammy couldn't see the other corners. The land was huge and they were far out of sight.

In fact, after their day's ride, he wasn't surprised to learn that they had only explored half of the land, with more unexplored pyramids rising into the distance.

'That was amazing,' Sammy thanked Vigor as he dismounted from his camel, Ramsey the Second. Much as he wanted to know, Sammy didn't dare ask what had happened to Ramsey the First.

'No problem,' Vigor flashed his gold toothed smile. 'Head for that pyramid there and you'll find the lift back to Dragamas inside.'

'Thanks,' said Darius as he leaped down from his camel. 'That was awesome!'

They met Dr Shivers standing next to Commander Altair and Professor Burlay by the square glass platform waiting for the lift to take them back down to Dragamas.

After a moment, the glass floor opened, the four triangles rose upwards, and the familiar face of Captain Firebreath appeared, his red hair matted as usual. He looked a little ill and mopped his brow with a checkered handkerchief.

'Too many times going up and down in the heat,' he grumbled, shook his head and threw up in the grey gargoyle.

CHAPTER 17

QUIET TIMES

Having forgotten the trip to the Land of the Pharaohs coincided with Halloween, Sammy was keen not to make the same mistake about Bonfire Night. He wrote to his parents, who obliged his requests and sent him a lockable box and a set of giant sparklers.

He locked his Dragon Minder pin, the map Dixie had redrawn and his bravery cross into the box and tucked it at the back of his drawer during an industrious clean-up of the tower room as instructed by Dr Shivers, who had come in one evening horrified not to be able to see the floor.

After a half hour lecture on the benefits of cleaning and Dr Shivers's warning that in his time at Dragamas boys were whipped for not keeping the room tidy, Jock had volunteered them to clean the room for inspection.

Dr Shivers had loved the idea and cast an oil slick across the door, sealing the five boys in so they could dust, polish and tidy the room completely undisturbed.

Sammy checked his area. Using his staff, he had managed to disintegrate some sticky sweet wrappers under his bed with one green spark.

Gavin had been impressed and swapped sorting out the pile of mixed up socks in return for a green spark to clean the stain on the wallpaper.

It was a fair swap. Sammy got all fourteen pairs of his socks sorted from the enormous pile of everyone's clothes on the floor and Gavin stopped moaning about sleeping in the dirty corner.

Toby found it hilarious that Gavin thought there were corners in their circular tower room.

'Lessons tomorrow,' said Gavin, ignoring his twin brother and handing Sammy fourteen pairs of socks. 'I wish we could have stayed longer at the Land of the Pharaohs.'

'Me too,' said Toby from under his duvet. 'Still at least it's Guy Fawkes this week.'

Fast asleep already, Jock snored loudly.

Sammy found he was thirsty and couldn't sleep until he had gone down to the bathroom to get himself a glass of water. The fifth year he held responsible for Mary-Beth's death was there, blowing smoke rings. He didn't look up when Sammy walked past him to fill his glass and accidentally splashed him as the water came out quicker than he expected.

In fact, he had almost made it out of the bathroom when the older boy called him back with an 'oi, squirt!'

Sammy froze. 'What?'

'Uh, nothing really,' said the cigarette smoking boy. 'Just thought I'd tell you Mary-Beth liked you. She thought you were cute.'

'Oh,' said Sammy. 'That's um, nice.'

'It's my fault she's dead,' he said, sucking in on his cigarette. He spat out the smoke. 'You want one?'

'Uh, no,' said Sammy, a little more sarcastically than he meant.

'You're sensible,' said the boy. 'They help me think,' he added, inhaling and coughing. 'Like, if I hadn't told her to play that game. It was just so I could see, uh, you know, her legs. She had nice legs she did, you know.'

'Yeah, well she wasn't your girlfriend,' snapped Sammy in spite of himself, 'serves you right.'

'She didn't want to play,' the boy rambled on, 'said Professor Burlay had said the game was dangerous, something in the stars. Stupid old goat, I said to her. Professor Burlay wouldn't know the difference between Dragonball and Dragon Dice.

'Mm,' said Sammy, feeling his bare feet going numb on the cold tiled floor. 'Maybe I'll catch up with you later,' he said backing out of the bathroom.

'Yeah right,' Sammy muttered to himself as he got back to the tower room. 'I don't think I'll speak to him again.'

He stared at his reflection in the tower window, imagining for a second in the candlelight, that instead of pyjamas, he was wearing a metal breastplate with the Dragamas logo and steel armour. He wore a metal helmet with an upturned visor and a green feather plume. In his hand he held a silver sword with blood dripping from his victory with the Shape.

Sammy reached into his drawer and picked out his medal for bravery cross from the locked box. He swung the rope cord over his head and checked the reflection again.

Even in his green striped pyjamas, the Celtic cross looked like it belonged around his neck. Sammy twisted it so it picked up the candlelight.

'For good not evil,' he whispered, holding it tightly in his right hand.

Lying down, refreshed from drinking the cool water, Sammy fell into a deep sleep, imagining he was riding Kyrillan and shooting goals in a ferocious game of Dragonball.

Monday morning began with a surprise theory test on the Art of Descaling in Dragon Studies. Dr Shivers handed out the papers with a flourish and paused at Sammy's table for an uncomfortable moment. Sammy knew he was still in Dr Shivers's bad books from the weekend at the Land of the Pharaohs.

Sammy sat between Gavin and Darius and they racked their brains to find an easy question on the test papers.

Dr Shivers asked for the lesson to be completed in silence so he could mark the third year "Lifespan of a Dragon" coursework, which sounded ominously difficult.

Sammy looked at the questions and puzzled over the name of the first ever dragon descaling champion of 1512. He leaned over to see what the others had thought.

Gavin had written King Arthur and Darius had written Maid Marian. Sure he could take neither answer seriously, he drew a line over his answer of King Serberon and Karmandor and left the question blank. He was glad when the bell above the door rang and they could go to Armoury.

Commander Altair's lesson passed unusually quietly. Instead of teaching them to block sparks or helping to create mental images to prevent mind reading, he had chosen to read them a story about Bonfire Night and how to take more care with fireworks.

Jock had fallen asleep half way through the lesson and Commander Altair woke him up with a series of dancing green flames fired on to Jock's textbook.

Commander Altair was surprised when Sammy lingered over packing his things into his rucksack, waited for the other students to leave, and volunteered himself to stay behind at the end of the lesson.

'Commander Altair,' Sammy began uncertainly.

Commander Altair looked keenly at Sammy, his hands clasped together as he sat at his desk. 'What can I do for you Sammy?'

'Um, I had a question...about my cross.' Sammy swung the cross out of his shirt and held it towards Commander Altair.

The cross itself was a mix of gold and silver with a run of coloured stones leading from a central white stone. It reminded Sammy of the Dragamas constellation from their Astronomics lessons.

Commander Altair leaned forward. 'Ah yes, the cross for bravery against untold danger. I am glad it went to you. It may just help you in unexpected ways.'

Sammy nodded. 'Um, I think it has. In the Great Pyramid when I was asked to join the...the...' a lump rose in his throat, 'Shape,' he said, choking on his words.

'I see,' said Commander Altair, intensifying his bright eyed stare. 'So you are aware of its powers.'

Sammy stared. 'Not really, um, I mean in the pyramid, the Shape they had Serberon. I thought if I joined them, they would let Serberon go. The cross burned and I remembered the Shape are bad.'

'And were you angry when the cross burned and reminded you to stay away?'

Sammy shook his head. 'No.'

'Even though you had been betrayed by your mentor, someone whom you trusted, you still wanted to save him?'

'Yes.'

'I see,' said Commander Altair scratching the back of his hand with an orange pencil. 'You were not even tempted to join the Shape when they asked you directly?'

'No,' Sammy said louder than before. 'So what? Serberon took me to the Shape. I'm here now.'

'He took you as a sacrifice,' shouted Commander Altair, standing up and snapping the orange pencil in half. 'He thought only of himself and how to get his girlfriend back. He didn't care about you.'

Sammy shook a little. 'So.'

'So!' shouted Commander Altair, rattling the windows. 'So,' he closed his eyes, shook his head, and relaxed. 'Nothing Sammy,' he said calmly. 'There will be a better time for this and a better place.'

'Why isn't anyone telling me anything?' shouted Sammy, thumping his fist on Commander Altair's desk. 'First Dr Shivers wouldn't tell me about my parents forgetting about dragons and now you won't tell me why it's so great I didn't want to join the Shape when I'd been allowed to get there as a sacrifice so Serberon could see Mary-Beth's legs.'

'Her legs?' said Commander Altair, hiding a smile in a fake cough.

'Yeah,' said Sammy, feeling very small. 'Her legs.'

'If you can keep it a secret,' Commander Altair leaned so close Sammy could make out faint blond stubble on his close shaven chin, 'I can tell you that the metal in your cross is made from the blade of a Dragon Knight's sword who died saving his dragon in the battle against the Shape.'

Sammy's jaw dropped open. 'Who?'

Commander Altair pressed his index finger to his mouth. 'Not yet.'

'A Dragon Knight's sword?'

Commander Altair nodded. 'Like your watch, you'll find it has hidden powers.' He held up his own watch, an exact copy of Sammy's and clicked one of the four buttons on the side. The dial faded and was replaced with a pool of oil slick blue Dr Shivers had created.

Sammy saw two dots in the pool.

Commander Altair nodded. 'It's us. Try it.'

Sammy squeezed the buttons on his own watch and found that he could find the same two dots.

Commander Altair leaned closer still. 'Sir Ragnarok thinks you need to know this so you can detect the Shape. If you can't see a dot on the screen but you can see a person in front of you then they are supporters of the Shape.'

'Oh.'

'Don't worry Sammy. While you're at Dragamas, we'll teach you all you need to know.'

'That didn't stop me getting into the pyramid.'

'You disobeyed Sir Ragnarok's direct rules,' said Commander Altair kindly. 'We will help you, but you have to meet us half way.'

'Why is this happening to me?'

'Trust Sir Ragnarok,' Commander Altair smiled. 'He's watching out for you.'

'But.'

'Meet us half way Sammy. Remember what I said to you about curiosity.'

'I need to know,' Sammy whispered as Commander Altair picked up an Armoury sword and tapped it on his desk.

'Don't we all. Trust Sir Ragnarok.'

'Put wrongs to rights,' grumbled Sammy. 'Maybe I should have joined the Shape.'

Commander Altair slammed the sword point down embedding it several centimeters into the wood. 'That's the last time you say that. Your dragon would be the first they'd kill.'

That jolted Sammy back to the classroom. 'Perhaps I'm not meant to be a Dragon Knight,' he mumbled, thinking he'd be grateful for Commander Altair to give him some stars and tell him to go to lunch.

'Maybe we should leave it there,' Commander Altair smiled, reaching for Sammy's watch and changing the pool of light to the normal clock face.

'Ok.' Sammy was grateful to be led out of the classroom.

'If you ever want any extra help with your staff, blocking sparks, self defence, just let me know.'

Sammy nodded. 'Thanks.'

Two days later, Professor Sanchez was demonstrating a new collection of fireworks in double Alchemistry. She had invited the first years into the lesson and Sammy found it was the first time he had actually met Nigel Ashford, the first year boy he was supposed to be watching out for.

Nigel Ashford was a small, dark haired, skinny boy who could have passed as Gavin and Toby's younger brother. He had a high pitched squeaky voice that got on Darius's nerves so badly that he had sat, for the first time, away from Sammy at the front of the class.

Dixie had taken Darius's place with Sarah Hillcroft, who had a voice shriller than Milly's and higher, squeakier pitched even than Nigel Ashford. They were giggling about the latest team strip that the Nitromen were wearing, which still seemed to be black leather trousers with a black and gold diagonally striped top, except the stripes were running the opposite way from before. If anything, Sarah Hillcroft liked the Nitromen and Firesticks as much as Dixie.

'Fireworks!' Professor Sanchez laughed. 'I have made my own creation,' she said, twirling her staff like a baton and casting out bright sparks like a catherine wheel.

At the front, Darius had to duck as some of the rainbow coloured sparks headed straight for him.

'The fireworks are good,' Simon nodded approvingly. 'May we do that with our staffs?'

Professor Sanchez was having none of it. 'You are still too young,' she cackled. 'The third and fourth years are doing the display.'

'This is not fair!' shouted Darius, mocking Simon's accent. 'The fireworks are the best bits.'

Professor Sanchez put down her staff and extinguished the sparks. She scowled at Darius. 'Perhaps you had better not go to the display. I will speak with Dr Shivers later today.'

Darius looked horrified. 'It was a joke. I'm sorry. Please don't stop me going.'

Professor Sanchez took out her notebook that Sammy recognised was used to store notes on students for their end of year reports.

She clapped the notebook shut. 'Where was I? Ah yes, the fireworks.' She handed round sheets of A4 paper with complicated diagrams. 'The fireworks.'

Sammy waited until the papers were passed to himself and to Nigel Ashford, who had fallen asleep. Sammy nudged him with his elbow. Nigel awoke with a start.

'Two stars from North Sammy,' barked Professor Sanchez. 'Don't let him fall asleep in my lesson again.

Sammy scowled at Nigel, who had promptly fallen asleep again.

'What's wrong with you?' he grumbled.

By the end of the lesson, they had constructed giant rockets with sparklers taped around the side, ready for the evening celebrations.

After lunch, Mr Cross had given the second years their first proper Dragonball game against the fifth years. Milly looked terrified when the cigarette smoking boy towered over her, however had surprised everyone by slapping him when he called her Mary-Beth by accident.

Sammy was pleased to see he was flying Kyrillan almost as well as Cyril Burns, Rachel Burns's older brother in the fifth year, who had been chosen to play Firesticks professionally for the Monk Titans.

Sammy had never heard of the Monk Titans but Dixie assured him that they were one of the teams that Nitron Dark had played for before he created his own team, the Nitromen.

Sammy scored twelve of the fifty-six goals that the second years scored and they won by three goals against the fifth years.

As Mr Cross blew the final whistle, Sammy saw Captain Duke Stronghammer and Captain Firebreath cheering from the sides.

The dwarves collected the eighty dragons and led them, accompanied by twelve of the thirteen Dragon Minders. Milly had fallen off when she dismounted and sprained her ankle. Mr Cross had sent her to Mrs Grock's house, escorted by the cigarette smoking boy and three of his friends.

'Thanks for your help,' growled Captain Firebreath as he waved the Dragon Minders away at the entrance to the Dragon Chambers. 'You can't come right in tonight.'

'Why not?' asked Simon Sanchez. 'We are normally allowed.'

'Security by Sir Ragnarok's orders,' said Captain Stronghammer. 'We have to make sure the Shape are kept out.'

'The rules are stupid,' said Simon Sanchez.

'Yeah,' agreed Captain Firebreath. 'That's why they make 'em. But they keep the dragons safe.'

'Protected from the Shape,' added Captain Stronghammer, taking a sip from his hipflask. 'Mm, that's a good 'un Firey.'

Sammy bumped into Dixie as he turned around. 'Uh, sorry.'

'It's ok, are we going to stand in the same place as last year to watch the fireworks?'

'Yeah,' said Sammy on auto-pilot, 'um, by the tree stump that moved.'

'Exactly,' Dixie whispered. 'I want to see where it goes.'

Sammy groaned. 'You're joking, right?'

Dixie shook her head. 'I checked it out. You need a Dragon Minder pin, which means we can get in. It goes down quite a long way, but there's a ladder and it's quite dark...'

'It's ok,' Sammy grinned, knowing Dixie hated the dark. 'I'll get Darius, we'll both come down with you.'

Dixie grinned as well. 'It's our first adventure as the passage spotters!'

CHAPTER 18

DRAGON POISON

As arranged, Sammy and Darius met Dixie in the clearing behind the Gymnasium. It was already dark with a light breeze in the air. Spots of rain were falling and splashing on to the leaves of the shrubs and trees.

'Over here,' Dixie hissed from behind a pink rhododendron.

'Ok,' said Darius, his voice muffled by a hot dog he had picked up on the way to the clearing.

As usual, Sir Ragnarok had arranged for some of the traders at the Floating Circus to come to Dragamas and bring refreshments for their Bonfire Night celebrations.

'This is so cool,' said Darius in a loud stage whisper.

'Shh,' hissed Dixie. 'You'll get Dr Shivers over here if you keep on being noisy like that.'

'Ok,' whispered Darius, a little quieter. 'Is it this tree stump?'

'Yes,' whispered Dixie. 'Move over, you put the Dragon Minder pin on the edge. There's a groove. It fits perfectly, I tried it earlier.'

Sammy stared. Dixie was carrying a small rucksack and had obviously planned their excursion in great detail.

She handed out a bar of chocolate and a large ball of bright pink string that Sammy and Darius took obediently. Sammy found himself privately thinking Dixie had lost the plot.

'We'll use the string to find our way back,' she explained, unpinning the silver dragon shaped pin from her jumper. 'Look, it goes here.' Dixie clicked the Dragon Minder pin into a groove in the tree stump.

Without making a sound, she lifted the top of the tree stump up on a hidden hinge.

Sammy knelt down and peered in. 'It's dark in there.'

'It's ok,' said Darius, 'I've got a torch.' He pulled his cracker sized torch from his pocket. 'Oh no,' he exclaimed.

'What?'

'No batteries. I took them out at lunchtime so Gavin could use them in his...'

'Never mind,' said Sammy, 'we'll use...'

'Fire,' Dixie finished for him.

'Oh yeah,' said Darius a little sheepishly. 'I guess, um, my fire doesn't always work. I carry a torch for emergencies.

'Emergencies,' giggled Dixie.

'I use it to do my homework under the duvet after lights out. You can't use fire under there.'

'Comics more like,' said Dixie. 'Don't you read Dragon Strike?'

'Sometimes,' muttered Darius. 'Let's go inside if we're going.'

'I'll go first,' said Sammy.

'No, I will,' said Darius.

'Ok,'

'Yeah, Darius you go first.'

Darius stepped up on to the edge of the tree stump. 'There's a ladder.'

'Yeah,' said Dixie sarcastically. 'What were you expecting?'

'An escalator,' said Darius, equally sarcastically, 'or a chairlift.'

Dixie climbed in after Darius, her green head disappearing down inside the tree stump. 'Come on Sammy!' she called up to him. 'It only goes down about ten steps.'

Sammy closed the lid of the tree stump behind him and made his way down. When Sammy got to the bottom, Dixie had lit a fire at the end of her staff. It was warm under his feet.

'What did you do that for?' said Dixie, pointing at the closed hatch. 'It's our only way out.'

'We don't want anyone following us,' Sammy whispered back. He handed her the Dragon Minder pin. 'We can get out again, I checked, you put the pin into a groove on our side.

'Are you sure?'

'Yes,' said Sammy firmly, although he wished he had double checked it as they started walking along the earthy passage.

'Suppose we get stuck,' whispered Dixie.

'It was your idea to come,' said Darius.

'It wasn't my idea to shut us in.'

'Sorry,' said Sammy, taking some of the fire and walking ahead.

'Stay together!'

'Go back if you're scared.'

'No way Darius. This was my idea. I'm going to find the end of the passage with you.'

'It probably just goes back to the school,' said Sammy. 'Maybe it links to the Shute or to Mrs Grock's house.'

'Suppose it's a dead end, or it caves in?'

Darius laughed. 'Are you sure you want to come?'

Sammy caught "My idea" as Dixie pushed past him.

'I'll start unraveling the string so we can get back,' said Dixie.

'Good idea,' said Darius laughing at her. 'So far it's a straight passage.'

Dixie shrugged and led them down the sloping passage until the earth walls turned to rock lined with gemstones that twinkled in the flames.

Some half an hour later, the passage was still straight and they hadn't seen any twists, turns or other passage openings.

'It doesn't feel real,' Sammy whispered to Darius. 'It's like we're walking forever. Ow! What did you poke me for?'

'Just so you know it's real,' Darius giggled. 'Hey Dixie, can we start the chocolate yet?'

'No, it's for when we get there.'

'Where?' asked Sammy. 'You said you didn't know where the passage went.'

'It has to go somewhere.'

'Suppose we missed something,' said Sammy. 'Up there in the passage ceiling. A trap door or something?'

In the flame light, Sammy saw Dixie and Darius go pale.

'Um, just a thought,' Sammy added hastily. 'Let's go on until the end of the string.'

Dixie held up the shrinking ball. 'There's only a little bit of string left. We've nearly used it all up.'

'If we're just going straight, it should be fine anyway,' Darius coughed nervously, 'we can't go wrong.'

Sammy nodded. 'We'll keep going.'

Dixie nodded and led the way into the passage. 'It's so dark,' she muttered almost every minute until the last centimetre of string had been unwound. 'There, that's it. No more string.'

'Are we going on?' Darius whispered. 'Without the string?'

'As long as it's straight,' said Dixie quietly. 'If the passage splits, or if there's a turn, we stop and go back.'

'Ok,' said Darius. 'You ok with that Sammy?'

'Ok,' Sammy whispered, finding he had butterflies in his stomach and a lump in his throat.

Dixie set down the pink string and took a deep breath. 'Ok, let's go.'

They carried on down the passage which although it sloped sometimes upwards, sometimes downwards, it was always straight.

Sammy checked his watch. They had been walking for close to an hour. The fireworks at Dragamas would be well underway. He found himself wondering who Professor Sanchez would choose this year to light the first firework and whether Dixie's brothers would have been allowed to create fireworks that spelt out their initials again.

He was carried away thinking about the firework display and his run-in with the Shape that he didn't notice that Dixie and Darius had stopped.

Sammy bumped into Dixie who dropped the fire. The flames went out.

Dixie squealed. 'Watch it Sammy!'

Darius waved his staff clumsily, clanking it against the tunnel walls.

'Ouch!' said Dixie.

Sammy guessed she'd been hit with the staff. He ducked as Darius's staff brushed the top of his head. He reached for his own staff and shouted, 'fire.'

'Yeah, fire,' echoed Dixie.

From the ends of their staffs came two warm jets of fire lighting up the passage.

Dixie shrieked making Sammy jump.

'What?' he snapped, turning to face her.

'Turns.'

'What?' Then Sammy stared. Dixie was right. The passage forked into two tunnels. 'Now what?'

'Let's go right,' said Darius, 'come on, we've gone a long way just to turn back. It's not as if it's tricky. Look, it's a "Y" shape,' he held his arms up to demonstrate. 'As long as we go straight when we come to this turn again we'll be fine.'

'I don't know,' Sammy started.

'Let's go back,' said Dixie firmly. 'It's cold, dark and it's getting late. We can come back again with more string.'

'We've walked miles,' said Darius. 'You have got to be joking. What do you think Sammy?'

'Um, we have come a long way.'

'Fine!' shouted Dixie, putting her hands on her hips. 'If we get lost down here...'

'Darius is right,' said Sammy. 'If we go straight on the way back then we can't go wrong.'

'Ok,' said Dixie.

Sammy thought he heard a tremble in Dixie's voice. 'It'll be ok,' he reassured her. 'Have you got anything else we can use to mark our way back?'

'Like a lipstick?' she laughed. 'Milly would have.'

'Ok, we'll just go on,' said Darius heading up the right hand passage. He returned seconds later. 'That way's no good. It's solid rock. There's no way through.'

'Let's see,' said Dixie, pulling the clump of flames into the right hand tunnel. She returned moments later. 'There's nothing there.'

'Ok,' said Sammy a little nervously. 'Let's try the other one.'

Sammy went no more than ten paces into the second tunnel and came face to face with a rock wall covered in damp lichen.

'It's a dead end,' he shouted.

'They're identical,' said Dixie. 'The tunnel goes nowhere.'

'It's a nowhere tunnel,' Darius laughed nervously. 'What a waste of time.'

'There must be something,' whispered Sammy. 'Let's have one last look.'

'It's a waste of time,' said Darius.

'It can't be,' said Dixie. 'Who would go to all that trouble to make a passage all the way from Dragamas just to finish in not just one dead end but two!'

'I suppose,' said Sammy, bending down to tie his shoelace.

There was a rumble overhead.

'Did you hear that?' said Sammy.

Dixie nodded. 'It came from the other tunnel.'

Instinctively, Sammy crouched and waved for Dixie and Darius to do the same.

'What?' grumbled Darius as he bent down.

'Shh,' whispered Sammy. 'Someone's coming.'

More creaks and rumbles could be heard from the other tunnel. Sammy could feel his heart thumping in his chest as he put out the fire. He felt Dixie and Darius draw close as they waited in the darkness. Voices came from the other tunnel.

'Are you ready yet?' came a deep gravelly voice that froze Sammy's blood.

'It's the Shape,' Sammy whispered, his voice shaking. He hunched back against the wall as the rumbling got louder.

'Must not be seen,' he heard Dixie mutter beside him and knew she had recognised the voice as well.

'I almost can't believe we will do this tonight,' came a second voice, female this time that sounded very much in command. 'Will you hurry up coming from down there. Any word from next door?'

Sammy's heart skipped a beat. This was it, they would come round the corner and see them crouching. He reached for his staff.

'No,' came a booming voice. 'He has visitors and cannot get away. We will complete the task without him.'

'It is not right,' came the gravelly voice. 'He knows the boy best. We cannot afford to fail this time. He knows too much.'

'Silence,' said the booming voice. 'Eliza is not here and neither is...'

'No names,' said the female voice, silky in the dark tunnel. 'You know better than that. Sir Lok Ragnarok is on to us. He will have already made checks.'

'You are right my dear, right as always.'

'To Dragamas then.'

'Where else,' said the gravelly voice with a cold laugh. 'This tunnel only leads from here to there.'

Crouched against the wall, the three figures swept past the opening.

'My staff,' said the silky voice. 'In my haste to fetch you, I have left it behind.'

'No matter my dear,' said the gravelly voice. 'You will be safe enough. After all, the staff is merely the instrument of the beginner.'

Sammy held his breath until the figures were out of sight. He saw them light a fire when they were almost out of sight. Gasping, he took several deep breaths and lit a small fire himself. Dixie was still shaking beside him and Darius had gone very quiet.

'The Shape,' whispered Sammy.

Speechless, Darius nodded.

'We can't go back,' whispered Dixie. 'Suppose we bump into them.'

'We can't go on either,' said Sammy. 'Both these tunnels were dead ends.'

'They can't be,' said Darius. 'If they were, the Shape wouldn't have been able to get into the passage.'

'Maybe there's a trapdoor, another tree stump?' suggested Dixie. 'Let's look first.'

'Yeah,' said Sammy, thinking out loud. 'They said one of them was with visitors.'

'The one from next door,' added Darius. 'Either they meant a house or that this tunnel was next door.'

Sammy stood up and pulled two flames out of the fire. He held them above his head and whistled as he saw a wooden square cut into the stone roof.

'Look,' Sammy whispered as Dixie and Darius stood up. 'It's a trapdoor.'

'How did we miss that?' whispered Dixie.

'Didn't look up, I guess,' said Darius. 'Wait there, I want to see if it's the same the other side.' He took a flame and disappeared.

Darius returned in under ten seconds. 'They're identical.'

'Are we going up?' asked Dixie.

'Yeah,' said Sammy, feeling a little reckless. He checked his watch. 'The fireworks are probably still going on.'

'Let's try this one first,' said Darius, swinging himself from tunnel to tunnel. 'If they've just come out, we can go in.'

'Mm,' said Dixie, 'there's still one of them left.'

'Two,' said Darius, picking himself up off the floor where he had fallen after a vigorous swing, 'if you count Dr Lithoman.'

'She probably projected herself to Dragamas,' said Sammy thoughtfully. 'I don't blame her, it beats walking!'

He followed Dixie and Darius into the other passage where the trapdoor was shut. It was identical to the first one.

'Do a crab, Sammy,' commanded Darius, 'I'll stand on you to get the door open.'

'Ok,' Sammy knelt on the floor and tucked his head under his arms. He felt less like a crab and more like a small boulder.

'That's not a proper crab,' said Dixie, arching her back and demonstrating one.

'You look stupid like that,' Darius laughed. 'Sammy's is better, he won't collapse when I do this,' Darius put his right foot on Sammy's back and reached towards the ceiling. He put his left foot on Dixie's stomach and she collapsed under him with a squeal.

'It's locked,' said Darius jumping down. He helped Dixie up.

'You squashed me!'

'Sorry,' Darius giggled, 'I told you Sammy's was better.'

'Locked?' said Sammy. 'But they just came out.'

Darius shrugged. 'So? Let's try the other one.'

Sammy led them back to the left hand tunnel. 'I wish Kyrillan was here. If this trapdoor opens, we can't all go up. One of us will have to stay behind.'

'Not me said Dixie, 'I can't lift you both up.'

'What good would Kyrillan be?' asked Darius.

'He'd help us all up,' said Dixie. 'Kiridor could do that too.'

'Yeah, well they're not here,' said Darius matter of factly. 'I'll help you up, Sammy can stay behind.'

'No way,' said Sammy. 'If it's open, I'm going up.'

'If,' said Darius. 'Ok, if not, we'll have to go back.'

'Hope it's open,' grinned Sammy. 'Come on, do the crab for me.'

'More like a snail,' laughed Dixie as she held out her arm.

Sammy took Dixie's arm to steady himself on Darius's back. He pushed up against the trapdoor. 'It's locked,' he muttered, steadying himself on a groove. His fingers closed round the groove and he recognized the shape of the indentation.

Instinctively he took off his Dragon Minder pin and clicked it into the groove. The trapdoor clicked and fell back towards them.

'It opens outwards,' exclaimed Darius.

'Duh,' said Dixie. 'Sammy must have used his Dragon Minder pin to unlock it. That makes sense as we had to use the pin to open the other end of the tunnel. What's up there Sammy?'

Sammy reached for the flames, guiding them up to the trapdoor. 'It's dark,' he muttered, hoisting himself up into the space above.

'What's up there?' demanded Darius. 'Let me up!'

'I can't lift you up,' said Dixie, 'you'll have to let me go up.'

'Ready?' Sammy called down. He found he was in a small room that reminded him of Mrs Grock's store room. There were sacks that felt like they had grain inside them. Probably dragon food he thought to himself, finding it strange that the Shape, who were trying to kill dragons would have food in this room.

He didn't have time to wonder for long as Dixie reached for his hand. It was really sweaty but he clasped it tightly and helped her up.

'Hey, it's dark up here.'

'It's dark down here too,' Darius called up. 'Send down some fire.'

'Create your own,' Dixie laughed, moving aside as Sammy swept a handful of orange flames past her and sent them down to Darius.

'Wait here, we'll explore for a minute then come back down.'

'Good point Sammy,' Darius called up, 'how are you going to get down?'

'I'll figure it out,' said Sammy. He turned to Dixie. 'Let's explore.'

He cast the flames at the end of his staff around the room. The flames flickered making long shadows on the stone walls. He pushed past a sack of grain.

'Haycorn,' he read out loud from the label. 'Hyperium Haycorn.'

'Dragon food,' said Dixie.

They crept deeper into the room and up to some wooden shelves that had dozens of bottles filled with a green liquid. There was a small skull and cross bones on the label of each bottle.

Sammy looked at Dixie. 'Poison,' he whispered. 'Food and poison.'

'They can't do that,' said Dixie.

Sammy felt another lump stick in his throat and he gulped. 'I don't know about this,' he said. 'I think we should tell Sir Ragnarok.'

'We have to find out more,' Dixie whispered. 'We need to know who put it here and why.'

'For someone who's supposed to be scared of the dark, you want to go on?'

In the candlelight, Sammy saw Dixie blush.

'I'm not afraid of the dark when I'm with...'

'Eugh!' called up Darius. 'I'm going to be sick!'

'Yeah, ok,' said Sammy, feeling his own cheeks burning. 'We'll try this way.' He turned around and bumped into a bottle of the poison, knocking it over with a clatter.

'Oh no,' whispered Dixie. 'Someone will have heard that.'

Overhead, they heard the creaking of floorboards. Sammy flipped the lid of the trapdoor and blew out the flames.

In the far corner, a horizontal beam of light appeared, it was a doorway. They heard a key grinding in the lock and the beam of light widened. Sammy pulled Dixie closer to him, checking they were both hidden behind one of the large sacks of grain.

'I told you I'm not coming tonight. You can do your dirty work alone.'

Sammy held his breath. If they were right and the Shape had built the tunnel direct to Dragamas with the intention of feeding all of the school dragons with poisoned food, he had to find out who it was.

'In fact,' went on the voice. 'You can stop using my house. I want no further part in this while they are here. Do you hear me?'

A torch shone down on the closed trapdoor.

'Oh I see. You've gone without me,' said the voice. 'Yes Julia, I'll be up with you and Charles in a moment.'

The door slammed shut, the key grating and turning. The light under the door went out.

When Dixie lit a small fire, Sammy found he was shaking from head to foot.

'What?' Dixie whispered.

'I...I know where we are...'

'Where?'

'I have to speak to Sir Ragnarok,' Sammy stuttered. 'This is too much for us to deal with.'

'Sammy, where are we?' Dixie sounded scared as she lifted the trapdoor. She jumped nimbly down and Sammy heard her telling Darius what he had said.

'Come down Sammy,' Darius called up. 'Dixie says the door is locked. We have to go back. Where are we anyway?'

'I think,' said Sammy, still shaking, 'I think we're at my Uncle's house in the village.'

'Your what?' exclaimed Dixie. 'That can't be right.'

Sammy swung his legs out over the trapdoor and grasped the other side. He swung out into the tunnel, narrowly missing Darius's head. He let go, landing on his feet.

Sammy dusted his hands on his jeans. 'My parents are called Charles and Julia. It sounded like my Uncle and it would make sense. We're in the right direction. He lives near Dragamas. Uncle Peter wouldn't have been able to poison our dragons while my parents were staying with him. It would be impossible.'

Dixie and Darius stared at Sammy, making him uncomfortable.

'It's not my fault. My parents never told me anything about dragons, remember?' he said, trying to justify things more for himself than Dixie and Darius.

After an uncomfortable silence, Dixie spoke first, 'so you're related to the Shape?'

'No wonder your parents forgot about dragons,' Darius laughed nervously. 'Probably safest. They'd be locked up.'

Sammy felt his eyes prickle. 'They can't be involved,' he whispered, tears forming in the corner of his eyes.

'Let's go back,' said Dixie quietly.

'Down the passage?' said Sammy.

'Yeah,' said Dixie, 'if we meet the Shape, just tell them your parents know you're down here.'

'I don't think that's a good idea,' Sammy whispered.

'Duh, even if we can go out of the other trapdoor, we know it's the house next to your Uncle's house. He'd see us leave and know we're on to him.'

'The Shape have already tried to kill me Darius,' said Sammy. 'Perhaps we should go in and find out why.'

'A vote,' said Dixie. 'I say go back down the passage.'

Darius raised his hand. 'Me too.'

Sammy shrugged. 'Fine.' He stomped down the passage.

Dixie ran after him. 'It's the right thing to do,' she whispered. 'We don't know where the other trapdoor leads.

'And we never will,' Sammy scowled. 'We should have taken some of the poison to show Sir Ragnarok.'

'It's too late now,' said Darius. 'Look, here's our string.'

'Look, here's our string,' cackled a deep voice in the darkness in front. 'I says to them, someone has been here but they says to me I'm being stupid, paranoid!' The voice laughed louder. 'Tell me children, where have you been? What have you seen?'

'Run!' shouted Sammy. 'Now!'

Sammy extinguished the fire and he, Dixie and Darius charged forward in the darkness. Sammy reached for Dixie's hand, his free hand scraping along the tunnel wall to check his bearings.

They barged past a fleshy person no taller than Sammy's waist that groaned as it was flung against the tunnel wall.

'Quick!' Sammy yelled. 'We have to get out of here!'

They ran as fast as their legs could carry them. Sammy fired green sparks back down the passage. Dirt and dust kicked up as the sparks ricocheted off the walls.

By the time they reached the ladder, the tunnel was almost on fire. Sammy and Dixie fired more green sparks back towards the figure who was firing great jets of black smoke towards them, making them cough and splutter.

Sammy helped Dixie on to the ladder and pushed her upwards. He fired another volley of green sparks into the thick black smoke.

Darius climbed up after Dixie. 'Quick,' he shouted down.

'Ok,' said Sammy, firing another three green sparks into the dense smoke. He reached up on to the ladder and climbed to the top as fast as he could.

The second he climbed up to the top and stuck his head out of the tree stump, he wished he had stayed down below.

Professor Sanchez and Commander Altair were standing over the tree stump, their staffs aimed directly at his throat.

'It's ok Simone,' said Commander Altair, lowering his staff. 'Sammy, you three have some serious explaining to do.'

'They shall go to Sir Ragnarok,' said Professor Sanchez, lowering her staff. 'He will know what to do.'

Commander Altair nodded. 'Dr Shivers will take you.'

Sammy looked up. Dr Shivers was standing behind Professor Sanchez, tapping his staff against his leg. 'Is this really necessary Simone? I'm sure they caused no harm exploring down there.'

Professor Sanchez looked frostily at Dr Shivers, then back to Sammy. 'Very well. Sammy may go back with his friends. I heard the tunnel was blocked on Sir Ragnarok's orders twelve years ago.'

Dr Shivers nodded. 'Exactly Simone. Even though they got down there, they would not have been able to go very far.'

Sammy opened his mouth ready to explain about the passage when Dixie nudged him.

She pulled her green ponytail straight, linked arms with Sammy and Darius and marched them back towards the castle.

Sammy looked back. Commander Altair had disappeared. Professor Sanchez and Dr Shivers were standing by the tree stump. Dr Shivers kicked it shut with a resounding thud.

'Wow!' said Dixie as they got back to the castle. 'How about that?'

'What?' snapped Sammy. 'My Uncle is part of the Shape. So what?' he said stalking off.

'Wait Sammy!' shouted Dixie and Darius, running after him.

'That came out wrong,' said Dixie. 'I meant it's cool that you can tell Sir Ragnarok we found another member of the Shape.'

Darius put his hand on Sammy's shoulder. 'You are going to tell Sir Ragnarok, aren't you?'

They reached the North tower door. Dixie pushed it open with her foot. It was almost pitch black. Lights had been turned out and there was only one candle flickering in the far corner of the room.

In an armchair next to the candle Sir Ragnarok sat quietly, his hands clasped together. He stood up as they entered.

'I've been waiting for you,' Sir Ragnarok said quietly, beckoning for them to sit down. He closed a shining gold Directometer. 'You've had quite an adventure.'

'It's not how it looked,' started Darius, looking petrified.

'Isn't it?' asked Sir Ragnarok, raising an eyebrow. 'You missed the fireworks I laid on especially for your entertainment. You follow underground passages out of the school grounds without permission and without a teacher. I'm most disappointed in the three of you. You especially Sammy. It may not have been your idea but I thought more of you.'

Sir Ragnarok turned to Dixie. 'You should know better too Dixie. Your brothers have turned you into a tomboy. Imagine how your mother would feel if she lost her only daughter.'

'It wasn't like that,' said Darius. 'It was my idea.'

Sir Ragnarok waved his hand. 'I know it was not!' he thundered.

'My Mum wouldn't care,' said Dixie. 'She would rather have Milly or Mary-Beth as a daughter.'

'Lies!' shouted Sir Ragnarok, his eyes blazing. 'Your mother would be heartbroken. First your father, then her son's girlfriend. Losing you would be more than she could take. As I said, I am disappointed in all three of you. Outside of Dragamas you are easy targets for the Shape. I sealed that particular passage for a very good reason.'

Sammy opened his mouth.

Sir Ragnarok raised his hand again. 'No more excuses. I have more important things to worry about now that I know you are back safely.

'Like the Shape?' asked Sammy.

'Yes Sammy. Like the Shape. I may as well tell you now as at a special assembly tomorrow. There is no good news I'm afraid.'

Sammy, Dixie and Darius stared at Sir Ragnarok.

'All of the fifth year dragons are dead,' said Sir Ragnarok quietly and somberly. 'Professor Preference has told us he is the "P" in the Shape and I have sent him under Captain Duke Stronghammer's guard to the Snorgcadell where he will perish in the cells.'

'It's not true!' shouted Darius. 'Sammy's uncle did it.'

'Food poison,' added Dixie. 'We saw it down the tunnel.'

Sir Ragnarok looked keenly at them. Sammy found himself thinking about the Shape, depicting them as giant sausage rolls flaking pastry as they chased him down the tunnel.

'Over excitement,' concluded Sir Ragnarok after a minute of staring. 'Finding things you are not ready to discover can do that to a young mind. Rest and I will explain more in the morning.'

Sir Ragnarok pulled his shawl close to his neck and left the room.

'You didn't tell him,' shouted Dixie. 'You were there. Why didn't you back us up?'

Sammy shrugged. 'I have to be sure,' he said, taking a note out of his pocket. 'I'm staying there at Christmas. Look, it came this morning.'

Dixie snatched the cream paper. 'So you're staying at his house?'

Sammy nodded. 'I'll be able to find out for sure.'

'Great,' laughed Darius. 'If all the dragons aren't already dead.'

'I don't think they will be,' said Sammy. 'They would have killed the fifth year dragons to prevent any of the fifth years from becoming Dragon Knights when they left school.'

Dixie looked at Sammy. 'Yeah and they caught Professor Preverence. It's safe now,' she snapped sarcastically.

'I'm not sure,' said Darius. 'I think it's a cover. Maybe Professor Preverence was framed.'

Sammy shook his head. 'Even if it is a cover, we can wait until Christmas. You can stay with me Darius.'

'Yeah,' added Dixie. 'My mum can drop me over from our house. We'll go into that room from inside your uncle's house.'

'If it was his house,' reminded Sammy. 'Now we're back, I'm not a hundred percent sure.'

Dixie yawned. 'It's nearly one am.'

'No wonder everyone's gone to bed.'

'Come on then,' said Darius. 'See you tomorrow Dixie.'

Dixie nodded. 'Goodnight.'

Sammy blew out the candle and followed Darius up to the tower room. Gavin, Toby and Jock were fast asleep. Without bothering to change, Sammy climbed into bed and fell asleep almost at once.

CHAPTER 19

SAMMY'S BIRTHDAY

Three weeks later, Sammy, Dixie and Darius were walking back from a freezing cold sports lesson where Mr Cross and Mr Ockay had asked them to fly as high as they could for the whole lesson. Mr Cross had spent the entire lesson firing sparks at the balls to keep them high in play.

Mr Cross had taken two stars from any student dropping to less than ten feet high. He hadn't blown his whistle until the sky had turned almost black with rain clouds and a flash of lightning had knocked Milly off her dragon.

It was cold inside as well, even though Tom Sweep the caretaker had promised every student and teacher in sight that the radiators were on at full power. Each time he said it, Sammy felt a pang of guilt. Everyone knew it was because the fifth year dragons were dead and the fourth year dragons weren't allowed to do more than two hour shifts on the heating system at a time.

Sir Ragnarok had also insisted on throwing out all their supplies of dragon food and had arranged for fresh food to be brought down from the Land of the Pharaohs which was still overhead.

It caused more upset when the food brought from the Land of the Pharaohs turned out to be camel fodder and caused severe cases of indigestion amongst the second year dragons who weren't used to the rich food.

As Dragon Minders, Sammy and Dixie had their work cut out trying to mop up dragon dung as regurgitated soggy pellets, colourful shades of sickness and diarrhoea sprung from both ends of their dragons.

Dixie caused such a fuss when Kiridor fell ill that Sammy had the feeling that Sir Ragnarok thought that all of the dragons at Dragamas were dying.

Coupled with individual ceremonies for the fifth years to grieve for their losses, Sammy found that he had completely forgotten that it was his twelfth birthday the following day.

He shivered in the passage as they half walked, half ran to their Gemology lesson. Dr Shivers's message about being one-one and then one-two sounded very much like a football score where one team lost. A Dragonball score, he corrected himself.

Mrs Hubar was sitting at her desk when they got there. There were several empty seats from other Dragon Minders and from students who had fallen ill after eating some of the Land of the Pharaohs camel pellets themselves before feeding them to their dragons.

Mrs Hubar looked up when she saw Sammy, Dixie and Darius and frowned.

'It's half a class today as it is. Please could you try to be on time?' she scolded.

Darius giggled as he threw his bag on the chair next to Gavin. 'At least we turned up.'

Mrs Hubar clicked her tongue and looked rather annoyed. 'We are looking at the ruby today. Do you have your staffs?'

They nodded and took out their red and black tipped wooden staffs.

Mrs Hubar circled the room, pausing uncomfortably at Sammy's table. 'My that's an old twig.'

Sammy didn't like the way she said "old twig" to him.

'I suppose,' he said coolly.

'Did you take it from the trees?'

'I did,' interrupted Gavin. 'My staff is pure oak. My dad said so.'

Mrs Hubar shot Gavin a dirty look and focused on Sammy.

Sammy shook his head. 'It was on the ground already. It was strange. I felt like it wanted me to pick it up.'

Mrs Hubar's eyes widened and Sammy almost held out his hands waiting to catch them. He could see the headline "Dragamas student catches teacher's eyeballs."

To his disappointment, Mrs Hubar closed her eyes.

'A fallen branch you say. One not taken from the tree.'

'It would have been on a tree at some point,' laughed Gavin.

'It was like it called me,' said Sammy and he wished he hadn't said it as Mrs Hubar snapped her eyes open suddenly.

'Then perhaps it is the one,' she whispered a look of horror in her eyes. 'The one who holds a fallen branch controls all nature.'

'Yeah right,' said Gavin. 'I bet someone else has a fallen branch as their staff as well.'

Mrs Hubar shook herself and let go of Sammy's staff.

Sammy picked it up, the staff seemed to be vibrating ever so slightly. He ran his hand from the onyx and ruby gemstones down to the blunt point, glad to see that it stopped shaking. He was annoyed to find himself quivering as well.

Mrs Hubar stayed away from the North table for the rest of the lesson. She even asked Amos to pass her handwritten notes to the four North students. Behind Mrs Hubar's back Amos crushed the paper into a ball and threw it on to the table so hard it bounced on to the floor.

Mrs Hubar took three stars from North when Gavin lobbed his copy of the notes over to the East house table, where it hit Amos on the end of his nose.

Amos looked furious and tore the paper into hundreds of pieces and scattered them all over the floor. Gavin snatched another copy of the notes and started to screw it into a ball ready to launch another missile.

Just as he was about to throw it, the end of lesson bell rang and the students packed their bags, scraped their chairs back and ran out of the classroom. Mrs Hubar scuttled into the mine. Sammy knew she would be changing for tea.

Dragamas teachers usually changed into casual clothes before eating. Students could choose whether to stay in uniform or not.

Knowing they were having Spaghetti Bolognese, which tended to be messy, Sammy went back to the North tower to change out of his school uniform white shirt and black trousers.

As he reached his tower room, Sammy noticed that there was an oil slick spun like a spider's web across the door blocking him from entering. Sammy leaned closer his nose almost touching the pool.

He reached out with his right hand. The oil was cold and clammy but it didn't stick to his hand when he pulled back.

Sammy pulled his staff from his pocket and assembled it with the ruby and onyx gemstones at the top.

He raised his staff and tapped the oil slick, focusing hard, wishing that he could control the oil and see what was inside the tower room.

Sammy closed his eyes. He heard a whooshing sound like the sea in his ears and jerked as he was thrown backwards into the stairwell wall.

When he opened his eyes all he could see was vibrant green grass stretching for miles in all directions. The tower room was completely gone.

Sammy walked forward, reaching out with both hands stretched in front of him. The air was sweet smelling and fresh in his face. He could smell the grass and see several sheep dotted on the hilltop.

On the horizon, Sammy could make out a figure, the shape of a man. Forgetting he was meant to be walking through dormitory door into the stone walled tower room, Sammy walked forward across the green grass towards the figure.

As he drew nearer, he recognised the shape. It wasn't a man. It was, in fact, the Stone Cross from his vision in the Great Pyramid.

Sammy walked towards it. The Stone Cross towered above his head. He could make out a tall pillar with the cross, like an "X", encircled in the stone wheel at the top. He could see the blue green draconite gems glistening at the top and for a split second he found himself thinking how pretty they were and how nice the cross would look when the circle of gems was complete.

As quickly as it had come the vision passed. Sammy felt his eyes spring open. He was in the tower room, standing on his chest of drawers, his hand clutching at the window.

'Ready to join me?'

Sammy thought the voice came from inside his head but as he turned around he saw Dr Shivers behind him, holding out his hand.

Sammy froze. He didn't know if he felt more sickened by his thought, his own thought, that draconite was pretty, or that he had been about to jump to his death from the fourth storey window.

'I've been calling you for nearly five minutes,' said Dr Shivers a smile on his thin lips.

Sammy climbed down from the chest of drawers.

'Draconite, the cross, I...' he paused seeing Dr Shivers's reaction. 'I'm sorry,' he stuttered. 'It won't happen again.'

'Good,' Dr Shivers smiled. 'I let you off at Bonfire Night and I will do so here. Next time, Sir Ragnarok will hear of it. You are after all one-two tomorrow aren't you.'

Sammy nodded. 'Good thing you were here.'

Dr Shivers smiled again. 'I was merely on a routine inspection to make sure your room is tidy. I've checked the first year's room is tidy as well. Professor Burlay lets anything go.'

'Ok,' said Sammy.

'So,' said Dr Shivers, 'no more jumping'

Sammy waited for Dr Shivers to leave before changing into a pair of navy jeans and a t-shirt.

Downstairs in the Main Hall, Dixie had saved Sammy a place as usual.

'What took you so long?' she grumbled.

'Uh, nothing,' said Sammy, thinking that the last thing he wanted to do was tell the second year North table about his adventure in the tower room.

Milly, Holly and Helana would have spent the evening giggling. Darius would have suggested a potion from his parents and Dixie would have been annoyed he hadn't called her into his tower room to share the adventure. All in all, he decided it would be better to keep quiet.

'Pass the salt Sammy,' Gavin woke Sammy from his thoughts.

Sammy picked up one of the dragon shaped containers.

'That's the pepper dopey'

Sammy checked, Gavin was right, he had handed over the large black pepper pot in the shape of a dragon's tail. He passed the salt, which was in the shape of a dragon's head.

'Cheers,' said Gavin, his mouth full of chips.

The next thing Sammy knew was a pair of cold hands on his shoulders. He flinched.

'Didn't make you jump, did I?'

Sammy turned round. Dr Shivers was behind him.

'Sir Ragnarok has seen fit to take twelve stars from you, Miss Deane and Mr Murphy for your escapades on November the fifth.'

Sammy's jaw dropped. 'You said Sir Ragnarok didn't need to know.'

'Yeah,' added Darius. 'That's not fair.'

Dr Shivers held up his staff. 'It is the way it is.' He frowned at the pepper pot. 'The dragon's tail,' he murmured walking back to the teachers' table.

'That's so unfair,' Sammy burst out when Dr Shivers was out of earshot. 'We'll have to do loads to get back those stars.'

'Thirty-four,' said Gavin. 'That's quite a lot.'

'Thirty-six,' corrected Dixie, 'between three of us. You got twenty-three stars deducted all by yourself on the first day of term.'

'Thirty-six stars,' echoed Sammy, deep in thought.

Gavin shook his head. 'You've lost it. You should be at Mrs Grock's like Toby and Jock.'

Sammy grinned. 'I know better than to eat poisoned food.'

Gavin suddenly bent over choking, his cheeks flushing bright pink. He put his hands to his throat.

'Gavin?'

'Are you ok?'

Gavin got pinker and pinker.

'Dr Shivers, come over!' shrieked Milly.

Dr Shivers appeared, his grey suit swishing as he pushed roughly between Sammy and Darius. Professor Burlay hustled over to the North table.

'Is everything all right?' asked Dr Shivers.

'No,' shrieked Milly. 'It's Gavin, he's choking.'

Dr Shivers leaned over and pulled Gavin's hands away from his throat.

'Another game Gavin?'

With a roar of laughter Gavin nodded. 'I got you. I got all of you.' He laughed, 'poisoned food, ha!'

Dr Shivers frowned. 'Thirteen stars Gavin.'

Sammy laughed despite himself.

Gavin shook his fist. 'It's not fair.'

'Going for minus points are we?' asked Professor Burlay. 'I hope you're not undoing the good work of my first years.'

Dr Shivers scowled. 'A troublesome class you have sent me John. The worst I've ever seen.' Dr Shivers picked up the dragon salt and pepper pots and clanged them together.

Professor Burlay smiled at Sammy. 'More adventures of the Dragon Knights,' he asked.

Sammy and Dixie nodded enthusiastically.

'Just be careful,' said Professor Burlay quietly. 'The mere mention of the Shape puts fear into the hearts of most men and women,' he added. 'Leave things to Sir Ragnarok, he will take care of it all,' Professor Burlay concluded and disappeared in a puff of silver smoke.

'I hate that,' stormed Dixie. 'If it hadn't been for Sammy, Dragamas would be closed.'

'He'd be out of a job,' Gavin laughed. 'No more school.'

'No more dragons either,' said Sammy somberly. 'Shall we go and check on them?'

'Ok,' said Dixie brightly. 'Then you've got to go back to your tower room with your eyes shut.'

'Why?'

'Surprise,' said Gavin, rolling his eyes. 'Might be something to do with tomorrow.'

'My birthday?'

'Shh,' said Dixie. 'You'll give it away!'

Feeling somewhat like a sheep, Sammy followed Dixie down to the Dragon Chambers. Kyrillan was waiting for him by the steps. Dixie whistled for Kiridor who bounded over and greeted her so vigorously that he knocked her over backwards.

Laughing, Sammy helped Dixie to her feet. 'Come on,' he said, 'what's my surprise?'

Dixie shook her head. 'I don't know!' she said and giggled.

'Liar,' said Sammy dusting some specks of hay off of Kyrillan's spiky neck.

'It's empty in here, isn't it?'

'Yeah,' agreed Sammy. 'I still can't believe forty dragons are dead.'

'Sir Ragnarok's speech at the assembly was good though,' said Dixie. 'All that stuff about looking out for each other.'

'Uniting to defeat the Shape,' added Sammy. 'I reckon by the end of the year we'll have found another person who's in the Shape.'

'Maybe Eliza Elungwen has a twin sister?'

'Sarah Shelby?' said Sammy picking the first name out of his head. 'If the names are all letters in the word Shape.'

'Then it could be someone like Steven Sturbridge, Sadie Storm, Simone Sanchez,' said Dixie thoughtfully. 'Hey, you don't reckon...'

There was a thud. Dixie fell to the floor.

'Nobody says my Mother is in the Shape,' shouted Simon Sanchez, holding the remains of a sack of dragon food he had burst open by hitting Dixie on her head. Grain scattered on the floor and Kyrillan started snuffling it with his long scaled nose.

'Kyrillan, no!' shouted Dixie. 'It's poisoned!'

'It is not!' shouted Simon. 'I have just fed my dragon and two others.'

Sammy kicked the grain away from Kyrillan. He held out his hand to help Dixie get back on her feet.

'Come on, let's go.'

Leaving Simon in a rage, they ran back up the staircase slamming the radiator closed behind them.

As instructed, Sammy held his hands over his eyes as he let Dixie guide him up into the boys' tower. From the "shh" and bumping, Sammy guessed Serberon, Mikhael and Jason were in on the surprise.

By the time they had climbed four flights of stairs Sammy had the impression that the entire North house was giggling and whispering behind him.

He thought he recognised the voice of the blonde haired girl he had bumped into on the first day of term. He remembered she had a high pitched laugh, like the tinkling of a waiter's bell.

'You're here,' whispered Dixie.

Unaware he had been holding his breath, Sammy opened his eyes and gulped.

Surrounding his bed were all his friends. Gavin, Milly, Darius, Toby with his throat in a neck brace (Mrs Grock's protection against food poisoning after he had eaten some of the camel food), Jock with his arm around the blonde haired girl with the tinkling laugh.

There were presents stacked high in rickety towers on a small table someone had brought into the tower room. Presents with blue paper and gold bows, others wrapped in coloured tissue paper and a small present wrapped in pink paper, which could only be from Milly. Sammy hoped it wasn't another set of Dragon Dice. He must have the whole set by now.

But what really got his attention was the way his duvet was suspended higher than normal and seemed to be rising and falling almost like breathing. As if there was something underneath.

A puff of white wisping smoke peeked around the pillows.

'Kyrillan?' said Sammy in surprise. 'How did you get him here? I just saw him a minute ago.'

Everyone laughed.

Serberon grinned and tapped his nose. He pulled off the green covers revealing Kyrillan's blue-green scaly head with his jet black watchful eyes.

'Special treat,' grinned Serberon. 'You have no idea how tricky this was.'

Sammy ran forward. 'Kyrillan,' he shouted and locked his arms around his dragon's neck.

'Yeah,' added Jason. 'Serberon got Dr Shivers out of the way by telling him to find Professor Burlay at Mrs Grock's.'

Sammy looked out of the window. Dr Shivers had Professor Burlay by the scruff of his neck, pushing him back towards the castle. Mrs Grock, wearing her usual flamboyant purple patchwork dress and spotted apron was standing at the door of her house Sammy had nicknamed the "Gingerbread House", shaking her fist.

'You told on her.'

'So,' said Serberon. 'Not everyone's relationship works out.'

Sammy stared. 'You knew they'd be there?'

'No,' said Serberon, 'not like that...honest. I thought it was the most likely place.'

Sammy frowned.

'Honest Sammy. If you think it's got anything to do with Mary-Beth...'

Aware that there were nearly thirty people bunched into the small tower room, Serberon stopped.

'Well it hasn't,' he snapped. 'Anyway Sammy, open this present first, it's from me, Mikhael and Jason.'

'Ok.'

Sammy pulled the wrapper of the parcel with the blue and gold paper. It was a leather and metal mass of chains.

'Wow! A harness for Kyrillan,' shrieked Dixie. 'That's so cool. I wanted one of them for ages!'

'Handmade,' said Mikhael. 'In Armoury. You get to do this sort of thing next year.'

'Yeah,' Serberon grinned. 'Commander Altair's lessons get more exciting as you go up the school.'

'Did you hear the rumour,' came a pipsqueak from one of the first year boys that Sammy recognised as Herbert Smythers, the first year that Gavin was supposed to be mentoring.

'Yeah, shut it,' sneered Gavin. 'What would you know?'

'Lots actually,' Herbert piped up.

'Let him speak,' said Serberon kindly.

'I heard Mr Altair.'

'Commander Altair,' corrected Gavin. 'See, what does Herbie know. He can't even get the name right.'

'Shh,' said everyone.

'He said he's picked a student with the makings of a Dragon Knight from last years first years.'

'Yeah that was Sammy,' said Gavin. 'Everyone knows that.'

Sammy felt himself blush. He twisted the harness from hand to hand aware that everyone was watching him.

'No,' squeaked Herbert going equally as pink. 'He said it was someone who least expected it.'

'Like Milly?' said Gavin making everyone except Herbert laugh.

Herbert sniffed loudly.

Sensing the first year was going to cry, Sammy pulled another present from the pile. It was the pink parcel he had thought had come from Milly but turned out to be from Dixie.

'Pink paper?' Sammy raised an eyebrow at Dixie.

Dixie rolled her eyes. 'Milly insisted.'

'Did not,' said Milly. She giggled. 'Well maybe.'

It was a small parcel about the size of a pencil eraser.

'It's kind of a useful present,' Dixie shifted her weight from one foot to the other. 'Something you know about.'

Puzzled, Sammy picked at the paper with his fingernail until it opened. He pushed the paper down revealing a two-piece small black tube with a gold band around the middle. He pulled the ends apart and laughed as he realised the present was a rose pink lipstick with flecks of glitter. He grinned and pretended to put some on his lips.

'Just perfect, thanks,' said Sammy.

Since Dixie was right next to him looking expectantly for his reaction he gave her a two-second hug.

'Useful,' said Sammy grinning at her.

'Sammy's got a girlfriend,' chanted Gavin peering over Darius's shoulder for a closer look. 'Sammy's got a...lipstick,' shrieked Gavin. 'You freak!'

'Are you sure you didn't get the presents mixed up Dixie?' asked Serberon. 'It's Milly's birthday the week after next.'

Dixie threw her hands on her hips. 'It's not for wearing! Sammy knows what it's for.'

'Oooer,' giggled Gavin and Darius at the same time.

'You're not, you know...are you?' asked Toby cautiously.

Dixie giggled louder than Gavin and Darius put together. 'It's for our club, the Passage Spotters. You mark the tunnels so you can find your way back.'

Sammy felt everyone in the room take a quick sigh of relief.

'Why didn't you get him chalk?' asked Herbert. 'You could have pinched some from downstairs.'

This was completely the wrong thing to say to Dixie as she clenched her fists.

'Are you calling me a thief?'

That did it. Herbert Smythers burst into tears. Bawling loudly, he made for the stairs but Sammy held him back.

'Get yourself together,' said Sammy, handing Herbert a tissue. The first year wiped sniffed and wiped his eyes.

Considering it was nearly eleven o'clock, Sammy was already surprised not to see any of the teachers coming up to check on them. He didn't like to think what would happen if he got caught with Kyrillan in his tower room.

'Shh,' Sammy hissed at Herbert. 'Why don't you open the next present for me?'

He gave Herbert a squishy parcel that turned out to be a Nitromen shirt, a combined present from Gavin and Toby. The black and gold coloured shirt did the trick and Herbert went quiet.

'That's so cool,' said Dixie. 'If it doesn't fit, can I have it?'

Sammy put the t-shirt on. It was a perfect fit.

'Sorry, Dixie, it fits perfectly.' He grinned at Dixie. 'Thanks guys, it's great!'

Serberon, Mikhael and Jason cast their staffs on the table to create food, drink and a small radio that played some quiet music.

'More fourth year tricks,' grumbled Dixie tapping her own staff on the table. 'Crisps, sandwiches, lemonade…it's no good,' said Dixie sounding disappointed when nothing appeared.

'Never mind,' said Serberon tapping his own staff on the table. A mountain of sandwiches appeared on a silver plate. 'Crisp sandwiches,' he said, grinning at Dixie.

'And lemonade,' said Mikhael, slamming his own staff on the table.

Three bottles of green lemonade appeared.

'Green lemonade?'

Mikhael nodded. 'It's my favourite.'

'It's supposed to be Sammy's birthday,' said Dixie critically.

Mikhael showed his sister his watch. 'Ten minutes to go!'

Sammy checked his own watch, it was nearly four minutes past midnight.

'Pharaoh time,' grinned Mikhael, 'and I like limeade,' he smoothed back his green hair.

'Figures,' said Gavin, who got a frosty stare from Dixie that faded when she saw Sammy was still wearing his new Nitromen t-shirt.

'That t-shirt suits you.'

Gavin grinned. 'Yeah we got you an extra large t-shirt!'

'Liar,' said Toby. 'It's ok Sammy, it's not really,' he apologised.

'Nitron Dark wears extra large,' said Dixie, a dreamy look in her eyes.

'Don't know what you see in him,' said Milly, leaning in to inspect the contents of the sandwiches. 'He must be at least thirty.'

'Twenty-four,' said Dixie, 'and, ooh Sammy, it's his birthday today too!'

'Great,' said Sammy, hiding a grin in his sleeve as Mikhael blew an imaginary kiss behind Dixie's back.

'I don't like him like that!' said Dixie hotly. 'He's a good Dragonball and Firesticks player.'

'Yeah, we know,' Mikhael laughed at his sister.

'Oh Nitron,' chuckled Jason, his mouth full of green jelly he had conjured.

'Shut up,' said Sammy, quickly remembering Dr Shivers's words at the Land of the Pharaohs. He had missed two chances to stick up for Dixie and he wasn't going to let this one slip through his fingers.

'Ooh err,' cackled Jason, ducking as Dixie threw a punch at him.

'Dixie's got a boyfriend!' shouted Gavin, Dixie's got...'

Gavin stopped short.

Still laughing, Sammy spun round. Everyone in the room had frozen solid. Jason had thrown his ponytailed head back in a huge laugh. Herbert and Montegue Smythers were playing crisp stackers, their tongues outstretched with different shaped and flavoured crisps piled high. Dixie had both her hands on her hips, her mouth open indignantly. Not one person in the tower room, apart from himself, was moving.

Slowly, stepping cautiously around the table, Sammy waved his hand in front of Dixie's eyes.

She didn't stir.

He shook her shoulder and pulled a strand of green hair away from her eyes. He touched her arm. She was warm but motionless.

"Like being in a dark tunnel" Gavin had described it, "you can't see or hear anything."

Sammy tested the theory, calling, 'Dixie? Gavin? Serberon?'

No-one moved. No-one answered.

Sammy wished Jock was there. He knew Jock could control the ruby stone to bring everyone back to life. He reached for his staff, pausing as he heard heavy footsteps on the stairs.

Kyrillan blew a puff of smoke. Sammy shivered. He suspected more than house stars would be taken for having an eight foot dragon hidden in the tower bedroom.

CHAPTER 20

SAMMY'S VISION

Checking Dixie and the others were still frozen solid, Sammy fastened his metal harness present from Dixie's brothers around Kyrillan's neck. It fitted perfectly, the loops of chainmetal clinking as they settled into place.

Using his staff, Sammy sent a volley of three green sparks over to close the door. It worked and as the sparks exploded, the door swung back on its hinges with a bang. The footsteps got louder and Sammy was sure within seconds a teacher would appear.

Without thinking too hard, he flung open the window and mounted his dragon, swinging his leg over Kyrillan's back and holding on tightly with his knees.

As if on cue, Kyrillan spread his green-blue wings and took off, knocking the cake and green lemonade on to the floor.

Sammy checked behind him, the tower door was opening slowly. He closed his eyes, sure Kyrillan couldn't squeeze through the narrow window but knowing they had to try.

With a "hurrumph", Kyrillan surged towards the window, his wings beating hard against Sammy's legs.

'Come on Ky,' whispered Sammy, watching as the bowl of green jelly created by Jason and the plate of crisp sandwiches went flying into the air.

Sammy pulled on the chain harness, lining Kyrillan up with the window.

'Go!' Sammy shouted and he had the feeling like he was being squashed by an invisible clamp. He shut his eyes, bracing himself to smash against the wall. He heard the door swing open, knowing it would be a teacher who would punish both him and Kyrillan.

The tight feeling increased and Sammy felt the breath squeezed out of him. He gasped for air that never came. Had he been frozen in mid-flight with Kyrillan? "No," he told himself firmly. "There was no red lightning."

He opened his eyes. Behind him by some distance was the tower room, the window wide open, two silhouettes staring at him.

In front of him, Sammy gasped and had to hold on tightly as he saw that the Dragonball pitch had disappeared. He let go of the harness to rub his eyes.

In place of Mrs Grock's house and the Dragonball pitch was the grassy valley he had seen in a vision first in the Great Pyramid and then in his tower room.

He looked back into the darkness. The figures were still at the tower window, but the tower itself looked different, older somehow.

The cone roof was missing and it reminded Sammy of the oil painting of Karmandor Castle in the school corridor. What he was seeing was almost identical to the picture and he was suddenly scared he'd gone back in time.

He leaned forward. 'Less trees,' he whispered to Kyrillan, who blew a puff of grey smoke in reply.

A horrible thought flashed through his mind.

'Supposing we can't get back,' said Sammy, gripping his fingers tightly on Kyrillan's harness, a lump forming in his throat. 'What if I'm stuck in the past?'

He clenched his knees together around Kyrillan's girth and guided his dragon down towards the endless silvery green grass.

Kyrillan landed surefooted on all four feet tucking his wings in tightly to his body. Sammy threw his left leg over Kyrillan's scaly neck and jumped to the ground.

They had landed, Sammy was pretty sure, exactly where Mrs Grock's house should have been. 'Will be in the future,' Sammy corrected himself, wishing Dixie or Darius or both were there with him.

'Both,' he whispered, remembering he had left his staff behind. He waited ten seconds before deciding neither Dixie nor Darius were going to appear out of thin air.

'Shall we go on or go back?' he whispered, more for his own benefit. Kyrillan seemed to be leading the way, almost pulling Sammy, into the thicket of trees.

'Woah there Ky,' whispered Sammy. 'I'm not sure about this.' He wrestled with his dragon who obstinately refused to go back towards the castle.

'Kyrillan, stop!'

Kyrillan ignored the command and plodded on towards the trees. Sammy stopped to tie his shoelace. He didn't want to admit it, but he was scared. His hands were shaking as they pulled the black laces tight. He looked up. Kyrillan was foraging among the bushes. Sammy got to his feet.

'It's quiet isn't it Kyrillan,' he whispered looking around.

Kyrillan plodded towards him and Sammy's blood ran cold.

Behind Kyrillan were two long black shadows staring straight at him.

Sammy froze. Kyrillan had taken no notice and was snuffling in the long grass.

One of the shadowy figures raised its right hand and thrust towards him.

A volley of sparks flew through the air. Sammy threw himself to the ground. The sparks grazed over Kyrillan's head, over Sammy's head and crackled in mid air behind him.

There was a horrific blood curdling scream and three more figures came into view, each carrying a wooden staff. A tall girl with caramel-blonde hair, perhaps a few years older than Sammy, was linked arms with a man Sammy thought looked like a younger version of his father.

They were standing next to a man with caramel hair who looked exactly like his Uncle Peter from the jewellery store. The second man had reflected the sparks with a disc on his wrist. Sammy checked his wrist, the watches looked the same.

'Sister,' said the man who looked like Uncle Peter. 'Come on, we cannot let them get away.'

'Sir Ragnarok will catch them,' said the first man. 'Sir..uh..save the..dragons...' he looked bemused.

'Dragons,' the woman giggled, 'what do you mean?'

'I don't know,' the first man laughed. 'Come on, let's go back to the castle.'

'What castle?' asked the woman, still laughing. 'I think you've had a touch of the sun Charles.'

'Perhaps I have,' said the man. He reached for her hand, 'shall we?'

The woman smiled. 'Why yes,' she said, rubbing her eyes as if she had just woken up. 'What are these funny sticks?' she asked, throwing down a wooden stick she had been carrying.

The man called Charles did the same.

The second man looked angry and sent a volley of green sparks in all directions. Sammy could only just make out a few words. The other words were garbled and spoken in a language he didn't recognise.

It was only when one of the stray sparks bounced right through his leg that Sammy realised he couldn't be seen by either the figures in the shadow of the trees, nor his uncle who was still catching sparks in the dial of his watch whilst sending a volley of green and red sparks with his staff back towards the trees.

Feeling braver than he had ever felt, Sammy stood up, apparently invisible to everyone. He picked up the twig sticks, the staffs his future mother and father had dropped. They were branches from young trees. One had a leaf he recognised as oak sprouting up towards the crystal stones at the top.

Sammy counted five stones, black, red, yellow, blue and green, which told him his parents must have been at the school for five years and must be at least fifteen.

'One - Five,' whispered Sammy.

His uncle strode forward towards Sammy and Kyrillan. He walked straight through Kyrillan, as though the dragon wasn't there, and disappeared into the wood.

Curiosity eating through him, Sammy followed his uncle, one hand clenched tightly around Kyrillan's metal harness, the other grasping the two staffs. The shadowy figures, his nerves told him, were the Shape, or at least a past incarnation of them. He took comfort in the fact that at least for now, they were as oblivious to his and Kyrillan's presence as the sparks that hit him were.

Uncle Peter disappeared between two bushes into the clearing Sammy recognised. Sammy's heart skipped a beat. It was the same clearing from his first day where he had picked up his own staff and first created fire. He crept forward. His uncle was standing on top of the tree stump surrounded by four hooded figures wearing long dark cloaks.

'By the powers of East and Air,' said one of the figures on his uncle's left hand side.

There was a rush of wind, almost like a small tornado, that swept through the clearing nearly knocking Sammy off his feet.

'By the powers of North and Earth,' said the next hooded figure.

Thunder rolled overhead and a fork of bright white lightning crashed into the ground inches from the tree stump.

'By the powers of West and Water,' said a third figure, tapping his staff on the tree stump.

Water fell from the sky in great raindrops. They pounded like the sound of a drum as they dropped heavily on to the grass.

'By the powers of South and Fire,' whispered Sammy, pretending to tap an imaginary staff.

'By the powers of South and Fire,' said a thick gravelly voice and great flames erupted in an orange ring around the stump.

Sammy's uncle's eyes rolled and he fell backwards on to the ground.

'No!' shouted Sammy, running forward.

The hooded figures stopped, sniffing the air.

'Lok Ragnarok! Run!' shrieked one of the figures and one by one they disappeared in four clouds of shimmering smoke.

When the smoke cleared, Uncle Peter had vanished as well.

Sammy ran a full circle around the clearing, shouting, 'bring him back! Bring him back!'

Out of breath, he stopped as another man, a young Sir Ragnarok, entered the clearing.

'I have failed!' shouted Sir Ragnarok, throwing down a long stick. 'I have failed!'

The trees swayed in Sammy's vision and suddenly he felt sick and dizzy. He saw bright lights flickering. He let go of Kyrillan to shield his eyes. Above him he heard the crackle of sparks. Sammy closed his eyes tightly, blocking everything out.

When he opened his eyes, a much older Sir Lok Ragnarok was standing in front of him. It looked like he was in Sir Ragnarok's office. Kyrillan was nowhere in sight.

Sammy blinked and rubbed his eyes.

'Where am I?'

Sir Ragnarok closed his eyes. 'You are in my office,' he said patiently.

Sir Ragnarok's grey cat Lariston wove between Sammy's legs.

'I...' started Sammy, stopping as Sir Ragnarok waved his arm.

Lariston purred and leaped on to Sir Ragnarok's desk. Sir Ragnarok stroked his cat, ruffling the downy hair under Lariston's chin. The silence was unbearable.

Outside, Sammy could see a glimmer of stars in the sky above. It was still night he decided. His twelfth birthday. One-Two.

Sir Ragnarok frowned. 'Quite an adventure?' he said, pointing to one of his TV monitor screens.

There were more screens than Sammy had ever seen displayed in a TV shop window. He looked up to watch what Sir Ragnarok wanted him to see.

In fast-forward, Sammy saw himself opening the Nitromen shirt from Gavin and Toby. On a second monitor, he saw a shadowy figure climbing up the tower stairs. He saw himself mount Kyrillan and take off.

'Watch closely,' commanded Sir Ragnarok.

Sammy clenched his fists. He remembered mounting Kyrillan, taking off, the wind in his hair and the fresh cool night air outside.

The figure on the screen stopped, it fell back on to the bed, cake, crisps and green jelly flying up in the air.

'But Kyrillan and I made it outside,' said Sammy going up to the screen and poking himself.

Sir Ragnarok cocked an eyebrow at Sammy.

'It was like,' Sammy paused composing himself, 'like stepping through time.'

There was another long pause. Sir Ragnarok scratched his beard.

'Was it now?'

Sammy nodded, sure Sir Ragnarok would say something else.

Sir Ragnarok frowned and Sammy felt like his mind was being rummaged through and it hurt.

'So you saw things?' asked Sir Ragnarok. 'Things from the past?' He handed Sammy a bowl of coloured sweets.

Sammy nodded and took two of Sir Ragnarok's sweets. Five minutes later he had told Sir Ragnarok his entire adventure.

'And these sticks?' asked Sir Ragnarok after another long pause.

Sammy checked his pockets. In his right hand pocket, was soft soil. He pulled out a handful and lay it on Sir Ragnarok's desk.

'Earth?' said Sir Ragnarok quietly. 'Funny how things travel through time.'

'Is it a clue?' whispered Sammy. 'Is it why my parents forgot about dragons?'

Sir Ragnarok paused. 'I think this can wait for another day. Sometimes you need to digest things before the answers are clear. Things are not always as they seem.'

Sammy stamped his foot. 'I'm twelve now. I'm old enough to know things. Is my uncle in the Shape?' He bit his tongue wishing the reckless words could be unsaid.

Sir Ragnarok stood up. 'Things are not always as they seem,' he repeated. 'There are ghosts in many pasts that are stirring. Things are changing.' Sir Ragnarok's eye glazed over. 'I believe in you Sammy. With the right guidance you will achieve great things.'

'Fine,' snapped Sammy, taking this to be another long winded headmaster speech. 'I'll find out myself. Put wrongs to right.'

'Ahh,' said Sir Ragnarok, snapping out of his trance, 'but please be careful which wrongs you put right.'

Sir Ragnarok clicked his fingers and Lariston jumped down.

Sammy felt like a sheep herded by Lariston to the door. He stopped, making Lariston bump into his calf.

'Where's Kyrillan?'

Sir Ragnarok waved his hand at the monitors. On each screen the Dragon Chambers appeared. In a corner Kyrillan was sound asleep, a towel plastered across his scaly nose. A flicker of light came from a small fire in the chamber and Sammy saw Dixie crouched over straightening the towel and stroking Kyrillan's scaly cheek.

Sammy returned Sir Ragnarok's smile and whispering, 'thank you,' he turned around and started the long climb back down to the ground floor.

It was nearly one o'clock in the morning when Sammy crept up the North tower stairs. He could hear Jock snoring in the tower room. He pushed open the door.

Three worried faces looked up.

Darius breathed a sigh of relief. 'We thought you were Dr Shivers.'

'Yeah,' added Gavin, who Sammy noticed had gone very pale, 'he went ballistic.'

'Course you don't remember anything,' said Toby. 'Knocked yourself clean out trying to get through that window on Kyrillan.'

Gavin gave a half laugh. 'Helps if you open the window first.'

'But I did,' started Sammy, his words drying up as Darius shook his head, a finger pressed against his lips.

'I know,' mouthed Darius.

Sammy nodded, sure he could hear Darius project "we'll talk later" in his head.

'Did Dr Shivers unfreeze everyone?' asked Sammy, changing the subject.

'Yeah,' said Gavin, 'and then he went ballistic.'

'Started chucking your cake everywhere,' added Toby, 'then he had the cheek to accuse us of making a mess.'

Sammy laughed. 'I saw the mess. Kyrillan knocked some drink over.'

Toby frowned. 'We cleaned it up.'

'By hand,' said Gavin. 'Every last drop wasted.'

'We didn't lose any stars though,' said Darius brightly, 'of course we might have, if you hadn't knocked yourself out.'

'Yeah,' said Gavin, his blue eyes wide, 'he was really concerned. Don't know why.'

'He knew,' said Sammy out loud.

Gavin tapped his head whilst suppressing a yawn with his pillow. 'Sammy got hit on the head.'

'He's lost it,' agreed Toby. 'Night all.'

'Night,' said Sammy, catching Darius's wink, he drew the green velvet curtain between himself and Gavin, leaving space for himself and Darius to whisper to each other from the warmth of their beds.

'Your shirt's dirty,' started Darius. 'I saw you go. Dixie did too. She went mad when she saw you go without her.'

'I thought the ruby affected you too?'

Darius shook his head. 'Dixie said she's been practicing with Commander Altair. My parents taught me ages ago.'

'So you haven't been...'

Darius shook his head again. 'It caught me off guard twice but I saw Mary-Beth die and I saw you leave tonight.

'How can I be in two places at once?' whispered Sammy. 'Darius, how can I...'

Sammy looked over. Darius wouldn't be answering his question tonight. His eyelids were shut tightly, his mouth ever so slightly open.

'Twelve,' whispered Sammy to himself, his head spinning as he recollected the evenings' events. One-Two.

The following morning Sammy woke to a violent shaking on his right shoulder. He opened his eyes.

'Morning Dixie,' he mumbled.

'Happy Birthday!' Dixie shouted in his ear. 'Ooh, you're still wearing your Nitromen shirt.'

Sammy checked. Dixie was right, he was wearing the gold and black Nitromen shirt over his school shirt and his navy jeans.

'You should have seen Dr Shivers last night,' said Dixie, her green eyes wide open. 'He dragged you by the back of your shirt to Sir Ragnarok's office,' Dixie paused for breath.

'Thanks for looking after Kyrillan.'

Dixie nodded. 'That's ok. Dr Shivers said to take him down to the chambers. I would have anyway. You'd do the same, right?'

'Sure.'

'When everyone, you know, woke up from the effect of the ruby stone, he sent us to bed.'

'Really?' said Sammy, yawning and screwing up his eyes. 'I wish he hadn't come up. The party was great.'

When he opened his eyes, Dixie was frowning at him.

'What?' asked Sammy.

'Nothing,' said Dixie. 'Just I wish I could have come on your adventure too. The ruby doesn't affect me. I've been...'

'Practicing with Commander Altair.'

Dixie nodded, surprised. 'How did you know?'

Sammy pointed to Darius. 'Did you see me go?'

'Yeah. It was so weird. Like you just shimmered and split in two.'

'I what?'

'Like, um,' Dixie scratched her head. 'Kind of like if you were running and your shadow stayed behind.'

'My shadow?'

'Mm,' said Dixie going pink, 'or you stayed behind and your shadow went on.'

Right,' said Sammy, privately thinking he'd never heard of something so stupid.

Be like that,' snapped Dixie. 'You find a better way of explaining it.'

Sammy grinned. 'I want to know why it happened.' He reached over and whispered everything he had seen into Dixie's ear.

Wow!' was all that Dixie could say. 'You reckon that's why your parents forgot about dragons.'

'I don't know,' said Sammy. 'But it looks like it was when they forgot about dragons.'

'We'll find out at Christmas,' said Dixie straightening her green ponytail. 'Has your uncle said it's ok for me and Darius to come over?'

'Yeah,' said Sammy, pointing to a letter on his chest of drawers. 'My parents said I have to wait until Christmas before I get my birthday presents.'

'That stinks,' said Dixie. 'Do you want to come down in a minute with me and Milly to check on Kyrillan?'

'Sure,' said Sammy. 'Thanks for looking after him.'

Dixie went pink again. 'Hurry up, I'll meet you down in the common room.'

'Give me five minutes,' said Sammy as he threw back the duvet.

CHAPTER 21

DESCALING

Three weeks later, Sammy was pleased that Kyrillan had only sustained minor bruising on his scaly nose. Several of the blue-green scales had turned crystal clear with yellow and red blood vessels showing through. Just three doses of Mrs Grock's healing potion had restored the shimmery scales to their normal pearlescent blue-green.

In the Dragon Chambers, it was Sammy and Dixie's turn to replace the dragon bedding. As well as feeding the dragons, one of their duties as Dragon Minders was to lift huge bales of dirty and wet hay between the chambers with three pronged steel pitchforks. They would then replace the dirty hay with fresh hay so the dragons always had clean bedding. It was a dirty and smelly task but it made sure the dragons were comfy and warm at night.

Simon Sanchez was in the corner feeding his black dragon a large slab of meat dripping with thick red blood.

'Kyrillan looks good,' said Simon turning around. 'Now his nose is better.'

Thanks,' said Sammy putting down his pitchfork and picking up a sack of food. He reached into the sack and scooped out some boiled oats, pouring them into a bathtub sized container for the North dragons.

There was still a strong smell of death in the air and so many empty caverns where the fifth year dragons used to live before they were taken and killed. For those who had wanted, Sir Ragnarok had given the fifth years a new dragon egg to hatch.

When the four bathtubs were filled with meat and boiled oats Sammy and Dixie led the ten North dragons to Dragon Studies, their last lesson before the end of term, Sammy paused and stared into Kyrillan's coal black eyes.

'You're not going to die,' he whispered.

In Dr Shivers's lesson, Sammy sat open mouthed as Dr Shivers demonstrated descaling using Mary-Beth's dragon, Goldie.

'Press here,' said Dr Shivers brightly, poking a pen shaped instrument behind Goldie's ears, 'and this is what we call the Domino Effect.'

The class watched open mouthed as all at once, crusty scales peeled off Goldie's neck and fell on to the swirl patterned rug Dr Shivers had placed under her four clawed paws at the start of the lesson. The scales fell tinkling as they clashed together in a pile on the rug.

Underneath the crusty scales, Sammy was pleased to see a new coat of pale gold scales already growing. Dr Shivers assured them they were smooth to the touch and invited Samantha Trowt to touch Goldie's back.

'These are just like the scales your dragons had in their first six months,' said Dr Shivers beaming at them.

'We're still on our first scales,' shouted Gavin sitting in the back row sandwiched between Sammy and Toby.

On Sammy's right, Dixie had her hand raised.

'Yes Dixie?' said Dr Shivers who seemed annoyed by the interruption.

'Are dragons who still have their first scales able to go through solid objects?' she asked innocently. 'Like walls?'

Dr Shivers stared hard, first at Dixie, then at Sammy. 'Like tower walls at birthday parties?' he asked cryptically his face giving nothing away.

Mouth set and eyes locked, Dixie nodded. 'Like Sammy did,' she said flatly ignoring Gavin as he let out a loud laugh.

Dr Shivers rubbed his chin. 'Perhaps you could demonstrate?'

'Fine,' said Sammy and Dixie together, grinning at each other as they shared a split second glance.

Dr Shivers outstretched his hand. 'Mrs Grock is winding patients down for Christmas. I'm not sure she'll be pleased to see you.'

'Pah,' snorted Dixie 'You watch.'

'Very well, try the wall here,' said Dr Shivers. 'The worst that will happen is that you'll interrupt an end of term mock exam the fifth years are sitting in the classroom next door.'

Feeling less confident by the second, Sammy climbed up on to Kyrillan. He held on to the scaly spikes on the back of his dragon's neck.

'Ok, Kyrillan, let's show them,' he whispered.

Dr Shivers folded his arms. 'When you're ready.'

Sammy pulled his arms back, gripped his knees tightly around Kyrillan's girth and with a beating of wings Kyrillan took off, circling the high ceiling with Dixie on Kiridor close behind.

'Two true on two blue,' murmured Dr Shivers, 'interesting.'

Sammy guided Kyrillan towards the classroom wall behind Dr Shivers, ready to try to pass through it. In a split second he hoped he would be knocked out again if they didn't make it. It would be more embarrassing to fail fully conscious in front of the whole class. He braced himself as the stone wall loomed close.

But at the last possible second, Kyrillan banked away and surged towards the tiny glassless windows. Sammy felt a pull behind him and without turning around, he knew that Kyrillan had circled his tail loosely around Kiridor's neck to guide him and Dixie to the other wall.

Feeling the same suction on his body that he had felt before, Sammy choked as the air squeezed out of his lungs. He shut his eyes in the split second they surged out into the open. Kyrillan swung his tail free and Kiridor flew forward so the two blue-green dragons were side by side.

'We made it!' shrieked Dixie 'We're through!'

Sammy opened his eyes. He could see the first years playing catch with Mr Cross on the Dragonball pitch. Smoke spiraled from Mrs. Grock's chimney. Snow lay on the ground.

'We're here,' he shouted to Dixie who had drifted away.

'Yeah,' she shouted back.

'No, Sammy paused, the cold air biting him. 'We're here, now, in the present, not in the past.'

Dixie wobbled on Kiridor. 'So?'

'There was no shimmery stuff. We just flew through the window.'

'So, what were you expecting?' Dixie flew closer. 'Oh...'

Behind them, the end of lesson bell rang out and Dr Shivers appeared at the window.

'See me after lunch please Sammy and you too Dixie. It's important to descale your dragons so you'll have to find a new way to do that trick.'

'No!' shouted Dixie. 'I don't want to.'

'If you don't take care of your dragons, I'm sure Sir Ragnarok will assign him to a fifth year who will.' Dr Shivers scowled and disappeared from the window.

'Sammy, no!' Dixie shouted across. 'He's trying to take away our dragons' powers.'

'There must be a reason,' shouted Sammy. 'Let's take Kyrillan and Kiridor down to the chambers. We can ask Captain Stronghammer.'

'What?'

'Ask Captain Stronghammer,' Sammy cupped his hands and shouted, pointing down towards the Dragon Chambers.

Dixie nodded, pulling Kiridor down towards the ground.

Sammy guided Kyrillan over to the bushes that hid the entrance to the chambers. Kyrillan landed gracefully, his large paws outstretched as they touched the ground. Sammy swung his leg over his dragon's back and jumped down.

They were met in the stone entrance by Captain Firebreath.

'Just the two of yer is it?' growled flame haired Captain Firebreath, any more an' I'll get Dukey to give me a hand.'

'Yeah, just us,' said Sammy. 'The others will bring the rest of the dragons down in a minute.'

'Captain Firebreath,' Dixie started hesitantly.

'That's my name,' said the dwarf.

'Is it true that dragons can fly through walls before they are descaled?'

Captain Firebreath threw back his head and laughed, spluttering into his ginger beard. 'Cobblers!' scoffed Captain Firebreath. 'Who's been filling yer head with that rubbish?'

'Dr Shivers,' said Sammy and Dixie together.

'We just flew through the tiny classroom window to get here.' said Dixie.

'Dr Shivers said once our dragons have been descaled we'll have to find another way to do it,' added Sammy.

'I see,' said Captain Firebreath taking a swig from his hip flask. 'Then yer'll be wanting to know about Karmandor then.'

'King Serberon's dragon?' exclaimed Sammy. 'But...'

'I'll tell yer what,' growled Captain Firebreath, 'yer find out who killed the dragons down here and I'll tell yer where yer'll find yer answers.'

'That's easy,' said Dixie. 'It was..'

'Professor Preverence said it was him,' finished Sammy, poking his finger into Dixie's back. 'He got the sack.'

Captain Firebreath sighed. 'I figured yer'd say that.'

'So it wasn't him?' asked Dixie, avoiding Sammy's furious stare.

'Nay so,' Captain Firebreath frowned. 'They say it was him, but he was here with me all along. I liked him, always brought me something, yer know, he was a sorta father figure to me after me dad got killed in the war.

'My dad might as well be dead too,' said Dixie making Sammy uncomfortable. 'He left on my seventh birthday, four and a half years ago.'

'Yer dad is still alive,' said Captain Firebreath coming up close. 'Last I heard, he was up country one of the last to get away but his dragon flew into an electric pylon.'

Sammy put his arm around Dixie.

'When's he coming back?' demanded Dixie, her eyes filling with tears.

'I bin speaking to Megan Burlay, yer know Molly and John's mother, Megan, yeah?'

Dixie nodded. 'She runs the ice cream caravan at the Floating Circus.'

'Reckons her old man will be home soon.'

'She said that last year,' snapped Dixie. 'Doesn't anyone know anything else?'

'Anything would be good,' added Sammy helpfully.

Captain Firebreath shook his head. 'Only Sir Ragnarok would know more. Rumour is he's going there over Christmas.'

'Up country?' asked Sammy.

'Nay so,' Captain Firebreath laughed. 'Aye they have dragons all over Britain, all over the world I suppose, but Sir Ragnarok is fighting the Shape before he gets into the rest of the world's problems. He's only going to the Floating Circus.'

'Oh,' said Sammy. 'So Dixie's dad is fighting the Shape too?'

'Aye and many of our fathers are fighting them. One by one the Shape are killing our dragons and one by one we are fighting the Shape.'

'Oh,' said Sammy feeling more foolish. He wished he knew more about dragons, making a mental note to read up on King Serberon and Karmandor over Christmas.'

'I'll help,' grinned Dixie pulling at Kiridor's scales. A couple fell away in her hand. 'So, how do we make sure our dragons can fly through walls?' she asked, flashing an innocent smile at Captain Firebreath.

Preoccupied with stopping Kyrillan from helping himself to a piece of hay caught in his hairy beard, Captain Firebreath didn't answer.

'We'll find out,' said Dixie stamping her foot defiantly. 'We'll find out everything.'

As Sammy nodded, he noticed a blur of black smoke stampeding on the ground towards them. He ducked as

Simon Sanchez with Amos riding pillion stormed in beside them. Following Simon and Amos were thirty seven slippery and slimy dragons, the second years' dragons coming in to rest after their descaling.

'Dr Shivers wants you to see you both after lunch,' said Amos grinning at Sammy and Dixie. 'You're in big trouble.'

'He didn't think it would work,' added Simon. 'He thought you would fall, boom!' Simon clapped his hands together.

'Well we didn't,' snapped Dixie. 'Come on Sammy, let's go.'

'Shouldn't we help get the dragons inside?'

'Not to worry Sammy, I'll see to them meself,' said Captain Firebreath. 'Go on, the lot of you, skedaddle.'

'Pah,' said Simon. 'Let's hope he gets all the dragons inside.'

Sammy stayed a few paces behind, making sure the North dragons were safely inside. He couldn't believe everything he'd just heard. The biggest problem would be talking about dragons with his uncle at Christmas without his parents thinking he'd gone mad.

At lunch, they found Sir Ragnarok had delivered the first of a series of special Christmas dinners he had promised to provide the school. Each of the tables was individually decorated with a crisp white Christmas tablecloth with brightly coloured patterns of reindeer, holly, angels and snowmen, a different design for each house.

Artificial snow was falling from the ceiling and mysteriously not landing in any of the food. Baubles and crackers filled the spaces between the plates and every few seconds there was a loud explosion as the crackers were pulled, followed by shouts of excitement as small gifts, hats and jokes fell out and then squabbles erupting over who had won the prize.

Sammy tucked into his roast turkey and seven vegetables with a hearty appetite. He pulled his cracker with Jock and lost the prize, which turned out to be a small sachet of Professor Sanchez's healing potion.

Sammy wasn't disappointed though as he easily won Gavin's cracker prize, a green plastic half-moon shaped Angel whistle. As Gavin and Toby already had an Angel whistle that would call their own dragons, Gavin had been more than happy to let Sammy keep the prize.

After lunch, Sammy went up to the East wing with Dixie and knocked firmly on Dr Shivers's door.

'Good afternoon Sammy and Dixie. Thank you for coming.'

'Do we really have to descale our dragons?' asked Dixie. 'I don't want to do it.'

Sammy was sure Dixie blinked twice at Dr Shivers, who appeared not to notice.

'Absolutely. It is a vital part of your dragon's transition from child to adulthood.'

'But I want Kiridor to stay the same.'

'Me too,' said Sammy, feeling he should say something.

'I understand,' said Dr Shivers kindly. 'But you'll agree that Sir Ragnarok can't have students squeezing through windows and disappearing through walls at will.'

'I'm sure he doesn't mind,' said Dixie.

'I'm sure he does,' said Dr Shivers resolutely.

'Can Sir Ragnarok do it?' asked Sammy. 'You know, go through walls on his dragon?

'What makes you think he has a dragon?' asked Dr Shivers with a hint of sarcasm. 'Perhaps he doesn't need a dragon.'

'But surely?' said Sammy pondering this, thinking of all he knew about Sir Ragnarok, all the times he had been in his office, he had never heard Sir Ragnarok mention anything but his students dragons.

'He has a cat,' said Dr Shivers.

'Lariston,' said Sammy.

'Indeed,' said Dr Shivers.

'Lariston?' asked Dixie.

'Yeah,' said Sammy, 'a smoke grey cat with yellow eyes.'

'My uncle's called Lariston,' said Dixie thoughtfully, 'named after...'

'King Lariston?' asked Dr Shivers sarcastically. 'Like your brother named after King Serberon. Perhaps you are suggesting your whole family is named after some royalty or another. Now, may we get back to the topic in hand, with your royal permission,' he laughed coldly.

Dr Shivers led Sammy and Dixie down the winding corridors to the Dragon Chambers. He unbuttoned his grey suit jacket to reveal a silver pin fastened to his shirt pocket. He removed the pin and pressed it against the fourth stone high on the castle wall, tucked neatly behind the bush.

Nothing happened. Dr Shivers took off his jacket and examined the pin.

'Strange, it worked this morning,' he muttered.

'Shall I try?' asked Sammy. He unclipped his own Dragon Minder pin from his shirt pocket.

'Or me?' said Dixie, pointing to her own pin fastened to her jumper under the Dragamas "D" logo.

'No need,' said Dr Shivers pulling a circular disc from his other pocket. 'Captain Stronghammer is on his way down from the canteen. He will let us in.'

Sure enough, Captain Stronghammer appeared from behind a large rhododendron accompanied by Mrs Hubar, Jock and a girl who Sammy recognised as the girl he had knocked over on their first day of term.

'Hi Sammy,' shouted Jock. 'This is my cousin. She wants to come and have a look.'

'Hi Jock,' said Sammy, grinning as Dixie frowned at him. She still hadn't got over the dwarves and trolls issues she had been teased about by Jock's family.

'Have you descaled yet?' asked Jock, playfully pushing his cousin forward. 'She thinks you're cute,' he grinned pointing at Sammy.

'Sammy isn't cute,' Dixie scowled, 'and yes, we're here to descale our dragons. Your Dad's going to let us in.'

'Sir Ragnarok shut down the chambers early has he?' Captain Stronghammer laughed. 'Thought he'd have at least waited until everyone's gone home at the end of the week.'

'Enough chatter,' said Dr Shivers, frowning at the dwarf. 'Perhaps you would be kind enough to open the chamber. Then we can do the descaling and move on.'

'Ah yes, Dr Shivers,' said Captain Stronghammer knowingly, 'you have the surprise party to set up.'

'Surprise party!' exclaimed Sammy. 'We didn't know anything about that.'

'That's why they call it a surprise,' said Dr Shivers stonily. 'Now open this door!'

Captain Stronghammer took out his own silver pin and scuttled over to the stones. He pushed the pin on the stone to open the doorway into the chamber.

'Looks like it iced over,' said Captain Stronghammer frowning. 'It shouldn't go like that. We've only had a light fall of snow this morning.'

'Hurry up man,' snapped Dr Shivers, pulling on a pair of black dragon hide gloves that didn't quite go with his grey pinstripe suit.

'I can't unseal it,' grumbled Captain Stronghammer. 'Eh, Jock, why don't you have a go son?'

Jock shuffled forward raising his staff. 'Fire,' he said weakly.

Nothing happened.

'Fire! Fire!'

'Stupid dwarves,' groaned Dixie. 'Let me try.'

In a split second, she had assembled her staff and pointed it high above Jock's head.

'Fire,' commanded Dixie and a surge of bright yellow and red flames poured from the end of her wooden staff, the onyx and ruby stones glowing as the fire burst out from between them.

Dixie's fire hit the wall with such force that the flames split into several clusters, fizzing and burning out before they touched the ground. Mrs Hubar looked on approvingly.

Captain Stronghammer pressed his rough hand against the stone wall.

'Good,' he growled. 'She'll open up now.'

Sure enough, the stone slabs creaked apart, revealing the sloping entrance to the Dragon Chambers.

'Kiridor!' called Dixie, running forward into the darkness.

'Duke? Is that you?' came a hollow voice from the depths of the chambers.

'Are you all right Firey?' said Mrs Hubar following Dixie inside, her daughter close to her side.

'Hullo everyone,' said Captain Firebreath, stumbling forward. 'Bin stuck in here for ages.'

'It iced up Firey,' soothed Mrs Hubar. 'All right now though.'

Captain Firebreath blew on his hands. 'That's good to hear, I ran out of rum just now.'

'Dwarf men,' Mrs Hubar giggled, 'don't you marry one Dixie, they'll cause you no end of problems.'

'Humph,' Dixie snorted, 'not much chance of that.'

Mrs Hubar gave her a disapproving stare and gathered her family together.

'If you're sure you're all right Firey, I'm taking Figgy and the family up to the Land of the Pharaohs.'

'Already?' spluttered Dr Shivers. 'There's three days of school left before Christmas. You'll miss the "surprise" party.' Dr Shivers threw Captain Stronghammer a dark look.

'Not to worry Dr Shivers,' said Captain Firebreath, 'they'll have just a good a time up there.'

'Sir Ragnarok will hear of this,' threatened Dr Shivers. 'I'll see to it.'

Mrs Hubar waved a dismissing hand at Dr Shivers and linked arms with Captain Stronghammer and her daughter.

Jock tapped his staff at Dixie, showering her with an embarrassing display of feeble flames. Bright red, he disappeared with his family behind some shrubs and on to the path to the Dragon's Cave.

'Not taking much are they,' said Sammy. 'I mean, if they're going for two weeks.'

'Never do,' growled Captain Firebreath. 'Did exactly the same twelve years ago, course it was just the two of them then. Came back with young Jock wrapped in a pink blanket if I remember,' Captain Firebreath chuckled. 'They were expecting a daughter to come first!'

Sammy and Dixie laughed until Dr Shivers gave them a disapproving look.

'May we have the two blue-green dragons please Captain Firebreath?'

'Yours is them?' asked Captain Firebreath, rubbing his beard with a gnarled hand. 'Not surprised really. They're the only blue-green dragons at the school now, since the Shape killed Mary-Beth's dragon, Kelsepe.'

'And Mary-Beth,' added Dixie. 'Serves her right for cheating on my brother.'

'I'd best get your dragons,' Captain Firebreath coughed, 'before the good doctor here starts taking stars away from you both. We can't have that, eh?'

Sammy grinned. 'Please may we go in and bring them out?'

'Sure,' said Captain Firebreath, blowing again on his hands, 'help yourselves.'

Sammy followed Dixie into the lantern-lit chamber.

'Brr,' it's cold in here,' said Dixie. 'Kiridor, come on Kiri, come here.'

Sammy reached into his pocket and blew the green plastic Angel whistle he had won in Gavin's cracker. He couldn't hear the whistle make any noise, but from the rumbling inside the chamber, it sounded as though all the dragons under the castle were charging towards them.

'Woah there!' squawked Captain Firebreath. 'What did you do?'

Sammy held out the green whistle.

'Blimin' toys,' growled Captain Firebreath as he singlehandedly held back the stampede of dragons charging towards Sammy.

'Interesting,' said Dr Shivers, walking into the chamber. 'I always wondered what would happen if one were to do that.'

'Do what?' snapped Dixie. 'We'll never find our dragons in this lot.'

'My dear,' said Dr Shivers smiling. 'You are supposed to blow the whistle in front of your own dragon for the first time. Once blown, any dragon who hears the sound at the first blow when the pattern is set is forever more bound to follow its tune.'

'So all the dragons in the school now follow Sammy's whistle?' asked Dixie, her mouth open.

Dr Shivers nodded. 'A tool such as this in the wrong hands would be fatal my dear.'

'It must be destroyed,' said Sammy, feeling suddenly sick.

'I will see to it,' said Dr Shivers holding out his hand. 'Perhaps Sir Ragnarok might be interested in keeping it. I believe he has Angel whistles to command all the dragons in each school year group. A historic collection passed down from headmaster to headmistress to headmaster.'

'No one should have one whistle for the whole school's dragons,' growled Captain Firebreath. 'I'm with young Sammy here. It should be destroyed at once.'

Sammy bent down putting the green whistle on a rock showing above the snow. He picked up a second rock and crashed it down splitting the whistle into tiny shards of plastic and metal.

Dr Shivers picked up the pieces and put them into a plastic bag handed to him by Captain Firebreath.

'Sir Ragnarok shall have the pieces,' said Dr Shivers.

'I'll see to it,' said Captain Firebreath. 'I'll see him before you anyway.'

With a pause noted by Sammy and Dixie, Dr Shivers handed over the plastic bag.

'Very well,' snapped Dr Shivers. 'Now do we have your dragons ready yet?'

As if waiting for some unimaginable pain, Kyrillan and Kiridor shuffled forward.

Dr Shivers unrolled a large black rug he had been carrying.

'Sammy, you may go first. Guide Kyrillan to the centre of the rug. Then with your first and second finger, just peel a scale from the top of his neck, like I showed you in the classroom.'

Sammy stepped on to the rug. It squished on the snow beneath his feet.

'If done correctly,' continued Dr Shivers, 'it will cause the Domino Effect and you will be left with just a handful of scales to remove.'

Sammy looked into Kyrillan's coal black eyes, silently apologising if he were to cause his dragon any pain.

He reached around the side of Kyrillan's head to the start of his spikes. Under the first spike, he felt a few scales that seemed to be looser than the others.

Following Dr Shivers's instructions, he pushed the fingernail of his index finger under the scale. It popped off in his hand. A single scale came off easily enough, but it was the only one to move.

'A good start,' chuckled Dr Shivers. 'Go on like that and you'll still be here next Christmas.'

Embarrassed by Dr Shivers sarcasm, Sammy reached under the next scale. It was firmer than the first and wouldn't budge. He fastened all of the nails of the fingers on his right hand under the tessellating tear pattern and pulled hard.

Kyrillan reared up on his hind legs, roaring in obvious pain. A fork of blood red fiery smoke poured from both nostrils and a shower of scales fell in blue-green shimmering rain on to the rug.

Dr Shivers drew his staff, flashing the ruby red crystal forward.

Sammy held up his hand, blood was trickling from under his nails where Kyrillan had been caught by surprise and ripped away from him.

Kyrillan snorted, stamping his feet on the ground. He was still moving and thrashing around. His tail swished violently, narrowly missing knocking Dixie over.

'Dratted dragon,' spat Dr Shivers, throwing down some green pellets.

Kyrillan crushed three pellets with his mighty foot and one flipped up into his nostril. As soon as the pellet entered his nose, Kyrillan snorted throwing back his head, then he became still and docile, standing with his feet squarely apart so that Sammy could reach forward and pull the remaining scales from his body.

'There,' said Dr Shivers smiling, some fifteen minutes later. 'Nothing to it.'

Sammy nodded bleakly. Even in the winter sun, Kyrillan seemed to have lost some of his magic and shimmer. The outline of his new scales was already formed as a smooth pattern on Kyrillan's skin, a little bit like a tattoo.

'No flying for six to eight months,' said Dr Shivers. 'That will give the skin time to heal and harden up ready for the adult scales to show through. It's a bit like teething,' Dr Shivers explained, 'you have to lose the baby scales to make way for the tough adult scales that will last for life.'

'But don't we do this every year?' asked Sammy.

Dr Shivers shook his head. 'Not from head to toe unless you have an unusual dragon. Most students will take off about half to a third of the number of scales you have there. Then it is carried out every two or three years. No more is necessary.'

Sammy bent down to ruffle his hand through the scales. Towering over him, Kyrillan looked bare.

Dr Shivers took out a brown sack bag with a rope drawstring from a pocket in his suit jacket.

'Use this bag to collect as many scales as you can,' instructed Dr Shivers. 'Some students sell them at the lands above the school to get extra spending money, but you'll need to keep a few for yourself when Professor Sanchez starts teaching you some of her potions.'

'Oh,' said Sammy, kneeling on the rug.

Dixie held the bag open and Sammy cupped his hands like a spade and shoveled the tear shaped scales into the open sack. The bag was no larger than a shoebox and felt as light as a feather when all of Kyrillan's scales had been safely stored away.

'Well done Sammy,' said Dr Shivers when they had finished. 'Take Kyrillan back into the chamber for Captain Firebreath to look after him until the end of the week and then you can take him home for Christmas.'

Sammy nodded. Kyrillan, looking a little the worse for wear, puffed a ring of smoke into the air and followed Sammy into the mouth of the chamber.

When Sammy came back, Kiridor was standing exceptionally still on the rug and looking very well behaved. Dixie was standing on tiptoe trying to pull a stubborn scale from behind her dragon's ears. The rest of the scales were on the rug.

Sammy felt a pang of jealousy and wished if Dixie was so good at descaling Dr Shivers should have let her go first to show him how it should be done.

Dr Shivers was smiling broadly, casting a string of three gold stars towards the castle.

'Well done Dixie, that was perfect,' said Dr Shivers, his white teeth gleaming.

Dixie scowled at him, her mind obviously on their previous conversation. 'Captain Firebreath says with the right magic you can still fly through solid objects.'

'You would be best to speak with Commander Altair about that then,' said Dr Shivers. 'I hear he's been giving you some extra tuition.'

'Yeah,' Dixie nodded uncomfortably. 'Come on Kiridor.'

Sammy felt more disgruntled when he found himself helping Dr Shivers pack Kiridor's scales into a sack for Dixie whilst she led her dragon into the chamber.

When she returned, Sammy hung back, following Dixie and Dr Shivers a few paces behind them as they walked back to the castle.

Dr Shivers escorted them back to the North Tower. He mentioned needing to mark some books and marched off alone down the corridor towards the East wing.

Without offering more than an encouraging smile at Sammy, Dixie engrossed herself chatting with Milly and the other girls from the North house who flocked to Dixie to hear about the descaling of her dragon.

CHAPTER 22

FIRESTICKS AND INVISIBALLS

Leaving the girls chatting in the common room, Sammy stomped back to his tower room alone to collect his Dragonball kit for the next lesson. With Kyrillan unable to be flown until after Christmas, he wasn't looking forward to playing catch in the freezing weather wearing just a thin t-shirt and shorts.

His mood didn't improve in the changing rooms where, when he had just pulled on his t-shirt, Mr Ockay came into the changing room to tell him that he should be watching a sports video in the Main Hall instead.

'I wondered where everyone was,' grumbled Sammy as he threw on his long-sleeved shirt, tie and school trousers.

Mr Ockay was waiting for him in the Gym foyer, keys in one hand ready to lock the building. In his other hand he was waving a sprig of mistletoe at one of the school cleaning ladies who was finishing polishing the floor around his desk.

'Don't you come any closer!' she squawked, threatening him with her mop.

Sammy slipped out unnoticed and walked back up the frosty path to the castle. He couldn't believe he'd been so stupid not to look at the noticeboard to find out the lesson had been moved, then to get fully changed into his sports clothes without anyone else in the changing room.

Still carrying his t-shirt and shorts, Sammy sneaked into the back of the Main Hall and perched on the wooden bench at the back next to Gavin and Toby.

Dixie was sitting at the front, chatting away with Milly and Holly. The three of them were giggling as sportsmaster Mr Cross was fumbling with the video remote control.

Gavin's arm shot up. 'I'll do it Sir.'

Mr Cross looked up slightly flustered. 'No need, should just take a second.'

Five minutes later, the picture flashed up on the school television. Mr Cross wiped his forehead with his wristband and sat down on a wooden chair at the front.

"National Firesticks Tournament" came up on the screen in big black letters, followed by the round face of a man whose name appeared in a blue bar at the bottom of the screen as "Bill Oaklock, Commentator".

Bill Oaklock had a ruddy red face from being out in all weathers. He wore a grey peaked cap over his piercing blue-grey eyes and had a short grey speckled moustache and a dimpled chin. He carried a large cone microphone in his right hand with the initials "F.S.L." on the stem.

'Firesticks Live,' explained Gavin when Sammy asked.

'There's Nitron Dark!' shrieked Dixie, jumping up from the front row. 'Look!'

Sammy and half the back row stood up. He couldn't fail to notice the tall handsome Nitron Dark with his smoldering brown eyes and strong jaw. Dixie had a life-size poster of him on her bedroom wall at the Three Chimneys that Sammy had seen when he and Darius had borrowed her room when they stayed over in the holidays a few months ago.

'Ooh Nitron!' yelled Gavin, and, copying Jason's chant to a furious glare from Dixie in her obvious humiliation, the boys from the houses, with the exception of Sammy and Darius, joined in singing.

'Ooh Nitron, ooh Nitron, ooh Nitron Dark!'

Mr Cross stood up after the third chant and switched the television off. The Main Hall fell silent. His eyes were glaring blue, half hidden under his sandy eyebrows.

'Never!' shouted Mr Cross. 'In all my five years teaching at Dragamas have I heard such rubbish. As you know, the Nitromen are useless without one player. They are not a balanced team. A bad example. If you must chant, shout for Bonny Jonny and our local team, the Woodland Ranchers who are,' Mr Cross consulted the newspaper he always carried, 'playing the Warriors, next Saturday,' he added gloomily, sitting down and fumbling with the remote control.

The television sprung back into life. The whispering stopped even in Milly's front row where Sammy caught the tail end of their conversation, "quite fit", guessing Milly had come round to the idea of Nitron Dark.

Sammy stared, his eyes fixed to the screen as Nitron Dark stood with his legs apart, his back to the screen engaged in a discussion of tactics with his nine teammates all dressed alike in their black and gold Nitromen shirts. He spotted a black armband with the word "Captain" written in red lettering on Nitron Dark's right forearm.

In the background, a man with bright red hair had a similar black armband with "Captain" on his right forearm. He was talking to a circle of men wearing blue and white striped shirts.

'Those are the Rainbow Wasps,' said Mr Cross, turning up the volume. 'Quiet everyone. It's about to begin.'

A whistle blew and Nitron Dark turned to face the camera. Up close, Sammy was hooked by the action. He could feel his knuckles clenching underneath the wooden bench.

'Hey Phil,' Nitron Dark spoke to the captain of the Wasps in his husky deep voice.

Wow, thought Sammy inside his head, Nitron Dark was so cool.

Next to him, Gavin and Toby were leaning forward, hanging on to his every word.

'Heads or tails,' shouted the referee.

'Lucky tails,' said Nitron Dark, getting approving nods from his team.

'Fine,' said Phil of the Rainbow Wasps.

The referee flipped and caught the coin. 'Tails! he shouted. 'Which end do you want?'

Nitron Dark surveyed the sky. 'North east,' he muttered. 'Wind's blowing that way so it should be easy to score.' He pointed to the far end of the pitch. 'We'll start there,' he said in his mesmerising voice.

'Raise the Dragon!' shouted the referee and the camera panned out to reveal a small stadium no bigger than the Woodland Ranchers stadium behind Dixie's house in the village.

In every seat and every spare gangway of the stadium floods of people wearing gold and black shirts shone in the winter sun. The camera swung round to the other side of the stadium, the end Nitron Dark had chosen to start, and there were hundreds upon hundreds of people wearing blue and white striped shirts shouting "Come on Wasps! Come on Wasps" and waving blue and white banners.

'He always starts at the opposition's end,' said Mr Cross. 'Most of his supporters are silent, then when the game changes to the opposite end, all his supporters have saved their energy and shout and scream the Nitromen through to win.'

'Does that work?' asked Sammy.

'Yeah,' said Toby enthusiastically. 'He's won almost every game like that.'

'He only lost when his brother was ill. Concentrated too much on that,' added Gavin. 'Dad went up the wall. He had a bet on with Euan that the Nitromen would win. That's his brother there.'

Sammy followed Gavin's finger towards a young man who couldn't have looked more different than Nitron Dark if he tried. He had dirty blond hair and bright blue eyes.

'Looks like your older brother,' said Toby. 'If you had one.'

Sammy stared, the likeness was uncanny, almost looking into a warped mirror of himself, only the reflected face was about ten years older.

The referee blew his whistle again and the two teams dispersed out at a trot. Nitron Dark waved for his men to spread out, his brother the farthest towards the edge of the pitch.

The camera came up close and the referee held out his hands to show everyone watching. The image flashed up on the big stadium screens. The referee's hands were empty.

'They're playing with Invisiballs,' whispered Gavin. 'Look.'

Sammy watched as a shadow appeared in the referee's hands and a black ball, like the ones Mr Cross had shown them appeared, flickered and disappeared. Then a second one did the same and a third.

Sammy counted five black-to-invisible balls before the referee marched to the centre of the pitch and placed the balls in the mouth of an enormous golden dragon, similar to the one on the Dragamas pitch.

'Go!' shouted the referee, covering his ears.

There was an explosion that literally rocked the television in the Main Hall. Or, as Sammy realised, the camera at the other end of the pitch filming the match. Five of the black balls flew high into the air in an umbrella formation, and disappeared as they hit the ground.

Nitron Dark stormed up the pitch and crashed his firestick at the space where the ball had been.

Sammy stood up to get a better look as the ball reappeared and sailed towards the spinning dragon. The ball landed neatly in the dragon's mouth and swung out through its tail up towards the crowd.

There was a roar of applause from the Nitromen's crowd and loud booing from the Rainbow Wasps supporters.

Unlike in football, Sammy noticed that the game didn't stop after each goal. With five or more balls in play and especially as each one seemed to have a mind of its own the game would never have got going.

As it was, Sammy found himself thoroughly enjoying the game and cheered with Gavin and Toby when any of the Nitromen scored and groaned when the Rainbow Wasps had a touch of one of the balls.

Mr Cross watched the game checking a piece of paper on his lap. When the referee blew his whistle for the final time Sammy agreed with the score table that the Nitromen had won comfortably with 105 points versus 83 points scored by the Rainbow Wasps.

Mr Cross consulted his paper, circled a result with a pen, smiled and tucked both pen and paper back into his tracksuit pocket.

'Did you enjoy that everyone?' asked Mr Cross.

'Yes Sir!' yelled Gavin.

Sammy checked his watch, he knew the two hour match had run into Gemology but with Mrs Hubar visiting the Land of the Pharaohs he guessed that Mr Cross had known and let the class watch the second half as well.

Mr Cross kept the television on for the commentary by ex-player Joe Northbrook and Sylvester Thomas who had played for the Chelsea Swans and the Warwick Bears.

Mr Cross was talking to the television, shaking his head and disagreeing with much of what was said.

He carried on talking as Captain Firebreath and two other dwarves came into the Main Hall to arrange the tables for tea.

In fact, Mr Cross only stopped talking and switched off the television when the rest of the school came in shouting and laughing.

The first years were clutching Christmas trees they had made with cardboard and tinsel. The third years charged in shouting about who had conjured the best reindeer.

Serberon and the fourth years were leaping from chair to chair sending new blue sparks Commander Altair had taught them in Armoury and the fifth years were quiet and calm, plodding in with their noses buried in text books, cramming in every possible minute of revision.

Mr Cross called the second years over to him and he handed out more leaflets for Excelsior Sports Supplies, urging them to ask for the combination wood and metal stick for Christmas.

'Best in the business,' he said looking keenly at Sammy. 'Definitely worth asking for.'

'It's too late,' moaned Milly. 'My parents have already got me a six storey mansion for my dolls.'

Mr Cross clicked his tongue as Gavin roared for laughter.

'Aren't you a little old for dolls?' asked Mr Cross.

'It's Willoughby Mansion,' said Milly, 'for Suzanne and James.'

'Friends of yours?' asked Mr Cross, raising an eyebrow.

'I suppose,' said Milly, 'they come as a set. My Daddy bought them for me.'

'Dolls,' snorted Mr Cross, 'you should get into Firesticks. You'll find it a lot more stimulating than dolls.'

Milly was nearly in tears. 'I'll tell my Mum about you. She won't get me some stupid Firestick for Christmas.'

'Fine,' snapped Mr Cross, 'use the school ones.'

'Ooh no,' said Milly earnestly, 'Mummy wouldn't have that.'

Sammy held back a giggle as he looked for a seat at the North table. With the end of the year, rules were more relaxed and Dixie had found a seat on the fourth year table sandwiched between Michael and Jason.

Feeling he had to say something to Dixie about descaling earlier, he deliberately walked past the fourth years.

'Well done descaling Kiridor,' Sammy muttered.

Dixie grinned at him. 'I just pushed the first one I saw and they all fell off!'

'Oh,' said Sammy, 'I thought...'

'Dixie doesn't show off,' said Jason turning round and speaking unexpectedly. 'She's grown up with dragons all her life. You can't expect her not to know how to do it. She helped our Dad descale his and Mum's dragons every year they needed it.'

'Oh,' said Sammy, feeling like he wanted the ground to open up and let him fall through into the mines below.

'Still friends?' asked Dixie.

'Yeah,' said Sammy. 'Are you still coming round at Christmas?'

'Try and stop me,' Dixie giggled, nudging Jason.

Jason stood up and let Sammy take his chair. 'Help yourself,' he muttered pointing towards his plate of roast dinner and walking off to get a second plate for himself.

'Wish the plates were still working,' Jason grumbled as he came back with a plate piled high with turkey and trimmings. 'Used to be great, sit down and then think about what you want to eat, then "pop" and there it was.'

'It's because of the fifth year dragons dying,' explained Mikhael.

'I know,' said Sammy. 'We're going to stop the Shape.'

Around him, all the students on the fourth year North table erupted in a roar of laughter.

CHAPTER 23

CHRISTMAS WITH UNCLE PETER

Sammy woke up the following morning in good spirits. The morning sun was pouring in through the window and there wasn't a cloud in the sky.

'Two and a half days to go!' Sammy said to no one in particular. He leaped out of bed, dressed quickly and went downstairs.

The common room was busy with students studying, chatting and playing games. He saw Dixie and Milly playing Dragon Dice at a table by one of the windows.

'Just going to check on Kyrillan!' Sammy shouted across the room.

Several fifth years looked up from their books and frowned.

They frowned harder when Dixie leaped up, scattering multi-coloured Dragon Dice into Milly's lap and shouted that she was coming too.

'Ug, it's so cold,' grumbled Dixie when they were outside pressing Sammy's Dragon Minder pin into the groove in the castle wall. She had her staff poised ready to light a fire in case the lock had iced up overnight.

Some of the snow had melted in the sun and showed patches of green grass underneath.

'Brr,' agreed Sammy, glad when the door to the Dragon Chambers opened. He and Dixie walked down the sloping entrance, into the Dragon Chambers, and out of the cold wind, blowing on their hands to keep warm.

Since the fifth year dragons no longer supplied heating in the school, Sir Ragnarok had given Tom Sweep, the caretaker, full permission to control the radiators.

On the first day of being in charge of the heating, Tom Sweep had prevented Dragon Minders from tampering with the controls. This meant that Dragon Minders could no longer use the hidden internal entrance to the Dragon Chambers and had to visit from outside instead.

As Sammy and Dixie walked deeper into the chambers they found Kyrillan and Kiridor sitting apart from the other dragons, feeding together from the cast iron tub.

Sammy scooped a shovel load of oats into the basin and checked Kyrillan's nose. It had healed completely from the tower room adventure and although the adult scales were not yet formed, his dragon looked none the worse for descaling.

'You taking 'em home for the holiday?' growled Captain Firebreath from deep within the chamber.

'Hopefully,' Sammy called back. 'If we're allowed to after the descaling. My uncle has three dragons.'

'Three?' asked Dixie, stopping in her tracks, nearly dropping the sack of hay she was carrying. 'What for?'

'His dragon and the dragons belonging to my parents,' Sammy answered, 'They've forgotten about dragons and my Uncle looks after them.'

Sammy paused, mid-scoop, 'It's strange because if what I saw in the woods was real then my uncle would have been looking after my parents dragons for nearly twenty years.'

'Wow,' said Dixie. 'That's a really, really long time.'

'Yeah,' agreed Sammy, suddenly feeling it strange that he didn't know the names of his parents' dragons or even what colour their scales were.

'Seems to me,' growled Captain Firebreath, 'there's a lot going on all of a sudden. What with the Shape reforming after such a long time of quiet. Makes jobs for us dwarves a darn sight harder.'

Captain Firebreath bent down and picked up an empty bottle.

'Darn Stronghammer, he makes my job harder every day. If he ain't leaving his rum bottles around, he's leaving the darn door open.'

'The darn door open?' said Dixie.

'Yes missy and don't let me hear that language from you. Yer dad wouldn't be a darn sight impressed.'

'Yeah? Well he isn't darn here is he?' Dixie stared at Captain Firebreath defiantly.

Captain Firebreath scratched his head. 'That's your business but if yer want some free advice, yer'll stop thinking bad of him. He left not outta duty but outta choice. There's a lot of dragons alive today all because of him and his Dragon Knights.'

'His what?' asked Dixie.

'Dragon Knights,' Captain Firebreath paused, 'don't tell me yer didn't know?'

Dixie shook her head, her eyes streaming suddenly with green tears. 'My Dad's a Dragon Knight?'

'Aye, actually he's a Dragon Commander, like Commander Altair,' said Captain Firebreath handing her his red and white neckerchief as a hanky. 'And a darn good'un at that.'

Sammy looked away, feeling his eyes prickle with tears too. He knew how much this meant to Dixie and her family and he wished he could say the same about his parents.

'Yours are fine folk too, I'm sure,' added Captain Firebreath rummaging in his pocket and finding a grubby tissue.

Sammy blinked and refused the tissue. 'My parents are a solicitor and a bank manager. I wish they could see dragons.'

'Maybe you should visit Mrs Grock and make a wish,' Captain Firebreath winked, 'now if yer don't mind I need to clean out the chambers as best I can by myself. All the other dwarves are working afrenzy in the mines. Sir Ragnarok's ordered us to top up the reserves of gems,' he explained, 'just in case the Shape do anything with that money he gave them.'

'Like what?' sniffed Dixie her eyes still wet.

'Like blood money,' growled Captain Firebreath. 'Paying folk to give up their dragons. Paying them to kill dragons and give up their draconite.'

'So the Shape can rebuild the Stone Cross,' said Sammy, finding the words jumping out of his mouth.

'Aye,' Captain Firebreath frowned, 'but what's the likes of you knowing about things like that?'

'Uh, nothing,' said Sammy quickly, 'just something I learned in Dragon Studies.'

'Humph,' said Captain Firebreath. 'You don't want to believe all you hear. Aye there's strange things about but if there's any truth in the stories of the Stone Cross I'll eat my boots!'

Sammy squeezed in a laugh at the thought of Captain Firebreath eating his black leather boots.

'And I'll shave off my beard!' added Captain Firebreath, stroking his flame coloured locks.

Sammy roared with laughter, glad Dixie and Captain Firebreath joined in. If only they'd seen what he'd seen, the Stone Cross could only be real, else why had the Shape stolen the draconite stones from Mary-Beth's dragon, from Toby and Gavin's Mum's dragon, from the entire fifth years dragons and countless other dragons if they weren't hoping to rebuild the Stone Cross and have power over earth, air, fire and water.

Sir Ragnarok's surprise Christmas party came and went and the last days before the end of term disappeared very quickly indeed.

Sammy found himself packing at top speed having overslept on the day they were going home for Christmas. He raced down to the Dragon Chambers to check on Kyrillan.

Captain Firebreath was preparing the dragons for the Christmas holiday and wasn't impressed to see Sammy but let him into the chambers, grumbling under his breath.

Sammy called for Kyrillan and found his dragon with some of the fourth year dragons, nosing for food in the bath tub full of oats. The fourth year dragons were much larger than Kyrillan and dwarfed him in size.

He suspected that their owners were staying in non-dragonish places over Christmas and had chosen to leave their fire breathing pets at Dragamas where they would be safe over the two and a half week holiday.

Satisfied Kyrillan was fed and would be ready for the holiday, Sammy ran back to the tower room to himself get ready to go.

Wrestling with a piece of tinsel hanging from his curtains, Sammy managed to be packed and ready to go as the midday bell sounded from above the tower door.

Gavin and Toby burst into the tower room to collect their things, laughing and joking about some tricks a group of fourth years had played on the first years, telling them that the first years weren't allowed home for Christmas.

'Monty was in tears,' laughed Gavin, 'and Herby. They both fell for it!'

Sammy grinned. 'Must be nice to go home for Christmas.'

'You're not staying here are you?' asked Toby, looking concerned, 'I mean, I'm sure it's ok but if you want you could come home with us.'

'Or Dixie,' added Gavin, 'I'm sure her Mum would let you stay.'

'Yeah,' said Toby, 'sorry, I forgot, I think Mum's still mad at you.'

'Not your fault though,' Gavin tried to reassure Sammy. 'Just she doesn't like the Shape and because of you...'

'Shut up Gavin,' said Toby.

'Well it's true, she said if Sammy hadn't stayed...'

Sammy shrugged. 'It's ok, I know.'

'No Sammy, Gavin didn't mean it like that. I'll talk to her, she'll let you stay.'

'It's ok, really,' said Sammy. 'My parents are staying with my uncle. He lives in the village. We're all staying there, Darius as well.'

'Oh,' said Toby. 'Well ok, if you're sure.'

Sammy nodded. 'If you like, I'll call you and you can come round.'

'Yeah.'

'Definitely.'

'Great,' said Sammy. 'Anyway, I have to go. My uncle's coming in a few minutes. Have you seen Darius?'

'Library,' said Toby. 'He said he was going to get a book on King Sellbegone or something.'

'King Serberon,' said Sammy leaping over Darius's bed to the door. 'Thanks, I'll see you in a minute.'

By the time Sammy returned with Darius, Gavin and Toby had packed their possessions higgledy piggledy into their suitcases. On the top were two cup shaped parcels wrapped neatly in green foil.

Gavin went pink. 'One's for you Darius and one's for Jock.'

'Oh,' said Sammy. 'Never mind.'

'No, it's ok,' said Toby, 'you have it. Jock's not here, he'll never know.'

'Are you sure? asked Sammy, handing over three Christmas presents of his own to Gavin, Toby and Darius and laying a fourth on Jock's chest of drawers. 'They're nothing much, but Happy Christmas anyway.'

Gavin tore off the paper. 'Cool a book on the Woodland Ranchers.'

'I'll save mine for Christmas,' said Toby, 'thanks anyway.'

'No problem,' said Sammy.

'Me too,' said Darius, going a little pink. 'Gives me time to um, wrap yours.'

Sammy knew Darius hadn't done more than Christmas cards for his friends. It wasn't that he couldn't afford it, just that in his house Christmas wasn't celebrated.

Sammy unpeeled the paper gently from his gift from Gavin and Toby. It was a mug with the initial "J" embossed in gold on the green ceramic.

Toby went bright red. 'I'm sorry Sammy, I didn't know.'

Gavin shook his head, 'me neither.'

Sammy didn't know whether to laugh or not, so he re-wrapped the parcel quickly and put it next to his present for Jock.

'That'll be nice for him,' Sammy muttered, 'a book and a mug.'

'Oops,' giggled Gavin. 'Well, we'd better go.'

Sammy looked out of the tower window. A striking blue Land Rover was pulling up inside the school gates. 'She's here!'

'Already!' screeched Toby. 'Come on Gavin, she'll murder us if we're late.'

Gavin and Toby charged for the door and smacked straight into Dr Shivers and Professor Burlay. From the window, Sammy saw Captain Firebreath standing with a herd of dragons, separating Gavin and Toby's dragons, Syren and Puttee, for Mrs Reed who tied them by the neck to the towbar on the back of her Land Rover.

'Enjoy your holidays boys,' Dr Shivers said, smiling at them, 'be sure to look over your notes on descaling. I hear Professor Sanchez is looking forward to teaching you some basic scale potions next year.'

'Ug,' groaned Gavin, 'we're going away for Christmas.'

'Skiing,' added Toby. 'Dad won a competition in the paper.'

'You never told us that,' said Darius.

'Are you still up for coming round and playing some Dragonball?' asked Sammy.

'Maybe,' said Gavin throwing his duvet crookedly on his bed and shaking crumbs off his pillows. 'We're going for ten days.'

'Be sure to leave some fresh meat out for your dragons. It makes their new adult scales tougher,' said Dr Shivers, looking mildly aware that his advice had fallen on Gavin and Toby's deaf ears.

'Fresh meat?' asked Sammy. 'Where from?'

'Normally you would ask your parents, but in your case...'

'I'll ask my uncle,' finished Sammy. 'I'm going to have to be a bit careful.'

'You could say it's for an imaginary friend perhaps,' said Dr Shivers with a smile.

'Yeah,' said Sammy. 'That should work.'

'Your mum will probably think you've lost it,' Darius grinned.

Sammy laughed. 'Are you ready? My uncle should be here soon.'

Darius nodded and they followed Dr Shivers and Professor Burlay down to the school courtyard.

Captain Firebreath was busy organising a group of three dragons and a dragon egg, belonging to the Griffin family whose parents had turned up in a giant double decker camper van.

By the time the four girls had hugged Captain Firebreath goodbye the dwarf was quite pink, half pleased, half embarrassed by the attention.

Mr Griffin shook Captain Firebreath's hand vigorously and leaped in front of Sammy to open the boot and let in all three dragons, one three years old, two monstrous four year old dragons and one dragon egg, belonging to Jane Griffin in the fifth year. The dragon egg was tucked safely into a brown shoebox that still had the label on.

When the camper van had gone, Mrs Deane was next to arrive. She pulled up in the layby opposite the gates in her rusty old Land Rover. She got out of her car and went over to Sammy and Darius.

'You got a lift honey?' she asked anxiously.

'Yeah,' said Sammy. 'My Uncle's picking us up.'

'Ooh the Jeweller,' said Mrs Deane. 'That reminds me, I must get my ring resized. My finger has been shrinking ever since Jacob went away and I nearly lost my ring doing the washing up only this morning.'

Sammy peered at the ring on her wedding finger. Mrs Deane was right. It looked loose even though she had wrapped a plaster under her finger to make the ring fit a little better.

But it wasn't the plaster that caught his eye. It was the blue-green stone set in the middle of the ring.

'Draconite,' said Mrs Deane, catching Sammy's stare. 'Given to me by my husband, Jacob, when his grandmother's dragon passed away.'

'Oh,' said Sammy, feeling uncomfortable.

'Natural causes,' Mrs Deane reassured him. 'Not like those poor dragons here. I tell you, if Sir Ragnarok wasn't running the school, I'd be sure to put my children into another school.'

'But dragons have died here,' started Darius, looking confused. 'Sir Ragnarok is running the school.'

'Oh yes,' said Mrs Deane, 'but so many more would be dead and who knows maybe the Shape would have rebuilt the Stone Cross.'

'How do you know they haven't?' demanded Darius, pipping Sammy to the question.

Mrs Deane pointed up into the sky. 'As long as the stars in the Dragamas Constellation are there, I know.'

Sammy followed her finger shielding his eyes from the winter sun. The Dragamas Constellation, four stars, one red, one green, one yellow and one blue circling a single white star. Beyond the five stars were the faint red dots that Sammy knew resembled the Shape.

'Will the dragons be safe here over Christmas?' he asked, looking over at one of the dragons chewing at a stone in the grass.

'Of course honey, the Shape are nothing to fear, they have bigger fish to fry than your baby dragons.'

'Nelson's not a baby,' said Darius indignantly.

'Of course, they're two now aren't they,' soothed Mrs Deane. 'You haven't seen Dixie, or the boys, have you?'

Sammy shook his head, half wishing he was staying at Dixie's rather than at his uncle's. At least her house was within walking distance from his uncle's house.

'Are you staying together?' asked Mrs Deane. 'Your mother's usually here first Darius.'

Darius nodded. 'My parents are up there somewhere,' he pointed to the sky. 'I got a postcard saying they were calling in at the Floating Circus but I've checked with Professor Burlay and it doesn't come overhead here until next summer.'

'I'm sorry honey,' said Mrs Deane, 'still, I'm sure you'll be welcome at Sammy's uncle's house. Oh good, here come the boys.'

Sammy turned around. Sat astride their green dragons, their suitcases suspended in mid air in front of them, upheld by some sort of magic, were Serberon, Mikhael and Jason followed by a crowd of fourth years shouting and shoving to see whose parents would arrive next.

Behind them, a rucksack and staff in one hand and an over-sized trunk pulled by the other was Dixie. Sammy ran forward to help with the trunk and found she was completely out of breath.

'Phew, that was heavy,' puffed Dixie. 'All the way from the tower.'

'You should have used magic,' said Serberon, grinning at his sister and deliberately avoiding Sammy's eyes.

'Yeah right,' said Dixie. 'They teach us how to make fire and put it out before we can do something simple like moving objects!'

'That's my girl,' said Mrs Deane. 'Strong as a herd of oxen.'

Dixie frowned. 'I hate being a troll. I wish I was normal like Sammy or Darius.'

Sammy grinned. 'I wish I had green hair!'

Dixie laughed. 'Yeah right! Come on, give me a hand with my suitcase.'

When Dixie and Sammy had loaded the four suitcases into Mrs Deane's Land Rover, Captain Firebreath returned with Kiridor.

'Nearly wanted to stay behind this un,' growled Captain Firebreath.

'Well, I guess I'll see you soon,' said Dixie as she played "rock, paper, scissors" with Mikhael and won the right to sit in the front seat.

Sammy nodded. 'I'll give you a call.'

'Yeah, or send over Kyrillan if you're busy.'

'You still want to do it, right?' asked Sammy, spotting a silver Volvo estate approaching the lay-by.

Dixie's eyes lit up. 'Yeah, definitely!'

'Bye honey!' called Mrs Deane as she started the engine.

'Bye honey!' mimicked Serberon, Mikhael and Jason to a flurry of giggling.

Sammy and Darius waved as Mrs Deane drove off, five hands waving back. The silver Volvo parked by the hedge and a tall thin man stepped out.

'Hullo Sammy.'

'Hello Uncle Peter,' said Sammy, glad not to be the last to be picked up. 'This is my friend Darius, you said it was ok for him to stay.'

Sammy's uncle paused and looked hard at Darius. 'I pictured him a little differently.'

'You mean white?' asked Darius, his black eyes glaring. 'It's ok Sammy, I'll stay here for Christmas. I'll see if I can get a crossing from the Land of the Pharaohs to the Floating Circus.'

'My boy I meant nothing of the sort,' Sammy's uncle, Peter Pickering, looked annoyed. 'Sammy's other friend, the young lady, is of troll descent. I somewhat prejudicially decided in my own mind that you would have green hair too.'

'Oh,' Sammy could see Darius didn't know whether to be put out or relieved.

'I don't have green hair,' said Darius, grinning.

Peter Pickering smiled. 'Indeed you don't. Now would you like to stop for some lunch before we go home?'

'Yes please,' said Sammy. 'Uncle Peter, is it all right to bring our dragons home?'

'Of course it is,' said Peter Pickering, 'just be a little cautious in front of your parents. Sammy's parents don't see dragons,' he explained for Darius's benefit.

Darius nodded. 'Sammy told me they forgot about dragons a long time ago.'

Peter Pickering's flinch went almost unnoticed. 'I see,' he concluded. 'Shall we pack your things into the car?'

In a short time, Kyrillan, Nelson, Sammy, Darius and Peter Pickering were squashed into the silver Volvo and making their way out of the lay-by, through the country lanes and into the village.

Peter Pickering treated Sammy and Darius to a café lunch where Sammy had a plate filled high with sausages and chips. Darius and Peter had pasta with a fiery red spicy sauce covering the seashell shaped pasta. The waitress was one of Darius's friends and she gave him a voucher for a free drink next time he was there.

They left the café and set off for Peter Pickering's home in the village. They parked around the back of the jewellery shop and Peter let them in through the back door, calling to Sammy's parents, 'Charles, Julia, I'm back with the boys!'

CHAPTER 24

PAPRIKA, CYNGARD AND JOVAH

There was a scurry of footsteps and Sammy lost his breath in a giant hug from his mother and a slap on the back from his father.

'How's school then Sam?' asked Charles Rambles.

'It's good,' said Sammy, grinning as he watched his uncle struggle with Kyrillan and Nelson in the back garden. Confused by their new home, Nelson had tried to follow Darius into the house.

'Mum, Dad, this is Darius,' announced Sammy, dropping his suitcase on the floor.

'Hello Darius,' said Charles Rambles, shaking Darius's hand. 'What do your parents do?'

'They're Healers,' said Darius, without hesitation. 'They make people better using potions.'

'Oh, you mean Doctors,' said Julia Rambles. 'How quaint to call them Healers.'

Sammy grinned, glad his parents couldn't see Kyrillan puffing smoke rings at his uncle through the shed window.

'It's a bit smoky out there,' said Julia. 'I must get that washing in.'

'Leave it Julia,' said Charles. 'Sam's back and I'm sure if his school's anything like my old one school, he'll have brought his washing home with him, so there will be lots more to do.'

Peter Pickering returned to the house a few moments later looking disheveled, a large spot of soot on his shirt that didn't go unnoticed by Sammy's mother.

'Honestly Peter, I can't believe you've been outside all this time. You're covered in mud!'

Peter Pickering laughed. He winked at Sammy. 'You've got a strong one there.'

Sammy's uncle and his father went into the sitting room whilst his mother gave Sammy another breathtaking hug and a plate of homemade chocolate chip cookies and two glasses of milk. Her mobile rang and she waved apologetically to Sammy and Darius before shutting herself in the dining room to take the call.

'Shall we unpack?' asked Sammy, biting into one of the giant cookies.

'Yeah, good idea,' said Darius. 'Are we sharing a room?'

'I expect so.'

'Race you!' shouted Darius.

Sammy pushed past the kitchen table, his suitcase in both hands, leaping into the dark hallway. He saw the doorway through to the jewellery shop in a blur as Darius overtook him to reach the bronze banistered staircase. Once Darius was on the stairs, there was no way past him and it was so narrow at one point Sammy doubted he would squash his suitcase up there.

As they reached the landing, Uncle Peter called up to tell them that they would be sharing the converted attic room up the stairs inside the airing cupboard.

Darius reached the airing cupboard first and dragged open the wooden door. A wave of sweet smelling air puffed towards them from the shirts and dresses hanging on the rails either side of the staircase. It reminded Sammy of the staircase that took you into Sir Ragnarok's office, going up seven steps and through another door that opened into pitch blackness.

'Is there a light?' shouted Sammy, hearing the hallway door click shut behind them.

'I don't know,' Darius giggled. 'Good thing Dixie isn't here. She hates the dark!'

'Move up, I'll get some fire going and see if there's a light switch somewhere.' Sammy raised his hand, balancing his suitcase on the top step. 'Fire,' he commanded.

A jet of yellow-orange flame appeared two inches from the end of his staff.

'That's amazing!' said Darius. 'Just like a torch.'

Sammy held the staff at arm's length, he had spotted the white square of the light switch just beyond his reach. He moved forward, stepping into the darkened room inches at a time, in case he bumped into something.

Just as his eyes grew used to the darkness, he noticed something moving out of the corner of his eye.

'Woah there,' Sammy muttered stumbling backwards.

'I saw it,' hissed Darius. 'Get the light on quick!'

Sammy thumped his hand on the rocker switch and gasped as he came face to face with the largest dragon he had ever seen.

It was bigger than the dragon Sammy had once seen underneath Mrs Grock's house and even bigger than Gavin and Toby's mother's dragon. It was a beautiful orange dragon, the colour of sunset, with streaks of pink, yellow and red running up from under its belly to its head, where orange eyes gleamed like lamps from above its fanged jaw.

The dragon opened its mouth and roared, shooting forked flames towards Sammy and Darius.

In an instant, Sammy grabbed his staff as tightly as he possibly could and with the red ruby crystal at the end flashing a fiery glow, he focused on stopping the flames.

The room burst into a cloud of red mist. Darius froze solid next to Sammy and fell backwards down the stairs as stiff as a board.

The fire froze in the dragon's mouth and it became motionless. A glint in its orange eyes and the rise and fall of its scaly chest were the only signs it was still alive. A thud came from the "L" shaped bend in the room and Sammy saw two more sets of orange eyes. Shaking, Sammy threw himself forward. He closed his eyes and gripped the stairs, wishing his uncle would come up.

Downstairs, a door clicked open.

'Sammy, what's going on up there?'

Sammy caught his uncle's voice and the next thing he knew was the crash as the airing cupboard door was flung open and then his uncle came bounding up the stairs.

'Ah, you've met Paprika, Cyngard and Jovah?' Peter Pickering said reaching for Sammy's hand. 'Let's unfreeze them, shall we?'

Sammy felt a surge of warmth through his uncle's hand, through him and through his staff. The red light evaporated and the large orange dragon shook itself, clattering its scales together.

Peter Pickering threw down some green pellets and the dragon bent down and ate one. The pellet took effect straightaway and the dragon yawned, showing off large white teeth. It lay down on the floor, bent its tail around its body and rested its head on Peter Pickering's shoulder. Within seconds it was asleep.

Peter gave the bag of pellets to Darius who had woken up and joined them at the top of the stairs.

'You might need some more pellets later,' said Peter Pickering with a knowing smile. 'They can be a handful at times.'

Sammy smiled politely, thinking his uncle was a little bit insane. He couldn't see how himself, Darius and three fully grown dragons would fit into the room, which although it wasn't small, would be cramped with just one fully grown dragon, let alone with three! There also needed to be room for Kyrillan and Nelson as well.

'This one here is Paprika, my dragon,' Peter Pickering announced cheerfully. 'The black dragon, Cyngard, belongs to your father and the green one, Jovah, belongs to your mother.'

'Oh,' said Sammy, trying to take it all in. 'Paprika, Cyngard and Jovah.'

'Sin-guard and Yo-vah,' corrected Peter Pickering. 'You'll soon get used to them.'

Sammy grinned weakly. He wasn't so sure.

Peter Pickering helped shuffle Paprika to the far corner where he explained that she would get to like Sammy and Darius after a day or two of getting used to sharing her home.

Darius seemed more at ease with the dragons. 'It's exactly the same as at my home,' he explained. 'Mum and Dad have all sorts of dragons to stay while they try to make them better.'

'I see,' said Peter Pickering. 'Hopefully you and Sammy will settle in straightaway.'

Sammy nodded.

'Good. Dinner's in one hour. A wash and a set of clean clothes should put you both in Julia's good books. She's cooking your favourite Sammy, fish fingers and smiley potatoes.'

Darius giggled and Sammy went red. 'Great,' he spluttered. 'We'll just go and unpack.'

'Open the window and I'll let your dragons fly up,' said Peter Pickering.

'You can't do that,' said Darius hurriedly, 'they've just been descaled. Dr Shivers said they mustn't fly until after Christmas to let their new scales settle.'

Peter Pickering nodded. 'Good thing you said that Darius. It might have hurt them. I'll call you half an hour before tea and keep Charles and Julia in the dining room to give you time to bring them upstairs.'

'Will they fit up the stairs and into our room?' asked Sammy anxiously. He remembered the narrow staircase and had visions of trying to explain why his parents couldn't come up to bed because there was an invisible dragon blocking the stairs.

'You'd be surprised how flexible my staircase can be,' said Peter Pickering, winking at Darius.

Half an hour later, Peter Pickering called up as promised and Sammy and Darius scuttled downstairs, through the kitchen, into the back garden and into the garden shed.

Kyrillan and Nelson were wedged inside next to a very rusty lawnmower, hoe, fork and garden rake stacked next to hundreds of coloured flowerpots all different shapes and sizes. An old coat hung on the back of the door and on the bench were several DIY tools, screwdrivers, nuts and bolts strewn across the work surface.

Sammy noticed a half built model. He stepped closer and saw that it was the makings of a castle with paper plans, a replica of Dragamas set in a model countryside. He also saw a diagram of a cross, dotted with blue and green chalk. There wasn't time to look properly but he made a mental note to come back and examine it in more detail.

Sammy led Kyrillan and Nelson outside to where Darius was keeping watch. Together they led their dragons back inside as quickly as possible and up the staircase which, as promised, seemed to take the width of the bulky dragons without them touching the wallpaper.

Secretly, Sammy was worried how the older dragons would take to sharing with his and Darius's dragons. By focusing his thoughts, he could tell Darius was nervous too.

Sammy froze when he saw his father emerge from the downstairs toilet and he pushed Kyrillan up ahead.

'Sneaking upstairs eh Sammy?' said Charles Rambles. 'Make sure your mother doesn't see you that dirty when you come down for dinner. She's cooking your favourite.'

'I know,' said Sammy, hurriedly. 'We'll be down in a few minutes.'

'Good lad,' called Charles Rambles, disappearing into the dining room.

Sammy and Darius led their dragons through the airing cupboard door and up the narrow flight of stairs into their attic rooms. Sammy found that the attic expanded into a rooftop suite complete with two bedrooms, a small kitchen, lounge and ensuite bathroom shared between the bedrooms.

'Must remember to lock both doors,' Darius giggled as Sammy accidentally walked in as Darius was washing his hands.

Sammy laughed. 'This should be good.'

'Yeah,' agreed Darius. 'Come on, are you ready? I'm starving.'

Sammy followed Darius downstairs, taking in the details of the upstairs hallway of his uncle's house.

Beyond the airing cupboard were two doors leading, he guessed, to his uncle's room and bathroom. A third door opposite the stairs was slightly ajar and Sammy could see his father's golf clubs stacked in the corner next to a dresser with a television perched on top.

A whiff of his mother's special "going out" perfume floated in the air and he was glad he had changed from jeans into his black school trousers with a blue-grey short sleeve shirt.

Darius was similarly dressed in a mauve shirt with his black trousers turned slightly up at the bottom to hide a last minute toothpaste stain.

'Don't you look smart,' said Julia, with a beaming smile. She welcomed them into the dining room to sit at a round oak table with tall oak chairs. 'Now who would like gravy?'

Sammy lifted the lid of the silver dome above his silver plate. There was a "pop" and a plate of golden fish fingers appeared with smiling potato circles beaming up at him.

Peter Pickering winked at Sammy and lifted his silver dome to reveal more fish fingers.

'Irritating isn't it Charles,' said Julia Rambles. 'That "popping" noise. I can't think where it's coming from.'

Across the table Darius giggled.

Charles Rambles clicked his tongue, not quite daring to reprimand Darius for laughing at the table. Sammy was sure if it had been him who had laughed then his father would have made him eat alone in the kitchen.

As they ate, Sammy recognised the five pronged forks and crescent shaped knives used at Dragamas. He had found an easy way of cutting things by spearing food with the knife point, then turning the crescent on to its serrated edge which enabled you to cut almost anything. Thinking of this reminded him of Dr Shivers's instructions.

'May we have fresh meat tomorrow?' Sammy asked after his father had finished telling them about a law that could be applied to illegally parked cars, the bane of his day when he had been blocked in by a car parking too close in front.

'And on double yellows,' Charles Rambles grumbled. 'A traffic warden got out and asked me to move!' he exclaimed. 'He said I'd been there for longer than half an hour.'

'Had you?' asked Sammy.

'I had just arrived! How was I supposed to move when I'd been blocked in? What do you want fresh meat for anyway? Are you going to cook us dinner?'

'It's for Kyrillan,' said Sammy, feeling reckless, 'my dragon.'

There was an uncomfortable silence.

'Your what dear?' asked Julia.

'My dragon,' said Sammy resolutely. 'You know, "flap flap",' he used his arms as wings and pretended to blow fire.

'Are you a little tired?' asked Charles. 'It's been a long day in a strange new place has it. When I came home from boarding school it always took a little while to settle in.'

'It's Sammy's imaginary friend,' added Darius, his helpful intention backfiring.

'His what!' roared Charles. 'Tell me boy, have you lost your mind!'

'He needs fresh meat,' said Sammy weakly, pointing to his uncle, 'like yours.'

'Perhaps you'd better go to bed,' said Julia reaching for Sammy's forehead.

'No! I want to hear this,' Charles Rambles slammed his fist down on the table making Sammy jump. 'Is this the kind of rubbish they teach you at Drabblers?'

'Dragamas,' said Sammy stiffly. 'It's not rubbish, it's all true.' He pushed back from the table and stormed upstairs. He had just reached the airing cupboard when his uncle appeared in a silver mist in front of him looking worried.

'You can't tell them. They won't believe you,' he whispered.

'But it's true.'

'I know,' said Peter Pickering. 'But for them, that time has passed. I'm sorry, there's nothing I can do. Come back down with me, apologise, say you were over tired, eat some dessert and we'll find a way to help them see again.'

Sammy sniffed, wiping the back of his wrist across his eyes.

'I know how important it is to you.'

Through his uncle's smile, Sammy detected something he couldn't place but he allowed himself to be led downstairs where his mother had cleared the plates and replaced them with bowls of strawberry trifle with a thick layer of custard and cream on top of the fresh fruit.

Sammy took a deep breath. 'I'm-sorry-I'm-tired,' he mumbled, grateful that neither his mother, his father nor Darius flinched or laughed at him.

He ate the large serving of strawberry, custard and cream trifle his mother dolloped into his dish and was pleased when his uncle turned the conversation to jewellery, telling them about a large delivery of precious stones a short bearded man had delivered to him in a wheelbarrow earlier in the week.

Eventually, after several hours of television and a long discussion about Dragamas in which Sammy made his lessons sound incredibly dull and dragon-free, Sammy yawned. Darius had already fallen asleep in one of the big armchairs in the sitting room and had to be prodded and carried upstairs by Sammy's father.

'I'll take him from here,' Sammy whispered as he opened the airing cupboard door.

'Thanks Sam. Your mother and I will see you in the morning. We're going for a spot of Christmas shopping.'

'Great,' said Sammy. 'Night Dad, see you tomorrow.'

Sammy pushed Darius in his zombiefied state up the last stairs into the attic rooms.

The large orange dragon, Paprika, was asleep at the top of the stairs. Sammy prodded Darius to climb over its scaly back whispering for him to be quiet. The dragon didn't stir.

He helped Darius into the larger of the two bedrooms, the one Darius had won from the toss of a coin, and slumped him on to the thick quilted bed, putting the pillows under his head. Darius snored gently.

Sammy closed the door behind him, catching sight of the shadow of Nelson slinking in through the bathroom so he could sleep at the foot or Darius's bed.

When Sammy walked into his own bedroom, he found Kyrillan curled up between his parents' dragons and felt a lump in his throat.

His small blue-green dragon was nestled under the paws of his mother's green dragon, Jovah, and had his head resting on the tail of his father's black dragon, Cyngard.

'A family of dragons,' Sammy whispered, changing into his pyjamas. 'I wish Mum and Dad could see this.'

In his mind's eye, he saw himself drop a coin into Mrs Grock's wishing well, watched by Professor Burlay, Commander Altair, Dr Lithoman, Professor Sanchez and everyone in his class.

'I wish my parents could see...draaaagons,' Sammy rubbed his eyes and fell asleep.

CHAPTER 25

A LITTLE CHAT

The following morning, Sammy woke to find his room had been covered with brightly coloured tinsel and sparkling baubles. It was like a grotto. He could hear his mother in the attic lounge making what smelt like warm toast and from the murmur of voices he could tell that Darius was awake too.

He got up, annoyed to find all five dragons were crowded in his room. Kyrillan was standing underneath the giant paws of Paprika, Cyngard and Jovah were lying full length at the end of his bed and Nelson was perched on top of a large wooden chest of drawers next to two wooden wardrobes.

'Morning Sammy!' shouted Darius as Sammy went through to the bathroom.

'Morning!' Sammy yelled back.

When he came out of the bathroom, he found his mother and Darius were sitting at the small table in the lounge. His mother looked at him with concern.

'Are you alright honey?'

Sammy nodded. 'I must have been tired. There's no dragons here.'

Darius giggled, stopping at a reproving look from Julia.

'I'm sorry Mrs Rambles,' Darius said apologetically.

'Call me Julia please honey. I may be European Manager of the largest bank in the world but there will be no "Mrs Rambles" from my son's friends, thank you very much.'

'Yes, Mrs um Julia,' said Darius.

Sammy grinned at Darius. 'No dragons here.'

To his mother's annoyance both Sammy and Darius erupted into hysterical laughter.

'Well really Samuel. This is hardly a laughing matter. Your father and I are quite worried.'

Sammy and Darius were still laughing as Julia stood up and left the room shaking her head in despair.

'Well really Samuel,' Darius laughed wiping a tear away. 'This is no laughing matter.'

Sammy stopped laughing. 'I wish they could see Kyrillan.'

Darius nodded somberly, 'I know.'

Sammy and Darius spent the rest of the day in the village with Sammy's parents while his uncle was at working in his jewellers shop, P. Pickering & Co.

They met Gavin and Toby briefly in the village café, where Darius used his voucher for a free drink, but since they were also with their parents, and especially since Anita Reed held Sammy responsible for the death of her dragon, they didn't have much time to talk other than to wish Gavin and Toby a good time on their skiing holiday.

After lunch in the café, Sammy and Darius were allowed to wander around the village, which since neither of them knew it very well, they were reluctant to go far beyond the Woodland Ranchers training ground, where they found the hole in the hedge had been repaired with a barbed wire fence with a wooden sign saying "Please Use The Main Entrance".

The evening passed quickly and Sammy found, as much as he pretended he wasn't excited, that he was really looking forward to spending Christmas day at his uncle's house.

Downstairs, Julia had sprayed the windowsills with powdered flour to look like snow. She had bought sparking lights and lots of garlands of tinsel which she placed in every room to make the whole house look very festive.

A warm smell from the real log fire in the lounge completed the Christmas scene. Even Peter Pickering was pleased to join in and helped to hang foil decorations from the ceiling.

Darius joined in too, although Sammy quickly got tired of him saying that he wished it was like this at his home. Having seen similar decorations all his life, Sammy took it for granted.

Every year, the week before Christmas the decorations would go up and every year the week after Christmas, they would come down again.

Sammy was glad when he could stumble upstairs with Darius. He carried a bag of presents to wrap in each hand and a roll of green and gold wrapping paper, complete with sticky tape and scissors hanging precariously on the end, tucked under his arm.

'I'll finish wrapping these tonight,' said Sammy.

'Aren't you leaving it a bit late?' Darius giggled. 'I'm going to bed.'

'Probably,' Sammy laughed. 'See you tomorrow Darius.'

'Night Sammy,' said Darius, disappearing into his bedroom.

Sammy curled up using Kyrillan as a backrest on the floor of his bedroom while he wrapped up the presents.

There was a book of professional golf tips from the antique bookshop next to the café for his father and a selection of bath salts for his mother. He had bought Darius a wind-up pocket torch and his uncle a pair of dragon hide gloves from the hardware store in a side street they had come across.

He wrapped the parcels as best he could in the green and gold paper. Kyrillan helped by putting his paw on the join ready for Sammy to put on the tape. He added a gold bow and streamers to the parcels and crept downstairs to put them next to Darius's gifts under the tree. He found a present with his name on it and gave the parcel a squeeze.

'Chocolates,' he grinned, moving round to the presents from his parents. Some of the presents were wrapped in birthday paper. With his birthday so close to Christmas it looked as though some of the parcels had been doubled up for both celebrations.

The first parcel was long and thin with knobbly bits underneath.

'Skateboard,' whispered Sammy. 'Like I need that when I've got a fire breathing dragon that can fly!'

'Is that you Sammy?' came a voice out of the darkness.

'Uncle Peter?' Sammy spun round.

His uncle was standing by the door dressed from head to toe in a long black robe.

'I think you and me need a little chat.'

Sammy froze, his blood shivered inside his veins. His uncle, the Shape, their mission. It all came flooding back.

'Don't you agree?' Peter Pickering waved his cloaked arm towards the sofa. 'Sit.'

Sammy put the skateboard down, wishing the ground would swallow him up. He reached for the replica of the stone cross around his neck, the cold metal giving him confidence. He stood up and walked over to the sofa without taking his eyes off his uncle.

'I know you know about my work.'

'The jewellers,' said Sammy, focusing on the black cloak, estimating the distance between the sofa and the front door. Twelve paces he reckoned, not enough.

'The Shape,' said Peter, giving a hollow cough. 'In the Great Pyramid, you considered joining our quest.'

Sammy felt his fingers twitch in his lap and held them tightly together, his left hand nested inside his right.

'When your friend betrayed you, I thought you would join.'

'You're not in the Shape,' stammered Sammy. 'You're my uncle.'

'I know you have seen how it happened. In the clearing.'

'It wasn't your fault, they made you...' Sammy faltered, 'you had no choice.'

Peter came over and knelt on the carpet beside Sammy, their eyes locked together. 'Don't be afraid. I will protect you where I can. A lot of people lost a lot of things that day. May I tell you the rest of the story?'

Sammy nodded, words drying up in his mouth. His hands, he was pleased to see, had stopped shaking and were getting hot and sweaty instead.

'Very well,' said Peter tapping his staff to conjour two mugs of hot chocolate. 'It's safe,' he added as Sammy looked at the thick brown broth suspiciously.

Peter tapped his staff again towards the fireplace and brought to life a roaring fire to keep them warm.

'The story starts about twenty years ago, several years before you were born, when your parents were at Dragamas together. Your father and I were in the same house.'

'My father was at Dragamas?' exclaimed Sammy, spluttering into his hot chocolate.

Peter nodded. 'Cyngard belongs to him. Raised from an egg much like young Kyrillan.'

'Oh.'

'Indeed. Your mother was there at Dragamas as well. She was in a different house, long before there were compass points and before Sir Ragnarok became headmaster.'

'Oh,' said Sammy, things slipping into place. 'When did you...'

Peter held up his hand. 'In good time.' He lit a pipe and began to smoke. 'Anyway, I introduced your parents to each other. I'd never seen my sister, your mother, so happy. Not even when she got her dragon necklace she'd seen in Dragon Today magazine.'

'Mrs Deane reads that.'

'I know,' Peter smiled, 'your mother still wears the necklace, it's blue-green.'

'Draconite?' whispered Sammy.

Peter nodded. 'The beginning of dark days.'

Sammy covered a yawn with his hand that Peter noticed.

'I'll cut a long story short. I traded myself for her.'

Sammy's mouth fell open. 'You...'

Peter nodded again. 'That ceremony you saw. That was when I did it. An initiation into a world of dark sorcery and magic you could only dream of. But,' Peter paused, 'it didn't suit me and I tried to escape, but it can't be undone...unless.'

Sammy was hooked. 'What?'

'Unless the stones are put back into the Stone Cross.'

Sammy gasped, his mind jumbled and tangled.

'Too much for one night I expect. Trust me.'

'Wait! You said you traded yourself for my mum?'

'I said that's enough for one night.'

'So that means she was in the Shape?'

Peter pressed his finger to his lips. 'I said that was enough for one night. Now would you like to watch some television with me?'

Sammy shook his head. He knew he'd heard enough for one night. He said goodnight to his uncle and, taking his mug of hot chocolate, he padded upstairs.

When he reached the airing cupboard he saw two green stockings, hanging on the door, one embroidered with a Father Christmas riding his sleigh and one with boughs of holly. He checked the tags and unhitched the Father Christmas sack, which had his name on the tag, and went up to bed.

Darius woke him at half past six in the morning by flinging his present filled stocking with a thump on to Sammy's bed.

'Morning!' shouted Darius. 'Look! I've got a stocking! We never have this at home!'

Sammy rubbed the sleep out of his eyes and reached for his stocking he remembered leaving at the bottom of his bed.

'You've got one too!'

'Yeah,' said Sammy sleepily.

'Mine was hung on the door! Santa-Claus has been here!'

'Mmm,' said Sammy. 'You know it's...' he paused looking at Darius's excited face.

'I heard reindeer hooves on the roof last night!'

Sammy grinned. 'I bet it's snowed. We can build snowmen.'

'Cool!' said Darius ripping open the coloured paper in his lap. 'Look it's some playing cards!'

'Wow!' said Sammy, the Christmas excitement getting the better of him. 'I think um, Santa's done a good job here, look, I've got a pair of socks!'

Darius giggled opening another parcel. 'They're gloves stupid. Look I've got some too.'

Sammy checked, they were indeed gloves. He rubbed his eyes again, still reeling from the conversation with his uncle last night.

'Chocolate snowmen!' shrieked Darius, opening another present. 'This is so cool!'

When all of the parcels had been opened, Sammy shared some of his chocolate snowmen with Kyrillan and Nelson, who had been eyeing them up, licking their lips.

The older dragons, woken by Darius's shouts, looked in but refused the chocolate, retreating haughtily as if it wasn't good enough for them.

The retreated further when Sammy taught Darius how to play a card game called "Slam" and they started shouting as they dealt cards on the duvet cover.

A short while later, Sammy's mother came in to wish them both a Happy Christmas and to take them downstairs for breakfast. Sammy couldn't believe that she couldn't see, hear or smell the large dragons that were only a few feet away from her.

They settled into sofas in the lounge eating chocolates by the fire and looking at the presents under the tree.

Uncle Peter came into the lounge with Charles Rambles. Their arms were full of logs and they had a light dusting of snow on their clothes and boots.

'We've got to keep the fire stoked for you boys,' Peter chuckled and heaved the logs into a wicker basket beside the fire. 'Happy Christmas Sammy, Happy Christmas Darius!'

'Happy Christmas Uncle Peter,' said Darius, grinning with his mouth full of chocolate snowmen.

'Uncle Peter,' Peter laughed. 'Now I have two nephews.'

'Double trouble,' said Charles. 'Let's get cracking opening all these presents!'

'Not until after lunch,' Julia called through the kitchen door. 'I need some volunteers to help peel some potatoes.'

Sammy gave the parcels a longing look and went in to the kitchen to help with the vegetables for the Christmas lunch.

'One of your friends called round earlier this morning,' said Julia, 'a girl with green hair,' she looked at Sammy, 'I hope you're not mixing with the wrong sort of people. It's nice of you to have girl friends but...'

'Dixie's all right,' said Sammy attacking a giant potato.

'Careful Sammy, if you peel it too much there won't be any left.'

'Why didn't you tell me she was here?' Sammy hacked at the potato.

'You were having fun with your stocking with Darius.'

'You should have said,' grumbled Sammy.

'She said she'd call again in a few days time. Something about seeing her grandparents. I'm not sure she's good company for you honey. She called them trolls.'

Sammy burst out laughing, then held it back. If his parents didn't believe dragons existed, they certainly wouldn't be happy that his best friend was related to trolls.

'Why has she got green hair?' asked Julia. 'I wouldn't have thought the school would allow that kind of thing.'

'It's genetic,' said Sammy, turning away and biting his knuckle to prevent himself laughing hysterically.

'Sammy really!'

'Sorry Mum,' giggled Sammy as he set to work on another potato.

When he had peeled the last of nearly thirty potatoes he passed them to his mum who sliced them into halves, smeared them with butter and put them into a roasting tin.

'I don't know what I'd do without you here sis,' said Peter dancing into the kitchen with Charles.

Julia blushed. 'It's not really my thing this. I prefer the city life myself.'

'Why are you here?' asked Sammy. 'You never used to take this much holiday.'

Julia shuffled by the sink making Sammy a little uncomfortable. 'I was going to tell you earlier...'

'What is it?' asked Sammy. 'Tell me!'

'Your mother's been fired,' said Peter grinning at Julia.

Julia slapped Peter's shoulder. 'Don't tease him. I was looking for the right moment.'

'Your mother's trying to tell you that she's on extended maternity leave. You're going to have a baby brother or sister soon,' said Charles Rambles.

'A what?' said Sammy, his jaw dropping. 'What if I don't want one?'

'It will be fun Sammy,' said Peter. 'Who knows, they might follow you to Dragamas.'

'Not if they can't see it,' snapped Sammy, surprised at himself and catching Peter's warning glance he added, 'um, I mean that will be great. Congratulations!'

A few hours later, Sammy found that after a large Christmas dinner, crackers, presents, where to his surprise he received a double ended Firestick, to use in Sports lessons, from his uncle and a small glass of wine that he was feeling very sleepy. He curled up in the armchair beside the fire thinking it had been the best Christmas ever and closed his eyes.

CHAPTER 26

GATHERING EVIDENCE

Four days later, he was still curled up in what had become known as "Sammy's Chair" watching the flames roaring in the iron grate.

Having fallen off trying to show Sammy a new trick on the skateboard, Darius had his wrist wrapped tightly in a bandage.

They were watching the chat show with Dr Livitupadup, who was talking to two men who were having a dispute over a garden fence.

A crowd of about thirty people had assembled to watch the argument escalate. Dr Livitupadup had brought in two JCBs and was offering a hundred pounds to the man who could knock down the largest part of the fence first. The crowd cheered as the men climbed inside the machines and charged towards the fence.

Sammy had just about given up all hope of seeing Dixie when the doorbell rang. He leaped up to answer it, but it was just his father back from collecting a newspaper and had forgotten his key.

At the same time, there was a knock at the back door that Peter Pickering answered.

'A guest for you,' said Peter, opening the door.

Dixie's green head bobbed around the corner.

'Hey Sammy! Hi Darius!'

'Are you North?' asked Peter. 'With green hair, you should be.'

Dixie nodded. 'Doesn't make me any different though.'

'I nearly married a troll,' Peter grinned, 'but she turned me down though.'

'Do you want to go upstairs?' asked Sammy, switching off the television.

Dr Livitupadup and the man waving his hundred pounds of winnings for demolishing the fence first disappeared from sight.

'Sure,' said Dixie.

'Come on then!'

Sammy led Dixie and Darius upstairs, across the hall and through the airing cupboard and up the flight of stairs into their attic suite.

'Wow!' said Dixie looking around. 'This is really cool. Are those your parents' dragons?'

Sammy nodded, a huge grin on his face.

'Have you explored downstairs? What did you find?'

Sammy paused, sharing an embarrassed look with Darius.

'We, um, kind of forgot about it,' mumbled Darius, 'look Sammy got me this wind-up torch.'

'That's great,' said Dixie, a little sarcastically, piecing together her staff. 'Like you need that.'

'I'm better with crystals,' snapped Darius, 'look!'

Sammy braced himself, Darius was holding the ruby, detached from the end of his staff. In the palm of his hand it gave off a swirling red mist.

'Yeah, that's so...oh...oh...good...Dar...i...us,' Dixie frowned stepping in slow motion towards Darius, 'un...do...it.'

Darius covered the stone with his free hand. 'See,' he snapped, 'I can do things you can't.'

'Are we going exploring?' asked Sammy, glad he hadn't been affected by Darius's stone. 'I'll see if my parents are going out.'

'Uncle Peter should be working by now,' said Darius. 'He usually goes into his shop about this time.'

'Yeah?' snapped Dixie. 'Since when has been your uncle? He's in the Shape.'

'You don't know that for sure,' snapped Darius angrily.

'I'll just see if they're going out...' started Sammy. 'I'll be back in a minute.'

Sammy met his mother in the landing. She was wearing a cream woolly bobble hat, matching cream gloves and scarf and a fashionably long thick black coat with gold buttons.

'Just popping out with your father. We're looking at prams in the sales, that sort of thing. I hear your friend has called round.'

Sammy nodded. 'Yeah, Dixie's here.'

Julia leaned in close to give him a kiss. 'Just don't go dying your hair green honey,' she whispered.

'I won't,' promised Sammy, skipping back upstairs to tell Dixie and Darius.

'Cool!' said Darius, pushing Nelson off his lap. 'Let's go!'

Dixie led the way downstairs into the hallway.

'Which way?' asked Sammy.

'At home, our cellar leads out of a trapdoor under the stairs,' said Darius.

'Let's try it,' said Dixie, pulling open the door to the cupboard under the stairs.

Pots and pans fell out and a spider scuttled past them into the kitchen. Cobwebs hung down from the ceiling.

'Spooky,' giggled Darius.

Sammy peered over Darius's shoulder. 'Look!' he whispered. 'Is there a trapdoor under that box?'

Darius kicked the box aside and crouched on one knee. 'You're right, it's here.'

'Open it,' said Dixie impatiently.

Darius creaked the trapdoor open, dust flying up. A set of stone steps like in Mrs Grock's house led down into darkness.

'Fire,' whispered Dixie, creating a series of flames no bigger than a candle that followed each other bouncing down the steps.

Sammy squeezed past the flames, holding on to a cold metal handrail for support.

He created his own, larger, fire and held it at arm's length using his staff.

The cellar was a large square room. Exactly as he had seen two months ago, there were shelves upon shelves of bottles of green liquid with the small skull and cross bones on the label. Some of the liquid had spilt on the shelf and was oozing and dripping to the floor.

On the opposite side of the narrow room were the brown sacks of Hyperium Haycorn with some of the oats scattered on the floor from a split bag.

'I've brought a camera, a bottle and a bag,' whispered Dixie. 'We have to show Sir Ragnarok this time.'

'I'm sorry Sammy,' said Darius. 'Your uncle is in the Shape.'

'Peter Pickering,' said Sammy, thinking of the expensive Firestick and Christmas presents his uncle had given him. 'It's not possible.'

'Look around you Sammy. This is poison. Dragons will die,' said Dixie. 'Remember the fifth year dragons. This stuff here, it killed them, he killed them for their stones.'

'He said it has to be done,' said Sammy, blinking away a tear, 'that the stones would help my mum see dragons.'

'Only dead ones,' said Dixie. 'He's lied to you Sammy. Can't you see that?'

Sammy paused, his eyes prickly, his hands shaking. 'I thought it was just a bad dream us seeing this on Bonfire Night. I didn't think we'd actually find it.'

'Are you ok Sammy?'

Sammy nodded. 'I just need to be alone.' In the darkness, he unstrapped his Casino watch and put it in his pocket.

'Ok, we'll just be a minute,' said Dixie, 'take a few photos, then we'll come up.'

'Or we could go out for a bit,' said Darius giving Dixie a nudge.

'Yeah, we could,' agreed Dixie.

'Ok,' said Sammy bleakly. He walked up the stone steps to the sound of the camera clicking at the evidence to prove without a doubt that his uncle, the man who he respected and who had promised to protect him from the evil in the Shape had lied to him and make him believe that dragons had to die. He stomped up to his bedroom and curled up using Kyrillan's paws as tissues to wipe tears from his eyes.

Several hours later Sammy woke to Darius knocking on his bedroom door.

'Come in,' said Sammy wiping his eyes as Darius's face poked around the door.

'Dixie's gone,' said Darius picking up a handful of chocolate snowmen. 'Can I have these?'

'Help yourself,' said Sammy picking himself up off the bed. 'I guess we should pack.'

'Last day tomorrow,' mumbled Darius his mouth full, 'It's been great staying here.'

Sammy nodded half-heartedly. He wished he could say the same.

After tea, Uncle Peter showed them how to build card houses seven storeys high. He handed out more chocolate snowmen, chocolate penguins, chocolate reindeer and steaming mugs of hot chocolate until the clock chimed midnight and they stood outside watching the fireworks in the distance and went in to watch the Queen's speech on television.

'Happy New Year,' beamed Julia, giving Sammy and Darius a huge hug. 'Make a wish!'

Sammy closed his eyes, jerking them open as a loud bang rocked the patio and a shower of coloured sparks fell around them.

'Peter, I do wish you'd say if you were going to do that!' scolded Julia, but she watched all the same as Sammy's uncle let off a display of coloured fireworks culminating in a seven foot catherine wheel that dropped fluorescent orange sparks all the way down the lawn.

'Back to school soon eh Sammy.'

Sammy looked up, his father never called him "Sammy".

'Make sure you work hard,' said Charles, 'do us proud.'

Sammy nodded, helping himself to a large hotdog freshly cooked on the barbeque.

'There's a good boy.' Charles sat back in a reclining garden chair, his hand fixed around a large glass of brandy.

It was nearly two o'clock when the rumbles, cheers and fireworks died down. Linking arms with Darius, Sammy stumbled inside with a few sausages wrapped in a purple serviette and went upstairs, just managing to avoid the sleeping dragons. Sammy found he only just made it to bed before falling asleep himself.

The last day passed at lightning speed. Kyrillan ate both the sausages and the purple serviette and Sammy was glad he'd managed to feed his dragon the fresh meat he had promised Dr Shivers.

By seven o'clock in the evening Sammy was hauling his suitcase downstairs.

In the hallway, Uncle Peter pressed a fat black leather-bound book with the initials "L.R." embossed on the cover into Sammy's hands.

'Late Christmas present,' muttered Uncle Peter, 'keep it secret.'

Without thinking, Sammy stuffed the book into his suitcase with a quick "thank you".

After a large evening meal Sammy and Darius went to bed. Sammy fell asleep easily having grown used to the gentle snores of the dragons who shared his room.

He woke early to find Darius jumping up and down beside his bed.

'Wake up! Wake up!' shouted Darius leaping from one side of the room to the other and back again.

Sammy groaned. It was so warm in bed and poking his toes out of the end of the duvet felt icy cold.

'Come on! I'll wait for you outside.'

Sammy forced his eyes to open. 'Ok, give me five more minutes.'

Downstairs, they ate a "goodbye" breakfast cooked by both of Sammy's parents. His father looked particularly impressed.

'Good to hear you're sticking with this school Sammy,' said Charles patting Julia's stomach. 'If you get some good results we'll send your new brother or sister there.'

'Sister,' said Julia laughing. 'I hope it's a girl.'

Peter laughed too. 'Got your suitcases boys?'

'They're in the hallway,' said Darius. 'Thank you so much for having me to stay over the holiday.'

'No trouble at all.' Julia smiled and bustled them out of the doorway. 'We'll see you at Easter Sammy.'

Peter held up a piece of paper he withdrew from an envelope. 'Not this time Jules, they can spend the holiday here if we sign this.'

Julia took the paper and looked at the pictures. 'The Land of the Pharaohs? Is that an adventure park?'

Thinking firmly of Hotel de la Pyramid and the Oasis pool with the ice-cream man he nodded, not daring to tell his parents what happened in the Great Pyramid.'

'Not just an adventure park,' Peter chuckled. 'It's educational too. They have a special section on Egyptology, Pyramids, Pharaohs, the whole works.'

'Educational you say,' beamed Charles Rambles, taking the paper and a gold pen from his shirt pocket. 'We'll have a bit of that.' He squiggled an illegible signature that Sammy knew would read "Charles Richard Rambles" when held upside down against a mirror.

Sammy forced a grin. He hadn't enjoyed the Land of the Pharaohs as much as the Floating Circus.

'I've got my signature,' said Darius. 'It came in the post this morning from my parents. I wanted to wait and see if you'd get yours signed too!'

'It's settled then,' said Julia. 'Let us know if you change your mind Sammy. If not, we might go back to Switzerland for a few weeks. I'd like to make sure they're still keeping my job open for me.'

Sammy swallowed hard. 'Ok, I'll go.'

'There's a good boy,' said Charles. 'Send us a postcard eh?'

Sammy nodded at his father, glad when his mother and Darius cleared away the plates and it was time to go.

He sat next to his uncle in the front of the silver Volvo. Kyrillan and Nelson were squashed into the boot. Darius sat between the two uprighted suitcases squashed shut more tightly this time since both cases were brim full with clothes books and presents. Sammy had insisted on taking his skateboard back despite Darius teasing "what do you need a skateboard for when you've got Kyrillan?" It was wedged between Sammy's knees and there was very little room for anything else.

The car creaked and grumbled but carried them through the village and out into the country lanes. They climbed the steep hill and stopped in the layby opposite the Dragamas gates.

'Here you are boys,' said Peter, parking his car in behind the Griffin family's campervan.

Sammy took out his skateboard and helped Darius with the suitcases. Kyrillan and Nelson shuffled forward when Peter Pickering opened the boot flapping their wings and shaking their tails.

CHAPTER 27

TOUGH DECISIONS

Dr Shivers was standing outside the school gates with Professor Burlay. They were ticking names off a register as the students came back from their holidays.

'Hello Sammy. Hello Darius,' Dr Shivers smiled, his eyes flickering in recognition as he saw Sammy's uncle.

'Zachariah!' exclaimed Peter. 'How nice to see you again,' he shook Dr Shivers's hand vigorously. 'We were at Dragamas together,' he explained to Sammy.

'No skateboards,' said Dr Shivers.

'No problem,' said Peter, reaching out to Sammy.

Reluctantly Sammy passed the skateboard back to his uncle.

'You don't mind if I help him do you?' asked Peter.

Dr Shivers smiled. 'Third years and above usually, but I'll look away for an old friend.'

'Do you have your staff Sammy?' asked Peter.

Sammy nodded pulling this staff out of his coat pocket and assembling it.

Peter's eyes lurched as he took in the wooden branch. 'My my,' he muttered clutching Sammy's wrist.

Using the onyx and ruby end of the staff he guided Sammy to tap twice, first on his suitcase, then on Darius's suitcase.

The suitcases shimmered, hummed and lifted off the ground.

'Focus Sammy and that should be enough to get you to the castle.'

'Thank you,' said Sammy and Darius at the same time, both very glad not to be lifting the heavy cases by hand.

'I'll see you in the summer perhaps,' said Peter, letting go of Sammy's wrist. He smiled at the boys. 'Goodbye.'

Sammy nodded, feeling the suitcases vibrating. It required his utmost concentration to guide them. He had to focus harder than anything he had tried in the past.

'It'll come naturally, eventually,' chuckled Dr Shivers. 'Off you go. I've ticked your names on the register so we know you're back safely. Walk up the driveway and concentrate on keeping the cases airborne. It will be much easier than using the Shute.'

'Bye Uncle Peter!' shouted Darius, waving as the silver Volvo turned around and disappeared back down the narrow lane.

Sammy guided the two suitcases in parallel up the rain soaked driveway, dodging the puddles. For January, it was quite mild but there were dark snow clouds overhead mingling with the golden mist that hung over the school.

'What land do you reckon is overhead?' asked Darius, squinting up at the sky. 'Land of Clouds?' he giggled. 'Oops sorry Sammy, concentrate on our cases. I don't want to carry them.' Darius paused to blow on his gloved hands to keep warm. 'Hey do you reckon that's why Dr Shivers said we couldn't use the Shute? If you drop them here we wouldn't be able to use to conveyor belt and it will be much harder.'

Sammy nodded feeling his knuckles press hard on the inside of his skin with so much concentrating. He couldn't see how Dr Shivers could think this could possibly become natural.

'Perhaps you shouldn't try so hard,' suggested Darius. 'Your hands are turning blue.'

Sammy dropped Darius's case on to the gravel courtyard.

'Hey!' exclaimed Darius. 'I was only joking.'

With Darius's case on the floor, Sammy felt ten times better. Just moving his own case was much easier than moving two. It was also easier than moving fire.

Mrs Grock appeared at the castle door with Captain Firebreath. She took one look at Sammy and his moving suitcase and held the door wide open for him.

'I'll get yer case,' Captain Firebreath growled to Darius.

Sammy bumped into Jock on the stairs.

'Thanks for the book Sammy,' said Jock grinning as he held out a small present for Sammy. 'It's just some coins from the Land of the Pharaohs. I thought you might like them.'

Jock put the parcel on top of Sammy's airborne suitcase and skipped down the stairs to the Main Hall.

Sammy was grateful to find their tower door open when he reached the second year dormitory inside the North tower.

It was empty, but from the mess of clothes and wrapping paper, Sammy could tell that Gavin, Toby and Jock had already arrived. On Gavin's table was a large framed photograph of him and Toby in the middle of a ski jump on a snowy mountain and a handful of gold, silver and bronze coins in a presentation box.

Sammy let his suitcase fall with a bang on to the stone floor and began unpacking his clothes, folding them and packing them away into his chest of drawers.

He took out the black leather book with "L.R." embossed on it that his uncle had given him and put it on top of the chest of drawers.

As he let go, the book bounced off and fell on the floor. Sure he had put it down securely, Sammy bent down and the book opened all by itself, it's pages fluttering.

Sammy took a step back. He had thought the book looked creepy when his uncle had given it to him in secret. He stared at the book.

Eventually, the pages stopped fluttering and Sammy saw that it had fallen open on a page showing some strange triangular diagrams. He didn't have a chance to take a proper look before Darius and Captain Firebreath arrived in the tower room, both completely out of breath.

'You got lead weights in there?' grumbled Captain Firebreath straightening his jacket and pulling his dungarees straps up to the top of his white shirt. Still muttering, he left the tower room and plodded upwards to help two first year boys with their cases.

'More presents!' shouted Darius catching sight of Jock's parcel on his chest of drawers.

'It's coins,' said Sammy staring at the book. It was very strange. The triangular diagrams had vanished. The page had gone blank.

'Coins,' said Darius looking at Gavin and Toby's drawers. 'Have we all got some?'

Sammy unwrapped his parcel and showed Darius the five coin collection.

'I've already got some of these,' said Darius, 'they're from the Land of the Pharaohs.'

Sammy nodded. 'Jock went there for Christmas.'

They had just finished unpacking when there was a knock on the door and Sir Ragnarok came in.

Sir Ragnarok looked gravely at Sammy. 'Would you accompany me to my office?'

Sammy shoved the book under his pillow and followed Sir Ragnarok back downstairs. Gavin and Toby ran past them followed in slow motion by Jock. Sir Ragnarok tapped Jock's shoulder, releasing him from the ruby crystal and he tore upstairs shouting after Gavin and Toby. Sammy wished he could go back with them.

Sir Ragnarok led Sammy up the twisting stairwell behind the tapestry in the Main Hall. Sammy looked as the Dragon Knight fell back into place and saw the five tables lined up ready for their evening meal.

'The second years are having a lesson with Dr Shivers this afternoon,' said Sir Ragnarok as they reached the top of the spiral staircase. 'I've told him I wanted to see you, so he'll know not to expect you.'

'Thank you,' said Sammy bleakly, feeling that this was the right thing to say.'

'Your uncle...'

'I know,' interrupted Sammy. 'He told me he's in the Shape.'

'Slow down Sammy, we'll come to that in a moment. I was saying that your uncle gave your dragon to Dr Shivers to take inside for you.'

'Oh,' said Sammy feeling foolish.

Sir Ragnarok took him up the seven stairs into his office. Lariston, Sir Ragnarok's smoke grey cat, was curled in a ball on the purple two seat settee.

'Ate too many mince pies,' explained Sir Ragnarok. 'Exactly the same as last year.'

Sammy smiled politely and sat down at Sir Ragnarok's invitation. Lariston cocked his head but made no move towards Sammy.

'Will he be alright?'

'Oh yes, he has a stomach as strong as a dragon. He's just looking for sympathy. Anyhow, to business.'

Sammy shivered, a swarm of butterflies kicked in his stomach. On Sir Ragnarok's desk he could see a bulging brown envelope.

Sir Ragnarok picked up the envelope, twisting and turning it in his hands.

'Would you like a spot of tea?' Sir Ragnarok asked, his eyes twinkling.

Sammy nodded. 'Is that from Dixie?'

Sir Ragnarok tapped his staff and a silver table with a silver teapot and two silver cups with silver saucers appeared from thin air. Sammy jumped as a silver bowl with sugar cubes popped on to the table between the cups and the teapot.

Sir Ragnarok poured the tea, handing Sammy one of the hot cups.

'Inside this envelope, I understand, is the evidence you withheld from me on Bonfire Night.'

Sammy looked at his shoes. 'We only saw it. I wanted to be sure.'

Sir Ragnarok put a finger to his lips. 'I haven't opened the envelope yet. It has to be your decision to hand it in.'

Sammy looked up and blinked in surprise.

'I want you to think of the consequences of your discovery. Your uncle has been helpful to Dragamas in the past. He took gemstones from the castle and sold them through his jewellery shop last year to give me some of the money for the ransom.'

'He would, wouldn't he!' exclaimed Sammy. 'He gets draconite by paying people or from our dragons if we didn't raise the money. He couldn't lose!'

Sir Ragnarok nodded. 'You are wise beyond the years of your fellow classmates. Yet is it in you to break your mother's heart?'

Sir Ragnarok tapped the screens behind him. As if filmed underwater, Sammy could see his parents and his uncle watching television at his uncle's house. Though he couldn't hear them, he could see his uncle patting his mother's stomach, laughing and joking. She was smiling.

'My uncle saved her from the Shape,' said Sammy.

'But at what cost?' thundered Sir Ragnarok smacking his fist on the table and making the sugar cubes leap out of the silver bowl. 'She lost sight of dragons. She lost her powers of healing with crystals. Through the swap your parents lost their places as Dragon Knights!'

Sammy choked on his tea. 'My parents were Dragon Knights?'

Sir Ragnarok nodded. 'Work we could have undone if they had merely joined the Shape under hypnosis but to strip them of their powers at the height of their success Peter would have been paid handsomely for that.'

'So he is in the Shape?'

'Part of the Shape, I believe. Your discoveries have helped but I am only beginning to put this puzzle together. I understand the vision you had was the ceremony orchestrated by your uncle to lure your parents and take their powers.'

'They walked away,' said Sammy, not daring to ask how Sir Ragnarok knew about the ceremony.

'Yes,' said Sir Ragnarok. 'They walked away with no recollection of Dragamas. No idea about dragons. Why would they stay? They got into a horse drawn carriage at the gates. Old Samagard took them home.'

'I didn't see that,' whispered Sammy, helping himself to a sugar cube.

Lariston looked over and purred. Sammy gave him a sugar cube as well.

'What will happen to him...if he is in the Shape?' asked Sammy.

'He will be sent like Dr Lithoman, Eliza Elungwen, to the Dragon Cells, the Snorgcadell. There he will be stripped of his powers and his staff will be crushed.'

Sammy thought for a moment. 'Can he use his star?'

'The red dots chasing our Dragamas constellation? Only if he has successfully performed the ritual to do so. If not, he will be kept in the Snorgcadell serving, I presume, a life sentence, however this would be decided in our courts.

Sir Ragnarok paused to drink his tea. He poured some into a silver saucer for Lariston.

'Have you decided?' Sir Ragnarok asked. 'Or would you like a little more time?'

Sammy fast tracked through his memories with his uncle, him coming upstairs to help him when his parents didn't believe in dragons, his Casino watch, his Christmas presents, being picked up and dropped off at school, letting Darius stay and Dixie visit. He thought back to the school terms, his room trashed, Kyrillan missing, leading Serberon to betray Sammy, killing first her dragon, then Mary-Beth.

'You may have more time,' said Sir Ragnarok kindly.

But Sammy shook his head. He had made up his mind. 'Open it,' he whispered.

'You understand what this means,' said Sir Ragnarok, peeling open the envelope.

'I want my parents to see dragons.'

'Very well,' said Sir Ragnarok, pulling out the photographs and bottles of oats and green liquid. 'These will be tested thoroughly. I'm proud of you Sammy. This must have been a very tough decision.'

Sammy stared into space numbly. In a voice that didn't sound like his own, far off and distant, he told Sir Ragnarok about the black book with the initials "L.R." he had been given and the powers in his watch.

Sir Ragnarok took a close look at the Casino watch that Sammy had put back on his wrist, tightly strapped.

'A book you say? Perhaps we could look through it together when you have found out more.'

Sammy nodded, watering his tea down with more sugar. 'Don't you want to see it first?'

Sir Ragnarok laughed. 'What harm can come from a book?' He stood up and tapped the screens. 'Yes, I thought it must be time for the feast,' he said smiling as the screens flashed and showed the Main Hall packed with students spilling into the room and sitting at the house tables.

'Go,' commanded Sir Ragnarok. 'I will join you in a moment.'

Sammy plodded downstairs thinking hard about his talk with Sir Ragnarok. He felt an urge to go back, to tell Sir Ragnarok that it was all a mistake, that his uncle was just a jeweller and that he had been wrong. But his feet took him down to the bottom of the spiral staircase, slipping out from under the tapestry, unnoticed in the riot by all except Dixie who waved to him.

'Saved you a seat!' she yelled, standing on a chair to be seen.

Sammy forced a grin, made his way to the North table, pulled up a chair and tucked into the feast.

CHAPTER 28

A GRUESOME DISCOVERY

Several weeks later, Sammy found time to look again at the mysterious black book. The thick snow had melted, revealing fresh green grass and early flowers springing up along the paths.

In their sports lessons, Sammy found that his Firestick from Excelsior Sports was ten times better than the school sticks. Disappointingly, Mr Cross wouldn't let them play Firesticks with the black invisiballs, claiming they were too dangerous for the second years to use.

Dr Shivers was pleased with everyone, except Gavin and Toby, for remembering to feed their newly descaled dragons fresh meat to strengthen their bones and put a shine on their scales.

Professor Sanchez and Mrs Hubar were already discussing what would be in the summer exams and making futile attempts to encourage rowdy second years to knuckle down and learn charts of gemstones, recipes for ailments and practice listening into the minds of others.

Sammy was particularly pleased to score top marks from Professor Sanchez for his focus on sausage rolls which prevented even her from guessing the sequence of numbers he had been asked to remember.

It was the sports lessons with Mr Cross playing Firesticks that Sammy enjoyed most. He loved listening to Dixie, Gavin and Toby talking endlessly about Nitron Dark. A keen sportsman, Mr Cross had let anyone with a team shirt wear it to games lessons and Sammy had soon picked up from the other boys which teams there were to support.

At Dixie's instruction, Milly had written home to ask her parents to send her a Nitromen shirt. They obliged her request and also sent four other Nitromen shirts for her to share with the girls from the North house.

As a result, with Jock receiving a Nitromen shirt for Christmas from his cousin and Darius asking his parents to send him one, the whole second year North house wore the black and gold Nitromen shirts which sparkled in the sun as they passed the balls up and down the field.

After a particularly grueling practice, Sammy hobbled with Gavin and Toby to Mrs Grock's house to repair his knee, which had been sliced open in a clash with Peter Grayling from the West house.

'Come on Sammy,' said Gavin skipping ahead.

'He can't run Gavin. Sammy's got a bust knee,' said Toby.

'She'll fix it in no time,' retorted Gavin.

'It's ok if you want to go back to the castle,' said Sammy, bending down to dab the cut with a tissue. 'I'll be ok.'

'No way,' said Gavin earnestly, 'if we're with you we might see the Shape.' He swiped his staff across the top of the bushes, taking off the uppermost layer of leaves. A flock of sparrows flew out of the bushes chirping angrily at him for disturbing them

'We're nearly there,' said Toby.

Mrs Grock's house loomed in the dusk, a dark shadow against the sunset. Mrs Grock was in her allotment pulling up turnips and carrots as they swung the gate open.

'Ooch, Sammy, you made me jump,' said Mrs Grock going pink. 'Ooch, Gavin and Toby as well. You'll be coming to me for my healing potion from a rough Firesticks match.'

'How did you know?' asked Gavin.

Mrs Grock pulled at her blouse. 'You're all dressed as Nitromen.'

Sammy held up his leg. Blood was dribbling down into his sock.

'Ooch,' said Mrs Grock. She beckoned for them to come inside. 'I'll have to ask you to help yourself, Professor Burlay is just with me.'

Gavin snickered and pushed past into the cottage.

Professor Burlay looked up from the sofa by the fire as they came in. He shuddered when he saw Sammy's injured leg.

Mrs Grock handed Sammy a sachet of her mixture and broke away part of the turnip with a kitchen knife she had been using to cut a large jam sponge cake she was sharing with Professor Burlay.

'That should do it,' said Mrs Grock.

Sammy took the turnip and mixture and pushed it as close to the cut as he could without wincing. As he swept it downwards away from the wound, the blood disappeared and his skin magically healed over as if nothing had happened.

'Good stuff that,' said Toby nodding approvingly.

'Let's leave them to it,' sniggered Gavin. 'Come on, it's fish and chips for dinner tonight.'

For the next three weeks, Sammy knuckled down with his lessons as his father had instructed. In the evenings when everyone had gone to sleep, he pulled out the black book and tried to decipher the strange symbols on the pages. He still hadn't told anyone apart from Sir Ragnarok about the book, mainly because the pages went blank whenever anyone approached, but also because Sir Ragnarok had entrusted it to him, for him to decipher.

Sammy had a strong suspicion that the triangles represented pyramids and the only pyramids he knew of were at the Land of the Pharaohs. There seemed to be a link between the dots shaped like the Dragamas constellation and the triangles, some kind of ancient alignment. There were also strings of Is, Vs, Cs and Xs that following a casual question in Dragon Studies, Dr Shivers had lent him a chart of Roman numerals to match to the letters.

If what he was reading was right, Sammy could see a link between his thirteenth birthday, the Land of the Pharaohs and Dragamas. He hadn't read the book for nearly a week after that, afraid that whatever would happen, would happen on the 30th of November later this year.

In fact, it was the morning before the Easter break when Sammy finally told Dixie and Darius about the book and his research as they left an Armoury lesson, where Commander Altair had let them practice defending against the ruby in pairs. Nearly all of the class could resist the ruby to some extent. Some could resist it completely and others were reduced to moving in slow motion.

'You should have said,' snapped Dixie. 'You promised you'd tell us if anything happened to you.'

'You can't have got it at Christmas,' said Darius indignantly. 'I was there the whole time.'

Sammy put up his hands in defence. 'So what? I'm telling you now. Something is going to happen on my thirteenth birthday.'

Darius looked at him disbelievingly. 'Two years ago, you didn't know anything about dragons. Now suddenly the Shape are after you?'

Sammy looked at Dixie and Darius, neither of them looked like they believed him. Darius had his concerned look and Sammy could hear in his mind that Darius was about to suggest that he and Dixie took Sammy to Mrs Grock's.

'Fine,' snapped Sammy, 'you think I've lost it but I haven't. My Uncle Peter is in the Shape. He is the reason why my parents can't see dragons. My parents were Dragon Knights!'

Sammy took a step back waiting for their reaction.

Dixie let out a laugh that set Darius into hysterical giggles.

'Your parents were not Dragon Knights!' Darius roared with laughter.

'They were so,' said Sammy feeling hot, 'Sir Ragnarok told me they were as much of Dragon Knights as your dad, Commander Altair and Professor Burlay's father too. They were Dragon Knights, I swear.'

Dixie squeezed his shoulder. 'I think you should see Mrs Grock.'

Sammy stormed off. He had already committed to staying at the school over the holiday to research the book without any interruptions. He didn't stop or look back until he was up on the seventh floor outside Professor Sanchez's classroom.

He could hear voices inside the Alchemistry room. Professor Sanchez was arguing with someone. His quarrel with Dixie and Darius was forgotten as he squeezed himself behind one of the long draping curtains to be out of sight.

'I will stay with Amos,' came Simon Sanchez's voice from inside the classroom. 'He will have me to stay.'

'Very well,' shouted Professor Sanchez. 'You know I have been asked to stay with the students over Easter.'

'It is not fair,' whined Simon, 'stay here or be abandoned.'

There was a crack from the classroom followed by a shout from Simon.

'I have given you the choice!' roared Professor Sanchez. 'Go and stay with your friend. I will have three girls and five boys to look after this holiday instead.'

Inside the classroom a door slammed and seconds later Simon emerged from the room holding his head in both hands.

'It is not fair,' he muttered slamming the classroom door behind him, 'we had plans to go to the Land of the Pharaohs like Mrs Hubar and Jock.'

Sammy waited for Simon to disappear from sight before sneaking out from behind the curtain. He wasn't sure if he'd heard correctly, but it sounded as though Professor Sanchez had gone down the secret passage hidden in the Alchemistry room that Sir Ragnarok had used last year. He didn't care if Dixie or Darius believed him, he was going to find a secret passageway they didn't know about.

'I'll show them,' he muttered, kicking open the Alchemistry classroom door.

As he had expected, the classroom was empty, the wooden desks looked lonely, forgotten in the rush to leave for the holiday. There were pencils under the desks and chalk writing about turning metal into gold on the blackboard.

Out of the sloping window Sammy saw two blue Land Rovers, Gavin and Toby leaving in their mother's brand new car and Dixie's family clambering into their ancient edition which was still on the road more by luck than mechanical engineering.

He remembered Dixie's mother telling him how every part that could be replaced had been replaced and how she would sell it when it reached eight hundred thousand miles on the clock.

Sammy felt a jolt in his stomach, neither Dixie nor Darius had said "goodbye" to him and he was now stuck at school waiting for them to return.

The Land Rovers sped away leaving a cloud of gravelly dust in their wake. A flock of shining dragons flew behind the cars and Sammy wiped away a speck in his eye.

'I'll show them,' he repeated. 'I'm a Passage Spotter. This is going to be my passage.'

He checked his watch. Commander Altair had shown him how to change the time into a portable Directometer that he was determined to try and see if he could make it work.

'Professor Sanchez,' he said out loud clicking the buttons.

A red dot appeared on the dial. Sammy moved his wrist to face the panelled wall. The dot turned green and he pushed past the desks.

He had an idea that the passage would be protected and he unclipped his Dragon Minder pin from his shirt pocket. Sammy felt around the corners of the panels for a ridge or dent, anything that could be used with the pin to turn or push to open the door into the secret passage.

He paused at a long thin panel stretching from the skirting board to just above his head where the paint began. The panel looked older and dirtier than the other panels with a light coating of dust. There were a couple of fingerprints at the top.

The green dot had faded from his watch which had gone back to display the time. He pressed the buttons but no combination would make either red nor green dot return when he said Professor Sanchez's name out loud.

He reached to the top of the panel and found what he was looking for. An inch long gash in the upper lip of the panel matched the shape of the Dragon Minder pin exactly. Unless you were looking for it specifically, you'd never know it was there.

Sammy pushed his Dragon Minder pin into the shape and turned it ninety degrees right until it would turn no further.

With a "click" the three panels to the right of him concertinaed together, leaving a gap that Sammy could easily walk through.

He picked up his Dragon Minder pin and lit a fire at the end of his staff to see into the darkness. Unlike the passage into the Dragon Chambers, there were no automatic lights.

A row of steps led down into a passage that seemed to run deep underneath the classroom and towards the centre of the castle.

Wishing suddenly that Dixie and Darius were with him, Sammy took a footstep down the stone stairs. Above him, almost as expected, the panel unstretched itself and closed over. No amount of tugging would bring it to open and panicking in the darkness, he dropped his staff and the fire went out. Sammy couldn't find anywhere to push his Dragon Minder pin and open the door.

Some twenty minutes later, he found his staff had rolled to the bottom of the steps and lined itself up with the passage wall which had made it nearly impossible to find.

'Gotcha!' said Sammy, praying he had picked up his staff and not a dismembered body part from someone or something wasting away in the passage.

The object did light a fire and Sammy was pleased to see his staff in the light. Several feet away, he found his two gemstones that had come off in the fall and reseated the onyx and ruby at the bulging end of his staff.

It was then that he noticed that the passage wasn't quite as he had expected.

Although it was panelled with wooden boards and appeared to run diagonally towards Sir Ragnarok's office, it had a horrible yellow slime running down the panels that smelt like sick.

Sammy held his sleeve over his mouth and nose. Taking a closer look, the slime didn't appear to be from damp or a leak in the roof. It looked almost as if it had been…splattered.

Sammy took a step back, his foot cracking on something. It looked like a rock. Sammy bent down and picked it up.

The rock glinted in the flames, shimmering like foolsgold, gold, green and blue.

'Draconite,' said Sammy, a lump in his throat. 'Dragon brains,' he whispered leaning closer to inspect the sickly yellow gel, his stomach turning. 'How many dragons have died here?' he whispered.

Sammy slipped the draconite into his pocket. Although it was only the size of a squashed tennis ball, it was as heavy as a lump of lead.

Sammy walked forward, keeping his free hand pressed against his mouth and nose. The passage widened into a bulging cavity.

Sammy tiptoed down more steps into the room. By the light of his flame torch, there were wooden benches dripping with the same yellow slime. Gold and blue glittering dust twinkled in the walls. In one corner there were pieces of slashed skin and rotting bones which made Sammy feel faint. A mass slaughter had occurred here.

Sammy crossed the slime ridden room to the passage on the other side, climbing more steps to get out of the grave. He paused as he heard footsteps behind him and turned around to face whoever was coming into the room behind him. He put out his fire so that the passage descended into darkness.

'She was here,' came a gravelly voice. 'You can see her footprints.'

'She doesn't know what went on here,' came a deep voice.

'You cannot rely on her to be blind and stupid. It is obvious she knows.'

Sammy melted against the wall, his heart racing, letting each breath out in near silence.

'We must remove the evidence. Do not follow her. She will be there already.'

'Why couldn't she heed her son and be gone? This would never have been found. We must clear this mess at once.'

Holding his breath, Sammy edged away. He didn't care how the Shape had got into the passage or how they were planning to get out. All he cared about was not getting caught.

If his uncle was down there, he wouldn't be best pleased with Sammy for turning him in and if he wasn't...well, Sammy didn't like to think what might happen.

'Let's get started,' said the gravelly voice. 'Wish Sweepy was here.' He laughed, a cruel laughter echoing down the passageway.

Sammy reached for his bravery cross, the cold metal crushing against his hand. He edged forward as quietly as he possibly could, sidestepping down the corridor in pitch darkness to the sound of a scraping broom and sloshing of water.

Taking confidence in the noise Sammy walked faster, not daring to light a fire and risk being seen. He kicked against some more steps and climbed upwards going higher and higher in the darkness. He almost froze when he came up to a dead end. He reached up, leaning forwards, careful not to tumble backwards.

His fingers touched something wooden with metal bars. It felt very solid. Sammy knocked on the panel in front of him.

It creaked away from him and he realised it was a door. A chink of light appeared and a shadow slunk out of the doorway. It wove around Sammy's ankles making him almost jump out of his skin.

Forgetting he was supposed to be quiet and invisible Sammy shouted "fire", stepping away from the doorway as a gust of flames licked past his arm illuminating a small four legged furry animal.

'Lariston!' he breathed as Sir Ragnarok's smoke grey cat locked eyes with him.

Lariston spat as a spark fell from Sammy's torch and landed on his head.

The door opened wider and Sir Ragnarok's grey bearded face looked down.

'Sammy Rambles I presume?'

Sammy nodded. 'Hello.'

'Ooo is it?' came Professor Sanchez's voice from inside the room. 'Is it the Shape?'

Sir Ragnarok held out his hand and Sammy pulled himself up the last three steps. Sammy gasped as he was hauled up into the room.

It was a circular tower room with a cone ceiling painted in gold and purple. The passage door opened next to a curved mahogany wardrobe and matching dresser unit, where clothes were draped over the back of a wooden stool half tucked under the dresser.

A giant four poster bed with purple and gold hangings tied in a gold bow took up the majority of the room. Fluffy purple pillows lined the top half of the bed and the huge headboard was painted gold with purple stars and curved in a semi-circle to tuck seamlessly against the curved wall.

Long slit windows were covered in purple curtains and a crystal chandelier hung from the coned ceiling high above. Sammy's jaw dropped. He had never seen a room like it in his life.

'My quarters,' said Sir Ragnarok. 'Come, Professor Sanchez is downstairs.'

Lariston pushed past Sammy, herding him down the metal spiral staircase into Sir Ragnarok's office below.

Professor Sanchez was sitting on the purple sofa. Her face was unusually pale under her dark hair. She glared at Sammy.

'Have you seen it?' she demanded.

Sammy nodded. 'They're there, cleaning it up.'

Professor Sanchez's eyes lit up. 'Then we must go. To catch them like this is an opportunity not to be missed.'

Sir Ragnarok came down the stairs looking somber. He put the key he was holding in a glass jar in one of the cupboards and waved his hand at the monitors.

'It is too late,' said Sir Ragnarok. 'They have gone.'

Sammy looked up, the room in the passage was spotless. He held up the draconite he had found. 'Here's one they won't be having.'

Professor Sanchez took the stone from him and laughed. 'They are already stealing jewellery from people's homes. One by one they will collect all the stones and rebuild the Stone Cross.'

'Not if I can help it,' Sir Ragnarok smiled and took the draconite. He put it in his mouth. 'They'll never have this one,' Sir Ragnarok gulped the stone down with a glass of his red berry juice.

Professor Sanchez laughed again. 'They know where every last dragon lives and when their draconite will be ripe for the taking.'

Sir Ragnarok looked at Sammy, his brows meeting in a deep frown. 'I don't want to know what you were doing in the passage, but I must know what you saw.'

Sammy took a deep breath and told Professor Sanchez and Sir Ragnarok his story.

At the end, Sir Ragnarok laughed. 'You should think more of your friends.' He waved to another of the monitors. Dixie and Darius were in the North tower sitting on Darius's bed playing Dragon Dice.

From the rucksack perched at the end of Toby's bed, it looked as though Dixie had moved temporarily into the boys' tower.

'They stayed?' whispered Sammy.

'Two more,' grumbled Professor Sanchez. 'Perhaps they will take extra Alchemistry lessons over the holiday.'

Sammy forgot his fear in the tunnels and grinned.

Sir Ragnarok reached for his staff and cracked it on to his desk.

Almost as Sammy had expected, a bag crammed with food and drink appeared.

'I'm sure you have things to say to your friends,' Sir Ragnarok smiled. 'Tell them I have organised a trip to the Land of the Pharaohs tomorrow. While it is here we may as well enjoy it.'

Sammy's eyes lit up. 'Cool!'

'On the contrary, it will be warm, so dress appropriately,' scowled Professor Sanchez eyeballing the bag of food. 'Perhaps we could discuss what will happen to the jeweller?'

'Not in front of Sammy,' said Sir Ragnarok. 'You can find your way back, can't you.'

Sammy felt a rush of relief when Sir Ragnarok pointed to his office door rather than to the stairs up to his bedroom and the passage door.

Even if the Shape and the horrific dragon remains were no longer there he didn't know if he could cope with going back through the dark passage to the Alchemistry room.

He walked slowly to the door with the carrier bag desperate to hear what Sir Ragnarok would say about his uncle, but most annoyingly, Sir Ragnarok seemed to read his thoughts and discussed the weather with Professor Sanchez until Sammy had reached the office door and was on his way down to the Main Hall and then up to the North tower.

Dixie and Darius jumped up from their game when Sammy staggered through the tower door clutching the food bag.

'We thought the Shape had got you,' Darius laughed.

Sammy grinned at them both. 'Not this time,' he said handing out chocolate, crisps, fruit and sandwiches.

CHAPTER 29

THE ANGEL OF 'EL HORIDORE

As promised, Sir Ragnarok took the students who were staying at Dragamas for the holiday up to the Land of the Pharaohs. He and Professor Sanchez wore shorts and t-shirts and spent most of their time in the Mummy Café that Dixie had branded a fake.

Sammy, Dixie and Darius spent most of the time examining the book with their feet dangling in the Oasis, drinking brightly coloured cocktails, swimming and having fun. Sammy wasn't the only one to be disappointed when Sir Ragnarok rounded them up to go back to the castle and the rest of the school arrived back at Dragamas.

The fifth years were unbearable, insisting on near silence to finish their coursework and revise for the summer exams. They hadn't taken kindly to a game of Dragonball organised by Toby that sent the first, second and third years crashing into the study tables in pursuit of the ball. As a result, Professor Burlay had been asked to stand guard in the evenings to ensure that the common room was peaceful.

Sammy snatched minutes here and there to talk to Dixie and Darius about the book and his uncle. Through school gossip, a fourth year whose mother was in government had assured everyone that a big legal case would be taking place in court over the summer.

Dixie had written home to ask if her mother could send a copy of "The Metro", her local newspaper so they could find out the details.

When the paper arrived, Sammy was extremely frustrated to find that a crossword had been done in felt tip over an article he wanted to read and a voucher for a free trip to a health spa had been brutally chopped out, cutting precisely through the date when the court case would be decided.

'Says here Peter Pickering has escaped,' said Darius, holding up the newspaper. 'The police lost him in a car chase. His car went over a bridge.'

'Your parents are ok though,' said Dixie holding up her mother's letter. 'Mum says your parents are a bit odd but they're safe in the village. She's seen them both since the accident and look, she's sent some fizzpoppers!'

'Cool!' said Darius folding up the newspaper and getting out his homework. 'I love those.' He put three fizzpoppers into his mouth and Sammy could hear the emerald green sweets fizzing and popping on his tongue.

'What's next?' asked Sammy, trying a fizzpopper and liking the soft peppermint taste as the sweet exploded on the tip of his tongue.

'Gemology, then Sports. Mr Cross is going to show us some new Firesticks moves.'

'Oh yeah,' said Sammy remembering, 'didn't he say we could play with the mighty Invisiballs.'

Dixie laughed. 'That's what Serberon calls them...um...sorry.'

'It's ok,' said Sammy, 'I know the Shape made him do it.'

'Have you got an answer for question four?' asked Darius.

'Yeah, it's ruby,' said Dixie, 'with your parents you should know that.'

'I know,' said Darius. 'Hey, did I tell you, they're coming here over the summer holiday.'

'Cool!' said Dixie.

Sammy didn't let on that he was worried about his uncle's escape. If Sir Ragnarok was right, the first thing Peter Pickering would probably want to do would be to complete the mission of asking him to join the Shape.

Sammy followed at a distance as they went down to the Gemology classroom.

Mrs Hubar had started the lesson when Sammy slipped behind the curtain and through the sparkling door. He sat down at the South table, unnoticed at the back.

They were copying notes from the blackboard about different gemstones. Every so often, Mrs Hubar would glance ferociously at the class, daring someone to interrupt.

Sammy was glad when the end of lesson bell rang, less pleased when Mrs Hubar called him back.

'I'm sorry to hear about your uncle,' she said kindly.

Sammy looked in her eyes. They were cold and didn't match her voice.

'I'm sure they'll find him,' said Sammy.

Mrs Hubar nodded. 'I'm sure they will. Oh and to remind you not to be late again, would you write up your notes from the blackboard.'

Mrs Hubar held her hand over the text book and words appeared on the blackboard.

Sammy waited for her to leave before copying the text from the book on to paper with his staff as quickly as she had. He tucked the paper into his rucksack and ran out of the classroom finding himself ten minutes late to their Sports lesson.

Mr Cross frowned at Sammy and waved for him to get changed. He then gave Sammy a hard time blowing the whistle at borderline fouls. If he'd had the opportunity, Sammy wished he could quit. The black-to-invisible balls were extremely difficult to play with and even they seemed to be picking on him, always landing under his feet to make him slide and then vanishing out of sight.

All in all, he was glad to be back in the common room drinking hot chocolate before bed.

'Exams in a few weeks,' said Darius.

Sammy nodded, questions and marks the least of his worries.

The summer term dragged on and on. From freshly mown grasses to boiling sunshine. Darius came down with a summer cold that, to his dismay, Mrs Grock diagnosed as hay fever and wouldn't let him off the summer exams.

Dixie wrote again to her mother to find out more news from the court case. Peter Pickering it seemed had been sighted in every town from Lands End to John O'Groats.

'They'll never find him,' she groaned as they sat together in a quiet corner of the school library looking at the black book.

'They will,' retorted Darius. 'Sir Ragnarok will see to it.'

Sammy felt Dixie staring at him. 'What?' he asked.

'Are you sure you're ok?'

Sammy nodded, although he'd felt funny since he'd said it was ok for Sir Ragnarok to open the envelope. 'It just feels weird you know, that Uncle Peter said that by rebuilding the Stone Cross my parents would see dragons again.'

'It was what you wanted most,' said Darius. 'He used that against you.'

'What if he's right?' asked Sammy.

'He's not,' snapped Dixie. 'My dad's a Dragon Knight. He's trying to stop the Stone Cross from being rebuilt.'

'Where is he then?' said Sammy and immediately wished he hadn't said it as Dixie's green eyes turned to water.

Dixie blinked her tears away. 'He'll be here. My dad and your parents will fight the Shape.'

Darius laughed. 'Is that when Sammy's parents can see the dragons they're supposed to be protecting?'

Torn between wanting to thump Darius over the head with his Gemology book and wanting his parents to see dragons, Sammy laughed. 'What do your parents really do as Healers?'

Darius's laugh faded. 'You know they help dragons,' he scowled.

Mrs Skoob the librarian tutted loudly from her chair. 'Quiet please or I'll send you to Sir Lok Ragnarok.'

'Yes!' shouted Dixie suddenly. 'L.R. Lok Ragnarok! No wonder he didn't want to look at your book. He wrote it!'

'Out!' shouted Mrs Skoob her hair unraveling from its bun as she shook her fist ferociously at them.

Sammy, Dixie and Darius scuttled past some fifth years down a staircase hidden behind a curtain that appeared on their "Dragon Minder Map" of the school. Unofficially, Darius had been made a Dragon Minder and none of the other North second years minded. "As long as he doesn't get a pin," Jock had said.

Dr Shivers was waiting in the North common room as Sammy, Dixie and Darius arrived, a little dirty from the dusty passage. Sammy passed the book to Darius for him to hold it out of sight.

'Two stars each,' snapped Dr Shivers, 'and an essay on how to keep quiet in the library.'

Sammy and Darius grinned at each other and walked up to the boys' tower. Sammy looked back to see Dr Shivers with his arm around Dixie's shoulders.

'He'll be back soon,' Sammy heard Dr Shivers say before pushing her gently towards the girls' tower staircase.

In the second year boys' tower room, Gavin and Toby were already asleep. Jock was reading by candlelight and blew it out as Sammy and Darius came in.

'I thought you were Dr Shivers,' grumbled Jock. 'Don't you think he's been acting strangely recently?'

'Yeah,' said Darius, 'ever since Sammy's uncle got arrested.'

'It was your uncle?'

Sammy nodded. 'I thought everyone knew.'

'I'll see to it,' said Jock tucking his book under his pillow.

'No, don't,' said Sammy, knowing it was no use talking to him since Jock fell asleep quicker than it took to blow out a candle.

'It'll be all round the school this time tomorrow.'

'Sorry,' whispered Darius drawing his green curtain around his bed.

'Night,' whispered Sammy, throwing on his pyjamas and tucking himself under his duvet.

It took ages for him to find sleep and when it came he woke in fitful sweats dreaming of his uncle and Dr Lithoman putting draconite into the Stone Cross one stone at a time. He could hear their voices chanting.

'By the power of East and Air. By the power of South and Fire. By the power of West and Water.'

Sammy found himself watching from the sidelines, bound in ropes like Serberon, helpless, unable to do anything. Everything went black.

The dream burnt against his eyes and he opened his eyes finding it as dark in the tower as it had been in the dream.

He reached for the black book with L.R. in the cover and traced his fingers around the letters. Why had Sir Ragnarok written the book and how had his uncle received it? He didn't like to think it, but he guessed his uncle had stolen it from Sir Ragnarok or maybe, just maybe, he had been given it.

Using staff, Sammy lit his bedside candle and opened the pages. Among the triangles and numerals, he was sure the clues pointed to the Land of the Pharaohs on his thirteenth birthday.

He turned to the back cover. Where he was sure it hadn't been there before, a list of names was inscribed in the same gothic text that appeared throughout the school. At the bottom of the list, Sammy read "Sir Lancelot Bonahue", "Sir Lok Ragnarok", "Peter Pickering", and Sammy blinked to double check, was he imagining it, his own name "Samuel Rambles" was written underneath Peter Pickering with the words "may you be successful".

'At what?' whispered Sammy, thinking the only way to be sure would be to see Sir Ragnarok himself. He checked his watch, it was nearly four o'clock in the morning. Not giving much thought to Sir Ragnarok's sleeping patterns, he threw on his jumper over his pyjamas and put on his shoes and tiptoed out of the tower room. At the bottom of the stairs, he paused. He had seen a shadow slip under one of the common room tables.

'Who's there?' he called, holding up his staff.

'Sammy?'

From under the table, Dixie's green haired head emerged.

'What are you doing Sammy? It's four o'clock in the morning.'

'I'm going to see Sir Ragnarok about the book.'

'Great,' said Dixie, 'I'll come too.'

Sammy nodded, not sure he wanted to ask what Dixie thought she was doing in the middle of the night under a table in the common room. He would never say it out loud, but he was pleased to have her with him.

In the darkness, Dixie grabbed his hand. 'Are you going to use your watch to check where he is?'

'How do you know about that?' asked Sammy.

Dixie let his hand go. 'Commander Altair told me. He's been telling me loads about my dad. The training he went through, all the missions he's been on. I want to be a Dragon Knight too.'

'Oh,' said Sammy clicking his watch. 'It doesn't always work.'

'Not when the Shape are around,' said Dixie heaving the common room door open. 'They fool it somehow.'

'Using the stars?'

'Maybe,' whispered Dixie. 'That would make sense, if they're not really there you wouldn't be able to detect them.'

'Sir Ragnarok must know that. Maybe that's why no-one's caught them yet.'

Dixie nodded. 'Hurry up. Where is he?'

'Sir Ragnarok,' said Sammy holding his left wrist out in front. The watch face flicked from the time to the blank screen with a green dot.

'This way,' said Sammy, leading them into the Main Hall.

'He's in his office,' whispered Dixie, checking the dial. She held the tapestry of the knight open and walked through to the staircase.

Sammy had to jog to keep up as Dixie leapt up the stairs two at a time.

Dixie knocked firmly on the door as Sammy climbed the last step completely out of breath.

Sir Ragnarok opened the door.

'Good morning,' he smiled. 'I've been expecting you.'

Sammy rubbed his eyes, he was tired and cold in his thin pyjamas that had seemed such a good idea to wear at the time.

'This won't take long.'

'We know that the book has been passed down,' said Sammy.

'Indeed,' said Sir Ragnarok, still making no effort to let them in. 'It has been passed down from generation to generation. I gave it to Peter Pickering when he left Dragamas as a sign of his dedication. I believed it would be him who would uncover its secrets.'

'And he didn't?' asked Dixie.

'No Dixie, indeed he did not.'

'It's going to happen on my birthday, isn't it?' said Sammy, feeling he had to say something for Sir Ragnarok to let them into his office or tell them to go back to bed.

'It happens on the same day every fifty years. This will be your one chance to find it.'

'Find what?' demanded Sammy, the cold wind sweeping up the stairs getting to him.

'The Angel of 'El Horidore,' said Sir Ragnarok, closing the door in their faces.

'The what?' Sammy looked at Dixie.

Dixie shrugged. 'The Angel of something.'

"El Horidore,' whispered Sammy. 'What do you think...'

'I'm cold,' interrupted Dixie, 'and tired. I'll see you tomorrow.'

Dixie pulled up her coat sleeves and said "North Tower" in a deep voice of utmost concentration. There was a crackling and she vanished leaving Sammy alone.

Sammy pulled his jumper up to his ears and said "North Tower" in the deepest voice he could muster.

A wind whistled about his ears and he felt like he was being squeezed in a vice. When he opened his eyes he was lying on the sofa in the North Tower common room on top of Dixie who pushed him away so he fell on the floor.

'How did you do that?' Dixie snapped. 'Commander Altair's been trying to help me do that for weeks.'

Sammy stood up and grinned. 'No idea. Is that what you were doing under the table earlier?'

'Yeah,' said Dixie, 'I was supposed to land on it but I fell through it instead. I think it's what Dr Shivers meant about being able to walk through walls now our dragons have shed their baby scales.'

Sammy stared. It hit him like being whacked with a cricket bat at just how unreal it was.

'Of course you have to know "where" you want to end up.'

Sammy nodded blankly.

'Could be nasty otherwise.' Dixie pulled her hairband out of her ponytail and let her hair hang loose, like a green curtain was framing her face.

'I'll see you tomorrow,' said Sammy. 'Night.'

'We'll figure it out,' Dixie whispered. 'North tower, second year girls' room,' and with a hiss she had gone.

Sammy plodded up the boys' stairs slowly. There was a chance someone would wake up if he appeared in the boys' tower room unannounced, even if he could do it again.

'The Angel of 'El Horidore,' he whispered to his toy lion when he finally got back into bed. It seemed a childish toy now and he decided he would give the lion to his first year, Nigel Ashford, at the next opportunity.

Between Jock and Darius's snores and Gavin moaning in his sleep about stars, Sammy was glad when he fell asleep, even if it was only for two and a half hours.

CHAPTER 30

EXAMS AND TELEPORTING

Term carried on for a few weeks and then came the morning Sammy had secretly been dreading.

He sat at the North table for breakfast in the Main Hall listening to Sir Ragnarok reading notices from a long scroll.

'There will be three Dragonball trials taking place over the summer holiday,' said Sir Ragnarok to tremendous applause. 'There will also be a reporter from "The Metro" attending as well as representatives from Excelsior Sports,' he added, his words drowned out with all the cheering.

Sir Ragnarok waved his hands for silence and Professor Sanchez stood up. She read a short article on a new healing potion from a scroll and finished with a strict warning for students not to leave the Alchemistry classroom in a mess.

She sat down to eat her breakfast and Professor Burlay took his turn to update the school with his news.

'Please watch the stars carefully,' said Professor Burlay. 'We need to you record the number of incidents involving the Dragamas constellation versus the number of red stars surrounding them.'

Sammy exchanged a worried look with Dixie and Darius. They knew the number of red stars was growing larger every day.

In some respects, Sammy wished he could turn on his visions of the Stone Cross to find out how many draconite stones were yet to be found.

Then Sir Ragnarok said the dreaded "E" word.

'Exams will take place in two weeks! Good luck everyone.'

The exams rolled round more quickly than Sammy had prepared for and he found himself sitting his Gemology exam flustering over the first question which was asking him "On which day in history were the gems ruby and malachite discovered?" followed by "Explain in two hundred words or more whether it is better to mine for gemstones in summer or in winter?"

Sammy was fairly confident of his answers when Commander Altair, who had been adjudicating, rang the silver bell on his desk at the front and picked up all of the papers.

'Thank you everyone,' said Commander Altair. 'Please leave using the doors to the left and right of the hall.'

Sammy followed Gavin and Toby out of the hall. Gavin was sure he had got all of his answers wrong.

'I put winter,' said Gavin, 'I'm sure that's wrong!'

'Why did you put it?' Darius sniggered.

Gavin shot Darius a dirty look. 'Just because my parents have proper jobs.'

Darius didn't need telling twice and he lunged at Gavin in a rugby tackle taking him to the floor. Other students stopped in the corridor as Gavin and Darius locked together rolled down the steps leading out of the Main Hall.

Sammy and Toby surged down the steps to pull Darius and Gavin apart.

Gavin had a swollen cheek and Darius's shirt was ripped.

Sammy locked his arms around Darius and Toby pulled Gavin away still kicking and shouting.

There was a single round of applause at the top of the stairs. Commander Altair was towering above them shooing the crowd away. When they had cleared, he checked his watch and Sammy knew he would be replaying the events.

Commander Altair relaxed as he clicked his watch. He stopped frowning and beckoned them. 'Gavin, Darius, ten stars each from North. Sammy follow me.'

Sammy stared at Gavin, Toby and Darius as the black stars flashed into the Main Hall towards the great noticeboards.

Commander Altair marched up towards the Armoury rooms, nodding to two professors in the corridor who were holding a gold crafted dragon harness.

'In here please Sammy.'

Like a sheep, Sammy followed Commander Altair into the darkened Armoury room. The fireplace still gave him shivers when he saw it, remembering how the Shape had stood in front of it.

'I know that you know about Dixie's extra lessons...where I have given her extra tuition.' Commander Altair paused, looking keenly at Sammy.

Sammy nodded. 'She can disappear from one place to another.'

'Teleporting,' said Commander Altair. 'I know you are very close to her. Sir Ragnarok and I are concerned about you and what might happen if you attempted to copy her without our guidance.'

'Oh.'

'You've already done it?'

'Yeah.'

Commander Altair frowned. 'Then what I have to tell you may be of little relevance or may be too late. Tell me, where did you go?'

'From Sir Ragnarok's office to the North common room.'

Sammy felt Commander Altair searching deep into his thoughts before he relaxed.

'Very well,' said Commander Altair, letting out his drawn breath. 'It is something that you will learn the theory of as a third year. I stress the word "theory". You must promise me you will not attempt this again.'

'In case the Shape get me?'

Commander Altair threw back his head and laughed. 'In case you get stuck somewhere.' He stopped laughing and leaned close to Sammy. 'You must always know where you will end up before you disappear.'

Sammy nodded. 'Will you teach me?'

'Sir Ragnarok doesn't think it's advisable.'

'But you're teaching Dixie!'

'And Simon Sanchez too, but that's another story. I need you to promise me you will not attempt it again.'

'No!' said Sammy, running out of the room.

'Then promise me you won't do it at the Land of the Pharaohs,' Commander Altair called after him.

Sammy stopped in his tracks. He had reached the top of the stairs. It would be easy to go down and pretend he hadn't heard anything.

He took one step down and paused. He couldn't do it. He had to know what Commander Altair had meant.

Commander Altair reached out. 'Do you want me to explain?'

Sammy nodded feeling suddenly cold. Shivers ran down his spine and his armpits and palms itched with sweat.

'Very well. We think there is something inside one of the pyramids that the Shape would very much like to get their hands on.'

Sammy stared. 'Do you think they'll use me to get it?'

'Your uncle was in the Shape,' said Commander Altair flatly. 'Sir Ragnarok agrees with me.'

'Fine,' snapped Sammy. 'I won't do it ever again.'

Commander Altair smiled. 'You can teleport any time I'm with you. Is that fair? That's what I've asked of Dixie and Simon.'

'We went without you to Sir Ragnarok's office,' Sammy backed away from Commander Altair into the corridor.

Commander Altair flashed an intriguing smile. 'What makes you think I wasn't already there?'

Sammy ran out of the corridor with Commander Altair's laughter ringing in his ears. He was determined to practice teleporting from the common room to the tower bedroom.

He marched down to the lower floor running into Dixie and Darius who were trying to collect a drink from the vending machine in the hallway.

Darius gave the machine a kick and two cans rolled out. 'Cool!'

'He's told me not to do it,' said Sammy.

'But you weren't fighting?' said Darius looking confused.

'To teleport?' asked Dixie. 'I said to Darius that's what it was.'

'You can't teleport!'

'Not anymore,' said Sammy gloomily.

'We both can,' said Dixie. 'Commander Altair taught me and Sammy just did it without any lessons.'

'That's not possible.'

'Watch!' said Dixie looking flushed. 'Dragon Chambers.'

The breeze swept around the corridor and Dixie vanished.

'Are you going too?' asked Darius.

'I can't,' said Sammy. 'Commander Altair made me promise. Dixie shouldn't really have shown you. We're only supposed to try it when he's here.'

'We?'

'Me, Dixie and Simon Sanchez,' said Sammy, feeling guilty he hadn't asked for Darius to be included.

'I see,' said Darius. 'I guess I'll see you in the library for revision this afternoon then. You'll probably want to teleport there.'

Sammy stared as Darius walked off. He wished he could have said something to make things better but he found that he couldn't. He walked outside to find a group of fourth year girls sunbathing on the grass verge. In the distance, smoke was spiraling out of Mrs Grock's chimney.

With Dixie and Darius away from him, Sammy felt alone like he had at his old school. He marched across the school lawns between the bushes and into Mrs Grock's garden.

Not knowing how or why, he knew that she would be the best person to talk to. He knocked using the golden dragon door knocker on her green front door and waited.

CHAPTER 31

PETER PICKERING RETURNS

There was a shuffling inside and Professor Burlay opened the door.

'Hullo Sammy,' said Professor Burlay pulling his tie straight and slipping on his grey suit jacket. 'Mrs Grock and I were just discussing things.'

Sammy nodded. 'Is Mrs Grock there please? I want to ask her about...'

'The Angel of 'El Horidore,' said Professor Burlay tapping his head, a faraway look in his eyes. 'There is a movement in the stars not seen since King Serberon's time. That's the answer to question four by the way, four hundred years.'

'Thanks,' said Sammy. 'The Astronomics exam was yesterday.'

'So it was,' chuckled Professor Burlay. 'How funny.'

'Ha,' Sammy smiled politely.

Professor Burlay let him inside where Mrs Grock was stoking a roaring fire despite the sweltering heat. By the items hanging on the string tied from one end of the mantelpiece to the other, she seemed to be roasting chestnuts.

'Ooch, good afternoon young Dragon Knight. Would you like some chestnuts? They're a bit on the bitter side this time of year but one of the trees has come early.'

'I'm ok thanks,' said Sammy watching as Mrs Grock unhooked two chestnuts with a pair of dragon hide gloves and dropped them into a silver bowl on her coffee table beside the fire.

'They're John's favourite,' explained Mrs Grock with a smile. 'It was where we first kissed, under one of the sweet chestnut trees. Near the tree your staff came from if I'm not mistaken.'

Embarrassed, Sammy nodded, he knew where she meant. It was one of the trees surrounding the tree stump where he had first created fire.

'Talking of trees, Professor Sanchez hasn't said anything to you about the damp has she?' asked Mrs Grock, quickly changing the subject. 'For a while now, I've been thinking summits not right down underground.'

Mrs Grock sat down on the purple velvet sofa adjusting her shawl around her shoulders. 'But that's just me thinking,' she chuckled. 'What canna I do for you?'

'I want to find out about the Angel of 'El Horidore please,' said Sammy, trying to ask as innocently as he could. 'It's for a summer project.'

'Ooch, there's a name I haven't heard in a long while. Take a seat and I'll find you what I can.'

Sammy sat on one of the beanbags nearest to the fire and helped himself to a chestnut. It was very bitter and he spat it out into his hand. Behind him, Mrs Grock was rummaging through her bookcases turning almost every book out of the shelves and on to her dining room table.

'Ah,' she said at last, pulling an ancient volume from the bottom shelf. 'There you are. "The Angel" by Helana Horidore, third wife of none other than King Serberon himself.

Mrs Grock paused, 'of course she was known as "El", not posh Helana, unless she was in the court of King Serberon. Ooch yes, she was "El" to the people all right.'

Sammy stared open mouthed. The book was covered in almost an inch of dust and as Mrs Grock dusted it with her handkerchief, it looked so brittle that she would never trust him to look after it.

'I got this from a jumble sale when I was about your age. An old gentleman sold it to me, ah yes,' she muttered, pushing her glasses up her nose, 'Humphrey Hoddle. Nobody ever forgets that name, that's what he told me.'

Sammy badly hid a laugh in a fake cough. 'Humphrey Hoddle and Helana Horidore.'

Mrs Grock chuckled. 'Ah know what you're thinking. After Eliza Elungwen, he may be the "H" in the Shape. But I'll not have you thinking that, a nicer gentleman you'd have trouble to find.'

Sammy stopped short, he had only thought of the name as amusing, not in terms of the ever-present threat of the Shape.

'I hear your uncle is the "P" in the Shape,' said Mrs Grock holding out the book. 'I hope you find your answers in there,' she added kindly. 'It must have been a hard decision to turn him in.'

Feeling his eyes prickle, Sammy took the book from Mrs Grock and thanked her before hurrying out into the sunshine. He paused by the wishing well, not quite ready to go back to the castle.

More students were lying on their jumpers on the grass. Several people were riding dragons in a procession to the grassy pitch where there was a game of Dragonball already underway.

As far as Sammy knew, the afternoon had been kept clear for revision or other entertainment. There were two more exams to go, then the much awaited summer party which Sir Ragnarok had promised they could have instead of a traditional ball.

Sir Ragnarok had asked every student to write down their own suggestions for what to have at the party on pieces of paper and hand them in to him at breakfast earlier in the week.

Sammy had requested to have the party outside, which he later found out was a wasted idea since Milly had already suggested it. He found out that Dixie's choice was to invite Nitron Dark and Darius had asked to have the dragons there as well. During the party, parents would arrive and take their sons, daughters and dragons home for the summer holiday.

Sammy wondered about the party, hoping it would be held outside and found himself walking towards the cool woodland shade, where he stopped in the tree stump clearing.

The trees sounded as though they were whispering behind him, leaves rustling, birds were chattering and singing their songs.

No-one else was around. Sammy was sure of that but he couldn't shift the shivers running down his back nor the feeling that from somewhere he was being watched.

He felt like the tall trees were watching him as he sat on the tree stump and looked at the purple and black book Mrs Grock had given him.

Humphrey Hoddle had obviously been an expert on this subject before discarding the book, since many of the paragraphs had been highlighted in faded yellow highlight pen once or twice per page, presumably by himself or previous readers. Sammy was interested to see that the book had once been the property of Ratisbury Library, his hometown library in Ratisbury.

Sammy sniggered thinking of the Rat-Catchers faces. If only they could see him now with his ability to create and control fire with his staff and teleport anywhere at will.

He froze as a stick cracked behind him. He closed the book and reached for his staff assembling it single handedly.

'Hi Sammy.'

Sammy spun round. Dixie and Darius were behind him. He dismantled his staff and stood up.

'Hi,' said Sammy awkwardly.

'What's the book?' asked Darius, reaching for Mrs Grock's copy of "The Angel".

'Does it say where to find it?' asked Dixie peering over Darius's shoulder.

'I don't know,' said Sammy, 'Mrs Grock has only just lent it to me.'

'Cool!'

Sammy watched as Dixie and Darius gently flipped through the flimsy pages.

'It says here the Angel belonged to King Serberon's wife,' said Dixie.

'Helana Horidore,' added Darius. 'It was a whistle they used to summon all the dragons in the kingdom together in times of dire emergencies.'

'So that's why the Shape want it,' whispered Sammy. 'To call all the dragons together.'

'It's got a shield of everlasting protection and can only be unsealed...'

'When?' asked Sammy impatiently. He turned around. Dixie and Darius were frozen solid and to his surprise Peter Pickering was standing before him.

'Uncle Peter? What are you doing here?'

'You have both the tools and the desire to succeed,' said Peter Pickering darkly. 'I am here to turn myself in. You will complete what I started.'

Sammy gulped thin air, his uncle was holding a ruby stone close to his chest.

'You are not affected, but I am not surprised considering who your parents once were.'

'A-r-e,' said Sammy in slow motion. He reached for his cross feeling the cold metal twinge slowly towards his fingers.

'Were,' snapped Peter Pickering. 'I saw to that myself twenty years ago. They cannot return and the irony is, they will never know that their only son will do the very thing they tried so hard to prevent.'

Peter Pickering laughed and shoved Sammy in the chest, knocking him over. Humphrey Hoddle's book fell out of Sammy's hands. It crashed on to the floor and disintegrated into fine powder.

Peter Pickering's laughter echoed as he shouted "Sir Ragnarok's office" and vanished in a grey mist.

Sammy held tightly to the cross, feeling the warm sun stretch across his back, regaining his feelings. He reached, still in slow motion for his staff to release Dixie and Darius.

'Your-uncle,' said Darius weakly in slow motion.

Sammy didn't have the heart to say that Darius had claimed Peter Pickering as his own uncle less than six months ago.

'Let's-go-to-Sir-Rag-nar-ok's-office,' puffed Dixie. 'Must-try-harder.'

'Teleport?' said Sammy, a glint in his eye. 'I'll have to explain to Mrs Grock about the book.'

'I-don't-care-about-the-book,' said Dixie. 'How-long-does-it-take-for-this-to-wear-off?'

Sammy held his staff closer to Dixie and Darius. He felt fine now and rubbed the ruby, concentrating hard to help Dixie and Darius move freely. Colour started to appear in Dixie's cheeks and she smiled, moving her arms slowly.

Five minutes later Darius was leaning on his staff like a crutch and walking around the clearing.

'I reckon we could make this into a den,' said Darius, struggling with his words. 'Bring a few of those branches around.'

'Add a roof of some sorts,' said Dixie enthusiastically.

'If your dad was here he'd have helped,' said Darius.

'Not a mushroom shape,' said Sammy sifting through the ash remains of the book.

Dixie mock punched him. 'We'll build a fortress. No one can come in unless we say so.' She lunged at a fallen tree that looked impossibly heavy and dragged it to the edge of the circle. 'Come on, we've got ages until tea.'

'But we've got exams tomorrow. I can't afford to stay down a year,' wailed Darius.

'It's only Armoury,' said Dixie. 'Commander Altair says we'll be fine.'

'Let's go to Sir Ragnarok's office first,' said Sammy mediating. 'You can pick up some books on the way back while we build it.'

'Ok,' said Darius brightly. 'Race you!'

Sammy caught Dixie's eye and together they shouted "Castle Courtyard" and landed between some bushes out of sight of the sunbathers.

Darius sprinted to them. 'Cheats!' he puffed.

'Let's go up to Sir Ragnarok's office,' said Dixie.

'Walking,' said Darius firmly. 'I'll figure out how to teleport over the summer.'

'Ok,' said Sammy, 'but quick, otherwise he'll have gone.'

They thundered up to the Main Hall and lurched through the tapestry on to the stairs.

They reached the top of the stairs out of breath except for Dixie who had climbed them as agile as ever, two at a time.

Sammy knocked firmly on the wooden door. Almost immediately it swung open to reveal Lariston's sleek grey head with his amber eyes trained firmly on the three of them. He purred and turned to climb back up the seven steps.

'Does that mean we can go in?' asked Darius.

Sammy nodded. 'I think so.' He pushed the door open to let Dixie and Darius through.

Inside Sir Ragnarok's office, Sir Ragnarok was pouring tea from his silver teapot for himself and for Peter Pickering. He looked up but didn't seem surprised to see Sammy.

'I was wondering when you would come.' Sir Ragnarok smiled. 'Your uncle has told me much of his plans for you.'

Sammy felt Dixie link hands with him, grateful for her support.

'He's lying,' said Darius raising his staff. 'Nothing's going to happen to Sammy.'

Sir Ragnarok stood up. 'I'm afraid you are wrong Darius. Because of Mr Pickering, everything is going to happen to Sammy.'

'You'll finish what I started,' laughed Peter, 'everything!'

Sammy shivered as he looked at his uncle. He despised everything about him, from his highly polished shoes to his slicked back hair. If he really had come to turn himself in, he had gone to a lot of trouble to look good while he was about it.

There was a thump from Sir Ragnarok's bedroom and Sir Ragnarok looked up.

'They are here already,' said Sir Ragnarok sipping his tea. He reached for his top drawer, pulling an old fashioned key out of a glass jar.

'Let them in Lariston,' said Sir Ragnarok to his cat. Lariston took the key in his paw and rubbed against Dixie's legs.

Sir Ragnarok smiled. 'He has chosen you my dear.'

Dixie let go of Sammy's hand and followed Lariston up the spiral stairs leading to Sir Ragnarok's bedroom.

From experience, Sammy knew that Lariston's key would open the door opposite Sir Ragnarok's four poster bed and let in the people who were going to take his uncle away.

Behind Sir Ragnarok, Sammy could see that the village maps had been replaced with a diagram of the Stone Cross. Flecks of blue and green had been chalked on to represent the draconite. Sammy guessed his uncle had given them to Sir Ragnarok.

On the purple sofa, his uncle was mopping his brow with a green silk handkerchief, mumbling to himself in a strange language that Sammy didn't recognise. Sir Ragnarok had his hands firmly pressed together, his elbows resting sturdily on his desk.

All eyes were on the spiral staircase as Dixie came down, her eyes wide, glistening with green tears.

Behind her came twelve men dressed in full battle armour, gleaming polished silver suits with golden dragons emblazoned on their chests, chains clanking, metal on metal.

They raised their visors to Sir Ragnarok and one tall man stepped forward, a scroll in his hand.

Sir Ragnarok nodded, pointing to Sammy. 'Mr Pickering is his uncle from his mother's side. He has a right to know.'

CHAPTER 32

GENERAL ALDEBARAN ALTAIR

The tall man took off his helmet and shook Sammy's hand.

'I am General Aldebaran Altair, son of General Arkabaran Altair, father of Commander Altair and my other sons Algol and Rigel of the Southern territories. It is a pleasure to meet you.'

The handshake was hard and Sammy looked up into his strong blue eyes, trusting him straight away.

'Your parents were fine people,' he said kindly. 'Put your trust in me to make sure Peter Pickering's life ends as quickly as the dragons he helped slaughter.'

Sammy took a step back to stand between Dixie and Darius, watching as General Altair and his men handcuffed his uncle and tied him to a metal stretcher. They put him in a straitjacket, tucking his arms into his body, so he could not escape.

General Altair saluted to Sir Ragnarok and marched to the spiral stairs. Turning Peter Pickering on his side, four of his men carried him away out of sight.

Sammy walked to the bottom of the steps in shock. Lariston was circling at his feet, preventing him from following.

At the slam of the door upstairs, Lariston went to Dixie, rubbing his head against her leg, silently asking for her to help him lock the door behind them.

Sir Ragnarok, Sammy and Darius waited in an uncomfortable silence for Dixie to bring back the key. She returned with Lariston behind her and from the way Lariston sat on the bottom step cleaning his paws Sammy knew no-one apart from Sir Ragnarok would be going up there again today.

'Well,' said Sir Ragnarok breaking the silence. 'Would anyone like a cup of tea?'

'Why did they take him that way? asked Sammy, shaking his head as Sir Ragnarok conjured cups of tea and passed round his bowl of sweets.

'I discovered a hidden exit,' said Sir Ragnarok, taking one of his favourite purple sweets. 'That room you discovered...'

'Where the fifth year dragons were murdered,' said Sammy.

'...there is a sliding wall that takes you down a long ramp to the ground floor under the North tower. I understand that the dragons were drugged and led there.'

Sir Ragnarok paused and Sammy knew he was wondering how much to say.

'Go on, please tell us,' said Dixie. 'We have to know.'

'Very well,' said Sir Ragnarok. 'For some dragons, the poison killed them in a matter of minutes, but for others, they may have lain there for days, unable to move as the poison took effect. Some may even have been alive when the stones were taken.'

'Hacked out of their brains,' spat Darius. 'They should do that to him. See if he likes it.'

Sir Ragnarok smiled. 'That would be his worst punishment. They will treat him fairly at the Snorgcadell. Sammy, you can trust General Aldebaran to be firm and fair.'

'Uncle Peter shouldn't have killed those dragons,' said Sammy. 'It's his own fault.'

Sir Ragnarok opened a notebook on his desk. 'Your uncle was a good man once Sammy. He has left it to me to tell you that his property in the village will, in the event of his imprisonment or death, be passed to your mother who is his next of kin.'

'You're going to live in the village!' squealed Dixie. 'That's so cool!'

'Your uncle will be tried fairly,' continued Sir Ragnarok, 'but remember that his crimes span a thirty year period. Many dragons have died at his hands.'

'I know,' whispered Sammy. 'I need to go. We've got exams tomorrow.'

'I can speak to Commander Altair and Professor Sanchez. Under the circumstances they would, I'm sure, excuse you from their tests. Commander Altair especially would consider this fair. After all, he is his father's son and General Altair is the fairest man you'll ever meet.'

'Cool! No exams!' said Darius. 'Go for it Sammy.'

Sammy shook his head. 'I need to take the exams. I have to prove to myself that I have the right to be here.'

'Then it is settled,' said Sir Ragnarok. 'There are three seats in an quiet corner of the library that you may use to revise undisturbed, if you wish.'

Sammy nodded, helping himself to a purple sweet as Sir Ragnarok passed them round again.

Sir Ragnarok stood up to show them out. 'I will see you at the party. I'm sorry to tell you Dixie that Nitron Dark is busy with a match, but he sends you his regards. However, the party will be held outside and it will be with our dragons.'

'Cool! Cool! Cool! Cool! Cool!' chanted Darius as he led the way out of Sir Ragnarok's office and down the twisting stone spiral stairway.

'I can't believe Nitron Dark isn't coming,' moaned Dixie. 'Hey, did you see how blue General Aldebaran's eyes were? Exactly like Commander Altair's.'

'Nitron Dark's got competition,' teased Darius.

'I heard that,' snapped Dixie as she held open the tapestry into the Main Hall.

CHAPTER 33

EXAMS

The following morning, Sammy woke to find his Armoury text book folded on his duvet cover from where he had fallen asleep. His mind churned. He was still digesting yesterday's events.

'Morning Sammy!'

Sammy looked over, Gavin and Toby were testing each other on questions from the Armoury text book.

'Iron,' said Toby.

'Right!' said Gavin. 'My turn!'

Opposite Sammy, Jock had his curtains drawn but could be heard muttering from behind the green velvet.

'I'm going to check on Kyrillan,' said Sammy. 'If I don't know it now, I never will.'

'Well said,' said Darius. 'I'll come too.'

'Uh ok,' said Sammy, 'just I was going to...'

Darius clenched his fist and outstretched his fingers using their secret sign for teleporting.

'It's ok, I'll walk,' said Sammy. 'Come on.'

'Yeah, you need your dragon to fly,' laughed Gavin. 'How else are you going to get there?'

Sammy grinned at Darius and put on his black jeans and a blue and green striped t-shirt. Darius was wearing his army green three quarter length trousers and a khaki shirt. With the end of term so close, the rules on wearing school uniform had disappeared.

In the common room, Dixie was playing Dragon Dice with the North girls. She wouldn't come down to the chambers when Milly nudged her, a mischievous grin on her angelic face.

Sammy just caught the tail end of a thought fired between Dixie and himself that told him she wanted to go. He grinned, projecting that he would put down some chocolate for Kiridor. He took Darius through the radiator door down into the Dragon Chambers.

When they got there, Captain Duke Stronghammer, his wife Mrs Hubar and Captain Firebreath were dropping oats into the "West" food tubs.

'Never feed them,' grumbled Captain Firebreath.

'He should'a let Jock take care of them,' Captain Stronghammer said bitterly.

'Morning!' called Sammy.

'Aha!' said Captain Stronghammer. 'Now here's two lads who know how to take care of their dragons.'

'Where's the troll?' asked Mrs Hubar, looking at them rather suspiciously.

'She'll be here later,' said Darius.

'Aye that's another good un,' said Captain Stronghammer. 'She'll be a Breeder if I'm not mistaken.'

'Babies!' said Darius. 'Yuck!'

'Dragons you fool!' snapped Mrs Hubar. 'It's a job well suited to their kind.'

'Like mining is to us,' added Captain Firebreath diplomatically.

'I'll tell her,' said Sammy. 'Please may we see the North dragons?'

'Quickly please,' said Mrs Hubar. 'You have exams this morning and if your Gemology marks are anything to go on, you'll both need all the time you can find to do a little last minute revision.'

Sammy picked up one of the sacks of oats and made his way through the now-familiar caverns under the castle. Darius followed with a bucket of fresh water in each hand. Water sloshed on the floor next to a group of fourth year dragons each the size of Mr Griffin's campervan.

'Healthy they are,' growled Captain Firebreath, mopping up the water behind Darius. 'Proper friendly to those who know 'em. Oi!' he grumbled as a large green dragon picked him up with its tail. 'Put me down!'

The dragon obliged by landing Captain Firebreath with one foot in Darius's bucket, which created more of a mess when, in hysterics, Darius dropped the other bucket and the water spilled and trickled amongst the straw.

'Right mess,' growled Captain Firebreath. 'I'll sort it.'

Sammy grinned as he shoveled oats with his hands into the stone basins. Kyrillan was blowing smoke rings around his feet and as he walked it looked like he was wearing slippers made from silver clouds.

The other dragons looked on as he scooped the contents of the sack into the basin and hand fed Kyrillan, Kiridor and Nelson pieces of chocolate he had bought from one of the machines in the corridor.

Only when Simon Sanchez's black dragon got too close for Kyrillan's liking did he blow a handful of flames out of his nostrils.

The flames landed in the water Darius had spilt at Captain Firebreath's feet, hissing as they extinguished themselves.

'I'll thank you for stopping that,' said Captain Firebreath. 'Singeing my beard. I don't know. Wait until I catch who did it!'

Sammy and Darius beat a hasty retreat up into the corridor above.

'That was close,' giggled Darius.

'Come on, we'll be late for the exams,' said Sammy pulling at Darius's sleeve.

They arrived at the entrance to the Main Hall as Professor Burlay was turning the "Exam in Progress" sign on the glass doors around so that it now read "Danger! Exam in Progress".

Sammy was grateful as Professor Burlay looked at them and let them inside with no more than a "shh!" and a pitying smile.

At the front of the hall, Commander Altair was standing on the adjudicators table holding his staff horizontally in both hands. He spotted latecomers Sammy and Darius and beckoned for them to come to the front.

'We have an unusual exam,' he thundered making the windows rattle. 'Everyone starts with 100%.'

'Yes!' shouted Gavin.

Commander Altair smiled and Sammy saw the same twinkle he had seen in General Altair's eyes. This exam wasn't going to be easy he could tell.

'I have arranged you in order of your ability, with the strongest at the front who will bear the brunt of the test.'

Sammy looked from side to side, he was the furthest forward in a line of himself, Dixie, Darius, Simon Sanchez and Jock.

'In this exam,' Commander Altair stared rock solid at the class, 'marks start at 100% for the first person to leave the Main Hall.'

As he said the words "Main Hall" Commander Altair cracked his staff on the table sending a bolt of red lightning around the room in a tornado mist catching each and every student in the room off guard.

Sammy fought to keep his eyes open, knowing that if he shut them, only Commander Altair releasing him from the red mist would wake him.

The mist gripped him. It held him in a cold vice. His arms were strapped to his sides, his feet like lead. Using the tiniest of movements, he rolled his right eyeball to see Jock take a shaky step forward, a look of intense agony etched on his face.

If this was Commander Altair's idea of a test, Sammy thought his teacher must have been fairly confident of his power with the ruby to generate such a concentrated mass of the red energy that could be used safely in the exam.

Sammy screwed up his eyes, feeling the skin on his eyelids chafe together as he lifted his right foot off the ground.

Jock had taken two steps towards the door. Sammy could feel Gavin and Toby moving alongside him, trying hard to fight the mist.

There was a clatter behind them and Sammy guessed one or more of his classmates had succumbed to the mist and fainted under its strength.

Sammy thought back to his first day of his second year when Jock had used the ruby to freeze everyone in the tower room except him.

Simon Sanchez was walking as if the floor was hot coals, tiptoeing to the door ahead of Jock. Other students were making their way in slow motion, some with their eyes closed and arms outstretched like zombies.

Sammy gave his right foot a rest and tried to lift his left leg from the thigh downwards. The red mist burned in his eyes and he couldn't see the floor.

'Simon Sanchez, 100%,' shouted Commander Altair. 'Come on the rest of you, under who scores less than 80% will fail this exam!'

'Half the class will fail,' Sammy heard Commander Altair shout and he dug his left foot down to take the weight of his numb body. He carried on moving forward without being able to see the floor.

'99%, 98%,' shouted Commander Altair. 'Well done to Simon Sanchez, Dixie Deane and Jock Hubar.'

Sammy pressed forward, Commander Altair's scores thundering in his head.

'93%, Toby Reed, 92% Gavin Reed.'

Sammy focused firmly on the door, or where the door should have been, imagining that the Shape were chasing him. He heard "Join Us" whispered from nowhere in his ears "He has betrayed you...let the girl die...poison the dragons...finish what we have started...".

'Noo!' yelled Sammy tasting the fading red mist. He shut his eyes, concentrating on the door, aware of a stampede around him.

'84%, 83%, 82%,' shouted Commander Altair from the tabletop.

Sammy was shoved from behind through the open door with Peter Grayling from West as Commander Altair shouted "80% End of the exam!"

Sammy clutched at one of the cold stone pillars at the top of the stairs feeling week at the knees. "Must not faint" he told himself as Commander Altair came out of the hall with his clipboard in hand.

'Sammy, you and Peter are joint 80%. If I haven't called your name then, everyone else, I'm sorry but you have failed this exam. If the Shape were really after you, then you'd already be dead.'

Sammy's jaw dropped and he was swept along by Dixie and Darius who told anyone who'd listen that he'd scored 89% for being the eleventh to leave.

It was only when they reached the North Tower that Sammy noticed that Dixie hadn't said anything the whole way back.

'What's up?' he asked, dropping back from Gavin, Toby, Darius and Jock.

'Nothing,' she said.

'Nothing means something,' said Sammy. 'You're never this quiet.'

'Really it's nothing, well just that I got out second to get my 99%, but I think the exam was more about saving everyone else...'

Sammy scratched his head.

'Like you did,' whispered Dixie. 'He put you right at the front so you'd be hit hardest, but you shook it off as easily as if me or Darius did it to you.' Dixie turned to square with Sammy 'Like it or not, you destroyed most of his mist.'

'Lucky I got out then,' Sammy grinned, 'I might have done all that and still failed the exam. Hey don't cry...' Sammy stopped short.

'He's testing you,' sobbed Dixie. 'I heard Professor Sanchez telling him to make it strong. To see what you're made of.'

'Oh,' said Sammy. 'I made it though.'

'This time...' sniffed Dixie, drying her eyes. 'Ug, can't let anyone see me like this. "Girls' Tower".' With a hiss, Dixie had gone.

'Girl stuff,' said Sammy quickly as Gavin opened his mouth.

Gavin opened his eyes even wider as he missed the point. 'Oh.'

In comparison, Professor Sanchez's final Alchemistry exam passed uneventfully with picture cards held up behind a screen.

Sammy found he had to choose his answers at random as she held the cards up so fast. In an hour and a half, she had held up five hundred cards depicting colours, shapes, buildings, people, cars, trains, planes, animals and Dragamas teachers.

Concentrating at ninety miles per hour took its toll on most of the class who, worn out from the Armoury exam, fell asleep after the first two hundred cards.

Sir Ragnarok had prepared a small evening meal, with the full celebrations taking place all day and all night tomorrow to allow parents to come from all over the world.

Sammy tucked into his beans on toast half-heartedly. Around him, everyone was talking about their plans for the summer.

Gavin and Toby said they were going to spend two weeks in the Caribbean and then another two weeks with their rich uncle in the south of Wales before coming home for the rest of the holiday.

However, it was Milly who seemed to be doing the most exciting thing. She explained in great detail how she was going on a jungle trip with stops at ancient ruins.

'It'll be awful,' she moaned. 'Daddy's doing it through work and there are these boys...so dirty...any mud and water...they'll want to push me in.'

Sammy tuned her out and turned to Dixie. 'What are you doing?'

Dixie grinned. 'I don't know yet. I expect Serberon, Mikhael and Jason will play Dragon Questers and probably make me stand in goal while they practice playing Dragonball.'

'We can fly our dragons again, can't we,' said Darius. 'Dr Shivers said it would take six to eight months for the adult scales to form.'

'Yeah!' said Sammy. 'I can't wait!'

Feeling fuller than he might have expected from beans on toast followed by chocolate mousse, Sammy checked on Kyrillan and then drifted into a dreamless sleep with his duvet pushed to one side. He insisted on all five tower room windows to be left wide open because it was so hot.

CHAPTER 34

PARTY TIME

Sammy woke to a huge bang from outside his window and to glitter and streamers hurling themselves one after another around the tower bedroom, weaving amongst the beds and the sleepers, scattering gold and silver glittery powder in a fine film over any free surface.

'Oi Sammy!' shouted Gavin.

Sammy looked up. Gavin was standing on his bed wearing his green duvet like a cape.

'It's party time!'

Sammy didn't need telling twice. He leaped out of bed and started throwing on his navy jeans and black and gold Nitromen shirt, which was covered in sparkling glitter.

It was already baking hot. There was the sound of laughter downstairs and outside. Taking a peek out of the tower window, Sammy could see groups of fifth year students congregating in the courtyard. This would be their very last day at Dragamas School for Dragon Charming.

Some of the fifth years had shoeboxes tucked under their arms with baby dragons inside, which reminded

Sammy of their loss and the tragedy earlier in the school year. They were stacking their suitcases and trunks in groups under a purple and gold striped canopy built by the dwarves.

Sammy's eyes widened as he caught sight of Mrs Grock's house. He was sure that the clouds of smoke whisping from her chimney were in hearts and star shapes. He grinned, flopping back on the bed to tie the laces on his shoes, thinking to himself that this would be his last time in the second floor tower bedrooms.

'Shh,' hissed Gavin.

Sammy looked over. Gavin had used his duvet to collect a load of the glitter ready to throw over his brother.

Gavin leaped on top of Toby and showered the mixture all over his brother in a brightly coloured glitter cloud storm.

Toby woke up coughing and spluttering.

'Oi!' yelled Toby, thumping Gavin with his pillow.

'Last pillow fight!' shouted Gavin. 'Me and Sammy against you and Toby,' he shouted pointing to Darius.

'What about Jock?' asked Sammy.

'Stuff him!'

'He's on our team,' said Darius, 'aren't you Jock?'

'Can't be bothered,' said Jock coolly. 'I'm going to see my Dad.'

'Good, you'll be gone first then,' said Gavin. 'He's already here.'

'We're staying at the Floating Circus,' retorted Jock. 'Bet you've never been there!'

'Wrong!' yelled Gavin flinging his pillow at Darius.

Darius held up his pillow getting into hysterics as both pillows exploded puffing hundreds of tiny white feathers up in the air.

'And you can keep your stinking mug,' added Jock, lobbing the "J" mug at Gavin. It cracked against the wall behind Gavin's bed creating a dark stain as hot chocolate spilled out dribbling down the wall.

'You'll pay for that!' shouted Gavin.

Jock smiled and rubbed the ruby on the end of his staff.

Gavin froze solid. Toby and Darius caught him as he fell.

'You'll pay for that,' echoed Toby, his face like thunder. 'No one does that to my brother!'

'Sez you,' sneered Jock. 'I'll see you next term.'

'Not if I see you first!' yelled Toby as Jock disappeared down the stairs armed with this staff and suitcase.

'Everything alright in here?' asked Professor Burlay stopping as he led the North first year boys down past the second year door.

'Everything's fine,' snapped Toby.

'I see,' said Professor Burlay, looking at the glitter and feathers floating down from the ceiling. 'I'm sure I'll see you downstairs in a little while.' He left with the first years in tow, each of them eyeing the second year boys in awe.

Sammy reached beside his bed for his staff and unfroze Gavin. Spotting his toy lion, Sammy leaped across his bed to the first years who were nearly out of sight.

'Hey Nigel!' shouted Sammy.

There was a pause and Nigel Ashford tottered back up the stairs. Sammy did a double take, with his jet black hair and sturdy frame, he looked as if he could have been Gavin and Toby's younger brother.

'Here,' said Sammy thrusting the toy lion at Nigel. 'I'm your mentor to help if you've got any problems.'

Nigel reached for the toy lion which, having been passed down from Serberon to Sammy, looked as though it had had a few adventures of its own.

'Is this Rolaan?' whispered Nigel. 'The lion you saved?'

Sammy nodded. 'He's yours now. Pass him on when you get your first year to mentor and look after.'

'Thank you,' said Nigel and from the look on his small face, Sammy knew he had just made his day.

'Anything you need, come and see me,' said Sammy. 'See you later!'

'Bye!' squeaked Nigel. 'Thank you!'

Sammy ran back up to the second year tower room to find Toby and Gavin sweeping the glitter and streamers over to Jock's bed.

'He'll have to clean this up before he goes home,' sniggered Gavin.

'How about you four do the cleaning instead?' asked Dr Shivers, appearing from nowhere in the middle of the tower room.

Sammy jumped back as Dr Shivers sidled close to him.

'I said this party was a mistake,' sneered Dr Shivers. 'Samantha Trowt's idea to wake up to glitter and streamers.' Dr Shivers kicked at the coils of foil and paper. 'You can clean this up before you wash and I'll have your Dragon Minder pins back so you don't lose them over the holidays,' said Dr Shivers marching out of the room.

'Well done Gavin,' snapped Darius. 'I wanted to be first outside.'

'If we don't wash,' said Toby thoughtfully, 'we could go anyway.'

Gavin leaped over the bed to give Toby a bear hug. 'Awesome!'

Sammy dusted his pillow and chest of drawers, checking under the bed for anything he had forgotten. He pulled out a pair of odd socks and a handful of sweet wrappers.

Gavin and Toby ran out of the room shouting and yelling to get the party started.

Darius made a half-hearted attempt to throw some of the glitter out of the window nearest to him. From down below an angry shout told Sammy that the glitter had landed like confetti on the party below.

'We're not getting married you know,' came Professor Burlay's voice, followed by a volley of "ooohs".

Sammy tapped his staff on his case bewitching it to lift off the ground two inches before it thumped back down again.

'Your uncle used his thoughts and power to help you before,' said Darius. 'You can't do it by yourself.'

'Watch me,' said Sammy trying again. He lifted the case to waist height, then, as his concentration broke, the case came crashing down again.

Thomas Oakes, a burly third year, stomped upstairs to see what was going on. He tapped his staff at the suitcase and made it somersault in mid air. The case wasn't shut properly and all of Sammy's belongings fell out in mid air.

'Sorry,' grinned Thomas. 'Guess you should practice with other stuff,' he said, lifting Sammy's chest of drawers at ninety degrees to make the empty drawers fall out.

'Get out!' shouted Sammy raising his staff.

'By the rule of three times three...' chanted Thomas falling over backwards as Darius lunged at him, narrowly avoiding a volley of green sparks Sammy had projected.

'Do you know what those do?' said Thomas, sounding genuinely terrified. He picked up his staff and ran downstairs leaving Sammy and Darius to pick up the fallen belongings and repack them at lightning speed.

Sammy grabbed his suitcase by the top handle and pulled it behind him down the four storeys of the North Tower.

He was greeted by a bear hug from Dixie.

'Look!' she squealed, pointing to the common room window. 'Nitron Dark couldn't be here so Sir Ragnarok's brought the Nitromen bear mascots and there's a shop with all of their kit!'

Sammy didn't like to tell Dixie that the shop was "Excelsior Sports Supplies" or that Mr Cross was handing out leaflets to parents who had arrived early. He had to admit that the dancing bears wearing black and gold Nitromen t-shirts were quite cool though.

'What time are your parents coming?' asked Dixie, making Sammy stop in his tracks.

'I uh, I don't know really,' said Sammy. 'My uncle would have picked me up, if, well, you know.'

Dixie grinned. 'I'm sure your parents will find it. They dropped you off here the first time, didn't they? My Mum's coming at five o'clock after she's had her hair done. She said it should give us plenty of time to enjoy the party without looking stupid if we're the last to leave.'

Sammy nodded. 'I hope my parents can find it,' he said anxiously.

'Of course they will,' said Darius heaving his suitcase behind him. 'My parents will find it with no problems.'

'Aren't they at the Floating Circus?' asked Dixie. 'I heard Professor Burlay say it's now overhead.'

Darius shifted his weight. 'I was just trying to reassure Sammy. My parents are coming down mid afternoon, then we're going um...'

'Where?' demanded Dixie.

'Trekking,' said Darius hesitantly, 'to find dragons who need healing. It's really interesting,' he added.

'Sounds good,' said Sammy. 'I don't know what I'm doing, probably waiting to hear about my uncle.'

'They should throw away the key,' said Darius. 'He'll never be allowed to work or live with dragons again.'

'That would be awful,' said Sammy, 'not for him,' he added hurriedly. 'Imagine if it was us, I don't think I'd ever want to be without Kyrillan.'

'I couldn't be without Kiridor,' added Dixie. 'I've always had dragons around me, but Kiridor is different. He's mine.'

Darius nodded. 'Hey come on, let's go outside!'

Ten minutes later, Sammy was sitting outside on the top of a giant pirate ship eating hot cross buns.

'Do you like my idea?' shouted Serberon from the crow's nest. 'I'm a sailor! Come on board!'

'Where's the sea?' shouted Darius, climbing up a rope ladder on to the deck. 'You can't have a boat without the sea!'

'Imagine it,' said Serberon shinning down the mast, 'rolling waves, sand the colour of vanilla essence, coconut trees.'

'And a nice man to share it with,' added Dixie dreamily.

'Not if I saw him first,' retorted Serberon. 'I just wish Mary-Beth could see this, she loved rough pirates and that stuff.'

Sammy nodded, thinking this added up to her relationship with the cigarette boy.

'Hey Sammy!' shouted Darius. 'It's my parents!'

Sammy checked his watch, it was barely ten o'clock. 'I thought you said they weren't coming until this afternoon.'

'Must be early,' said Darius. 'Hopefully they'll stay for some of the party.'

'Introduce us,' commanded Dixie, dressed like a pirate in her black and white striped t-shirt and blue shorts. Her costume was complete with a telescope, pirate hat and eye patch. She climbed down the gangway on to the grassy lawn.

Darius leaped down the ladder and landed in front of his parents, who were being escorted to the castle by Captain Firebreath.

Darius received two hugs from his mother before she let him introduce Dixie.

'How nice to meet you,' said Darius's mother stroking a bead necklace around her neck. 'Darius has told me so much about you. You are just as he described,' she chuckled.

Dixie patted down her green hair. 'It's genetic.'

'Quite remarkable,' said Darius's father. 'Trolls and dragons and humans.'

'I'm as human as you are,' said Dixie.

'I'm sure you think you are,' said Darius's father, 'still, we must be getting along. Fetch your things Darius please.'

Darius rolled his eyes at Sammy. 'I've gotta go.'

'We'll see you soon,' said Sammy encouragingly, 'maybe at the end of the summer?'

'Unless the Shape get me first,' Darius grinned. 'Let me know when you hear about your uncle. Have a good summer holiday!'

Darius waved to Sammy, Dixie and Serberon as his father picked up his suitcase and put an arm around his son's shoulder, leading them down the driveway.

At the end of the school driveway, Sammy watched as Captain Stronghammer fetched Nelson from the pack of dragons and gave Darius some rope to walk Nelson to the gates.

As Sammy and Dixie walked with Darius and his parents, a brightly coloured orange, purple and green minibus stopped at the gates. Overhead, the minibus was being followed by ten dragons equally as bright, their scales shimmering in the morning sunlight.

'My "real" uncle's dragons,' explained Darius, 'and my six cousins!'

'Makes me having three older brothers look easy!' Dixie grinned as she waved with Sammy as Darius and the brightly coloured minibus rumbled away down the country lane with navy blue Nelson following the pack of dragons and soared high into the sunlight.

'What's next?' asked Sammy, feeling a bit deflated when the minibus disappeared from sight.

'Ice creams,' said Dixie. 'Molly's serving. I'm going to ask her about my Dad.'

Sammy smiled, knowing that Molly wouldn't be able to satisfy Dixie unless she let Jacob Deane out of her deep freeze where she stored the ice-creams. Dixie hadn't given up hoping and spoke as often as she could to Commander Altair, Professor Burlay and Mrs Grock who also had family fighting the Shape and protecting dragons throughout the world.

Dixie skipped ahead to the caravan where Molly Burlay was setting out white plastic tables and chairs with pink and white striped cushions.

As usual, Molly was wearing her pink knee length dress with a pink and white striped apron and pink and white striped hat. Even her shoes were pink with pink and white bows.

A pink and white striped awning was spread over the window of the caravan, where an old lady was unpacking boxes of cones for the ice-creams.

'Where's John?' the old lady shouted to Molly.

'He'll be here,' said Molly, shouting even though her mother was only ten feet away. 'She's hard of hearing,' Molly explained as Sammy and Dixie sat down at one of the tables.

The two Floating Circus clowns, Philippe and Borjois entertained them by somersaulting over each other and larking around with a juggler who had seven balls in the air that turned into doves and flew into the trees.

'Reminds me of when they went to war,' whispered Molly as she brought over two colas and a bowl of pink and white ice-cream for them to share.

'When are they coming back?' asked Dixie.

Molly looked up at the sky. 'Your guess dearie is as good as mine. They said they would return when the Shape had been defeated.'

'We've caught two of them,' said Dixie. 'It can't be that hard.'

Molly looked over. 'It's not just the people in the Shape that must be stopped. It's their actions, the knock on effect, the people they have bribed, the stones they have collected. One day, it will take everything we have to stop the effects and it may be too late.'

'Do you mean about the Stone Cross?' asked Sammy.

Molly threw her hands up to her face. 'You shouldn't know about that,' she said, looking horrified. 'Whatever is Sir Ragnarok thinking of, worrying you children with these problems.'

'My uncle was in the Shape,' said Sammy. 'He wasn't too worried about that.'

Molly looked kindly at Sammy, her brown eyes a little tearful. 'There are some very wicked people in this world Sammy, but there are good people too.'

Molly turned at a shout from her mother.

'I'll be there Mum,' shouted Molly. 'She can't manage so well on her own these days. John and I will probably end up running the caravan and ice cream stall when she's gone.'

'But John, uh, Professor Burlay I mean,' said Sammy, 'he...'

'Wouldn't know the first thing about ice cream,' giggled Molly. 'I know, since he's so good with the stars, Mum's always wanted him to work in the fortune teller's tent...All right! I'm coming!' Molly scuttled back to the caravan.

'How did you get the caravan down here?' shouted Gavin, feeding his dragon some pink candy floss.

Molly raised her right hand and the caravan slowly lifted two feet into the air.

'Put me down!' shrieked Megan, appearing at the window armed with two chocolate flakes the size of drumsticks. 'Put me down at once!'

Molly lowered her hand and the caravan bumped back on to the ground. 'We flew here!' she chuckled.

'Bunch of freaks,' said Gavin. 'Hey Sammy, do you want to play Dragonball?'

Despite having only just started his cola, Sammy nodded, the chance of playing one last game of Dragonball with everyone from the school who wanted to play was too big an opportunity to miss.

He ran with Dixie in hot pursuit to Captain Firebreath at the school gates to pick up Kyrillan and Kiridor. As they got there, Syren and Puttee, Gavin and Toby's dragons took flight and soared skyward to where Gavin and Toby had blown their Angel whistle.

Sammy leaped onto Kyrillan's back and kicked off from the ground. Kyrillan spread his blue green wings and swooped gracefully in an arc to join Gavin and Toby on the Dragonball pitch.

Several students were circling the golden dragon and the two goals. They were playing catch with the basketball sized balls covered in black leather.

'We'll play with the school balls,' shouted Toby. 'My Excelsior XR2 set is packed.'

'Fine,' shouted Sammy doing a loop the loop to catch a ball passed between Ern and a girl from the South third year.

'Oi!' shouted Ern. 'Oh, it's you Sammy. How's it going?'

'Fine,' shouted Sammy as he carried the ball high towards the clouds throwing it towards the goal. As he let go, Kyrillan swung round flicking the ball with his tail, correcting the offset and flinging the ball past the goalkeeper.

'Kyrillan's playing!' shrieked Dixie from the goal. 'Sammy, he's playing!'

Sammy felt his cheeks glowing. 'Kyrillan's playing,' he thought to himself, ducking as a wild pass from Gavin just missed him.

'Catch it you idiot!' yelled Gavin. 'You're useless!'

From an ant sized person on the ground came a reproving squawk.

'Gavin! I will not tolerate your language!'

'Stuff you!' Gavin shouted downwards, then to Sammy he called, 'it's my Mum! I've gotta go!'

Sammy followed Gavin to the ground, keeping out of sight behind two stocky fifth years as Mrs Reed with a face blacker than thunder roared at Gavin and Toby, clutching each of them by the shoulder until they were whisked away in her shiny blue Land Rover.

Dixie joined Sammy with Serberon, Mikhael and Jason hovering at eight feet. Sammy looked at the four of them with their green hair, Dixie and Jason looked a little windswept with hairs straying from their ponytails.

'Great shot Sammy,' said Mikhael, 'that was an awesome goal, you can be on my team.'

'Me too,' said Dixie.

'Nah, no girls,' said Mikhael. 'Miranda should be around somewhere. You can be on her team.'

'Don't bother,' snapped Dixie. 'I'll create my own team. Sammy you'll be on it yeah?'

'Uh, sure,' Sammy grinned. 'Do you want to be on Dixie's team?' he asked Mikhael.

'For you Sammy, alright,' conceded Mikhael. 'That goal was awesome.'

'You can go in goal,' said Dixie looking thoughtful. 'Serberon and Jason can follow Sammy.'

'I'm not going in goal!' shouted Mikhael. 'You can!'

'Are you playing or not?' came a shout from the other end of the pitch.

'Yes!' shouted Sammy and Dixie together.

'Come on then!' shouted Mikhael, curving his dragon in an impossibly steep angle to catch a shot that had been aimed at their goal.

'59-72,' shouted a blond haired boy several hours later.

'Tea anyone?' called another voice from the ground.

Sammy looked down, recognising Mrs Grock standing by a stall selling helium balloons shaped like the Dragamas twin tailed "D" logo. He followed Serberon down to the ground and dismounted, swinging his left leg over Kyrillan's neck and sliding down his scaly side.

'Ooch Sammy, I didn't realise it was you up there. That was a marvelous goal you and your dragon scored,' Mrs Grock chuckled. 'Ooch, have you got my Humphrey Hoddle book you could give back to me before you go home for the holiday?'

Sammy looked at his feet, his blush of pride about the goal swapping for a cringe of embarrassment.

'You've lost it,' said Mrs Grock nodding understandingly. 'No matter, I'm sure it will turn up.'

'Um,' started Sammy unsure whether to tell Mrs Grock or not.

'Yes dearie?'

'It kind of broke,' said Sammy shifting his weight uncomfortably. 'My uncle appeared and we dropped it and the book turned to dust.'

'The Shape,' breathed Mrs Grock, 'here? Oh my.'

'What's for tea?' demanded Mikhael. 'Green jellies and limeade?'

'Whatever you like,' said Mrs Grock looking totally preoccupied.

'Cool!' said Serberon. 'What do you want Sammy?'

'Pink ice cream with two flakes,' said Sammy after a moment's thought.

'So long as it isn't poisoned,' said Jason.

Serberon cut his brother a venomous look. 'Like I'd do that.'

'You tried to give Sammy to the Shape,' added Mikhael. 'That's what Miranda said.'

'Stuff the lot of you,' snapped Serberon marching off.

'Oooer,' grinned Mikhael. 'Like he'd know how to poison food anyway.'

'Sammy's uncle knows,' said Jason.

Dixie linked her arm through Sammy's. 'Come on,' she whispered, 'we'll build some more of our den while they squabble. Mum won't be here for ages.'

Taking two Dragamas "D" shaped helium balloons and some sandwiches and crisps from the stands, Sammy followed Dixie into the woods where she began lugging branch after branch, weaving them together to form a tight tepee around the tree stump while Sammy ate a few of the sandwiches.

That should do it,' puffed Dixie as Sammy stood up from shoveling mud in the cracks between the branches.

'Professional,' agreed Sammy. 'Now we just need to cast a spell to stop anyone but you, me and Darius from getting in.'

'Serberon would know how to do that,' said Dixie, 'but then he'd have to know about our secret den.'

Sammy shrugged. 'It's not a problem for me.'

'He tried to kill you!' exclaimed Dixie. 'You can't want him in here.'

'Either we tell him, or anyone who wants to get in can come in here,' said Sammy.

'Fine, I'll get him.'

Sammy sat on the tree stump listening for the sound of footsteps outside of the den. He held his staff across his knees, a flame dancing around the doorway ready to light up the faces of anyone who came near.

He stood up as a twig cracked outside.

'Hey Sammy,' said Dixie. 'Come out and Serberon will put on the spell.'

Sammy ducked out of the den. 'Ok.'

Serberon nodded raising his staff, humming a single low note, he cast the staff over Sammy, Dixie and himself, closing his eyes as he waved the staff from side to side. From the end of his staff came a silvery grey oil slick mist that swirled around the teepee.

Serberon opened his eyes. 'That should do it,' he said walking in and out of the teepee. 'It won't last forever but it should be good enough until you can do your own.'

Dixie gave Serberon a hug. 'Thank you!' she said, grinning at her brother.

Serberon shrugged her off. 'Of course you know I'll bring my friends here too.'

Sammy nodded. 'That was the deal.'

'Thanks. Just don't do anything I wouldn't do,' Serberon grinned. He turned to his sister, 'Dixie, Mum should be here soon.'

'Cool!' said Dixie. 'How come your parents are taking so long Sammy?'

'I don't know,' Sammy smiled, 'but they can take as long as they like,' he said jumping on the tree stump inside the teepee. 'This is our den!'

'Cool!' said Dixie jumping up on to the tree stump as well. 'Do you think we could do with some more balloons?'

CHAPTER 35

A BABY IS BORN

They went back to the castle courtyard. Captain Firebreath had only a few dragons left and was tucking into some sandwiches that smelled strongly of fish.

'Alright Dixie,' growled Captain Firebreath. 'There's a green haired woman looking for you.'

'My Mum?' asked Dixie.

'Prob'ly,' growled Captain Firebreath. 'She went up behind the pirate ship.'

'Come on Sammy!' shrieked Dixie. 'My Mum's here!'

Sammy ran after Dixie as she vaulted over an empty table that the two Floating Circus acrobats were dismantling and helping with the clearing up after the party.

In the distance, Sammy could see the Floating Circus Ringmaster, Andradore Havercastle, talking with Sir Ragnarok beside the empty Dragonball pitch.

Mrs Deane was wearing her usual blue denim skirt and striped blouse. She was running a hand through her dark green curls and looking all around her.

She turned around looking extremely anxious as Dixie crept up behind her mother and tapped her on the shoulders shouting "boo!" in her ear.

'Ooh,' squealed Mrs Deane. 'Oh hello Sammy,' she smiled. 'As long as Dixie is with you or the boys I'll know she'll be safe.'

Sammy grinned and shook Mrs Deane's hand. 'Nice to see you,' he said meaning it. 'My parents haven't turned up yet.'

Mrs Deane frowned. 'They should have turned up otherwise it will be dark soon. I'll go and see Sir Ragnarok. Leave it with me.'

She marched over to Sir Ragnarok. Three more students waved to Sammy and Dixie as a shiny Mercedes rolled up with their parents coming to collect them.

'We're almost last,' said Dixie.

'We are last,' said Serberon. 'The Griffin family left ten minutes ago. Miranda's staying with Shelley for the first week.'

'She wouldn't let me stay with them,' grumbled Mikhael, 'apparently I'm a bad influence.'

Sammy grinned. 'I wonder what your Mum's saying to Sir Ragnarok.'

'I don't know,' said Dixie. 'but it looks like they're coming over.'

'Hope it's nothing serious,' said Mikhael. 'I can't wait to get home and play Dragon Questers.'

'Maybe Sammy has to stay here,' laughed Jason.

Sammy laughed nervously. 'I hope not. Not by myself.'

'I'll stay with you,' grinned Dixie. 'You're nicer than my brothers.'

'Oooh,' laughed Serberon. 'Hear that Jason, Dixie fancies Sammy!'

Mikhael, Jason and Serberon fell about laughing.

Sammy found his cheeks flushing. 'Cool!' he grinned, catching Dixie's horrified look.

'I don't!' she said looking indignant.

Sir Ragnarok, Andradore and Mrs Deane came over and they all fell silent at the adults' worried faces.

'Sammy,' said Sir Ragnarok, 'are you parents not here yet?'

Sammy shook his head.

'Wait here please. Sylvia, would you mind waiting with Sammy. I'll give Mr and Mrs Rambles a call from my office.'

Mrs Deane nodded. 'My pleasure,' she said, squeezing Sammy's shoulder. 'I'm sure everything will be fine.'

Andradore gave Sammy a wink. 'That job I offered is still open to you. Anytime you want to be a lion tamer, just let me know.'

Sammy nodded, a pang in his stomach worrying about his parents, hoping they hadn't had an accident, or worse, the Shape had made them forget about him or worse still, they had been taken prisoner by the Shape. His eyes glazed over.

'Sammy?'

Sammy focused. Sir Ragnarok was standing beside him. Serberon, Mikhael and Jason were standing open mouthed. Dixie and Mrs Deane were smiling.

'He didn't hear you,' giggled Dixie. 'Tell him again.'

Sir Ragnarok smiled. 'I have spoken to your father, on his mobile. They're at the hospital...'

Sammy felt his jaw drop, his stomach churning. 'Are they...are they...ok?' he whispered.

Sir Ragnarok laughed taking Sammy's hands. 'They're fine Sammy, your mother has had her baby...you have a baby sister.'

'Oh,' said Sammy, relief hitting him like a cold shower.

'They have called her Eliza.'

'And you're staying at ours for a week!' shrieked Dixie. 'Get your stuff!'

To his horror, Sammy found he had tears in his eyes that he fiercely blinked away. 'A baby...'

'And you're staying at our house honey,' said Mrs Deane kindly. 'You'll see your parents tomorrow and you can stay with us as long as you want.'

Sammy looked from the smiling faces of Sir Ragnarok, Andradore, Mrs Deane, Serberon, Mikhael, Jason and Dixie to the rising turrets of Dragamas, swirling in and out of the golden mist.

He had finished his second year at Dragamas, his parents were staying in the village hospital, he was staying with Dixie and her posters of Nitron Dark, sleeping in her brothers' bedroom on the camp bed listening to the sound of Dragon Questers, playing Dragonball on the Woodland Ranchers pitch. It was perfect.

'Thank you,' whispered Sammy as he harnessed Kyrillan and climbed into the back of Mrs Deane's battered Land Rover, holding on as Mrs Deane put her foot down, the five dragons flying strongly overhead.

Behind him, Sammy saw Sir Ragnarok wave before returning to the castle armed with some of the remains of the food from the party. Overhead, a stunning display of fireworks creating the shape of a golden dragon lit up the night sky.

The End.

Dragon Talks

The journey writing the Sammy Rambles series has been full of ups and downs. It has been an adventure starting with a pen and a piece of paper, through to publishing and promoting the books around the world.

I've created a series of Dragon Talks and Writing Workshops to share my experiences and help inspire children in their writing. In the sessions everyone is encouraged to create their own story with memorable characters, layers of detail and inventive plots.

Dragon Talks and Writing Workshops are available for schools, libraries and clubs with tailored content suitable for children from Year 1 to Year 6 (KS1, KS2, KS3) either as a full school assembly or class sessions.

Find out more about:

- The inspiration behind Sammy Rambles, the reason for writing.
- Philosophical influences, mythology, love of words, hidden meanings within the stories.
- Writing the stories using pen and paper in every spare minute and very unusual places.
- Editing, proofreading, aiming for 95%.
- Agents, Publishers, Rejection and the route of self-publishing.
- The reason for publishing the books in quick succession.

- Promoting the stories, creating the website and Facebook page.
- Visiting fairs, events, schools, meeting the readers.
- Writing more stories in the future.

In the Dragon Talks, children are encouraged to create their own dragons and their own fabulous stories to share.

These are some of the comments following Dragon Talks in schools, libraries and clubs.

"The Canadian and British Sections were delighted to welcome JT Scott, author of the Sammy Rambles series of novels, to SHAPE International School. Over the course of two days, the children were privileged to experience a series of writing workshops designed and delivered by this celebrated British author. The two sections learned all about the grit and resilience required to get a book published; how to structure and develop a story arc; and how to utilise a rich and powerful vocabulary to engage and enchant the reader. The children were also enthused to learn a plethora of facts about everybody's favourite mythical monster: dragons! The two days were an unqualified success and packed full of exciting writing experiences. It also allowed the British and Canadian Sections the time to start developing the close relationship that will be an incredible boon of their new shared school. This was an amazing learning opportunity, and both Sections would like to extend their gratitude to JT Scott and to Common Services for making this unforgettable two days a possibility." – SHAPE International School.

"The children enjoyed creating their dragons. Some really good ideas." St. Nicholas Church of England School.

"Thanks a lot for coming in yesterday. It was lovely to meet you and thank you so much for coming to talk to the children. I know the children found it really exciting and got loads of great ideas from it." - Pelynt Academy.

"In Jenny's Sammy Rambles Dragon session boys who usually refuse to write anything spent the hour engrossed and they did not stop writing. Thanks for all the work and time you've given us. I will recommend you to our other schools! All my class were motivated and it was great to see their creative ideas." - Looe Primary School.

"Jenny came to visit our vibrant Year 4 class of 37 pupils and had them truly engaged with her stories. It was thoroughly enjoyable to have Jenny share her writing tips and enthrall our students with extracts from the books. The children relished the chance to write their own dragon stories, based on the adventures portrayed in Sammy Rambles and now they can't stop talking about dragons! Thanks Jenny, please come again." - Elmhurst Junior School.

"Thank you so much for coming over, sharing your work and inspiring our children. I know the visit was a huge success from our point of view and both children and staff, from both the British and Canadian Schools, loved the experience." – Acting Head, SHAPE International School.

Dragonball

Dragonball is the sport played by Sammy Rambles and his friends in the Sammy Rambles books.

It's a hybrid of football, netball and rugby where players use their hands or feet to kick, throw and pass the seven Dragonballs to score goals and the team with the most Dragonballs in the opposition goal wins.

Although in the books Dragonball is played whilst riding on a dragon the ethos of Dragonball translates into real life and Dragonball is a tactical game for social and competitive teamwork, fitness and entertainment.

Dragonball is a sport anyone can play. It's for all ages and all abilities. There's no "you're not good enough", "you can't play", "we don't want you on our team".

It's all inclusive and a great way for children and adults to keep active, fit and healthy, to make friends and work together to score goals and win games.

For more information or to book a Dragonball game or tournament, please visit www.dragonball.uk.com.

These are some of the comments from recent Dragonball taster sessions, sports lessons and tournaments.

"We are thrilled to be endorsing, promoting and delivering Dragonball as one of our inclusive sport options in The South West." - Sports Way Management.

"I think it's a really good game. Everyone is running about. It doesn't matter if it's crowded, there's loads of space and everyone's around the balls." – Oliver, Dragonball Player

"Your visit was brilliant, thank you so much for inspiring our pupils. Just to let you know that our KS2 children have all been playing Dragonball this morning courtesy of our Sports Coach! It has been great fun!" - Headteacher, All Saints CE VC Primary School, Dorset.

www.dragonball.uk.com

Dragon Shop

You'll find lots of exciting things in the Sammy Rambles Dragon Shop and also in the Dragonball Shop.

Sammy Rambles Books / Audiobook
Sammy Rambles and the Floating Circus
Sammy Rambles and the Land of the Pharaohs
Sammy Rambles and the Angel of 'El Horidore
Sammy Rambles and the Fires of Karmandor
Sammy Rambles and the Knights of the Stone Cross

Sammy Rambles Kyrillan Soft Toy
Sammy Rambles Fridge Magnet
Sammy Rambles Keyring
Sammy Rambles Standard Mug
Sammy Rambles Colour Changing Mug
Sammy Rambles T-shirt
Sammy Rambles Hoodie

Dragonball Fridge Magnet
Dragonball Keyring
Dragonball Standard Mug
Dragonball Colour Changing Mug
Dragonball Kit
Dragonball T-shirt
Dragonball Polo
Dragonball Hoodie

Dragonball Equipment and Coaching Workpack

www.sammyrambles.com | www.dragonball.uk.com

Sammy Rambles and the Floating Circus

J T SCOTT

Sammy Rambles is given a dragon egg on his first day at his new school. The egg hatches into a dragon called Kyrillan and Sammy learns to look after his new pet.

He makes new friends, a girl with bright green hair called Dixie Deane and Darius Murphy, a boy with unusual parents. Things are going well for Sammy Rambles, until he learns of a dark fate hanging over the school.

An enemy, known only as the Shape, wants to destroy all of the dragons and close the school. It is up to Sammy Rambles and his friends to try and stop this from happening.

www.sammyrambles.com

Sammy Rambles and the Land of the Pharaohs

J T SCOTT

Sammy Rambles is keen to return to the Dragamas School for Dragon Charming for his second year with his friends Dixie Deane and Darius Murphy. There are new lessons, new teachers and new skills to be learnt.

On the school trip to the Land of the Pharaohs, Sammy learns his parents once knew about dragons but cannot see them any more. He finds out about the Stone Cross and discovers the enemy, known only as the Shape is trying to rebuild it.

When the fifth years' dragons are poisoned, Sammy has no choice but to find out more about the Shape and uncover why the Stone Cross is so important.

www.sammyrambles.com

Sammy Rambles and the Angel of 'El Horidore

J T SCOTT

A wedding gift from King Serberon to his future Queen, the Angel of 'El Horidore is an ancient whistle used for calling dragons. With one single blast, the whistle will call all of the dragons in the world together.

The Shape want to find the whistle and use it to kill the dragons, steal their draconite, rebuild the Stone Cross and obtain the powers of immortality and invincibility.

Sir Ragnarok cannot let this happen. He is sure the Angel of 'El Horidore is hidden near Dragamas and sets a task for his students to find it so he can protect it from the Shape. Sammy Rambles and his friends Dixie Deane and Darius Murphy embark on their most serious quest so far.

www.sammyrambles.com

Sammy Rambles and the Fires of Karmandor

J T SCOTT

Tying the past and the present together, Sammy Rambles needs to find his best friend and uncover the link to the ancient Queen Karmandor.

He must use all his skills and attempt a daring rescue, whilst staying on top of his schoolwork. As the legend of Karmandor comes true, it begins the systematic destruction of everything Sammy Rambles cares about in the Dragon World.

He finds himself yet again in the hands of the Shape and almost powerless to do anything about it.

www.sammyrambles.com

Sammy Rambles
and the
Knights of the Stone Cross

J T SCOTT

Bringing everyone together one last time, Sammy's final year at the Dragamas School for Dragon Charming sees him fight his fiercest battle yet.

Can he find the last member of the Shape?

Can he free Karmandor?

Will he escape with his life?

www.sammyrambles.com

Printed in Poland
by Amazon Fulfillment
Poland Sp. z o.o., Wrocław

57328049R00226